THE
PURSUIT

PETER SMALLEY

Typeset by SX Composing DTP, Rayleigh, Essex
Printed and bound in Great Britain by
CPI Bookmarque Ltd, Croydon, CR0 4TD

arrow books

Published in the United Kingdom by Arrow Books in 2011

1 3 5 7 9 10 8 6 4 2

Copyright © Peter Smalley 2010

First published in the United Kingdom in 2010 by Century

Arrow Books
The Random House Group Limited
20 Vauxhall Bridge Road, London, SW1V 2SA

Addresses for companies within The Random House Group Limited can be found at:
www.randomhouse.co.uk/offices.htm

The Random House Group Limited Reg. No. 954009

www.randomhouse.co.uk

A CIP catalogue record for this book
is available from the British Library

ISBN 9780099513650

The Random House Group Limited supports The Forest Stewardship Council
(FSC), the leading international forest certification organisation. All our titles that are
printed on Greenpeace approved FSC certified paper carry the FSC logo. Our paper
procurement policy can be found at www.randomhouse.co.uk/environment

What shadows we are, and what shadows we pursue.
(Edmund Burke, 1780)

For Clytie, with whom I cross the sea

SPRING 1792

Lieutenant James Hayter, RN, and his wife Catherine were in the blue drawing room at Melton House, his father's seat near Shaftesbury in Dorset, and they were discussing, with increasing hot vigour, Catherine's late social activity.

'Why must you harry and press me so, again and again, when—'

'You say that you have never seen this man?' Over her. 'Never at any time?'

'As I have said – not as I collect.'

'I am obliged to say, painful though it may be to both of us, that I do not believe you.'

'You dare to say that? You dare to accuse me of lying to you!'

'I should not wish to, were I able to call it by another name, but I cannot. I am a plain-spoke man, and I must speak plainly now. I think that y'did see this man, at the Bell at Warminster, by arrangement.'

'I have not been near to Warminster the entire spring!'

'Not in April? Not then, with your friend Mrs Swanton?'

'I have met Fanny Swanton on many occasions. She is my dearest friend. Why should not I meet her? Do you forbid even that?'

'In course I have never forbidden any of your pleasures, when they have been above reproach, but in this instance—'

'Above reproach! Fanny and I have been friends since we were children together. How could you begin to suggest that she—'

'Mrs Swanton has wrote to you from Warminster, has not she?'

Catherine shot him a dark glance, then her gaze faltered and she looked away from him, disconcerted.

'Yes, I have found it.' James nodded, his eyes still hard on her, and he took from the pocket of his coat a folded letter, and held it up. 'I have found the letter.'

'You have searched through my private things?' Again staring at him, anger and confidence returning.

'I am your husband.' Holding up a hand before she could continue, shaking open the letter in his other hand and glancing at it. 'Mrs Swanton writes very favourable about him, don't she? Mr Bradley Dight? "My dear, what a handsome fellow he is." And then . . . yes, here it is: "I will see to it that you are introduced to him, when you come to me next. I know that you will like him, and he you."' James looked up from the page, and tilted his head a little. 'Do you still say that you never met the fellow?'

'When? Where? These insistent questions are very vexing. I have already told you, I do not recall—'

'I warn you, Catherine, do not play childish games! If you did not meet him at Warminster, then you met him at Bath!'

Shaking her head, and feigning exasperation: 'Often, when I was with Fanny at Bath – at home, or at the play, or the Assembly Rooms – we did meet a great many people, yes, both ladies and gentlemen. What could be more usual? I cannot absolutely *swear* that I did not meet him, nor absolutely that I *did*, even if Fanny wished it. And when—'

Over her, holding up a small pasteboard card: 'Is this not Mr Bradley Dight's calling card, left at Mrs Swanton's house at Bath? A card you have kept hidden?'

Catherine now rushed toward him, and tried to snatch the card from his hand. He jerked his hand away.

'Ahah! No, you don't, madam!'

'Well – what if I did meet him!' Her dark eyes openly defiant now. 'In least he is amusing, and gentlemanly!'

'Ahh.' Quietly, fiercely, holding the card. 'And I am not?'

'Not at present.' Defiantly. 'Not for some little time since, neither.'

'Ahh.' Again, with a little nod. 'I see. I am not amusing, nor gentlemanly, nor witty, nor urbane, nor have I the easy charm of a damned foppish wastrel – not *at present*. But I am still your husband, and I command—'

'You may command nothing, sir.' Sharply. 'You are not at sea now, snarling orders upon your quarterdeck.' She turned her head away, her slender neck rigid with anger.

James saw the curl of soft dark hair at the nape of her neck, and was at the same moment furiously angry with her – and filled with sudden long-absent desire. A sharp breath to steel himself, and:

'You had better tell me the truth, Catherine. Is he your lover?'

'My *lover?*' Turning on him in furious astonishment. 'You believe *that* of me?'

'What else am I to believe? Letters, and cards, and secret assignations! Am I to be made a cuckold, without a murmur of complaint!'

'Ohh!' Again turning away.

'Answer me! Deny that he is your lover! Deny it to my face!'

'I will do nothing of the kind, sir.' Bitterly. 'You may think what you like, now.'

'You do not deny it! Goddamn your faithless impudence, madam!'

Without another word Catherine snatched up her bonnet from the arm of the sofa where she had laid it with her basket of fresh-cut flowers, and swept from the room. The basket slipped and tumbled to the floor, spilling blooms wide across the palmetto-patterned rug.

'Hell and fire!'

James kicked savagely at scattered stems of flowers. He turned this way and that, took a great breath, and slowly let it out. His anger had vanished like mist on the wind, and he was left with a sour taste on his tongue, mingled with the fragrance

of his wife's cologne in his nostrils, and the heavy sweet scent
of the flowers at his feet. He felt exhausted, and low in spirit.
The flash of her dark eyes as she had left him, a flash of scorn
and contempt, had wounded him, even as he had wounded her
by his accusations. In truth he had very little against Mr
Bradley Dight, beyond a single letter from a mischievous
woman, a calling card hidden among gloves in a drawer, and
the fact that he had indeed met Catherine – by her own
admission. He had very little against him, except a poisoning
suspicion. Bradley Dight was a prosperous young man who
had that season taken a house at Bath; his name had been
widely mentioned as one of a group of fashionable and
amusing people whom society wished to acknowledge; he was
much admired, it was said, by young ladies, including –
presumably – Mrs Swanton. "My dear, what a handsome
fellow he is." And Catherine? He could not be certain
they were lovers. Not absolutely. In fact – he could prove
nothing.

James slumped down in the wide-shouldered chair by the
fireplace and stared into the empty grate. It was mid-spring,
and his father Sir Charles Hayter – ever acute in economy –
had ordered that no fires were to be laid in any of the
downstair rooms save his library, and Lady Hayter's private
parlour. The Dorset air was not chill today, yet neither was it
warm. The quiet ticking of the long-case clock. The still,
enclosed air of the room. James lifted his head. The tall
window at the end, new green leaves pressed close, framing
the panes. A coaltit fluttered briefly at the unyielding glass,
and fled. Broad lawns beyond, and away in the west white
clouds slowly piling, against looming blackness.

'It will rain.'

James and Catherine had come to Melton for a fortnight,
at Lady Hayter's invitation, while minor refurbishments were
carried out at Birch Cottage, their home at Winterborne
Keep, south of Blandford. In truth they could have remained
at Birch Cottage without inconvenience, but Catherine had

wished for a change. Things had not been right between them for many months.

A year ago they had lost their only son to an outbreak of typhus, and Catherine herself had been gravely ill. Subsequent to that calamity, James was embroiled in a hazardous clandestine mission in revolutionary France, during which he had become romantically entangled with a Frenchwoman, who had later been killed, and the mission had failed. Downcast and bereft, James had returned to his ailing wife in England, and tried to find harmony and hope anew. Alas, far from achieving a renewed bond of tenderness and affection, they had drifted apart. When she had recovered her health, Catherine determined on a life of gaiety and distraction to counter the grievous loss of her son, and James – unable to match her mood, which he found frivolous and self-indulging – turned in on himself and grew increasingly morose. He became suspicious of his wife's frequent absences at Wells, and Bath, and Lyme, and fell to questioning her at length upon her return from these excursions, and for her own part Catherine grew increasingly resentful and reluctant to answer him, and relations between them were first strained, then fractious, and at last hostile. For months now, they had slept in separate bedchambers. Both of them felt that the fortnight at Melton was their last real chance of reconciliation, yet neither was prepared to concede anything to the other, so bitter had the differences between them become. And then he had found the letter, and the card.

Now as he sat low in his chair James reflected on the overwhelming love and desire they had felt for each other in the first years of their life together, the warmth of their affection and the passion of their embraces. He thought of how they had rejoiced in the birth of their son. Of how, each time he came home from foreign service, they had rekindled the fire of their early attraction, and made it blaze again.

'God's love, how could we have come to this . . . ?' Murmured on the quiet air.

Presently he got up on his legs, went outside and sniffed the approaching storm. A breath of cold wind cleared his head, and he became resolute.

*

'Bring her a point closer, if y'please, Mr Loftus. If we are to board short we must make headway, you know.' Captain William Rennie, RN, came aft to the wheel. He braced himself on the tilting quarterdeck, hands clasped behind his back.

'Ay, sir.' Bernard Loftus, his sailing master, turned and gave the instruction to the helmsman. HM frigate *Expedient*, thirty-six guns, heeled into the stiff westerly and beat close-hauled six points off the eye of the wind on the starboard tack, sails quivering taut on bowlines, and seamen of the afterguard hanging their weight on the falls to trim her to an exactitude.

'Hold her so, just so.' Rennie sniffed the wind, smelled rain, and: 'The glass has not lied to us, Mr Loftus. There will be a storm of rain.' Nodding westward, where cumulo-nimbus stood broad and tall and threatening on the sky.

'Ay, sir. That will likely become a storm of wind.'

'Indeed. I was of a mind to exercise the great guns today, but now I do not think so.'

'Had you meant to fire the guns, sir?' Bernard Loftus turned his face to leeward as a glittering smash of spray flung aft from the dipping bow and swept across the quarterdeck.

'Did y'say fire our guns?' Rennie ducked his own head, then lifted it, his thwartwise cockaded hat dripping. 'Nay, Bernard, I meant merely a running-out exercise, quoins pushed. We must not waste powder in home waters, hey?'

'No, sir, in course not.'

'The Ordnance don't like it, and neither do Their Lordships.'

'No, sir.'

'Hm. I expect you will say that I have ignored such strictures often, in the past.'

'I have no observation to make, sir. My business is navigation, not gunnery.'

'Hm. Hm.' Rennie glanced at him and smiled. 'Very wise in you, Bernard.' Now he looked round, and frowned. 'You said Mr Leigh had gone below very brief. Where is he?' He meant the ship's first lieutenant, who had the deck.

'In truth Mr Adgett had wished me to go below, sir, but Lieutenant Leigh said that he—'

'Adgett? What is the trouble?'

Mr Adgett was *Expedient*'s carpenter, and had been with Rennie since the ship's first commission in '86.

'I do not know that there is any trouble, sir. I think he wished merely to show me something in the water tier. When Mr Leigh said that he—'

'Water tier?' Rennie's affable demeanour had disappeared. 'If I know anything about Mr Adgett, that is his way of saying there is a leak. Christ in tears, did not the damned dockyard men tell her off to us as sound? What was they about all these last weeks, when they had her shored up in the bloody dry dock?'

'I am nearly certain Adgett would have told me if there was a leak, sir. With your permission I will jump below at once, and—'

'No no, Mr Loftus, y'will remain on deck, if y'please, and con the ship. I will go into the hold myself.'

'Very good, sir.' Stiffly, gripping a backstay as the bow dipped deep in a sudden trough, and the sea thudded in heavy under the cutwater. An explosion of spray across the forecastle.

'You there, Mr Foster!' Rennie, to one of the duty midshipmen.

'Yes, sir.' The boy attended him, removing his hat.

'Find my steward and tell him that I want a can of tea directly. Steaming hot, say to him, with a splash of rum in it. Jump now.'

'Ay, sir.' The boy departed at a run, dropped his hat, retrieved it, and fled down the ladder.

There was no leak. Mr Adgett had merely been overcautious in drawing their attention to a modicum of water in the well, which he believed might possibly have come from leaking water casks.

'What made ye think the casks had been damaged, Mr Adgett, good God?' Rennie asked him in the glow of lanterns. 'There is no sign of any damage at all, man.' Glancing at Lieutenant Leigh, who nodded in confirmation.

'No, sir.' Mr Adgett. 'But as I say, there is always the possibility of it, when there is more in the well than we would like. Either that, as I say, or a leak forrard. Which we has had in the past, sir, as you will be aware.'

'Yes yes – what is the depth of water in the well today, Mr Adgett?'

'Well, sir, it ain't above a foot, but that—'

'A foot only?' Another glance at Mr Leigh, who gave an apologetic shrug.

'Yes, sir, yes.' Mr Adgett gave a little exasperated sigh. 'But we was near dry when we weighed at Spithead, and even if it is only a foot now, what will it become if we continue to beat west into the wind, with a storm approaching?'

'Yes, yes, well well, very good, Mr Adgett.' A sniff. 'You did right to draw it to Mr Leigh's attention. But we will not allow ourselves to grow timid our first day at sea, hey? We must find out how she handles after the large repair, and shake her down in all distinctions. Water will get into a ship, Mr Adgett, when she puts to sea after a long absence, that is inevitable. That don't mean she is suffering serious indisposition. It is entirely usual, and I am at my ease about twelve inches in the well, today.'

'Yes, sir. Thank you.' Another sigh, scarcely audible.

'We will go on deck, Mr Leigh, wear ship, and run before.'

'Very good, sir.' Following the captain to the orlop ladder.

As they ascended, Rennie: 'Backstays, Mr Leigh. That is what concerns me.' Over his shoulder. 'I shall say a word to Tangible. Backstays, and vangs, and the driver boom sheets.'

'You wished me to remind you about gunnery, sir.' As they came on deck, into the bracing saline air.

'Yes, Mr Leigh, so I did. I have changed my mind. We have enough to do today without we—' A terrible frown. 'That man, there! Make fast that loose swinging block, before it carries away someone's head!' Striding aft from the waist ladder. 'Mr Tangible! Mr Tangible! – Where is my boatswain when I want him!'

'Stand by to wear ship!'

Mr Leigh stood at the breast-rail and bawled a series of commands through his silver speaking trumpet, which caught and reflected a flash of sunlight through the towers of canvas as he turned forrard. *Expedient* lost way, pitching on the increased swell, swung wide by the stern to face east, the sea lacing and seething along her wales, and caught the following wind. Soon she was sailing away from the storm, flying fair and true across the broad-rolling, wind-beaten sea at better than eleven knots.

At seven bells of the afternoon watch, *Expedient* tacked north round the Foreland of the Isle of Wight, and beat nor'-nor'-west to her mooring number at Spithead, making her signals. The flagship HMS *Vanquish*, one hundred, acknowledged.

Heavy rain was falling as Captain Rennie went ashore in his launch, wrapped head to foot in his new boat cloak. He went alone, leaving Lieutenant Leigh in command of the ship. As Rennie had gone down the side ladder he had called up to Mr Leigh at the rail:

'Anchor watches, Mr Leigh, and make it your business to keep the middies on their toes, you and Mr Loftus both. The wind may well increase overnight. You will need to double-breech your guns. Say so to Mr Storey. I shall return on the morrow, before the noon gun, and take divisions.'

'Ay, sir.' His hat off and on, making his obedience. Rennie had already given him these instructions, but Lieutenant Leigh had come to know that his captain was not a man to leave anything to chance, or misinterpretation, at sea.

'And Mr Leigh . . .' Rennie, calling up from the stern sheets of his boat.

'Sir?'

'Defaulters, too, hey?'

'Very good, sir.' Again making to lift his hat, and then merely touching it. Good heaven would the man never give his officers any credit for their intelligence and sense of discipline? Had he no regard for their experience and knowledge of the sea, and ships, and men? A sigh, and he sent a boy to find the gunner Mr Storey. Presently Mr Storey came on deck, wiping his hands free of blacking with a piece of cotton waste.

'You wished to see me, sir?' Ducking his head against the rain.

'No, not really, Mr Storey. You know what to do, in all particulars. But I must enter in my journal that I have spoke to you about the double-breeching, else I shall be found wanting should the captain ask to see what I have wrote. You know what he is, hm?'

A nod, a little pursing of his lips. 'I do, sir, indeed. Shall we say that you has told me that due to adverse weather we must by all means – without fail – double-breech our great guns, and shroud the flintlocks.'

'By God!' In mock alarm. 'I had nearly forgot that! The flintlocks!' A nod, a chuckle. 'Thankee, Mr Storey, you have saved my life.'

Mr Storey went forrard to see about the double-breeching, and Lieutenant Leigh went below to look at the defaulters' book, shaking his head and smiling to himself.

Ashore Captain Rennie stepped on to the Hard from his launch, sent the boat back to the ship, and made his way to the Marine Hotel, where he expected to find his wife Sylvia. She had not arrived, and he was at first puzzled, and then downcast. To the head porter:

'The coach did not come, last night?'

'Oh, yes, sir. It did come, all right.'

'But my wife was not among the passengers?'

'No, sir.'

'There was no message, no written note, or anything, with the coachman?'

'No, sir. Not as I am aware of.' Shaking his head with dignity and sympathy in equal measure. He was very familiar with this sort of thing.

'Ah. Hm. Very well, thankee. I will just go up and write a letter. I will ring presently, when I want a boy to take it up to the George.' The mail coach departed from the George Hotel in the High Street.

'Very likely Mrs Rennie will be on the coach from London this evening, sir.'

'Yes . . . yes, very likely. I hope so.' And he climbed the stair to his room. Captain Rennie kept a room at the Marine Hotel so that when he was in Portsmouth and could live ashore, his wife could join him from their home at Middingham in Norfolk, in order that they should not be apart unnecessarily. For the past month, while *Expedient* had been undergoing large repair at Portsmouth Dockyard, Sylvia had been detained at Norwich by the illness of an elderly cousin, who had since recovered, and she had lately written to say she would at last be coming to Portsmouth. Rennie and his wife were very fond. They had both been widowed, and by happy chance had found each other before life could attach them to that sad race of beings – the lonely.

However, he was not writing a letter to his wife today, but to the Lords Commissioners of the Admiralty in Whitehall. Certainly he hoped that his wife would join him late tonight, but in the meanwhile he had important business. He threw his boat cloak over the back of a chair, shrugged out of his undress coat, and settled at the writing table in the corner by the window in his shirtsleeves. Presently, as he found quill pen and ink and drew a sheet of paper before him, there was a knock at the door. A frown.

'Yes?'

The knock was repeated. Rennie sighed, rose from the table and went to the door. Opened it, and:

'Ah. It is you, is it?' Not with joy.

'And good day to you, Captain Rennie.' Mr Brough Mappin gave Rennie a polite half-smile, and raised his eyebrows a fraction. He had already removed his hat, and stood waiting, lean and dapper and at his ease in dark grey silk coat and waistcoat, his shirt and stock snowy, and his silver-buckled shoes discreetly gleaming. His hair was cut and arranged to flatter the shape of his head. From his fob pocket hung a neat little seal. Everything about him said that here was a dandy, a man of the coffee houses and gaming clubs and salons of London, given to witticisms, and elegant compliments, a social diplomatist with just a hint of the rake, and much admired by the ladies. It was an appearance he took great trouble to cultivate. In his other hand he held a silver-capped ebony cane. Rennie frowned at him.

'I am – just writing a letter, you know.'

'Even so, I wonder if you will spare me one moment of your time? Or even two?'

'Oh, very well.' Stiffly, stepping aside to allow Mr Mappin into the room. Then, unstiffening a little: 'I hope y'will not think me unwelcoming. Sea officers are apt to sound blunt-spoke, ashore, and brusque-seeming. That was not my intention, sir.'

'Thank you.' Mr Mappin stepped down the room, and turned. 'A pleasant view, even in wet weather.' Nodding toward the casement, which overlooked the glistening cobbled street, and the rainswept darkening harbour beyond.

'They know me here. They are very accommodating, always.'

'Ain't that their business?' Mildly.

'Eh?'

'To accommodate. This is an hotel, after all.'

'Ah. Hm. Just so. Erm, how may I serve you, Mr Mappin?'

'You said you were writing a letter, Captain Rennie. To Their Lordships, perhaps?'

'I hardly see how that concerns you, Mappin, you know.' Again stiffly.

'Come now, Captain Rennie. We have had dealings in the past, you and I. We know each other tolerable well, I think.'

'It was, as you say, sir – in the past. Now, today, I am a serving sea officer and nothing more. Your connections in London are not mine, and never will be again.'

'You are quite certain of that?'

'Quite certain, thankee. I have accepted my present commission in *Expedient* on the strict understanding that never again will I, nor my officers, be plunged unknowing into wickedness and foolishness abroad, in pursuit of fanciful notions invented by political men. Men acting behind, in shadow and deceit.'

'And does that include the Prime Minister?'

'I will not engage in this. I will not debate and dispute with you, Mappin. My position could not be plainer. If you must know, I am writing to Their Lordships today to inform them that I am at their disposal, now that my ship has been released by the dockyard after undergoing large repair. Repair, I may say, occasioned by inimical activity I undertook at your behest, all in vain. Well well, never again, sir. I have Their Lordships' assurance as to that, firm and secure.'

'Ah, have you? Then perhaps I waste my time, today.'

'There is no perhaps. You do waste your time.' Lifting his chin.

'On t'other hand, you know, Captain Rennie – if I was you I should not bother to write the letter quite yet. Not quite yet, until you have heard me out.'

'Nothing you could say to me will in any way change my position. Must I repeat it? You are wasting your time, sir.' A sniff, and an irritated little shake of the head. 'And you are contriving to waste mine.'

'Two thousand pound.' Another glance out of the window, then he turned his gaze again on Rennie. The half-smile.

'I don't understand you, Mr Mappin.' Curtly.

'D'y'not? Two thousand pound sterling of money, in specie.'

'Pfff.' Rennie returned to his desk, banged out his chair and sat down, and took up his quill.

Mr Mappin waited, patiently waited, and when Rennie turned his head irritably at last, and said:

'Are you still here, sir?'

Mr Mappin nodded politely, put his hat and cane on the settee, and drew from the inner pocket of his coat a folded document. There was no seal, Rennie noted.

'May I read to you from this paper?' Waving it briefly.

'You may not.'

Ignoring him, and opening the fold: 'Oh, well, I need not trouble you with all the intricacy of language.' Glancing at the paper. 'The Whitehall clerks will have their way, in all such official utterance. Prolixity is their bread and butter. What it says, in little, is that if you will sign your name on the paper, 2,000 of money is yours.'

'I want no part of such idle bloody nonsense.'

'It ain't idle, Captain Rennie, you know. Nor nonsense, neither. It is plain fact, wrote out.' And again he held up the document. No seal, and no signature.

'Did not y'hear me, sir?' An exasperated, dismissive sigh.

'Are not you curious, even a little, as to what you are asked to accomplish for this payment?'

'I am not.' Curtly.

'I feel it my duty then – before you refuse absolute – to acquaint you with—'

'Mr Mappin!' Angrily, turning in his chair. 'You will cease these blandishments at once, or know the consequence!'

'Consequence?' A bemused frown. 'That sounds very like

to a threat. My dear fellow, I am trying to help you.'

'No, sir, no! You are not!' Getting up. 'You are attempting to importune, and to suborn, and I will have none of it! Go away now, will you!'

'I do not think I can. I would be failing in my obligation to you if—'

'Mr Mappin!' Holding up a hand, breathing forcefully through his nose. 'You have said that we have had past dealings, and that is true. They was wholly inimical to me, to my ship, and to a great many of my people. They cost shame and humiliation, they cost suffering, they cost lives, sir. – Be quiet! – When I accepted this new commission I was given absolute and unconditional assurance that my duties would be entirely naval in nature, in waters close to home. The protection of coasts, and sea lanes, the general oversight of the eastern shores of England, necessary to the nation's interest in these or any other days – necessary but dull. And do you know, I welcome such opportunity. I wish to be a very dull fellow indeed, because by God I have earned that right. To go to sea without the smallest possibility of excitement, nor upset, nor alarum, is a delight to me, sir. I crave tedium, I embrace monotony, I love to be dull more than anything in the world. More than gold.' Again holding up a hand as Mr Mappin began to interject. 'More than any bribe or temptation you could offer me, however grand, however glittering, nor tremendous, nor astonishing. And now I will like to sit down and write my letter to Their Lordships, vouchsafing the intelligence that my ship is repaired and ready for sea, and that I await my final instructions. Good day t'ye, Mr Mappin.' A sniff, and he sat down and once more took up his pen.

And Mr Mappin, being not unintelligent, saw that for the moment he had better retreat, since no good would come of pressing Rennie further today. The matter he had in mind was urgent, but could be postponed a short time – a few days. Mr Mappin folded up the document, returned it to the inner pocket of his coat, took up his hat and stick, bowed, and:

'Your servant, sir.'

'Servant.' Rennie did not even look up as Mr Mappin departed.

*

Lieutenant Hayter stood by the slipway at Mr Redway Blewitt's private shipyard at Bucklers Hard, on the Beaulieu River in Hampshire, on a warm afternoon. Gulls turned and wheeled overhead, floating south toward the mouth of the estuary. The tide was low, and the smell of fishy mud lay heavy on the air. Mr Blewitt stood beside the lieutenant, a clay pipe fixed in his big yellow teeth.

'Yes, sir, yes. Last time you was here, I repaired your cutter.'

'Ay, the *Hawk*. But I do not come here today about cutters, Mr Blewitt.'

'No, sir, as you said in your letter, you have a mind to purchase the *Firefly*.' He nodded at the small merchant brig that lay shored up at the top of the greasy slip. 'Her coppering is near complete. That had to be undertook, come what may. It will be done by the end of this week. Saturday forenoon, in fact.'

'Excellent. And how long until her standing rigging is rove up?'

'Hold fast a moment, Mr Hayter.' He puffed at his pipe. Blue smoke wreathed his head. He removed the pipe and jabbed the stem at the brig. 'There *Firefly* lies, naked except for her lower masts, and there she will remain, sir, without further moneys lavished upon her . . . unless you was certain of your intention.' Replacing the pipe. 'Which I would oblige you to confirm with your deposit of ninety pound, the remainder of the whole – 810 pound – to be paid in full by month's end. Those are my terms.' Another puff. 'Well, now. Are you certain, sir?'

'I am, Mr Blewitt.' He gave into the shipwright's hand a tied leather purse heavy with coin.

'That is well, sir. That is very well indeed.'

They shook hands.

'Will not you count the money, Mr Blewitt?'

Mr Blewitt puffed his pipe, and hefted the purse in his hand, making the coins chink, then he drew open the top and peered in. Presently:

'It feels like ninety pound, sir. It sounds like ninety pound. And it looks like ninety pound. Therefore I am certain that it is ninety pound.'

'Very good. I shall return on Saturday at noon, when the standing rigging will be complete, and her copper. Hey?'

'That it will, sir. My rigging crew will begin the work at once.' A nod, a puff, and he held up the purse and shook it.

James made his way to the water's edge, clambering over greasy slip timbers, to where his wherryman waited in the boat. A final wave to Mr Blewitt, and James went aboard and settled himself on a thwart. He clutched at his hat as a rippling breeze came down the estuary, and:

'Give way, there. And row dry, if y'please, I have no boat cloak today.'

'Yes, sir.' The wherryman fitted his oars into the thole pins, and bent his back. As they progressed into the broadness of the river, James:

'I will add a shilling if we arrive at Gosport by five o'clock.'

A grunt. 'I will do my best, sir, but that is a good twelve mile, and I cannot guarantee it.'

'It is a pity we cannot step a mast and bend a sail in this boat. That would aid us greatly.'

'A light little boat such as this could never wear canvas with safety, sir. We should likely fall down in the first gust of wind on open water, and be drowned.'

'Hm, no doubt. – Two shillings, then, above the agreed fare, if you put me ashore at the Haslar wharf by five o'clock.'

Another grunt. 'I will do my best. That is all I can say.'

James had an appointment at the Haslar Hospital with Dr Stroud, the eminent physician and disciple of the great

Dr Lind. These two medical men had instigated between them a regime for the Royal Navy – now beginning to bear fruit – of both rigidly maintained cleanliness between decks, and the regular addition of anti-scorbutics to the diet of seamen. In those ships where this regime was followed a notable improvement in the health of the people had been observed, most particularly in the elimination of scurvy.

James's concern today was not scurvy, or the health of sailors in general, but the condition of one man, his old friend and shipmate Dr Thomas Wing. Dr Wing had been surgeon in *Expedient* since her first commission, when James had joined the ship as first lieutenant under Captain Rennie. Dr Wing – himself a pupil and follower of Dr Stroud – had been a success in *Expedient* from his first days aboard. He and James had seen much of the world together, and bitter bloody action on several occasions, and James had been saddened to hear, only a fortnight ago, that his friend was laid low at the Haslar with a serious illness. He determined then to visit him, and cheer him if he could, and do him any service he was able. He had written to Dr Stroud, and the physician had replied, naming the date and time James should call.

The wherry reached the wharf at twenty minutes past five, and James was at first not minded to pay the wherryman the extra two shillings, but when he saw that after twelve effortful miles the man's face was haggard and filmed with sweat, he relented and gave him the full amount.

He came to the hospital gate at half past five, was admitted, and a moment after was received by Dr Stroud. The doctor was tall and lean, his rimless spectacles and close-cropped grey hair lent his face austerity and severity, and he could have made a forbidding figure. The warmth and liberality of his character gave the lie to this appearance; his smile was full of welcome.

'My dear Lieutenant Hayter, come in, come in.' Beckoning him into his private office. 'I am right glad to see you looking so hale.'

Dr Stroud had treated James for wounds a year or two before, after a savage encounter in the Channel between his cutter and a smuggler. James did not linger over reminiscence.

'How is Thomas, Doctor?'

A sigh, and a little grimace, that the doctor quickly made into a smile. 'He is much improved, Mr Hayter, I think.'

'He is – he is not mortally ill?' Alarmed by that sigh.

'The disease has greatly weakened him, and recuperation may be protracted, but he improves every day.'

'What is the nature of the illness?'

'It was a fever, a peculiarly pernicious fever. For nearly a month he was very ill indeed, and then by a miracle he began to rally. In course we kept him in strict quarantine, in an upper room where the air might penetrate and aid his recovery. Clean sea air can work wonders, you know. Well, but in course you do know, when you have spent so long in ships. But fever is a troublesome thing, a fickle and spiteful thing, and just when you consider that a patient is mending – he is gone in the space of an hour. Thomas nearly did depart permanent, upon two occasions, the last not above a week ago. He has rallied again, and I am very hopeful, but he is skin and bone – having eaten next to nothing for weeks – and there was little enough of the poor fellow when he was healthy and strong.' A grim chuckle, and another sigh. 'You will be very shocked by his appearance, I think, but you must not show it.'

Dr Stroud led the way from his office to a separate wing, and up the stone stair to the quarantine quarters. Over his shoulder:

'Very likely he is no longer a risk to others, but we must ever be vigilant in fever cases. I will prefer that you refrain from proximate conversation, and ask that you talk across an intervening space. You apprehend me?'

'Yes, Doctor, I understand you.'

Dr Stroud opened the door at the end of a long passage, and James saw a wide, whitewashed room, empty except for a narrow bed by the open window. Dr Stroud called across the room:

'Thomas . . . I have brought an old friend to see you.'

The covers of the bed moved, and a tiny figure was revealed, the head on the bolster turning toward the door. The figure was so obviously frail, and the effort of turning so severe, that even that small movement seemed to exhaust him. The face was sallow, the eyes and cheeks sunken, the teeth and jaw showing through the taut skin.

'Who is it . . . ?' The familiar voice, with its familiar precise enunciation, was today so weak it was little above a washing whisper.

James instinctively began to move toward his friend, but Dr Stroud seized his arm and restrained him. Pointed to a red chalk mark on the floor halfway to the bed, and:

'That is the demarcation line. Please not to go beyond it.' *Sotto voce*.

'Very good, Doctor.' Also very quietly. 'May I talk to him?'

Dr Stroud nodded his approval, and James moved to the red mark. 'Thomas, can you hear me, old fellow? I am here.' The smell came to him now, at first faint, and then sharper and stronger – the stale ammonia reek of urine combined with foul breath to produce a wafting miasma that seemed to hang above and about and just beyond the bed. James suppressed an impulse to retch, swallowed and made himself determined.

'Thomas? It is James.'

The sunken eyes focused on James, and slowly recognition came there. A croak of breath, and another little heave of the covers.

'By God . . . hhh . . . it is really you . . . James Hayter . . .'

'Ay, Thomas. I have come to revive you, you know, and get you up on your legs. You have lain abed too long. I have a job of work for you – if you want it.' As soon as he had said the words he was ashamed of himself for his attempt at jocularity. Mock heartiness and banter would not do here. The response surprised him.

'Then do not hang back. Come close by me, and tell me all about it.' And the sick man raised a thin arm and beckoned. When James hesitated, glancing over his shoulder toward Dr Stroud, Thomas Wing slapped feebly at the covers, and:

'Damnation . . . hhh . . . I am not a contagion on mankind . . . In spite of what my colleague Dr Stroud may have told you . . . the fever has died off, and I will soon be hale . . . Come by my bed and cheer me up, now, will you, James? Tell me what work you have for me.'

James did not glance again at Dr Stroud, but heard him sigh his assent, and moved beyond the red line to the side of the bed. The smell there was very penetrating, and he had to breath through his mouth to avoid the gagging reflex. When the sick man held out his hand James felt obliged to take it, and grip it gently, for fear of crushing the bones. To his surprise the hand was not feverish hot, nor even warm. It was, on this mild early evening, porcelain-cold.

'I have bought a ship, Thomas, and I would like you – when you are quite well, in course – to act as surgeon in her. That is, if you have a mind to.'

'D'y'mean . . . that it is a private ship? A merchant vessel?'

'Ay, that is what I mean, exact.'

'You have resigned from the navy?'

'It is a long story. I will tell it to you another day.'

'Oh, but I should . . . hhh . . . to hear it now . . .' A rattling breath.

James heard Dr Stroud clear his throat from near the door, and he smiled at the diminutive figure in the bed, that was like an ancient child in its cot, and shook his head.

'Nay, Thomas. When you are well again – when you are strong.' He patted the cold hand in what he hoped was a kindly gesture, a touch of brotherly love, and continued:

'You will in all likelihood wish to join Captain Rennie in *Expedient* again. I know that he has got a new commission in her. But if by a happy chance you found yourself free of naval duty – happy for me – then I would like it very much if you would come to me in *Firefly*.'

'*Firefly*. Yes, a pretty name. Well, Captain Rennie has not asked for me, and I am ready to go to sea with you, certainly, James. Only tell me when, and I shall come.'

Dr Stroud cleared his throat behind James, and said:

'You remember, Lieutenant, that we must meet that other gentleman at six o'clock. It is nearly that now.'

This was Dr Stroud's signal that his patient had had enough excitement for one evening, and must now be allowed to rest. James made his farewells at the bedside, and rejoined the physician at the door. As Dr Stroud began walking away down the long passage, James turned a last time to wave to his friend, and was dismayed to see tears in Thomas's eyes, that spilled down his cheeks as he lay back mute against the bolster and stared up at the white featureless ceiling.

'Christ's blood, he is dying – and knows it, poor wretch.' Not aloud.

He followed Dr Stroud. At the foot of the stone stair he caught him up.

'It cheered him to see you, Mr Hayter.'

'I think he will not recover his health.' Not a question, very subdued.

'We must never despair of him. We must never give up hope.' Sharply.

'Nay, nay, you are right, sir.' Looking at him. 'We must always wish him well.'

'I have known Thomas since he was a boy. He came to work in the hospital as a porter, and because of his very small stature I thought he hadn't the strength for such arduous labour. I was proved wrong entire. He was strong as an ox, with a mind as keen and sharp as a scalpel. I trained him from the beginning, you know, I taught him everything, and am now proud to call him "colleague". While I have breath I will never abandon his care.'

'And in course I should feel the same, in your shoes, Doctor.

He is my greatly valued friend, also, and I—'

'I will save his life, you may depend on it.' A vigorous nod.

Dr Stroud came with James to the gate, a hand on his shoulder. 'Come again as soon as you are able, will you? Tomorrow?'

'Yes, tomorrow.'

'It lifts him so to see old friends, even if they cannot stay overlong. Well, you saw that, hey? You saw how he responded.'

'Good evening, Doctor.' They shook hands again.

'Goodnight.'

James came away to the wharf, deep in his thoughts, and sad, found a boatman free, and had himself rowed across to Portsmouth Hard.

As he stepped from the boat there was another boat just coming ashore, a naval launch, the seaman in the bow jumping into the shallows. James saw the officer in his thwartwise hat and boat cloak, moving forward from the stern sheets to step ashore, and was about to turn away and walk up the shallow slope, then paused. And turned back. At the same moment the officer in his boat cloak looked over at James, and together:

'Good God, James!'

'Is that you, sir! Good heaven!'

In ten minutes they were sitting in the small parlour at the Marine Hotel, Rennie drinking tea and James drinking coffee.

'I must chide you, James.' Not severely. 'Y'never replied to my letters, dear fellow. I had hoped we might serve together again. You knew I had got a new commission in *Expedient*, I expect?'

'Yes, sir, I did know. Congratulations, by the by. And I am very sorry that I did not take time to reply to your letters. I have had . . . there have been certain difficulties of late.'

'D'y'mean with Their Lordships? Then you must allow me to intervene in your behalf, and—'

'No, sir, it ain't the Admiralty. Nothing to do with Whitehall.'

'What, then? Perhaps I may be able to help you. If I can I certainly will.'

'That is kind in you, sir, very kind – but I fear that these are matters of a personal nature.'

'Ah.'

'I must resolve these things by myself. They are troubles all of my own making, d'y'see?'

'Well well, I am very sorry to hear it, James.' Rennie was anxious to know more, but at the same time he did not wish to pry. He sucked down a mouthful of black tea, and was silent a moment, then:

'Catherine is now quite well? She has recovered her health, and her spirits?'

'Yes, yes, she is fully recovered, thankee.' He said it in such an emphatic way that Rennie was at once alerted to the difficulty James had spoken of.

'And is she with you at Portsmouth?'

'Nay. Nay. Catherine is at Shaftesbury, just at present.' Looking down into his cup.

'Ah. Hm.' Another swallow of hot tea, and Rennie changed the subject. 'What brings you to Portsmouth, James? I see you ain't in uniform, but then you was never inclined to wear even an undress coat if you was not absolutely obliged to.'

'I have bought a brig.'

'Eh?' Rennie stared at him.

'Yes, I have bought her off Mr Blewitt, at Bucklers Hard. She is called *Firefly*.'

'You have bought a brig!'

'I have, sir. I intend to become a merchant master.'

'Merchant master . . . ?'

'You stare at me as if I was the worst kind of villain, sir. It is a perfectly respectable thing, ain't it, for a sea officer to go into the merchant service when the navy has no further use for him?'

'No further use for you? I cannot believe that! I refuse to believe it! We was both assured that we would be favoured,

after the sufferings we endured our last commission, and
I—'

'You forget that I held no commission in *Expedient* during
our last venture, sir. I was employed by the Secret Service
Fund.'

'Yes, that damnable bugger Mappin!'

'Oh, I don't blame Mappin for anything. I accepted his offer
readily enough, after all, and his money. And is he a bugger?
D'y'know that for a fact? He may be many things, but I doubt
that he is a sodomite.'

'He is worse, the fellow. He thrives upon deceit and trickery
and sharp practice, with the slippery cunning of the viper, and
the honeyed words of the pimp.'

'All in the nation's interest, I expect he would say.' With a
shrug.

'I am in no doubt that he would. It don't make him an
honourable fellow, all the same. I cannot bear him, the
preening wretch, skulking about.'

'Skulking about? D'y'mean – he is here, in Portsmouth?'

'I do. He had the effrontery to come uninvited to my room
in this very hotel, and to attempt to bribe me.'

'When? And why? What did he say?'

'Never mind him, he don't matter. I sent him away right
quick.'

'Ah. So you do not know, then, why he tried to bribe you?'

'Nay, I don't, and don't want to, neither.'

'Was it a large sum?'

'What?' Frowning.

'That he offered you, sir.'

'I am surprised y'would ask me that, James. The fellow is a
wretch and a scoundrel, as we both know to our cost. Was it
one guinea, nor an 100,000, my answer would be the same.'

'Hm. By the by, I had just come from the Haslar when we
met. I had been to see Thomas there.'

'Thomas Wing? So he is at the Haslar, is he, assisting Dr
Stroud, as of old? I wrote to him about the new commission,

but he never replied. You are both very poor correspondents, James, you and the doctor, and I ought—'

'No. No.' James, shaking his head. 'He does not assist Dr Stroud, sir.'

'Then . . .?' Noting James's subdued tone, and peering at him closely. 'You do not mean, I hope, that Thomas is a patient?'

'Yes, he is very ill in the quarantine quarters. Dr Stroud has every hope that he will recover – but I fear it may be touch and go.'

'That is sad news indeed.' Putting down his teacup. 'Y'said quarantine. That means fever, I expect.'

'Yes, fever. Dr Stroud permitted me to go into the quarters to see Thomas. His appearance was very shocking to me. He is skin and bone, and no colour in his cheeks. When I touched his hand there was no hint of fever present. It was deathly cold. And his voice – in usual, you remember, so strong and clear – was so weak I had to bend down to the pillow to hear him.'

Rennie was silent a moment, looking away down the room, then: 'I must go there myself, James. I should have gone there long since, had I known of this.'

'I am going there again tomorrow, myself. We could go together. I am sure it will lift Thomas up to see two old friends and shipmates.'

'Let us go together in my launch. It comes for me at the Hard well before the noon gun each day. We will make a detour to see Thomas at Gosport, and then I should like you to come with me to *Expedient* and join me in the great cabin for dinner, James.'

'Thank you, sir, you are kind. I should like that very much.'

'Where d'y'sleep tonight?'

'Oh, well, I had not arranged anything as yet. I came to Bucklers Hard only this afternoon, and from there by wherry to Gosport, and across to the Hard.'

'Leave everything to me, will you? I shall take a room for

you here, and ye'll join Sylvia and me for supper. She came from Norfolk to join me t'other day, thank God.'

'You are very good, sir, but I had thought to go to the White Hart, where—'

'Damnation to the White Hart. It is miles away, out on the turnpike. Ye'll stay in Portsmouth tonight as my guest.' Holding up a hand, brooking no further protest. 'My guest, James – we have much to talk over between us, hey? And Sylvia will be very glad to see you, in the bargain.'

At supper James endeavoured to be cheerful, and to keep up with the conversation, but in truth his heart was not in it, and neither was his mind. His thoughts and emotions were far away from the private dining room at the Marine Hotel, and the excellent things Rennie had provided. He ate and drank little, and more than once, when Rennie asked him a question, he looked blankly at his friend and was obliged to say:

'I beg your pardon, sir. I did not hear what you said to me.'

'Will you tell me, Mr Hayter,' asked Sylvia Rennie, at one of these embarrassing moments, 'why my husband calls you "James", but you never call him anything but "sir"? Should not you call him "William", when you are such old friends?'

James looked at the handsome woman who had made Rennie so happy, and felt himself a fool. He did not know how to answer her. Rennie himself spoke up, and denied that there was anything odd about it.

'My darling, in course we are friends, but first and always we are sea officers. It is an entirely traditional circumstance, like the Prime Minister and his close colleagues.'

'Surely they are not sea officers, William?' Her face straight.

'Mr Pitt and his Cabinet? Good God, no. But it is very like the navy, all the same. They would not call him "William", I think, but "Prime Minister", or "sir". It is a mark of their respect for his rank, an acknowledgement of it, d'y'see? In the same way . . . He broke off when he saw that his wife was smiling at him, then:

'Yes, hm, you was teasing me, my dear.'

'Only a little, William, only a very little.'

'Was I being pompous, my love?'

'I would not say pompous.'

'Something worse, hey?' A chuckle, and he glanced at James. But James had again departed the supper in his head, and was now absent elsewhere. Rennie cleared his throat and refilled Sylvia's glass, then his own.

'James? More wine, dear fellow?' Holding the bottle.

'What? Oh, no thank you, sir. I must have a clear head tomorrow.'

'Come, one more glass will not fuddle you.' He refilled James's glass. 'I will like to hear about your new ship, now. Will you tell me all about her?'

'Yes, my brig.' A brief smile. 'Well, she is called *Firefly*. She is quite elderly, but Mr Blewitt is refitting her, and she will serve very well.'

'Ah. Very good. What are her dimensions?' Taking a pull of wine.

'She is seventy-four foot overall, sixty foot in the keel, twenty-one in the beam, and nine foot in the hold. She is 148 ton by builder's measure. By all measure she should be a sturdy sea boat, and right handy. She is mine for 900 pound, a very fair price, I reckon.'

'Very fair, by the sound of it.'

'I hope to engage in the coastal trade.'

'Home waters, hey? What will you carry?'

'Whatever I may be asked to carry, I expect. Timber, tallow, even coals.'

'Will she make a collier, d'y'think? Ain't that dirty work?'

'It may be dirty. In least it is honest.'

'I did not mean it as a rebuke, James.' Mildly, then:

'And . . . will you sail her yourself?'

'Indeed, yes. As I told you earlier today, sir, I mean to be her working master.'

'So y'did, James, so y'did.' Another pull of wine, and he set down his glass. 'Hm. Hm. But will that answer, d'y'think?'

'Answer, sir?' Looking at him.

'Will that suit you, a sea officer, RN? Slogging up and down the east coast, from Newcastle to London, with dirty sails and dirty decks, your person forever grimed head to foot, staring grim into filthy weather, for a few pound of money here and there, and never a hope of anything better? Is that the life for you, James, I wonder?'

'Everything you say does sound like a rebuke.'

'Well well, it ain't meant to be. But I cannot stand idle on the side while my friend makes his life into a misery.'

'Misery? Misery? Christ's blood, what was our last little venture together! Death and suffering all around us, harsh and brutal treatment, imprisonment in a filthy, rat-infested dungeon! Was that delightful pleasure, exact!' Catching sight of Sylvia Rennie's shocked face he broke off, and after a moment: 'Please forgive me, Mrs Rennie. I did not mean to – to shout so, and upset you.' Rising and dropping his napkin on his chair. 'I have outstayed my welcome. I must go.'

'James, James.' Rennie, hastily getting up on his legs. 'Don't take it ill, what I just said, I beg you. I meant well, I swear to God. I meant well, and if I expressed myself clumsy then I beg your pardon. Sit down and drink your wine, and forget everything I said about your brig and your brave new venture. Will you?'

Seeing Rennie's obvious sincerity in wishing to make amends, James: 'If you wish it, then in course I will sit down, sir.' To Sylvia Rennie: 'I must ask your pardon again, madam, for my intemperate outburst.'

'Do not trouble yourself, my dear Lieutenant Hayter. I am used to naval men.' She smiled at him.

James bowed to her, and sat down. Rennie sniffed, drank off the last mouthful of his wine, and:

'Will you permit me to say one final word, James? I promise to say nothing untoward about your brig.'

James inclined his head politely and kept his expression

neutral. He wished to hear nothing more at all as to his circumstances, but felt he could not now – having just apologised – demand that his host be silent at his own supper table. Rennie nodded, and continued:

'I will say only this, James. I assume ye've had no communication with Their Lordships for some little time, and do not know therefore what might or might not have been offered you in the way of a commission. Now then, should anything go wrong about your present venture, should anything go ill with you, then I will make it my particular business to intercede with Their Lordships and ask for you in *Expedient*.'

'Ask for me . . . ?' James frowned, then raised his eyebrows.

'I don't say that anything will go wrong – and let us hope nothing will. However, should ill luck befall you in *Firebird*, then—'

'*Firefly*, sir.'

'Just so, *Firefly*. If it did, then you would be very welcome by my side.'

'Nothing will go wrong, I think.' Politely, but firmly. 'The deposit is paid, the other part of the money arranged, and I am to take possession of her on Saturday next, at noon.'

'In course, in course, just so. I am merely speculating, you know, on a question of if. If something should happen, if it should, you are welcome in *Expedient*.'

Again James raised his eyebrows. Politely: 'In what capacity, sir? Surely I could not hold a commission in a frigate that has already been assigned her full complement of officers?'

'Well well, we should have to decide about that. Yes. But it could be managed, and would be managed . . . if.' He refilled his glass. 'There, I have finished.'

James stared down at the table a moment, and again politely: 'Forgive me, sir, but I do not see quite how it could be . . . managed.' Lifting his gaze.

'I assure you, my dear James, that—'

'You will recall, I am in no doubt, sir, that when during your last commission I had occasion to make just such a request –

could you put me on your books as your first – you felt yourself obliged to turn me down flat?'

'Yes, well well, the circumstances was entirely different, James. When you—'

'Different? Again forgive me, but how, exact? I was at a loose end, and wished to find employment as a sea officer, and I came to you. You said, quite candid and blunt, that since Their Lordships had given you your full number of officers by commission, you could find no place for me.'

'Yes, so I did. But at that time, if you will recollect—'

'Then how I wonder could you find such a place for me now, when all of your officers have been assigned to you, exactly similar?' James, over him, with an edge on his voice. 'I do not follow.'

And now Sylvia Rennie intervened, seeing that such an exchange could not end well unless it ended at once. Smiling at each in turn:

'William. Lieutenant Hayter. I am used to naval manners, certainly, but I am used also to other things – diverting things – and I demand that you entertain me, else I shall languish and grow fatigued and disconsolate. Do you see, against the far wall, the pianoforte?' Pointing at the instrument half-hidden by a screen in the corner.

'What? Pianoforte?' Rennie peered across the room.

'Do not you see it there?'

'Yes, my dear, I do see it.' A nod, a forced brief half-smile.

'And you, Mr Hayter?'

'I see it, madam.' Clearing his wind.

'I am glad. I have a proposal to make. If one of you plays, will the other one of you sing?'

'Eh? Play the pianoforte?'

'Sing?'

'Yes. Sing. And play. Will you play, Lieutenant?'

'Oh, well, madam. Mrs Rennie. In truth, you know, I cannot play a single note.'

'Have you no sisters, sir?' A smile.

'Nay, I haven't. I have cousins, though.'

'And did they not ask you to play by their side at the pianoforte, when you were children?'

'I have seen them play, and heard them, but I was never – I never did attempt to emulate them, madam.'

'Ah, a pity.' A little sigh, then: 'Then you shall sing for me, both of you.'

'Oh, no, my dear, really I cannot.' Rennie shook his head, discomfited.

'Nor I.' James.

'But do not sea officers often sometimes sing after dinner in the gunroom, or the great cabin? My late first husband said so, and I am certain he was telling the truth.' Turning to Rennie. 'Have you never sung, my love, after dinner at sea?'

'Hm. Well well, very rarely. I have never cared for it, at any rate. Most sea officers cannot carry a tune.'

'No, that is true.' James, in agreement. 'That is very true, they cannot. I cannot.'

'Oh . . .! Oh, gentlemen, I am so disappointed. I had thought to be entertained.'

'Mrs Rennie, may I be permitted to make a suggestion?' James rose.

'Mr Hayter?'

'If you yourself will consent to entertain two unworthy sea officers at the pianoforte, I will like humbly to offer my services as turn-page.'

'Very prettily said, sir. I bow to your request, and accept your offer.'

And he escorted her, that handsome, clever woman in her low-cut gown, gallantly into the corner, and moved aside the screen, gratefully aware that she had averted a rupturing of the most important friendship in the life of either man.

On the morrow, at ten o'clock in the forenoon, the two sea officers went into Captain Rennie's launch at the Hard, and were rowed across double-banked to the Haslar wharf. At half past ten, Dr Stroud took them up the stone stair to Thomas Wing's room.

Wing was deeply asleep, a pale diminutive figure in his cot by the window, and Dr Stroud advised:

'Gentlemen, I think we should not wake him. His condition is still very feeble, and the more restful natural sleep he can get the better things will go for him. I am sorry you have had a fruitless journey, Captain Rennie, you and the lieutenant both, and I hope that you will return another day. I know it lifts the patient to see familiar faces.'

'Very good, Doctor.' Rennie, as they followed Dr Stroud back along the passage. 'I will endeavour to do as you suggest, and so no doubt will Mr Hayter.' Glancing at James as they reached the top of the stair.

'Yes, indeed, so I shall.' James, as they went down.

Outside the gate Rennie sniffed the air, and:

'We'll step our mast and bend sail, and beat across to Bucklers Hard. What say you?'

'Do not you wish to take divisions aboard your ship, sir?'

'My ship? She is our ship, James. I will always like to think so, anyway. And she will manage very well without me a further hour or two. I should very much appreciate sight of the brig, if you will permit it?'

'In course I shall be delighted to show her to you, by all means.' Noting that Rennie had not said 'your brig', whereas he had said 'our ship' of *Expedient*.

They returned to the launch. Rennie's new coxswain, a sturdy young man called Clinton Huff, quickly complied with Rennie's orders; mallets were produced, the mast stepped forrard, and clamped. The boat was pushed clear.

The duty midshipman, in his cracking pubescent voice, called: 'Give way together, lads. Let us row dry.'

And soon, as the boat pulled into open water off the fort and came round the point into a freshening westerly breeze, he called to the men handling the sails: 'Make sail! Starboard tack, full and by! Trim sheets, and keep your luff, there! Cheerly, now!'

Presently, as the two officers settled in the stern sheets, ducking their heads in the wind and spray, Rennie:

'He looked so damned reduced in that room.'

'Thomas? Ay, it is a cheerless, bare, bleak sort of place, that seems to diminish the human spirit.'

'I had forgot quite how small in stature he was.'

'But he is not in any other way a small man.'

Rennie looked at him, and: 'Nay, you are right. As strong and brave and loyal a man as I have ever met. I hope with all my heart that he may come back to us.'

'To *Expedient*?'

'To *Expedient*. Just as I hope that you will come back, Mr Hayter.'

James said nothing, but he was now very displeased with Rennie, and felt that he had been hoodwinked into this trip to Mr Blewitt's yard. Rennie had said he wished to have sight of *Firefly*, but what he wished in truth was to find fault with her, to cast doubt on her seaworthiness and design, weaken James's resolve, and attempt once more to persuade him to give up his new venture, and return to the king's service.

'Damn his impertinence, and his importuning, bullying pride!' raged James, but not aloud. 'Why will he not see that I am my own man, and not his nor the navy's, neither!'

'Has the swell made you queasy?' Rennie, peering into his face.

'No no, I am quite all right.'

'It always takes a day or two for a sea officer to reacquaint himself with his chosen element. There is no shame in it.'

'I tell you, I am quite all right, sir.'

'Very good, Mr Hayter, very good. There is no need to bite off my head.'

'God damn the meddling fellow!' James, furiously, in his head.

The wind now steady, and presently they set a course west

across the Solent for Bucklers Hard.

When they arrived Mr Blewitt took James aside, looking very solemn, and:

'She is took off the market. She is withdrawn.'

'What!'

'In course I will return your deposit in full, there is no question, but the—'

'Took off the market! Withdrawn! But how can that possibly be, Mr Blewitt, when you owned the vessel, and have sold her to me!'

'Ah, no, well, you see . . . never did own her outright, sir. No, I never did. She was put in my hands to sell. I was to bring her up to a certain condition of repair, and offer her for sale – but I never had my name on her papers, no. And now, she ain't for sale no more. There it is, Mr Hayter, there it is. I am very sorry for all your trouble, and as I have told you, I wish to return your deposit in gold. Return it in full.' He reached inside his coat, and withdrew the small bag of coins.

'This is infamous, Mr Blewitt. It is wretched and underhand and wrong. I demand to know the name of the true owner. Give it to me.'

'Alas, sir, I cannot do that. I am not permitted to give out his name. Not to anyone at all.'

'Hell and fire, Mr Blewitt! I am not just "anyone at all", sir. I am the purchaser of this vessel. I do not want my deposit returned, I do not want the gold. I want my ship. I want *Firefly*.' Pointing up the slip to where *Firefly* lay shored, individual new sheets of coppering shining amid the dull mass of the old along the curve of her hull.

'What is the difficulty, James?' Rennie, anxiously, coming to James's side.

'Nothing that you can remedy, sir.' James, curtly. 'Kindly do not interfere.'

'I had no wish to interfere. I simply saw your distress . . . Good day, Mr Blewitt.' Nodding to the shipwright, who stood nervously fiddling with the money bag. 'You remember me?'

'I do, Captain Rennie.' A grimacing uncomfortable smile, touching his hat.

'That is the vessel?' Pointing at her.

'Ay, it is. As I was just now explaining to Mr Hayter—'

'That will do, Mr Blewitt, thankee.' James took Mr Blewitt's arm and led him abruptly away toward the yard sheds, several low timber buildings beyond the slip. Rennie saw that he could not easily go with them, and remained where he was. When they reached the sheds, James still had hold of Mr Blewitt's arm, and:

'Now then, Mr Blewitt. Now that we are private again, I will like you to understand me. I have no intention of allowing you, nor the secret owner of *Firefly*, to hoodwink and cheat me. The vessel is mine, legally and fairly purchased.'

Mr Blewitt shifted the sack of coins from one hand to the other. With evident discomfort and apprehension:

'Well, sir, well . . . I am obliged to ask: where is your wrote-out proof?'

'My what? What did y'say?'

'You say you bought her . . . but there is no contract in writing, sir, no bill of sale. Is there?'

'But good heaven, I gave you that money! I gave you ninety pound in gold!'

'You did, sir, yes, and now I—'

'Yes, indeed, you know very well I did. So how can you talk of "proof", and so forth, when you accepted the money, and even now hold it in your hand?'

Mr Blewitt held out the bag of coins, almost in supplication. 'And I am now returning it in full, look. Take it, sir, take it, if you please.'

'This is nonsense, Blewitt.' With steely menace, ignoring the proffered money. 'And by God you know it, too.'

'I know only that I – I am now returning this money, that was held in l'oo of a transaction that has not took place, subsequent.' Holding out the sack again. 'A transaction that never occurred. Here, take it. I do not want it. It ain't mine.'

'You knew very well what "occurred". A payment was made in consideration, that constituted the purchase of that vessel.' Pushing aside the money. 'We made a bargain, Blewitt, and by God you are going to stand by it.'

'There is no call to grow violent, if y'please. There is no need for threats.'

'Threats! I will show you what a real threat is, you miserable bloody wretch!' Putting a hand on the hilt of his sword.

'Reuben! Will! Noble! Come here to me! I need you! I am being assaulted!'

Three muscular men in leather aprons emerged from the sheds, carrying adzes. They advanced toward James and Mr Blewitt. Rennie now moved rapidly forward, leaping over the slip, and stood by James's side. Quietly to him:

'We must get away out of this. No good can come of swordplay, here.'

'But the damned bloody bugger has cheated me! I am not afraid of his ruffians, neither! I will run them all through, then spill his guts in the bargain!' Making to draw his sword. Rennie's firm hand closed over his and prevented it. In James's ear:

'Step away down to the launch with me, now. They will not follow us to the boat, with so many of our people waiting there.'

And gently, carefully, he drew a reluctant and furious James away from the low, shabby buildings, the leather-aproned men with their adzes, and Mr Blewitt, who still held the sack of coins in his hand as the two sea officers reached their waiting boat.

In mid-afternoon they sat down to a very late dinner in *Expedient*'s great cabin. James was still tremulous with rage, and his hand shook as he took up his glass. He sucked down wine, scarcely tasting it.

'More wine, sir?' Rennie's obsequious steward Colley Cutton, with the wide-bottomed decanter.

'Stop fussing, Cutton, and go away.' Rennie, not harshly. 'I will call you when I want you.'

'Just as you like, sir.' Cutton left the decanter and sidled out, his slicked-down hair clinging to his head. Rennie waited until he had closed the door, then:

'How much did you pay Blewitt, James? I hesitated to ask in the boat.'

'Hm? Oh, ninety pound in gold.'

'Well well, even though you refused it today, I expect you will wish to have it back some time – but not at the point of a sword. Perhaps you will allow me to intercede in your behalf?'

'Intercede how?' Moodily. 'You heard what the blackguard said. He wished to return the gold – which I don't want – because we had not made a contract of sale, when we most certainly had.'

'He was discommoded at having been caused to withdraw the vessel from sale. Often a man that feels himself put in the wrong will resort to bluster.'

'You cannot mean that you think he was telling the truth?'

'About the abortive sale? Very like.' A nod.

'You cannot believe in this third party, surely? This fictitious hidden owner? Good heaven.'

'I cannot see why Blewitt himself would wish to cheat you, James. You have had dealings with him in the past, have not you?'

'Yes.'

'He behaved honourably?'

'Yes. Then, he did.'

'It ain't his doing the real owner don't want to let *Firefly* go so cheap. If you will permit me, I shall make certain of the return of your money, another day. Will not that satisfy you?'

'No, it will not.'

'But surely, my dear James—'

'Thank you, sir, for your kind offer.' James, over him. 'You are very good. I fear I cannot accept. I wish to pursue the matter. I am absolutely settled on the purchase of *Firefly*. I do not want my ninety pound returned. I shall force the sale. I shall prevail.'

'Well well, you was ever a determined fellow, James, in usual an admirable thing in a sea officer. But I must tell you that in this instance you are wrong. By attempting to—'

'Sir. Please. I beg you, do not continue.' Staring down at the table intently.

'As your friend, I think I must. In my opinion—'

'I do not want your opinion!' Banging down his glass and standing up. His chair fell backwards with a clatter. 'You are determined to take Blewitt's side because you wish my private venture to fail! You wish me to come crawling back to the navy on my knees, and beg for employment like some snivelling halfwit scullion! Damnation to that!'

'James, James, my dear friend . . .' Rennie, very shocked. 'I have nothing but your best interest at heart, whichever course your career may take. I have no wish to thwart you in anything.'

'Hah!' Fiercely. 'Then why did you insist on taking me in your boat to Bucklers Hard?' Before Rennie could reply: 'I will tell you why, exact! Because you wished to belittle the whole enterprise, condemn my ship out of hand, and make me see the error of my ways! Nay, do not deny it!'

'Good God, I had no such motive. You are mistook. Wholly mistook.'

'Did you call for me, sir?' Colley Cutton, coming in with a tray. 'Only I has the first remove, piping hot broff, sir. I had great difficulty in persuading the cook Mr Swallow to return to his duty so late, but he has done so.' He carried the tray to the table, and set down two bowls of steaming broth. Neither officer said a word. Silently, dutifully, Cutton retrieved James's chair, and held it behind him. 'Will you be seated, sir?'

Very stiffly James sat down, and allowed Cutton to push the chair comfortably in under him. 'There we are, sir.'

Opposite James, Rennie allowed himself to relax a little. He took up his spoon.

Timbers creaked as the ship rode a swell and eased in a slight drift to leeward at her mooring. Reflected light rinsed bright across the deck head from the stern gallery window.

Rennie addressed his broth, dipping, blowing upon, then sucking at the brimming spoon. James sat mute and unmoving. Cutton waited, and when Rennie looked up and flicked his eyes toward the door, the steward took his tray and departed, closing the door softly behind him. Rennie sucked up another spoonful of broth. James sat still, his hands resting in his lap. Presently:

'I beg your pardon, sir.'

'Nay, nay, it was nothing at all.' Rennie, dismissively.

'As your guest in the ship I have behaved abominably bad, and I am very sorry.'

'I am at my ease, entire.' Rennie smiled, and shook his head, his eyes closed. A further spoonful of broth.

'I am thoroughly ashamed of myself.' James looked at his own broth without appetite, then blurted: 'Catherine and I are to part.'

'What?' Rennie put down his spoon and stared across the table.

James pushed his bowl away. Broth slopped and rode and spilled on the cloth.

'Ay.' A sigh. 'It has come to that between us.' Quietly.

'Oh, my dear fellow, I am so very sorry for you both.' Sincerely.

'Thank you, sir.'

'I should never have thought it possible.'

'It has not happened all at once. But we have now reached an impasse, I believe. We are quite out of sympathy one with the other, and there is no way forward, nor back, neither.'

'I wish there was something I could say, James, or some kindness I could do for you. Perhaps – after our little exchange this afternoon – I had better say nothing.'

'You may say anything you wish, sir. Anything at all. I could not think less of myself than I do at this moment.'

'Nay, do not punish yourself. And never think that I would wish to. If ever I say things that seem to you clumsy, or interfering, or ill-judged – then all I am guilty of is a fervent desire for your success and happiness. We have served together many years, we have seen and been obliged to do terrible things and known much hardship and danger, and you have never failed me. You are my truest and dearest friend, before God.'

'You do me a great kindness by saying that, and I thank you for it, and echo it.'

'Hm. Hm.' He cleared his wind. 'There is no possibility that things might come right between you and Catherine, given time?'

'I fear not.' A breath, and he shook his head. 'I will not burden you with my private troubles.'

'If it will help you to speak of them – I am here.'

'Thank you, sir. I do not think it will help.'

'No? Ah. Well.' Rennie waited.

James sat silent a few moments, then looked across the table, and:

'I had thought she was the most faithful and loving wife a man could hope to have – and in course as you know I do not deserve her.'

'How so?'

'I was not faithful myself. That affair in France . . .'

'Men are men.' A shrug. 'Most of us fail in these things, and you had strayed in Jamaica, as I recall, long before France . . .'

'Oh, that. That was nothing, a foolishness. I had forgot all about it. But what happened in France was a love affair, that I felt very deep.'

A sniff. 'Did Catherine know anything of what happened in France?'

'Nay, nothing, I am quite certain. But I was burdened with sorrow, and guilt.'

Rennie regarded James a moment, and wondered if he should ask his next question. Presently:

'You said just now that you had thought Catherine was the most loving and faithful wife. Do not take offence, but had you any reason to change that view?'

'She took to a life of gaiety and pleasure, and I did not like it, always rushing off to Lyme, or Bath, with her friend Mrs Swanton. Meeting great throngs of worthless, purposeless people, idle gossipmongers and their silken fripperies. People with too much money and nothing to do but waste it, taking the air, taking the waters, going to the play.' Dourly.

'But . . . had you any – particular intelligence?'

'Intelligence?' A glance, a frown.

'I see that you had.'

'Well, there is a fellow. I've never met him, or seen him, only heard of him. Bradley Dight.' Scowling.

'No, don't know the name.'

'Nor did I. Never heard of him at all, until a few weeks ago.'

'You had reason to suspect him of making advances to her?'

'A strong suspicion.'

'What sparked it?' Sharply.

'I found a letter.'

'A letter? From him to her?'

'No no. From her friend Mrs Swanton.'

'And his name was mentioned specific, in this letter?'

'Very specific, and I knew then that Catherine had met this fellow, and quite deliberately said nothing to me about it. About him. In fact she denied it, at first.'

'At first?'

'When I confronted her. And she had hid his calling card among her private things. I found that, too.'

'Will you tell me what the letter said, exact?'

'That he was a very handsome fellow, and that Mrs Swanton proposed to introduce him to Catherine, very soon.'

'Nothing more? No other letters? Notes? Billets-doux?'

'No.'

Rennie sniffed, then: 'I fear I must ask a very direct question, James. Again, pray do not take offence.' A breath. 'Do you and Catherine still share the marital bed, as a couple?'

James looked quickly at Rennie, not quite a glare, then he looked away, and very subdued: 'Nay, we do not. Not for months.'

'Hm. I thought not. You have neglected her, and she has not unnaturally sought comfort elsewhere . . .'

'There!' Bursting out. 'You think the same thing! That they are lovers! Any man would think it, in my position!'

'Nay, I don't.' Calmly, but firmly. 'I think that like any beautiful young woman who feels herself neglected by her husband Catherine was flattered by the attention paid to her by a handsome young man – but nothing more. Mrs Swanton introduced them, and he left his card. If there had been anything more, you would have found more, I think. Trinkets, gifts, billets-doux. I do not believe she has strayed, nor committed hot-fleshed treason. She wished merely to warm herself in the glow of life, after everything she had suffered.'

'What? D'y'mean the loss of our son? What had she suffered that I had not?'

'James, my dear friend, I know that you have suffered much else beside.' Sincerely, leaning forward. 'That poor wounded wretch you was obliged to shoot dead to end his agony, your first command at sea. I know that cut you to the quick, and made ye doubt your fitness ever to be a sea officer again. Then you lost your only son, and Catherine herself nearly died. And then . . . there was France.' Sadly, quietly: 'I think that both you and Catherine needed to be healed and renewed, together. Perhaps you should have gone with her to Lyme, and Bath, and to London even. Gaiety and pleasure ain't a sin, you know.'

'Sir, I think you do not – cannot – understand everything that has happened. It ain't just Bradley Dight, even if he is not her lover. For weeks and months Catherine has sought to breach the trust and understanding that once bound us together. She refused to answer any and all of my careful questions about her activity, she did nothing to disabuse me of my increasing misgiving, nothing. In truth she fanned the flames deliberate. She provoked me. When I am her husband, that had every right.'

'Every right – to what?' Gently.

'To demand answers to my questions, to pursue her.'

'Ah. Hm. Like a magistrate, d'y'mean?' Again, not harshly.

'No no, nothing like. Not at all.'

'Ah. Well.' Quietly.

'I – I may have spoke harsh on occasion, when I was most vexed with her. But she would never address my questions honest and direct. She sought always to deflect my purpose, to obfuscate and dissemble and discommode me at every turn.'

'Hm. Poor Catherine.'

'Poor Catherine . . .' James's face clouded, and began to be very angry with Rennie. And then he checked himself. He looked away toward the stern-gallery window, and bit his tongue. Presently, in a quiet and reasonable tone, Rennie:

'You had not considered, I expect, that she felt herself hounded, poor girl? Under the circumstances, had not she the right to remain silent, to refuse to submit? And had not you considered, in addition, that your own feelings of guilt was behind much of your suspicion of her, James?'

'My own guilt? You think so . . . ? Well, perhaps I may have pursued her too sedulous, on occasion . . .'

'I think perhaps ye did.' A sigh, raised eyebrows, a little nod.

'You are anxious to find fault with me today, sir.' A grimace, and he dipped his head.

'I am anxious to do nothing of the kind, James.' Kindly. 'I wish to see you and Catherine reconciled, that is my sole motive.' Another nod. 'I wonder, now – will you permit an old friend to intercede in this?'

'Twice in one day, sir . . . you will like to intercede in my behalf?'

'Oh, forget about Blewitt for the present. Ninety pound is

nothing at all – compared to your wife and her happiness.'

'You are very patient and good. But I fear you can do no good in this, sir. Our life together is broke in fragments, and they lie scattered on hard and bitter ground.'

'Will not you let me make the attempt, in least?'

'How? What will you say to her?'

A brief glance. 'Leave that to me – will you?'

A hailing shout now on deck, the sound of a boat approaching, and accompanying commands.

'Oars!' The bumping and nudging of the boat alongside.

'Who the devil is that?' Rennie stood up, pushing back his chair. 'Sentry!'

The Marine sentry put his head in the door. 'Sir?'

'Pass the word to Mr Leigh – nay, I had better go on deck myself. That is a launch or a barge, if I am not mistook, carrying a senior personage. James, will you excuse me?'

'By all means.' Standing up politely.

'Or better still . . . come on deck with me. Let us see who it is together, hey?'

'Oh, but I am not in uniform. I am only a guest.'

'Uniform or not, you are a sea officer, RN, and you have every right to stand at my side on the quarterdeck of a ship of war. Come on, then.' And he jerked his head toward the door, took up his hat and sword, and strode out.

Coming up the side ladder into *Expedient* – as Rennie and James appeared on deck – were Mr Brough Mappin, and the newly knighted Admiral Sir David Hollister, vice-admiral of the white and commander of the Channel Fleet. They had come together in the admiral's barge from his flag, HMS *Vanquish*, one hundred. The admiral was in dress coat, and stooped though he was he cut a striking figure in his cockaded hat and gold lace. Mr Mappin was dressed today in blue. Captain Rennie came forward to greet them as they were piped aboard. A line of Marines had been hastily assembled by their officer, Lieutenant Harcher. As he passed him, Captain Rennie murmured:

'Where is your hat, Mr Harcher? You have forgot your hat, sir.'

And moving beyond the hapless officer, and removing his own hat, Rennie formally welcomed the visitors aboard. James hung back and kept out of the way, in spite of what Rennie had said about his having the right to be present on the quarterdeck.

The party went aft to the great cabin, and James remained on deck.

'I do not belong here any more.' To himself.

An officer shrugging into an undress coat approached. 'Is it Hayter? Lieutenant James Hayter?' James turned, and recognised him.

'Mr Leigh.'

'I had heard you were aboard, but I was detained – business in the hold, you know – else I should have saluted you before this. I am just going below to the great cabin, we have important guests. Do not you join us there?'

'Nay, I – I think not. I wonder, Mr Leigh, if you will do me a kindness? I notice the jollyboat is moored astern. D'y'suppose you could spare me two men to take me ashore?'

'Yes, yes, in course, I expect it can be arranged.' Puzzled. 'But ain't you the captain's guest, though? I had understood—'

'I am wanted ashore urgently.' Over him, and glancing at his pocket watch. 'It is later than I'd thought. Be a good fellow and haul in the jollyboat, will you?'

'As you wish.'

And James went quietly and quickly ashore, without making his farewells to Rennie. In spite of his friend's wish to help, James felt that he could not impose himself on Rennie any longer, and that he must now take charge of his responsibilities, and make the best of his circumstances, alone.

'Else I am not my own man – nor even a man at all.'

*

'Brandy, if you have it?' Admiral Hollister with a nod, in reply to Rennie's question. He sat down at the table, glancing round the great cabin. Without being asked, or even noticing what he did, he took Rennie's chair at the head of the table. Rennie and Mr Mappin sat down, facing each other across the table.

Rennie, to his steward: 'Brandy, Cutton.' And to his other guest: 'For you, Mr Mappin?'

'Nothing, thankee.'

'Nothing at all?' A frown of surprise.

'Nay, I take nothing before six in the evening.'

'Ah, well well.' He became aware of Colley Cutton's head immediately behind his own, whispering. Irritably, *sotto voce*:

'What?'

'Hair his no hrandy hin the hip, hir.'

'Well well, bring us – bring us wine, then.' Turning in apology the admiral: 'Unfortunately, sir, I regret to have to tell you that—'

'Yes yes, I heard your steward. Madeira, if you have that.'

'Madeira, Cutton. Jump now.' And as his steward departed: 'Gentlemen, I am at your service.'

'Let us wait for our wine, and then to business, hey?'

Rennie glanced across at Mr Mappin, saw no indication of what that business might be, then inclined his head to the admiral.

'Very good, sir.'

The admiral again looked round the cabin, and he nodded. 'Yes, frigates. They are austere little ships. I have grown used to comfort, I confess. Is that a good thing, I wonder?'

'Sir?'

'It is fitting that frigate officers should live austere, though. It keeps you alert, and ready for anything you may be called upon to do, at a moment's notice.'

'Indeed, sir. Just so.'

Their wine came. Aside to Cutton, Rennie: 'Find Mr Hayter, or send a boy to find him, and ask him with my compliments to join us in the great cabin.'

'But he hain't in the ship no longer, sir.' Pouring wine.

'What? Nonsense. Go and find—'

'He has gone ashore, sir, hin the jollyboat.'

'Good God, why? – Forgive me, sir.' Rennie, to the admiral. 'Ship's business, you know.'

'Did I hear you say the name Hayter, Captain Rennie?'

'Well, you did, sir. He was my guest in the ship, but he . . . he has evidently took himself ashore.'

'Was not he your first, in an earlier commission?'

'He was, sir, yes. In several commissions.'

'But no longer? Yes, now I recall. He has got his own command, in course. The *Harrier*, cutter, ten guns.'

'*Hawk*, sir. That was sold out of the service. Mr Hayter is presently on the beach.'

'And who is your first, now?'

'Lieutenant Merriman Leigh, sir.'

'I am surprised ye did not ask for Hayter again, when you made so admirable a pairing of sea officers, in the past, hm? If he is on the beach, and thus available to you . . .'

'It was – it was not my decision, sir.' Stung by the implied rebuke.

'Nay, I expect it was not.' A pull of wine. 'Mr Mappin has something to say to you, Captain Rennie. I shall stay on the side while he says it.'

A knock at the door, and Lieutenant Leigh presented himself, very correct, his hat under his arm, and apologised for his late arrival. When the formalities had been observed, and Mr Leigh had taken his place at Rennie's side, Rennie:

'You have no objection, Mr Mappin, I hope, to Mr Leigh's presence? He is my right arm in the ship, and must know and be party to our duties and obligations in all distinctions.'

Rennie had decided on this, and it was difficult for Mr Mappin to object. In fact he would have liked to oblige both the admiral and Merriman Leigh to absent themselves. However, Admiral Hollister had not disagreed with Rennie's assertion, and was a man of great and powerful connection.

He had brought Mr Mappin to *Expedient*, and Mr Mappin thought that he could not insist – in least, not yet. And now the admiral:

'Pray proceed, Mr Mappin.'

'Thank you, Admiral. Captain Rennie – and Lieutenant Leigh – I am given authority to offer you a duty quite separate from your general duties of coastal patrol, that will I think be more fitting to your abilities than that mundane though necessary task.'

'Yes?' Rennie, politely.

'Yes. You are to find and follow a particular ship.'

'A chase?' Both Rennie and Mr Leigh leaned forward a little, and the admiral cocked his head attentively.

'Well, no, not in the sense that you naval men mean "chase", exact. I do not mean "chase and engage". I mean – follow the ship, very discreetly follow her, and find out where she goes.'

'What is the ship? Who commands her? Follow her where she goes? How far?' Rennie, with keen, rapping insistence.

'We do not know who commands her, because we do not yet know the name of the vessel. As to where you will be required to follow . . . that may be very far away.'

'Out of home waters, d'y'mean?'

'Almost certainly.'

'Well well, I must disappoint you, Mr Mappin. As I have already told you in an earlier meeting ashore, when you offered me a sum of money, Their Lordships have given me the firmest possible assurance that my duties in *Expedient* would keep me in home waters all the present commission. In view of what we was obliged to undertake on our last commission, I think that eminently fair and just. Therefore, with regret, I must—'

'Perhaps you have not perfectly understood me.' Mr Mappin gave Rennie a chilling half-smile.

'Eh? What is this talk of money, Mr Mappin?' Admiral Hollister put down his glass.

'A sum of money was mentioned on an earlier occasion.' Mr Mappin, turning his head politely. 'As a consideration.'

'How much?'

'It was 2,000 pound, sir.' Rennie, very matter-of-fact.

'Two thousand! Good God, on whose authority?'

'No transaction took place. The offer was subsequently withdrawn.' Mr Mappin.

'I asked you a question, sir.' The admiral. 'By whose authority was this money offered?'

'So you did, Admiral. And I am obliged to reply: I cannot divulge that intelligence.'

'You refuse to answer? When I have extended you every courtesy, and brought you here to *Expedient* in my own barge, and lent you my authority in so doing?'

'Because you were asked to, sir.'

'Asked?' Admiral Hollister's blue eyes had turned to ice. 'I was required, sir, required. By official letter from Whitehall.'

'Sir David.' Mr Mappin had in turn grown icily correct. 'I thank you for attending to my comfort and safety in giving me passage to *Expedient*. Perhaps you will allow me now to conduct my business with Captain Rennie in his ship – I think in the navy it is called an independent ship, unattached to any squadron or fleet – in private? If you please.'

'No, sir. I am not pleased to do anything of the kind. Ye've contrived to involve me in this business, and I mean to understand it.'

'Ah. Then I fear I am unable to proceed, today.' Mr Mappin pushed back his chair and stood up.

'Sit down, sir! You ain't ashore now, where you may throw your weight about so damned presumptuous. You are in a naval ship, a ship of war, where matters are conducted according to the wishes and requirements of those in command. You will answer my questions, sir, or know the consequence.'

Mr Mappin then did a very foolish thing. He smiled at the admiral, and shook his head, and said:

'You naval men are very fond of that word. Consequence. You think that I am in any way intimidated by such empty threats as "consequence", Sir David? Hm?'

'Captain Rennie.' The admiral did not stand up, but his manner now was one of cold fierce authority. 'Who is your Marine officer?'

'Lieutenant Harcher, sir.'

'Summon him.'

'Very good, sir. Sentry!'

Lieutenant Harcher came to the great cabin.

'Mr Harcher.' The admiral did not look at him except fleetingly, and then returned his cold blue gaze to Mr Mappin.

'Sir?' His rediscovered hat clamped under his arm.

'You will escort this gentleman into my boat, and require him to remain there until I am ready to go out of the ship.'

'Very good, sir.' Lieutenant Harcher moved to Mr Mappin's side.

'Admiral Hollister,' said Mr Mappin, and again he smiled. 'This is an empty gesture, entirely lacking in reason or purpose.'

'Be quiet, sir! Else I shall have you placed under close arrest!'

'This way, sir, if you please.' Lieutenant Harcher urgently touched Mr Mappin's elbow, and guided him from the cabin. As they went out of the door, Mr Mappin again shook his head, and:

'A wholly futile gesture . . .'

When they had gone, Admiral Hollister turned to Rennie. 'Now then, Captain Rennie. You will make your report to me, sir. You will tell me everything that has happened in regard to that fellow and your association with him.'

'D'y'mean – everything, altogether, sir?'

'I do.'

'I have known him before this. My last commission came under his direct influence.'

'In what way?'

'Well, sir . . . I fear that I am unable to acquaint you with all the circumstances.'

'Unable? What d'y'mean, Captain Rennie?'

'I am – I was forbidden to reveal the circumstances.' Rennie was now very uncomfortable.

'By whom was you forbidden?'

'Well, among others – by the senior naval lord, sir.'

'Hood?'

'Yes, sir.'

The admiral was silent a moment as he considered the implications of what he had just been told. At last:

'Captain Rennie, I am aware in course that you have been independent in previous commissions, but while you are here at Portsmouth you are under my command as a ship attached to the Channel Fleet. I will not like to be thwarted in my command, sir. I will like to have answers to my questions, when I ask them.'

Rennie felt that they were now in less troubled waters. He drew breath, and:

'As to my present commission, and Mr Mappin's presence here, I know no more than you do yourself, sir. Until today I had heard nothing of the chase – the pursuit of this mystery ship. A few days since Mr Mappin came to my hotel uninvited, and offered me 2,000 pound if I would sign a paper he had in his pocket. I refused outright. Did not even look at his paper. And he went away. I have not seen him again until he came here in your boat today, sir.'

'Why should he offer you so large a sum, Captain Rennie? Tell me that.'

'I do not know, sir.'

'Has he paid you large sums in the past?'

'He has not, sir.'

'It is a riddle, then. I don't like riddles. They ain't the business of sea officers. Our proper work is the handling and fighting of our ships, by command of Their Lordships, in the service of the king.'

'Yes sir, I . . .'

'Well?' Peering at him.

'Well, I think that Mr Mappin would very likely say in his defence that he too serves the king, sir.'

'You wish to defend the fellow?' The blue stare.

'Nay, I do not. His conduct is very – very vexing.'

'Ay, vexing is the word, exact. I was obliged to bring him to your ship, Rennie, in compliance with an official letter from the Admiralty. Signed by a fellow called Soames. Don't know Soames, never met him. Know Stephens, in course, First Secretary, and know the Chief Clerk Wiggin. Don't know Soames.'

'He is the Third Secretary, sir.'

'So his letter states, yes. He writes very elaborate, and flowery, whoever he is. Not a form of expression I favour, neither in letters, nor written instruction. However, his meaning, and the will of the Admiralty, was plain enough. I must welcome Mr Mappin into *Vanquish*, afford him all assistance I was able, and bring him to *Expedient*. Not send him in my boat, you mind me. Bring him myself. It is obvious the fellow has political connection. The whole damned thing is political, in my humble opinion.'

Rennie thought, but did not say, that the admiral could not be described as humble in anything, least of all his opinion.

'I expect I shall be obliged to beg his pardon.'

Rennie said nothing.

'I should not have threatened him with arrest. That is what y'are thinking, ain't it, hey?'

'I have no thoughts upon the matter, sir.' Rennie, carefully neutral.

'That is a slippery answer, Captain Rennie, but I cannot blame ye for giving it. We will go on deck.' Getting up on his legs.

Rennie motioned to Lieutenant Leigh, who had sat silent throughout, and the young officer followed his superiors out of the great cabin, and up the ladder.

Presently Mr Mappin was readmitted to the ship, and Admiral Hollister went out of it, and away in his barge to *Vanquish*, his gold-trimmed cockaded hat thwartwise on his head in the stern sheets.

'Mr Mappin.' Rennie nodded to his guest, turned abruptly on his heel, and led the way aft to the tafferel. On Rennie's instruction Mr Leigh attended them as far as the wheel, where he remained.

At the tafferel Rennie turned and:

'You have caused me great trouble this day, Mr Mappin. I don't know what to do with you, I confess.'

'Must we discuss our business on the open deck?'

'There is no business to discuss, sir. I have declined your proposal. There is no mention of it in my commission papers, so there the thing ends. I should have preferred it was you to have gone away with the admiral. But he has left you here. The jollyboat has been took, else you could have gone ashore in that. I expect I must take you in my launch, when I have looked to my other duties aboard. In the meanwhile you must wait your turn, sir, out of the way aft. Further, I will like—'

'Captain Rennie,' over him, 'you do not yet quite understand your position, I think. You cannot simply send me away. I have not come to you with a proposal, at all. I have come with an instruction.'

'Well well, if you mean—'

'I mean, sir, that you will prepare and store your ship for a long voyage, a voyage of pursuit. We expect the ship you will follow to depart from the Thames estuary within a week. You will depart Portsmouth on Saturday, sail to the Nore, and there anchor and wait. A description of the ship – tonnage, design, paintwork – will be sent to you there. When the ship passes on her way out to sea, you will discreetly follow.'

'Hm. You have all this wrote out official, have you, Mr Mappin? Wrote and sealed official? Hm-hm, I do not think so. Nay, I don't, sir.' He sniffed and turned to look astern at gulls wheeling and dipping over the sea. Behind him:

'Do you not? Then you are mistook.'

Rennie turned to look at him, and Mr Mappin drew from inside his coat a folded document. With dismay Rennie glimpsed the seal attached. Mr Mappin gave him his cold half-smile, and the document.

'But, good God, Saturday is the day after tomorrow . . .'

'Good God, so it is.' Mildly. 'You have much to do, hey, Captain?'

*

Lieutenant Hayter had packed his few things into the small valise he had brought from Melton House to Portsmouth. He went downstairs in the Marine Hotel to pay his bill, but was told by the head porter:

'The bill has been settled in full, sir.'

'Eh? Settled? But I have not—'

'By Captain Rennie, sir.'

'Yes, I know he engaged the room in my behalf, but I never expected him to pay for it. Look here, now then, I will pay, and you may return Captain Rennie's money to—'

'Nay, he will not, you know.' Rennie, behind James. And to the porter: 'All right, Joseph, thankee.' The porter touched his forehead and left them. 'James, a word with you, if y'please.' And they went into the small parlour.

'I am embarrassed.' James, as they sat down. 'You will think that I ran away.'

'I am at my ease, James. You came ashore. Mr Mappin has come ashore, and so have I. Coffee for you? Or chocolate?' He rang the table bell.

'Nothing, thank you. I am going to the White Hart, directly.'

'Are ye? Ah. Hm. Will you allow me five minutes, to say something?'

'In course I will.'

Rennie ordered tea for himself, and when the girl had gone:

'I have agreed to Mappin's proposal. Well – proposal. I have agreed to obey my instructions. I did so on one condition. Since it was not to his advantage to refuse me, he has accepted it. I want you with me.'

'Sir . . . I am again embarrassed. I am certain you have my best interests at heart, but you know very well I am not commissioned in *Expedient*, and that I mean to force Blewitt to sell me the brig, and that therefore—'

'Blewitt will not sell you that vessel, and you know it.' Firmly, over him. 'Your one chance to save your career lies with me, and by God I will not allow you to fail. I have this afternoon obtained an extraordinary warrant of commission from the Port Admiral, upon Mr Mappin's express authority, that obliges you to report for duty aboard *Expedient* upon the morrow. I will just drink my tea, James. Thank you, my dear . . .' To the girl who brought the silver pot, and he gave her a coin. 'And then we will go to Bracewell & Hyde.'

'Your tailor?'

'My tailor, who will provide you with everything you will need. There is no time to send for your uniforms.'

'Sir, I am very well aware of all the trouble you have taken in my behalf . . .'

'Do not think of it, James. I am—'

'. . . but you have not asked what I will prefer to do.'

'Eh? Prefer?' Over the rim of his cup.

'Yes, prefer. With great respect, you do not govern my life, sir. I am my own man, you know, and—'

'Nay, you are not.' Briskly, putting down his cup. 'You are commissioned in *Expedient*, sir, and you are the navy's man, and mine.'

'And if I refuse?'

'Then you will be in breach of the Articles of War, by God.' Nodding, and getting up on his legs. 'Article 34 in specific. I think I can quote it accurate: "Every person being in actual service and full pay who shall be guilty of mutiny, desertion, or disobedience to any lawful command, shall be liable to be tried by court martial, and suffer the like punishment for such offence . . ."'

'You do not seriously say that you could apply the Articles of War to me, do you, sir? When I have not yet decided to accept this commission?'

'My dear James . . .' Rennie put on his hat. '. . . What alternative to this commission lies before you?' And before James could reply: 'Only the beach.' The twitch of a smile. 'That ain't for you, hey?' And he turned for the door. 'Come on, then!'

*

At sea, rounding the North Foreland of Kent, *Expedient* beating into a brisk north easterly wind close-hauled on the starboard tack. Rennie had been particularly anxious to steer away from the Goodwin Sands, that lay just east of the Downs and had been the graveyard of so many unwary ships, and he had tacked nor'-east in the Channel off the South Foreland, to within clear sight of France, before turning again toward the coast of Kent. Throughout the afternoon watch he had kept the deck with the officer of the watch, his third lieutenant Mr Trembath – who had been a middy with him in an earlier commission, had recently passed his Board of Examination and had his name attached to the Lieutenants' List; Rennie had seen his name, and asked for him. The quarterdeck had become nearly overcrowded, so anxious had Rennie been for his ship in these narrow, turbulent waters. His sailing master Mr Loftus; the quartermaster Patrick Clift; two helmsmen; the duty mids; a busy, heaving and hauling after-guard; and a scuttering ship's boy bringing cans of hot tea for Rennie from his steward below; all milled about on the heeling deck; and the boatswain Roman Tangible was a frequent attendant. But James Hayter was not there.

Captain Rennie had thought it impolitic to invite James on deck at all since they weighed and made sail at Spithead on the

previous day. Rennie had not yet satisfactorily resolved the
difficulty of having four lieutenants aboard a thirty-six-gun
frigate that rated only three. James had continued to protest
from the moment Rennie had revealed his new status, in the
parlour of the Marine Hotel. At Bracewell & Hyde, where he
was obliged to order for immediate delivery shirts, waistcoats,
stockings, dress coat, undress coat, and cockaded hat – all on
account – James made clear his discomfort, unease and
unwillingness of compliance:

'Sir, in stark practical terms, what will be my place in the
ship? I am in effect a warranted supernumerary, a damned
frockcoated idler.'

'Nay, you are not. You are a commissioned sea officer, that
will be invaluable to me at my side.'

'As what, sir? Your fourth? When I have been your first
many times, and have had my own command?'

'We will find you a title and a role, James, do not exercise
yourself unduly. – Nay, Mr Bracewell, that is a post captain's
coat.'

Mr Bracewell helped James out of the offending coat. 'I was
merely trying to get an idea of the officer's size, sir. Across the
shoulder.'

'Yes, well well, he ain't quite a post yet, Mr B, and we must
not flatter him, hey?'

James peered at Rennie over his shoulder as Mr Bracewell
busied himself with his tape measure. 'I do not wish to be
flattered, nor made the butt of jokes, thankee, sir.'
Straightening his arm for the measure, then bending it. 'And
what of this warrant of commission of mine? I have not had
sight of it. Have you, sir?'

'Mr Mappin has arranged it. He has great influence, the
fellow. Even the Port Admiral could not gainsay him, though
he did his best, I understand. Happy Hapgood ain't a man to
be complaisant in anything, but Mr Mappin made certain he
wrote out the warrant in full, signed and sealed it.'

'D'y'mean . . . Admiral Hapgood himself sat down with a

quill and wrote the warrant?' James turned, delaying Mr Bracewell a moment.

'Good heaven, no. His clerk Pell wrote it out, I am in no doubt.'

'Yes, I expect you are right.' A sigh, lifting his chin as Mr Bracewell hooked and then unhooked a stock at his neck, and added it to his list. 'I expect it is all official and correct, even if it was not done in London.'

'In course it is correct, James.' Rennie, sharply. 'Come on now, Mr Bracewell, we haven't got all day, you know. There ain't a moment to lose.'

'Very good, sir.' Mr Bracewell draped the measure about his own neck, added something else to his list, and suppressed an irritated sigh.

Presently James twisted this way and that in front of the long glass, peering at his new undress coat in reflection, then:

'When will I have sight of it . . . ?'

'What?' Rennie, pacing to the window.

'My warrant, sir. When shall I see it? After all, it is my name wrote on it.'

'Just as soon as it has been delivered. We must go and see Thomas again, before we weigh. We had better do that now. Are you done, Mr Bracewell? Good, good. Pray send everything to the Marine Hotel, as quick as you like.' He strode to the door, James shrugged into his civilian coat, nodded his thanks to Mr Bracewell and followed, and the two sea officers went out into the street to the clanging of the above-door bell.

They had gone briefly to the Haslar, found Dr Stroud, who had told them that Thomas Wing was again sleeping – his condition unchanged – and they had come away.

And now as Rennie ducked his head against the whipping blasts of the wind, he came to a decision. He nodded to Mr Trembath, and to Mr Loftus, and went below to the great cabin. He made an entry in his journal, then summoned James.

'I have found a title for you, James.'

James straightened his stock and smoothed his hair, and

stood very correct, his hat under his arm. In truth he had been asleep in his cabin when the summons came. He had had little to do but sleep and pick at his meals in the gunroom since he was piped aboard with Rennie early yesterday morning. He felt a little queasy. He had not yet quite regained his sea legs, after many months ashore.

'Thank you, sir.'

'No doubt ye've been hard at work wondering why I haven't permitted you to go on deck.'

'Is that a question, sir?'

'Fact, ain't it? Well well, I have decided you are to be my Officer of Pursuit. Should any one of the other officers be indisposed, and so forth, you will be expected to stand in his place and take his watches, until he is again fit for duty. In usual, however, your duty will comprise the pursuit itself, in all distinctions. From the moment we have sighted the ship we are to pursue, everything pertaining to that vessel – her bearing, speed, handling, what sails she bends – will be pertinent to your attention. Nothing about her will escape your notice. You will report directly to me all of her actions over the preceding twenty-four hours, at noon each day, in a comprehensive written account.'

'Am I to keep the deck, sir?'

'I don't mean you to be on deck all the time, in course. As I have said, y'will take another officer's watch if he is indisposed – but y'may tread the deck or go aloft at any hour, as you please. Each officer of the watch will keep you informed of the pursuit, and allow you to have sight of his glass-by-glass notations, to add to your own observations. In addition you may choose the lookouts for each watch, to aid you, and I will expect you to know to a certainty where the pursuit is at any given moment, should I call on you to give me a verbal report at any hour. I will also like you to give me your sense of what the pursuit may do.'

'May do, sir?'

'You have been in a number of chases over the years. Do

not you find, when you have been chasing a particular ship across the sea for a long time – days together – that you are able to anticipate, to guess and predict what the chase will do next? It is like the instinct of a beast of prey. You apprehend?'

'Yes, sir, I do.' Nodding.

'Very good. I will like to hear what your instincts tell you. – Sit down a moment, will you?' Motioning James to the table.

'Thank you, sir.' James sat down, and laid his hat beside the chair on the decking canvas.

'Two matters remain unresolved, that I had meant to attend to, but in the rush of departure was unable. The first is the question of your gold, which I had undertook to recover for you from Blewitt.'

'I will recover it myself when we return, sir.'

'The other matter – infinitely more important – concerns in course your wife.'

'That was the reason I went out of the ship in the jollyboat, sir. I had decided I must deal with this alone. I wrote a letter to Catherine accordingly, before I left the Marine Hotel, and sent it off.'

'Ah.' He did not ask what the letter contained. 'Then I am forgiven for failing to intercede, as I had said that I would?'

'There is nothing to forgive, sir.'

'Hm, very good.' A deep, relieved sniff. 'We must now turn our minds wholly upon our task. I do not – as y'know – think very high of Mr Brough Mappin, but the more I think about this pursuit – the more engaging it becomes.' He looked across the table. 'And I am right glad to have you with me, James.'

'Thank you, sir.'

'We will go on deck, and see how the ship lies. Ye've earned a breath of fresh air.'

Night was falling as *Expedient* dropped anchor at the Nore, off Sheerness, and hammocks were piped down immediately afterward, at two bells of the first – night – watch. *Expedient* was one of several and many naval ships lying at anchor, among them three brigs, a supply ship, and the guard-ship, but beyond making her signals in the gathering gloom *Expedient* did not try to speak to any of them, obeying Mr Mappin's specific request. She was to wait, patiently and quietly and unobtrusively, for the pursuit. And now Rennie saw the particular point of anchoring here. *Expedient* was among naval ships, and thus would not be remarked.

At supper in the great cabin, where James was Rennie's guest:

'Sir, given my new responsibilities, I must raise a question. What if the ship we seek should slip down the estuary at night, and be gone away out to sea before we even knew she had passed us?'

'Intelligence will come to us, James. We will know when she approaches from the west, and be ready to weigh and proceed at a moment's notice. Cut our cables, if we must.'

'In darkness? In the Thames estuary? Ain't that a very great risk, given the shoals and sandbanks at the mouth?'

'It is a risk we must take. You as Pursuit Officer must prepare for all such exigencies, James.'

'Yes, and in course I am ready to do all in my power to aid us. However, another difficulty arises, sir . . .'

'What? Don't talk womanish when we have scarcely begun, good God.'

'I hope I will never do that. I must ask: am I to have duties of navigation and ship-handling, in addition to my duties of pursuit? In little, am I to be given the deck if I request it? Over Bernard Loftus? Who knows these waters as a pilot?'

Rennie sniffed, raised his glass then put it down without drinking, and:

'I am obliged t'admit you have a point there, James. Bernard Loftus is a very able man, an invaluable man, and I must not slight him nor deprive him of his standing in the ship. You was right to draw it to my attention.'

Colley Cutton came in with their next remove, a plum duff. On the tray he brought their cheese also, and a decanter of Madeira.

'Duff, is it? Good, very good. Mr Swallow makes an excellent plum duff, and his suet pudding ain't t'all bad, neither. Thankee, Cutton.'

'Will you be wanting me for anythink else, sir? Only . . .'

'Only you wished – if I did not – to go to the fo'c'sle and smoke. Yes?'

'You are very kind, sir.'

'Haven't said I did not want you, though. What about our tea and coffee?'

'Ho, I shall return in time to serve that, sir.'

'Very well. Y'may go forrard one glass. No longer, d'y'hear?'

When the steward had gone, James ate a part of his pudding – which he did not greatly enjoy, since for him plum duff had always lain stodgy and heavy on the stomach – and returned to his role in the ship:

'It is not only Bernard, sir. On the open sea, should the pursuit grow difficult or problematic, am I to be given the deck then? Over Mr Leigh, or the junior lieutenants?'

'There will be no difficulty about young Mr Trembath, who has passed his board only a few months since. The other fellow Mr Tindall was pressed upon me. I don't know him, and don't greatly like him. He will do as he is told, and like it too.' Rennie finished his pudding, and drank off his wine.

'And Lieutenant Leigh?'

'Leave that to me, leave that to me. The thing will be managed. And Bernard Loftus. It will all be managed. Light along that cheese like a good fellow, will ye? Give y'self a glass of Madeira.'

Later, as he lay in his hanging cot, James could not help but reflect that very little had been decided, after all. His duties, and his status in the ship, were at best makeshift. And there remained the very real possibility that the vessel they were to pursue would give them the slip in darkness. As for his warrant of commission, Rennie had not only failed to allow him to keep it in his possession, but even to have sight of it. A sigh, and to himself:

'In truth, I do not know to save my life what I am doing here, lying again in a ship of war, far from home.'

He thought of Birch Cottage, of happy days roaming over the hills with his dog and his gun, of his dead son, gone for ever, of all the things he had held dear – and of Catherine, and that last letter, in which he had offered, after much heart-searching, to release her to a wholly independent life, without conditions or recriminations – if she wished it.

'She is lost to me.'

And quietly in the darkness he wept.

*

No word came to *Expedient* about the pursuit, and the ship lay riding at anchor all next day, her cables slowly lifting and dripping as she turned a little on the tide, a reefed topsail aback to aid her in keeping to her mooring place, so that she did not drift athwart the hawse of the guard-ship. In early afternoon a boat was lowered from the guard-ship and approached *Expedient*. Rennie was on deck, and saw in the boat a man he thought he knew, or had once known – a stout, red-faced post captain in undress coat and an old-fashioned wig. The boat was hailed, and in response a very young lieutenant called up:

'*Obelisk!*'

Now Rennie remembered. As the stout occupant of the boat came puffing up the side ladder, Rennie greeted him:

'By God, Captain Paxton, it is you, sir. I thought I recognised you in your boat.'

'Captain Rennie, good day to you.'

He was piped aboard, and when the formalities of the deck had been observed Rennie took his visitor aft to the cabin. The two posts had got to know each other years ago, when both their ships were refitting at Deptford. Rennie had gone on to several far-flung commissions in *Expedient*, and Captain Paxton – who had even then, when they first met, lamented his lot as commander of a guard-ship – had remained at anchor here at the Nore, his elderly seventy-four gradually deteriorating under him, leaking, rotting and:

'Stinking, sir. She stinks like an open sewer, below. Yet I do not dare pump ship for fear she will straightway sink under my legs.'

'I am sorry for you, Captain Paxton. Will you drink a glass of wine with me?'

'I will, thankee. Madeira, if you have it.'

'We have it. – Cutton! Colley Cutton!' And when his steward appeared, after a slight delay: 'Bring us a bottle of Madeira wine. Jump, man, jump.'

'Yes, sir. I shall leap.'

'You are here to escort ships, no doubt, in these troubled days?' Captain Paxton looked about him with evident approval as they waited for their wine.

'Troubled days? D'y'mean . . . the troubles in France? So far as I am concerned, they are far away. I will not like to have anything to do with them. Until we are at war, in least. And we are not at war as yet, thank God.'

Their wine came.

'Your health, Captain Paxton.'

'Your health, sir, and damn the French – war or no war.' They drank, and Captain Paxton: 'So you are here to go into Sheerness, then?'

'Nay, I am not. I am under orders to – await orders.'

'Await orders, hey?'

'Just so.' In fact Rennie was under orders to speak to nobody, but since he could not have prevented Captain Paxton from paying him a visit, he must now do his best to be hospitable.

'This is all very mysterious, ain't it?'

'Is it?' Mildly. 'I don't think so. We are newly commissioned, newly repaired and refitted, and I await my instructions.'

'Where did you refit?'

'At Portsmouth.'

'Portsmouth. And then you came here . . .'

'It is all quite usual, you know.' He pushed the bottle across the table.

'Nay, but it ain't. A single frigate, lying unattached . . . ?' He refilled his glass.

'I know no more than you do, Captain Paxton. We learn in the navy, do we not, never to anticipate Their Lordships' wishes too acute?'

'Yes, yes . . . I expect you are right.' Captain Paxton gave a puffing sigh, knowing that Rennie would and could tell him nothing, but resenting it all the same, and finding in his heart a deeper resentment. He felt that Rennie had been favoured, and had made a considerable success of his career as a sea officer, with a string of exotic commissions to his name, all officially denied but much talked of in the service. Whereas he, Captain Paxton, as worthy and capable a post as any in the Royal Navy, had been left miserably to rot. He sucked down a great draught of wine, emptying his glass. He nodded at Rennie, and made himself smile.

Rennie smiled in return, and in his head: 'How can I get rid of the fellow? He is determined to pump me, and I am equally determined to say nothing. This can only lead to resentment on both sides, unless I can deflect him somehow.' Aloud he said:

'Will you allow me to show you over the ship, sir? There are one or two things that will spark your interest, I think. The Ordnance have given us the new eight-foot eighteen-pounders.'

'D'y'mean the guns with a loop on the button for the breeching rope?'

'Nay, it is the conventional button, but the gun is shorter

and lighter, enabling a frigate thirty-six to carry a greater weight of powder and shot.'

Captain Paxton forgot his resentment, and followed Rennie out of the cabin and forrard into the waist. Soon the two officers were discussing gunnery and tactics, full as opposed to reduced allowance cartridge, trajectory, accuracy of fire, and the like, and Rennie – who made most of the running – felt that he had achieved a successful diversion.

Captain Paxton stayed to dinner, and although once or twice he did attempt to steer the conversation back to the purpose of Rennie's visit to the Nore, he was again deflected – Lieutenant Leigh amused the table by imitating first a horse, then a duck, then a barking fox – and returned flown with wine to *Obelisk* in his boat, at seven bells of the afternoon watch.

At eight bells a cutter was sighted running down the estuary on the tide, and half a glass later she went neatly about – nearly in her own length – and came dashing in under *Expedient*'s stern.

'I have a dispatch for *Expedient*!' The lieutenant in command, through his speaking trumpet.

A weighted canvas packet was flung up over *Expedient*'s tafferel, and the cutter swung away, her great tall mainsail bellying taut, and flew back the way she had come, the sea curling and lacing under her transom and her gold-lettered name:

SWIFT

James had come on deck when he heard the commotion of the cutter's approach, and now as he watched her heeling away his heart lifted a little as he remembered the *Hawk* cutter, his first command. Quietly:

'There is nothing handles quite so true, by God.'

'Mr Hayter.' Rennie's voice behind him, and James turned. 'We will go below, if y'please.' Holding the packet. 'If I am not mistook, this is what we have been waiting for.'

*

The dispatch, written in Mr Mappin's own meticulous, wholly unflowery hand, read:

> BY HAND as per the cutter *Swift* to:
> Captain William Rennie, RN, aboard HMS *Expedient* at the Nore.

> The name of the vessel is the *TERCES*. She is a small three-masted ship, square-rigged and light-built for speed, painted black so that her gunports are not clearly defined.
> Her dimensions as described to me are:
> 118 feet in the lower deck, 101 feet keel, depth of hold 11 feet, 451 tons & 28/94ths BM.
> 'She is believed to carry eighteen 24-pounder carronades.
> Latest intelligence indicates she will sail with the tide early upon the morrow, from Gravesend, bound for Norway.
> You are to pursue her with all diligence, & the greatest possible discretion, at a suitable distance, so that you are never seen to be in pursuit, & your presence goes unremarked upon the sea, until you learn her final destination, which you will convey to me forthwith.
> Her master is named to me as one Denfield Broadman, aged 35 years. He is medium tall, black-haired, sturdy-made.
> Brough Mappin (and his seal)

' "Unremarked upon the sea",' said Rennie, handing the dispatch to James in the great cabin. 'Does he have the smallest notion what he asks of us, the fellow?'

'Nine twenty-four-pounder carronades per broadside is 216 pound weight of metal. Captain Broadman will very nearly be a match for us in armament, sir. That is what concerns me.'

'Good heaven, James, we are not going to engage his ship in an exchange of fire. Our purpose is to pursue, not engage.'

'And she is fast, by the look.' Tapping the dispatch.

'Hm. Well well, *Expedient* is no laggard, she is a damn fine sea boat. No no, our greatest difficulty will not be keeping station astern, but remaining out of sight.'

'Why d'y'suppose he carries such heavy armament, sir? Eighteen carronades, in a little ship sloop?'

'How should I know, James? Even brigs carry them of late, so I am told.'

'Ay, naval brigs. This is a private ship, a merchant ship.'

'What point d'y'attempt to make, James?' Pulling charts across the table, and weighting one at the corners with leads.

'A little merchant ship like this could not have good intent upon the high seas, with that number of great guns. Ain't that so, sir?'

'There is any number of questions we might ask. Why do we pursue the *Terces*? What is her destination, and purpose? What does her master eat for his dinner?' Opening a pair of dividers, and turning them in a line across the chart. 'I go where I am told, James, and do as I am told, and you must do the same. Puzzles, and riddles, and other vexatious enquiry – I leave to others.'

'Very good, sir. Erm . . . since you have given me the duty of Pursuit Officer, am I to have a certain leeway in how I prepare us for the ch— . . . the pursuit?'

'Yes yes, in course y'are to do everything you think necessary, as I have said.'

'Then I will like a good supply of full allowance cartridge filled, and I am minded to double-shot our guns.'

'What on earth for?' Rennie lifted his head from the chart, and stared at him.

'Let us just call it – instinct.'

A grim little smile. 'Well well, that was a word I used,

certainly.' A sniff. 'Do as you think best. I will not stand in your way.'

'Thank you, sir. I will say a word to Mr Storey, with your permission.'

'Yes, very well.' Again peering at his chart.

'I had meant to ask – what became of young Richard Abey, that was senior mid and master's mate the last commission? You did not want him again, sir?'

'I looked for his name on the Lieutenants' List, and could not see it. Mr Abey has clearly not yet passed his board, and so I could not ask for him. I asked for Mr Trembath instead.'

'Could not you have asked for Abey again, simply as senior mid?'

'Eh? Why? The boy should have took and passed his board when we paid off. Clearly, he did not do so, and therefore lacks purpose and ambition.'

'But did not you appoint him your acting third, last time, when Lieutenant Souter was killed? Was not that to show confidence in him, and—'

'Mr Hayter.' Firmly. 'Perhaps you have forgot yourself, sir. This is my command, not yours. I think y'have something to say to the gunner. Kindly go to him and say it, if y'please. And from now on you will keep your lookouts sharp.'

'Ay-ay, sir.' Very correct. James made his back straight and departed the cabin, putting on his hat.

When he had gone Rennie sighed and tapped the table with his fingers, made a face and bent once more to his charts. A moment, and he lifted his head and asked himself:

'Have I made a mistake in bringing him back?' And twice tapped the table again.

Colley Cutton appeared. 'You called me, sir?'

'Nay, I did not.'

'I fought you was making a signal, sir. Calling and rapping.'

'Well well, I was not. – Where is my cat?'

'Dulcie, sir? Why, she is snug in the fo'c'sle.'

'The fo'c'sle? I do not want her there. She should inhabit my quarters, when I am aboard. Bring her to me.'

'Yes, sir. Only, I fear she may wish to return to the fo'c'sle, where she has become a-ccustomed to the warmf of the Brodie stove, sir.'

'Am I to be contradicted at all points, good God! Find my cat and bring her to me, you idle bugger!'

'As you wish, sir.' Departing, and closing the door behind him.

Rennie bent once more, straightened, and threw the dividers down with a clatter.

To himself: 'Y'must not start and reprimand so severe. It is a failing, William Rennie, a failing. Look to it, and improve.'

In the early hours of the following day fog drifted in from the sea across the broad Thames estuary, shrouding and silent, and in the hour before sunrise *Terces* slipped downstream on the tide and away, while *Expedient* lay blind. This was so bold a move, so daring a feat of navigation, that Captain Rennie was at first loath to believe it when later it began to dawn on him what must have happened.

As a precaution he had ordered anchor watches in addition to the regular sea-keeping watches, and at seven bells of the morning watch, as up hammocks was piped, Rennie came up on the newly washed deck with his glass. The fog had scarcely begun to clear, and Rennie was quite at his ease. To the officer of the watch, Lieutenant Tindall:

'No man would risk his ship in this, hey, Mr Tindall?'

'No, sir.' With a confidence he did not feel.

'All quiet?' Glancing forrard through the slow swirling mist.

'All quiet, sir. Erm . . .'

'Yes?' Turning his head.

The stout, fair young man hesitated, then: 'I . . . I thought I heard something at two bells, sir, to the north. I made a note in my book, sir, under the binnacle light.' He showed Rennie the note.

'You heard a muffled cry?' Peering at him.

'Yes, sir.'

'What was it, d'y'think?'

'I cannot be certain. It was very muffled, deep in the fog. I am not even certain it was a human voice. It may have been a bird of some sort. A goose.'

'You heard nothing else, Mr Tindall? No other sounds?'

'Nothing else, sir.'

'Hm. Then likely it was a goose. Very well, thankee, Mr Tindall, y'did right to bring it to my notice. We will keep sharp from now on.' From behind them:

'Good morning, sir. Good morning, Tindall.'

'Mr Hayter.' Rennie nodded to James as he joined them.

Today James was wearing his working rig of old leather jerkin, rough seaman's pantaloons, and a blue-and-white chequered kerchief tied on his head.

'All you require to complete the disguise is a cutlass gripped 'tween your teeth,' observed Rennie, not harshly. He was quite used to James's working sea clothes. Mr Tindall stared in astonishment at the rig, and said nothing.

James had posted only one lookout – on the fo'c'sle – through the morning watch, given the density of the fog, and this man had already reported to him that he had seen and heard nothing. James was now on deck to observe the condition of the fog, and place lookouts in the tops as soon as it cleared.

By eight bells it had begun to lift, and as hands were piped to breakfast Rennie went below to his own breakfast, with the instruction that he was to be called at once if anything was seen. In the past it had been usual for him to invite James to breakfast with him, but today he did not. James remained on deck, and at two bells of the forenoon watch, when the fog had lifted and thinned in the morning sun, revealing the broad stretching calm of the estuary, he went aloft, climbing to the main crosstrees. His mainmast lookout came with him, and together they scanned the estuary in an arc of 180 degrees, from the marshes on the Isle of Grain in the west, to the beaches of the Isle of Thanet in the east, and saw nothing but fishing boats – other shipping having been port-bound by the fog. By three bells of the watch James was beginning to be concerned. Merchant ships had begun to venture up and down the estuary, but in the main they were colliers – stout, dirty little vessels – and none remotely resembled the ship *Expedient* sought. At four bells James stepped off the crosstrees, clapped on to a backstay, slid rapidly to the starboard chains, and went below to the great cabin.

Rennie was feeding his cat Dulcie.

'The fog has cleared, sir.'

'As I see.' Putting down the dish on the canvas squares, and glancing at the stern gallery window. The cat bumped against his leg, and settled to eat. 'In course ye've seen nothing, else ye'd've called me, hey?'

'Nothing, sir.'

'Hm.' Putting on his coat. 'I will go on deck with you. It may be that he will run north a little as he makes east, and try to evade us over t'ward Shoeburyness.'

'I doubt that he'd risk the Maplin Sands, sir, but even if he did I have men aloft. He could not escape our attention, no matter how far north he dared to run.'

They went on deck. At five bells, Rennie looked at his pocket watch just as James slid to the deck from the mizzen crosstrees, where he had gone with his glass.

'Sir, I am very concerned, now.'

Rennie looked at his Pursuit Officer, frowned, and:

'Could he have given us the slip, after all, Mr Hayter?'

'I think that very likely he has, sir. In darkness and fog.'

'It is nearly beyond belief. How did he manage it, the villain?' Then:

'By God, Mr Tindall's goose.' He had made his own note of the lieutenant's observation, and now found and confirmed it. 'Two bells – five o'clock.'

'Goose . . . ?'

'Ay, that Mr Tindall heard in the early morning darkness. An echo across the water, deep in the fog. But it was not a goose, it was a muffled shout of command from that damned ship as she went down on the tide, right under our noses. God damn that wretch Broadman, he has outfoxed us! Mr Trembath!'

'Sir?' The officer of the watch, attending.

'We will weigh at once, if y'please, and make sail.' Urgently.

'Ay-ay, sir.' Touching his hat, shocked at the suddenness of the departure. 'Mr Tangible! Hands to weigh, and make sail!'

Mr Loftus ran on deck, cramming on his hat. Pounding feet, curses, men pulling themselves up hand over hand in the shrouds, their feet dancing on the ratlines. The foretopsail falling in a great grey expanding tumble from the yard. Waisters hauling. The bellowing of the fo'c'sle petty officer. Rennie stood at the breast-rail in a fever of urgency, and presently, with a drumming of his fingers:

'Nay, nay, this will not answer. – Mr Tangible!'

'Sir?' The boatswain.

'We will cut our cables if y'please! Cheerly now! We are in a chase, and there ain't—'

'– a moment to lose.' Roman Tangible finished for him, and turned to give the orders at the roaring top of his voice.

Sea axes thudded in a hacking rhythm, *Expedient* swung away from her severed cables in the light morning breeze, and caught it, and begun to run before, east-nor' east toward the open sea, under spreading canvas.

'Stunsails, Mr Loftus! Alow and aloft, if y'please! Let us crack on!'

Half a glass, and Rennie:

'Mr Loftus, I will like to find that bugger before sunset today, just to make certain he is going where I think he is.'

'And where is that, sir . . . ?'

'Set me a course for Norway, Mr Loftus. Mr Hayter! You there, Mr Madeley.' To the duty mid nearest him. 'Find Mr Hayter, and—'

'He – he is aloft, sir.' Pointing high. Rennie looked, and saw James foreshortened far above in the canvas tower, a tiny figure clinging to the mainroyal mast, his feet braced on the narrow yard, and his glass to his eye.

The swell and chop of the open sea, and *Expedient* began to lift and roll as she came round on the new heading, the wind on her larboard beam and quarter.

'Hold her so, just so.'

And feet apart, hands clasped behind his back, Rennie sniffed in a deep, exhilarated breath.

*

The ship – three-masted, painted black – was sighted late in the afternoon, at three bells of the first dog watch. The mainmast lookout hailed the deck and reported the sighting, and added that she was heading east-nor'-east toward the Netherlands, under all plain sail.

James jumped into the main shrouds and ran aloft with his customary quick agility – first acquired as a midshipman – to the crosstrees, where he joined the lookout and focused his glass, and found the quarry. He peered a few moments, then to the lookout:

'What colours does she wear? Can you make them out?'

'I cannot make them out distinct, no, sir.' Peering through his own glass.

'Neither can I.'

James slid by a backstay to the deck, and informed his captain, who:

'Ay, he is a wily fellow, the villain. His colours are false, very like.'

'Well, false colours or not, he certainly makes for the Netherlands coast, on his present heading.'

'Hm. That surprises me.' A sniff. 'However, we will follow. We must not overhaul him, though. We must maintain station at a discreet distance astern.'

'Very good, sir.' Lowering his voice: 'Am I to have the deck, sir?'

'What? Dressed like that? I think not, Mr Hayter.' Also lowering his voice.

'You wish me to shift into undress coat, sir?'

'Mr Trembath has the deck.' Pointing to the young lieutenant, who stood at the weather-rail with his glass, looking at the pursuit ship. 'You will consult with him, if need be.'

'Consult . . . ?'

'Just so.'

James found this very disconcerting, and vexing. The question of his status in the ship had even now – when they were at sea, and in pursuit – not properly been addressed, and he felt that he was being left to dangle and swing like a loose block in the wind. He opened his mouth to say something further, but at that moment Lieutenant Trembath rejoined them, and a moment after Rennie stepped away aft, and stood alone on the quarterdeck near the tafferel. James knew that in keeping with the tradition of the service he could not follow the captain there, unless he was asked, and so he exchanged a few words with Mr Trembath, and went again aloft to observe the *Terces* as she continued steady on her course, east-nor'-east toward the Dutch coast.

'Why does she make for the Netherlands?' To himself, raising then lowering his glass. 'Denfield Broadman ain't a Dutch name, and Mappin said nothing about a Hollander connection. He said Norway.'

It became clear as twilight approached that the ship they were following had altered course a little and was now heading due east, in all probability making for Rotterdam. James studied her carefully through his glass while the light held, and after a time became certain that the ship he was observing could not be the *Terces*, after all. Her lines were different from the description given in the despatch. She was a long way ahead, but he thought she had more the look of a fluke than a ship sloop. Her bow was bluff, and her stern rounded, without the angular transom of a lighter-built vessel. She looked to be heavy-laden and lying low in the water. James descended once more and went to Rennie in the great cabin, where the captain was writing in his journal.

'That cannot be *Terces*, sir, I fear.'

'What?'

James gave his reasons, and Rennie:

'Then why did you identify her as *Terces* earlier, good heaven?'

'She was a small three-masted square-rigger, painted black, and I thought that given her position it could only be *Terces*. I was mistook.'

'Have you discussed this with anyone else in the ship?'

'Nay, I have not. I thought it my duty to inform you at—'

'Good, good.' Over him. 'Do not do so. I do not want the people discouraged so early in the commission. Nor do I wish the quarterdeck to be seen as a tribe of damned fools. We will continue the pursuit until nightfall, then anchor off the Dutch coast. We cannot risk falling on a lee shore in darkness. With any luck the master of the Dutch ship will slip through the channel on his way in to Rotterdam, and there will be no sign of him in the morning. We will then give it out that we think *Terces* tried to fox us into believing she made for Rotterdam, and has again headed into the North Sea, making for Norway, and make sail in pursuit.'

'Could not we simply alter course now, sir, and try to find *Terces* while the—'

'Did not y'hear me, James?' Brusquely. 'We will resume the pursuit at first light. Sailing on blind now will not answer.'

'With respect, sir, we have already lost time in following the wrong ship, and—'

'Yes, and whose fault was that? Hey? Yours, sir, yours.' Again brusquely.

'I admit it. It was my fault. But as Pursuit Officer I think I must indicate that—'

'Indicate, Mr Hayter?' A glint in his eye. 'D'y'presume also to contradict?'

'No, sir, in course I do not. However, it is my strong—'

'You do not contradict me,' over him, 'and yet you continue to express a contrary view – to indicate?'

'Sir, if I am to conduct myself efficient as Pursuit Officer, I think I must be permitted to—'

'You are made efficient by obeying orders, sir. Pray do so.'

'Very good, sir.' James bowed stiffly, and left the cabin.

Rennie shook his head, expelled a forceful breath, and walked away from his table to the stern-gallery window. Presently he turned and peered round the cabin:

'Dulcie . . . Dulcie . . . where are you, my dear?'

His cat did not come to him.

*

The open sea, under a hazy early morning sky, the water glittering and dull in turn as each wave of thousands and tens of thousands rose and folded into the next, the waterscape stretching away at all points of the compass to the hazy horizon. Fishing boats, and away to the west, heading north and south in the lifting south-westerly breeze, small merchant ships. *Expedient* on the larboard tack, sailing four points large with weather stunsails bent, and the weather clew of the main course hauled up.

Captain Rennie emerged on his quarterdeck, and asked the officer of the watch Lieutenant Leigh – in *Expedient* the first lieutenant always took his watch – how the ship lay. Lieutenant Hayter was already aloft in the maintop. Lieutenant Leigh gave the captain all the information he required – sails, trim, the direction of the wind and the speed and position of the ship – and called for the duty mids to run out the logship again.

'Nay, Mr Leigh. You have told me the speed of the ship at the last glass, and I am content, until the bell sounds again.'

'Very good, sir.' Tucking away his notations in his coat. Lieutenant Leigh was always very correct in his dress when he had the deck, and never came on duty other than in frockcoat, waistcoat and breeches and cockaded hat, and his glass under his arm. He dismissed the mids for the moment.

Rennie stepped to the weather-rail, then aft to the tafferel. He observed the line of the ship's wake a moment, then turned and walked forrard to the wheel. Lifting his head:

'Aloft there! Mr Hayter! What ships in sight!'

In answer James slid down a backstay and came aft.

'Any number of small merchant ships, sir, sailing north and south – most of them to the west of us.'

'Any number?'

'Twenty . . . twenty-three, sir.' Consulting his own notes. 'Twelve sailing north, and eleven south. No sign of the ship we seek.'

'She has pressed on north in the night, as I feared at first light.' Loud enough for the people nearby to hear him. 'We will follow, and find her, right quick.'

'Very good, sir.'

'You wear waistcoat and breeches today, I note, Mr Hayter. And a clean shirt. This is a miracle of dandyism, eh, Mr Leigh?'

'I had not really noticed, sir. Mr Hayter has been aloft all the time I have been on duty, until now.'

'Ah. Hm. Is it a celebration of some sort, I wonder? A saint's day? A feast day?' Turning again to James.

'I am not a papist, sir, as I think you know. I am merely . . . I had thought that as Pursuit Officer, with very grave responsibility and obligation in the ship, I should best honour my position by being properly dressed.'

'Ah. In course, there are saints' days, and feast days too, in the Church of England. I should've thought ye'd've known that, Mr Hayter – you that read Divinity at Cambridge University.'

'You were going to be a clergyman, Hayter?' Mr Leigh, in surprise.

'No. I was not.' Discomfited. 'Well, for a very short time, you know, I thought . . . and then I changed my mind.'

'He changed his mind, Mr Leigh.' Rennie, sagely, nodding.

'I am just going forrard to speak to my fo'c'sle lookout – with your permission, sir.' James, punctiliously.

'Certainly, Mr Hayter, certainly. And then perhaps you will join me for breakfast, hey?' Including his first lieutenant with a turn of his head. 'You and Mr Leigh both, at the change of the watch?'

Seven bells and hammocks up, and James came aft through the bustle of the ship's new day, the washed deck still damp under his feet. He stood talking to Mr Leigh abaft the skylight on the quarterdeck, and at eight bells, as the watch changed and the bulk of the people were piped to their breakfast, the two lieutenants went below to the great cabin, and eggs, toast and marmalade.

'No doubt you are wondering, gentlemen . . .' Rennie, motioning them to chairs at the table, '. . . why I have not displayed particular urgency this morning? Why I have not marched the deck shouting let-us-crack-on, and so forth, hm? I will tell you. – Pour yourself some coffee, Mr Leigh, and pass the pot to Mr Hayter. – Yes, the reason is that rushing about a ship very agitated, with anxious expression and fidgeting hands, don't inspire confidence among your people. We will find the *Terces* today, I am entirely certain. And then we will settle to our task of quiet pursuit, just as we have been instructed.'

Less than half a glass after came the call, from high on the foremast:

'De-e-e-eck! Sail of ship, three points on the starboard bow!'

James at once went aloft to have a look for himself, and was soon convinced that the small three-master better than two leagues ahead was indeed the *Terces*; she fitted the description in Mr Mappin's dispatch:

'Exact, sir.' James to Rennie, on the quarterdeck, a few minutes after. Rennie finished his tea, wiped his lips and gave his cup and napkin to his steward, who had followed him on deck.

'Thankee, Mr Hayter. If you are certain – this time, certain – that the ship is *Terces* . . . ?'

'I am, sir.'

'. . . then I am satisfied.'

'Will you go aloft yourself, sir, and make your own—'

'No.' Abruptly, over James. 'No no, I am satisfied entire. I will just . . . keep the deck a glass. Proceed with y'duties, Mr Hayter, if y'please.'

James touched his hat, and went forrard. He had forgotten Rennie's fear of heights, until the captain had reminded him with that brisk rejection of the invitation to go aloft. He hid his fear well, but on the rare occasions when his going aloft became an absolute necessity, Rennie did so trembling in every limb, half-blinded by nausea and the dystopian sense that if he looked down even for one second, he would plunge instantly to his death. As a midshipman he had lived in an agony of terror when his fellows leapt aloft to skylark, and had had to invent an extraordinary array of excuses to avoid these more or less imperative games. Fortunately he had been in every other way an admirable student of seamanship, and had duly passed his board, and subsequently been made post, without his superiors ever becoming aware of this fundamental impediment to a sea officer's career.

At six bells of the forenoon watch, Rennie was still on deck, and:

'Mr Tangible!'

'Sir?' The boatswain, attending.

'We will pipe to divisions.'

The command repeated, the boatswain's mate lifted his call, and the high-pitched summons echoed along the deck. Rennie duly inspected the ship by assembled divisions, inspected between decks, and dealt with the list of defaulters. A brief lull, then at midday the half-hour glass was turned, the duty marine on the fo'c'sle struck eight bells, and the official ship's day was about to begin.

Expedient at 53 degrees and 22 minutes north, 2 degrees and 59 minutes east, lying on the larboard tack in a sou'-westerly breeze at a steady six knots.

'Noon, sir.' Mr Tindall, standing very straight, the mid assisting standing at his side with the sextant.

'Noon declared. Thankee, Mr Tindall. Y'may pipe the hands to their dinner.'

Throughout these rituals – divisions, defaulters, the declaration – James's lookouts had kept a close eye on the ship ahead, which seen from the deck lay hull down, a point off the starboard bow; at intervals they hailed the deck to confirm that no change had occurred to her course. When the hands had gone below to their messes Rennie stood with James on the fo'c'sle, both with their glasses trained ahead. Presently Rennie:

'We will hold station just as we are, well astern of her, and match her speed, but no more.'

'Should we beat to quarters, sir?'

Rennie lowered his glass and looked at James. 'Beat to . . . ? Good heaven, no. I am minded to exercise the great guns during the afternoon watch, but not before. Five bells, say to Mr Storey. Or, no, wait – that had better come from Mr Leigh, I think.'

'Very good, sir.'

'Erm . . . who is your mess president, by the by? You have elected your president in the gunroom, I assume?'

'Mr Leigh, sir.'

'Well well, that is fitting. The first should in usual be made president, or secretary, or whichever term ye prefer. I was wondering . . .'

'Sir?'

'In course I will like to give dinners myself, in due time. However, I was wondering if it might be possible for the gunroom to invite me to dine, to begin?'

'Certainly, sir. I will say a word to Mr Leigh.'

'I have a particular reason for this request, James. I want to get to know my junior officers, and I fear that asking them to dine in the great cabin may perhaps be intimidating to them, all at once. They would not likely be at their ease. I was a little down on young Mr Tindall, at first. I thought him unprepossessing as a sea officer.'

'Unprepossessing, sir?'

'Lazy and fat, in little.'

'Oh.'

'That was unjust in me. I no longer think it of him – that he is indolent. He is a conscientious and intelligent young fellow, and I will like to drink a glass of wine with him – if you find it acceptable among you to invite me to dine.'

'I will say a word to Mr Leigh. I am sure it can be arranged at your earliest convenience.'

'That is kind in you.'

Captain Rennie was finishing a late dinner alone in the great cabin at four bells of the afternoon watch when one of the lookouts hailed the deck from the mainmast crosstrees:

'Ship ahead has altered course! Beating south toward us!'

Rennie pushed aside his cheese, shrugged hastily into his coat, and ran on deck. James met him as he reached the wheel.

'May I have the deck, sir, with your permission?'

'Nay, nay, Mr Hayter, Mr Trembath has the deck, and there is no reason to relieve him of that duty.'

James leaned closer to the captain, lowering his voice and speaking urgently in his ear: 'Sir, the pursuit ship is coming directly at us. As Pursuit Officer I see inherent danger to us in that, and I suggest we alter course at once, and beat to quarters.'

Rennie took James by the elbow and led him abruptly aft

toward the tafferel, out of earshot of the group at the wheel –
helmsman, quartermaster, lieutenant.

'James, you must not make these precipitate judgements and
assumptions. This is not a chase. It is a pursuit, over long days,
to discover one fact, and then report it to Mr Mappin – and
Their Lordships. We are to find out Captain Broadman's
ultimate design, his destination. That is the whole of our duty.'

'Sir, you said that you would value my instincts as Pursuit
Officer. I beg you to listen to me, now. Captain Broadman
clearly knows our intent, or has guessed it. By running at us he
probably means us harm, and I most earnestly—'

'We will proceed upon our present course.' Rennie, over
him firmly, still with his hand at James's elbow. 'If *Terces*
approaches us, we are one of His Majesty's ships cruising in
the North Sea, an entirely usual duty. It is not for us to alter
course and dash hither and thither in anticipation of – what,
exact?'

'An attack. I feel a twinge in my bladder.'

'Then ye'd better find your pisspot, and make use of it, Mr
Hayter.' And Rennie left him, walked forrard to the wheel as
Bernard Loftus joined the knot of men there, and nodded to
his sailing master. Mr Trembath touched and lifted his hat,
and:

'She is one league off, sir, beating directly toward us. Shall
we hold our present heading, sir, or—'

'Certainly, Mr Trembath, certainly. So far as that ship is
concerned, we are not in pursuit of her, not at all. We are
minding our own business.'

But as the minutes passed, *Expedient* keeping steady to her
course and the *Terces* rapidly closing from the opposite
direction, something about the smaller ship began to make
him uneasy. The heeling of her masts, and the speed of her
approach under a stiff spread of canvas, lent an insistence to
her actions which could mean only one of two things: an
urgent desire to speak, or the intention to attack.

Rennie had asked his Pursuit Officer to follow his instincts, and had then rejected them – because he hated to be told his duties by a subordinate officer. But was not that bloody damned foolishness, with a well-armed ship running straight at *Expedient*? Was it not pure bravado?

'Can he be right, by God?' Not aloud. 'Or does she wish to speak?'

The *Terces* closer and closer. Five bells struck. Now she was nearly within range.

'She is coming off the wind, and going about, sir!' Lieutenant Trembath, lowering his glass and pointing.

Rennie had seen it. The little ship sloop was now cutting across *Expedient*'s path at an angle, her larboard side exposed.

A bright orange flash. Then a whole series of flashes along her black port strakes.

BOOM   BOOM-BOOM-BOOM   BOOM-BOOM

At the same instant as the thudding wave of sound reached them a storm of iron struck, and *Expedient* shuddered from stem to stern.

The broadside had been aimed at her mainmast, but the mast was not hit. Two of *Expedient*'s boats, resting on skid beams over the waist, were torn out of their gripes in a whirling eruption of shattered timbers. The breast-rail disintegrated in a spasm of lethal splinters, sending sand-vomiting buckets tumbling into the sea. A midshipman was cut in half on the gangway in a smacking spray of blood. Halyards, jeers and shrouds were cut, snapped, shredded. Torn courses billowed and lifted, cut loose from sheets and tacks. A whole section of hammocks was torn from the netting and hung trailing down over the side. Seven waisters were killed outright, and three fo'c'slemen cut down with frightful injuries. Two died within moments, the other a moment after, retching blood and staring. Captain Rennie was flung to the deck, knocked unconscious by the shockwave of a twenty-four-pound roundshot that hit nothing and nobody aboard, droned away to larboard and struck a lifting sea in a thump of spray.

Groans, shrieks and screams the length of *Expedient*'s deck. The sea riffled and whitened by splinters and other debris – fragments of iron hammock cranes, chains, port cill hinges. Three of *Expedient*'s starboard eighteen-pounder guns had been smashed off their carriages, and a fourth shattered from the muzzle to the reinforcing rings.

Terces continued on her short lateral run, smoke boiling and drifting all round and away from her on the wind, and floating in shadows over the sea.

James had been struck by a length of planking a glancing blow to the back of the skull, had fallen half-stunned, then stumbled up on his legs. Mr Trembath he could not see, nor Mr Loftus. He could see the captain lying still, one arm flung out. Blood ran all over the deck, amid bloody bits of men.

'I am the one officer left alive . . .' James, to himself. A breath, he glanced fore and aft and saw the extent of the destruction, and aloud:

'Beat to quarters! Clear the decks for action! Cheerly now, lads!'

Groans and screams.

'Come on, now, we must man our guns and fight! You there, corporal of marines!' To a red-coated marine, who staggered to his feet, leaning on his musket. The man clearly could not hear. His eyes were glazed, and blood ran down his cheek from a wound on his scalp. James ran aft to the wheel. The helmsman had not been hit, and now clung to the spokes in white-faced fear, certain only of the fact that his wheel was not destroyed, and thus his world was still intact. A lookout, from far aloft:

'She is tacking away! She is escaping to the north!'

Later, as his people attempted to recover from the devastation all about them, and his ship limped half crippled across the sea, Rennie castigated himself, having recovered consciousness after being carried below. Bitterly:

'You should have beat to quarters. You should have listened to James Hayter, your most loyal and tactically experienced officer, and you did not. You behaved acutely irresponsible, lackadaisical, and foolish, you bloody wretched buffoon you! You don't deserve command of a ship of war, you don't deserve command of a fucking harbour hoy! And ye'll pay for this, by God. Ye'll suffer, you mump!'

His new surgeon, a bald, bespectacled, thin man of thirty called Elias Empson, came to the door of the great cabin to make his report. Rennie had been assigned this man by the Sick & Hurt when Dr Wing was unable to rejoin the ship. Rennie knew nothing untoward about him, but the very fact of his not being Thomas Wing counted against him in Rennie's eyes. The captain rose on his legs and:

'I will go below with you, Doctor, and see for myself.' Staggering a little.

As they went, the surgeon: 'Eleven killed, sir. And eighteen wounded severe enough to require continued attention.'

'Amputations? Head wounds?' They went down the ladder.

'I fear there may be two men that I must cut, yes. Else gangrene will result. As to injuries to the skull – one man has lost an eye, and another has a very disfiguring wound to his lower jaw, but likely will live.'

'Thank you, Doctor.' As they moved among the groaning patients in the confined space the surgeon had utilised forrard in the lower deck. And to himself, in terrible dismay and shame, Rennie: 'It is all my fault, my fault, my fault.'

Later still he conferred with his officers in the great cabin, all excepting Lieutenant Trembath, who lay with an injured leg below. He asked each in turn for reports of damage, and an assessment of the position. Mr Leigh confined his remarks to the bare facts: damage to the boats, upperworks, masts, rigging and guns. Mr Tindall added his own observations. Mr Loftus gave his, as to trim, seaworthiness, &c. And James, as Pursuit Officer:

'*Terces* has made good her escape entirely undamaged, since we did not fire upon her, not even a pistol shot, sir. In my opinion *Expedient* is not in a condition to resume nor maintain the pursuit.'

'Not in a condition, Mr Hayter?' Rennie turned to look at him.

'No, sir. The damage is very extensive, as Mr Leigh has—'

'I will not like to hear that we are powerless. I will not like to hear that we are beat. What does the boatswain say, Mr Leigh? And the carpenter?'

Merriman Leigh cleared his wind, and: 'We would – we will require very considerable repairs before we could proceed at all, sir. We are merely limping at present, with the wind behind us, and—'

'Limping? We are making headway.' Curtly. 'No great damage was done below the starboard port strakes, since the broadside we took was aimed at our mainmast, and did not strike home.'

'Well, yes, that is so, sir . . . but we sustained very great damage elsewhere in the ship, and we are making headway only in so far as the wind—'

'Am I surrounded by fainthearts, good God? The ship swims, and we are not all dead, we are alive and able. We will proceed as ordered.'

'To what purpose?' James, flatly.

'What did y'say?' Rennie, turning again to James.

'What purpose is served by our proceeding, sir? When we—'

'What purpose! Overhauling that bloody villain Broadman, and teaching him that he cannot attack one of His Majesty's frigates with impunity, by God!'

'Surely . . . that cannot be our true purpose, sir, when our written instruction is merely to follow and report the *Terces'* destination . . . ain't it?'

'Y'will kindly allow me to know the purpose, Mr Hayter, and all of you.' Glaring round the table at them.

'Very good, sir.' James, politely inclining his head.

Rennie stood, and walked to the stern-gallery window. At last turned, and:

'Very well, thank you, gentlemen. You have made your reports. Return to your duties, if y'please.' And as they all made to leave: 'Mr Loftus, will you pass the word for the gunner, the carpenter and the boatswain to attend me in the waist in half a glass? And Mr Hayter, I will like you to remain.'

When the others had gone, Rennie returned to the table, sat down and rubbed the back of his neck. James remained standing. Rennie did not look at him, and called:

'Colley Cutton! Bring me a pint of grog!'

A brief delay, and still Rennie did not turn his gaze on James, but sat quietly at the table, staring at his hands in front of him. Cutton brought his pint of grog.

'Is it three water?'

'Hit is, sir, yes. Three parts water and one part spirit, sir.'

'Very well. Y'may go.'

The steward departed. James shifted his feet, and looked up at the deckhead immediately above. And waited. Rennie took up his grog, and sucked down a draught. Sniffed. Sucked down another draught, then set the tankard down.

'Mr Hayter . . . James.' At last, lifting his eyes to look at his lieutenant.

'Sir?'

'I did not mean to bite off your head, just now. Sit y'down, will you?'

'Thank you, sir. I prefer to stand.'

'Oh, good God, I am about to make you an apology. Will not y'sit down while I do it?'

'If that is your wish . . .' And James did sit down at the table.

'I am at fault, James.'

His companion said nothing.

'I should have listened close when you wished us to clear for action. You were quite right. You were quite right, and what has happened to *Expedient* is very dreadful, and I deeply regret it.'

James remained silent, and waited.

'However, we cannot lie motionless upon the sea, waiting for providence to come to our aid. We must resume the pursuit, and repair as we proceed. There is nothing else to be done. We must make amends for our folly. My folly.'

James took a breath, but did not speak.

'You ain't in accord with me? Hm?'

James was obliged to answer this direct question, and: 'I do not think, sir, with respect, that *Expedient* can be made whole enough, at sea, to continue the pursuit in anything but name, given the very great damage she has took.'

'You don't think it right we should pursue this wretch Broadman, that has had the temerity to fire on one of His Majesty's ships unprovoked?'

'In course, sir, had *Expedient* weathered the encounter better, we should be obliged to pursue him and fulfil our duty of commission. However, we were not in a position to engage, and now we are crippled.'

'We are not crippled! Good God, Mr Adgett has made repairs to *Expedient* at sea when she was damaged worse than this!'

'Sir, will you allow me as Pursuit Officer to advise you?' Then he swiftly added: 'I do not mean to tell you your duty.'

Rennie, with the ghost of a smile, and a sigh: 'Well well – say what you must say.'

'You asked me to apply myself to my task with all my powers of attention and concentration, as to the activities of *Terces* and her master. To use my instincts. I have seen Mr Leigh's list of injuries to the ship, and Mr Loftus's. I have observed these same injuries myself, when you had not yet regained your senses, sir, and were carried below. If we were to pursue *Terces* in our present condition – even if we made some little improvement by repair – *Terces* could well turn on us again, attack and inflict further terrible damage. Perhaps sink us. We could not hope to match her in handling nor manoeuvre, given our present impediments. Our starboard battery is gravely reduced, four of our guns broke or smashed entire.'

'Have you finished?' Rennie, raising his eyebrows.

'Not quite yet, sir, with your indulgence. It ain't for me to say what was in Mr Mappin's mind when he gave us this task – nor Their Lordships'. I do not know why we pursue this ship, why it is so vital to the nation's interest that we discover her destination. I do not know why she fired on us. Nay, I do not. I do know that to attempt to carry through this task, when we have suffered such grievous harm – would be folly.'

'Yes, well well. Thank you, James. You have succeeded in iterating your case with great vigour and determination, great soul. You are very eloquent.' He drank off the remainder of his grog.

'Then . . . you will order us to return to the Nore, and go into Sheerness or Chatham to undergo repair?'

'Very eloquent, indeed.' Setting the empty tankard down on the table. 'Was you not an exceptional sea officer, I should say that you had missed your calling, you know.'

'Calling?'

'Ay – of theatrical. Haven't heard such a moving soliloquy since I went with Sylvia to the play in London, months since. There is only one flaw. A ship of war ain't a theatre. Make-believe and tearful beating of the breast will not answer here.'

'Make-believe!'

'James, James . . . hhh. Why must you always and always make it so difficult for yourself to be complaisant and obedient? You must know that I value your loyalty and experience above all of my other officers. I asked you to remain because I felt that you was owed an apology, and I have done my best to make it. In addition I must tell you that in fact I have seen for myself the damage to the ship, when I came to consciousness, and before I called all of ye to come here to the great cabin. I am well aware of it, well aware.'

'Sir, I—'

'God's love, will y'keep silent for one moment! Will not you apprehend, will not you grasp – that I am in command? That I must make the running – in everything? Now then.'

'Sir?'

'Will you please – in light of all I have said – allow me to do my duty, my dear James, while you attend to yours? Hm?'

'We do not return to port?'

'We do not. We pursue.' He rose, and reached for his hat. 'I am going on deck.' And then he staggered very slightly, and touched a hand to his forehead. James at once moved forward to aid him. Rennie stood straight, and:

'Nay. Nay. I am all right.' And he strode from the cabin, leaving James to take up his own hat and follow.

HM frigate *Expedient*, thirty-six – bloodstained and limping, trailing debris – sailed on.

*

At first James was very angry with Rennie, and very disappointed in him. Since he had no distinctive duty in assisting with repair to the ship, and it was conveyed to him on deck that he was in the way, James went below and lay disconsolate in his hanging cot in the cabin that had been give him on the starboard side of the lower deck, between those of Mr Tindall and the gunner Mr Storey. In usual this cabin would have been occupied by the captain of Marines, but this commission there was no such officer, only Lieutenant Harcher. In her recent refit *Expedient* had been afforded for the first time timber partitions, bulkheads and doors for the officers' cabins on the lower deck, replacing the original canvas screens. Space was minimal, but at least there was some measure of privacy. Now, today, as *Expedient* echoed to the sounds of urgent repair, James found himself entirely alone. He lay gently swinging with the movement of the ship, and his anger and resentment simmered.

'He don't hear a single thing I say to him, because he will not listen.' Muttering. 'My position as Pursuit Officer is a sham, an invented nonsense of a duty that he has disguised as something vital and profound. My work could be done as a matter of routine by any of the other officers. His only wish was to oblige me to return to *Expedient* as his glorified bloody clerk, and sounding board. He has no pertinent understanding of this commission. It is pure blind arrogance that drives him on. When we are smashed and beaten, for Christ's sake! Because of his own blockhead deafness to all opinion above his own, including that we should protect the ship by beating to quarters. A fundamental thing, known to the dullest middy in the service! – I turn my back. I can do nothing, I am absolved of all responsibility.'

Presently he swung his legs to the deck, found his copy of Milton, and lay down again to read by the light of the lantern. Turning a page at random he read:

He asked the waves, and asked the felon winds,
What hard mishap hath doomed this gentle swain?
And questioned every gust of rugged wings,
That blows from off each beaked promontory:
They knew not of his story,
And sage Hippotades their answer brings,
That not a blast was from his dungeon strayed,
The air was calm, and on the level brine
Sleek Panope with all her sisters played.
It was that fatal and perfidious bark
Built in th' eclipse, and rigged with curses dark
That sunk so low that sacred head of thine.

His anger subsided, faded, and disappeared. He put the book aside, and:

'Very probably he meant what he said in apology. In truth, he must feel desperate sad about the killed men. Very probably I was wrong in thinking he wished me to return to duty solely for his own gratification and comfort. Likely he wished only to aid an old friend, and went out of his way to get him a commission. Ain't it? Ay . . . ay, it is. I must not think ill of him, in that regard.'

He heard the striking of the bell, and the changing of the watch.

'I had better go on deck, and offer my services. Even if I do not agree with him in resuming the pursuit, I must not be petulant. I am a sea officer, and must behave accordingly. There will be something for me to do, I am in no doubt.'

He put on his hat and went up the ladder.

On deck he found that his lookouts had already been sent aloft. He busied himself by asking questions. His brother officers, sorely pressed, virtually ignored him, and he was left with only the midshipmen on duty, and Captain Rennie, who paced his quarterdeck alone abaft the skylight. James exchanged a few words with one of the duty mids, Mr Madeley, but the boy was so clearly upset at the death of one of his companions in the middies' berth, and so monosyllabic in his replies, that James let him be. At that moment Rennie turned at the tafferel, lifted his head and saw James, and beckoned him.

When James was by his side Rennie nodded forrard and:

'There is nothing too fierce nor terrible, you see?'

James looked, saw destruction everywhere – torn rigging, torn sails, shattered boats, shattered breast-rail, the starboard gangway hammock cranes ripped away, everything splashed and stained with sprays and blotches of dried blood – and lied through his teeth:

'Indeed, sir, we are nearly restored to full health.'

Presently: 'The starboard battery must be brought into a fighting condition.'

James waited, hoping that Rennie would assign him this task. Rennie sniffed, and:

'Mr Leigh must undertake this, just as soon as he has—'

'With your permission, sir, I should like to propose myself for this task.'

'No no, James, that will not do, you know. You are Pursuit

Officer, and cannot deviate from that duty. No, Mr Leigh must consult with the gunner, find out which of the damaged guns may be repaired, and which must be got into the hold by tackles. It may be that he will need to send guns from the larboard battery across the deck, and place them in the starboard ports where the damaged guns have been took away.'

'Balance the batteries?'

'Exact. An equal number of guns for each side of the ship.'

'If I may make a suggestion, sir . . .'

'Eh? Well?' Looking forrard anxiously as a shout went up and a block fell.

'Send down the nine-pounders from the fo'c'sle and the quarterdeck, sir, and make up the full number of guns in the starboard battery with these. Then the larboard battery need not be reduced. Treble-shot the nine-pounders, and they will be nearly as effective as our double-shotted eighteens.'

Rennie turned to look at his lieutenant. A frown, then:

'That is a damned good suggestion, by God. Very well, James, I will take you up on your offer. Find Mr Storey directly, choose a crew of men between you – as many as y'need without grossly impairing other working parties – and go to it with a will. Your pursuit duties may be neglected for the moment. Our guns, and weight of metal per broadside, may not.'

'And Mr Leigh . . . ?'

'I will say a word to Mr Leigh.'

'Very good, sir.' His hat off and on, and he hurried below before the captain could change his mind. As he went it occurred to him that the slightly lower weight of each nine-pounder that replaced an eighteen-pounder might well cause a difficulty in the trimming of the ship on the starboard side.

'I had better say a word to Bernard Loftus.'

As always in a ship of war the burial service was conducted with the minimum of delay. Rennie read from his prayer book over the bowed heads of the assembled people, and the eleven corpses, sewn in their shot-weighted shrouds, were duly committed to the depths of the North Sea. In the brief lull, all repairs temporarily halted, the ship was sombre, but once the dead were out of her the mood almost imperceptibly lifted.

*

Expedient, still very slow, now at 54 degrees and 35 minutes north, 3 degrees and 28 minutes east, the wind getting up from the south, and the sea grey, white-capped, beginning turbulent, with a swell running. The ship rolling and pitching more than Captain Rennie liked, with stays and shrouds weakened and her masts therefore vulnerable. Repairs continuing apace, men a-swarm in the tops, on the fo'c'sle and along the gangways, and the rippling crack of mallets and adzes. Tackles rigged amidships to send down the injured guns into the hold, and James came to Rennie, touched his hat, and:

'Sir, I will like to make a further suggestion.'

'Well?'

'That we put the damaged guns over the side, sir.'

'What? Nay . . .' Shaking his head, making a face.

'Sir, it will aid us in recovered speed, in pursuit. Eight ton less of metal to propel through the sea. We have sufficient armament, with the nines on the upper deck, and our carronades in addition, on the quarterdeck. The smashed guns are merely dead weight.'

Rennie thought a moment, turned briefly to look aft, then:

'Very well, ye've carried your case, Mr Hayter. The four eighteen-pounders that are broke to go over the side. Make it so.'

'Very good, sir.'

'Only we had better catch this bugger Broadman, else I shall be hard pressed explaining to Their Lordships why I have lost two best bowers, and four of my great guns too, without result.'

Bernard Loftus now approached, as James retreated.

'We cannot give up hope. We will not.'

'No, sir.' James, half attending, distracted by a further thought.

'Even if you think it.'

'Erm . . . think what, sir?'

'Come, James, do not be coy. You do think this duty is damned foolishness, in spite of what I've just said. It is wrote all over your face.'

'May I be candid, entire?' Before Rennie could reply, James leaned forward earnestly and: 'What I think, what I believe, is that since we have both of us accepted this duty, we must see it through, whatever our private doubts.'

'I am glad to hear you say that, James.'

'Further, I am nearly certain—'

'Ah.' Over him, a little grimace. '"Further." Now, the caveat.'

James shook his head, and hurried on. 'I am nearly certain, the more I think on it, that *Terces* does not go to Norway as her final destination, but instead calls there to collect something – goods, or a passenger, I don't know which – and that Captain Broadman's intention is then to transport his cargo far away. I think Mr Mappin knew it, and that is why he told us to store for long foreign service – and he did so, did he not?'

'Ay, he did.' Rennie inclined his head. 'We are stored for four months.'

'At his particular suggestion – four months?'

'I did ask him how long as we went ashore at Portsmouth, you are right. Yes, the notion of four months' stores came from him.' He sat up a little, and the cat, disturbed from comfort, dug her claws into his leg.

'Then it is the North Atlantic.'

'Oh? Why?'

'Anywhere further away would require a greater weight of stores. Six months, eight. And nearer – the Mediterranean, say – would require less. My strong belief . . .'

'Yes, James?' Rennie leaned forward, and his cat, with a

murmer of complaint, jumped down on the canvas squares, and fell to washing herself.

'My strong belief is that *Terces* will go to America.'

'Then we are in accord.' Rising and coming to the table.

James, astonished: 'Eh? We are?'

'And first she will go – not to Norway's principal city, nay, not to Oslo . . .'

Rennie pulled a chart toward him on the table, and spread it open.

'. . . but here.' He tapped the place with his finger. 'To Bergen.'

*

'Why Bergen, Mr Leigh?' Rennie, dining in the gunroom at the invitation of the mess president, put down his glass, and turned in his chair to address his host. 'Because it gives Captain Broadman exactly what he wishes. A superb natural harbour, close to the open sea – much closer than Oslo – from which he may sail direct into the North Atlantic, and thence to America.'

'D'y'mean that he will sail between the Shetland Isles and the Orkneys, sir?'

'Nay, he will not do that, I think. He will sail north of the Shetlands, and then head west-sou'-west, south of the Faroes, and away into the Atlantic.'

'To Newfoundland?'

'I doubt there is anything for Captain Broadman at so remote a place as St John's. He will likely head for Boston, or New York, I think.'

'With respect, sir, we cannot know that he will, when we do not know his purpose in crossing the Atlantic, to begin. Or do we know it . . . ?'

Rennie sniffed, took up his glass, refused the cheese offered him by the steward, and waited for the man to return to the pantry. Then:

'We may only guess at it, Mr Leigh.'

'In my own view—' began James, and was immediately silenced by a warning glare from Rennie.

'Everything that we do is based upon guessing, for the moment, gentlemen.' Glancing along the table to include all present. 'He outfoxed us once, and dealt us a heavy blow, from which we have near recovered.' He nodded approvingly at Mr Trembath, who had risen from his hanging cot to attend the dinner, his injured leg yet heavily strapped. 'We have not been able to pursue him direct, therefore, but Bergen is his immediate design, I am in no doubt.' Confidently.

'Nor am I.' James took up the decanter pushed along to him by Dr Empson, and refilled his glass. The doctor had not refilled his own glass. Nor had Mr Trembath, who looked – and felt – rather frail still. Mr Loftus was in his cups. Mr Tindall, as officer of the watch, was entirely sober, and in order to attend the dinner had briefly left the deck in the charge of the master's mate. The purser Mr Trent – a stout, rubicund figure – was today absent, laid low by a stomach ailment. Mr Harcher, the Marine officer, made up an even number of eight at table. He was very flushed, beginning voluble, and quite unaware of it.

'I wonder if you have had occasion, sir, to examine my plan?' To Rennie.

'Your plan, Mr Harcher?' Turning politely.

'Yes, sir, yes. I gave it into the hand of your steward, who said he would pass it to you at the earliest opportunity, since you have no clerk this commission. The plan is this. It is . . . there is some slight difficulty of tackles, but it may be managed, I am entirely certain. It is this . . . and it would not, by the by, entail great trouble, just because there would be two. I do not think it is has ever been done in the Royal Navy, in fact I am not aware of it ever having been thought of at all, and I—'

'Mr Harcher.'

'And I think, therefore—'

'Mr Harcher.'

'Sir?'

'Two of what?'

'Why, carronades, sir. Hoisted into the tops.'

'Hoisted . . .'

'Yes, sir, yes. The effect of smashers in the tops would be double devastating to an enemy. Naturally, they would not fire roundshot. They would fire grape.'

'The enemy . . .'

'No, sir, no, ha-ha. The carronades.'

'Carronades. In the tops. Firing grapeshot. Is that what you are proposing?'

'Indeed, sir, yes. I do not think it has ever been done before, and—'

'And we must hope very fervent that it is never done at all, Mr Harcher.'

'Never done . . . at all?' Flushed, puzzled.

'Never, Mr Harcher.'

'Oh, but sir, I assure you, the difficulty of the tackles may be—'

'Your proposal is wretched, sir. Wretched, and lunatic. Y'would set the courses and topsails afire, blast away the tops altogether, and all of the rigging, kill your own people, and render the ship defenceless.'

'Oh, but I assure you—'

'Y'may assure me of nothing, Mr Harcher, except that y'will never mention the scheme again, in my hearing.'

A brief, uncomfortable silence, during which Mr Harcher buried his face in his glass. Then Mr Leigh:

'I wonder what reason lies behind the *Terces* going to Bergen?' Asked of nobody in particular. Rennie answered.

'To take aboard cargo of some kind, Mr Leigh.'

'A heavily armed ship?' Tilting his head. 'Timber, sir? Dried fish?'

'I do not think she will carry timber to America, Mr Leigh,

where there is ample forests of all kinds.' Tartly. 'Nor fish, neither. We do not know her cargo.'

'Forgive me, sir, but it would seem that we are more or less wholly in the dark about this dangerous ship – ain't we?'

'Mr Leigh, our task is to pursue the *Terces* until we find out her ultimate destination – in America. Shedding further light on the question ain't our work. That is for others to undertake.' With effortful patience.

A further brief lull, and now Bernard Loftus turned his head in a sudden loose swivel, took a moment to focus on the first lieutenant, and:

'We are too solemn. Time for jollities, eh? We must liff up our spirriss and-and-and . . . Mr Leigh, will not you entertain us? Give us a tortoise, as an isstance! Hey?'

'Eh? A tortoise? I don't know that a tortoise makes any kind of a sound, except shuffle . . . shuffle . . . shuffle . . .' He crouched very low, hunching his back, peered out as if from under a shell, craned his neck, withdrew his head, and was still.

'Hhh-hhh-hhh . . .' Bernard Loftus wheezed with bibulous laughter. 'Give us a nelephant, now, willee?'

Mr Leigh straightened himself, and shook his head. 'Nay, I cannot.'

'Eh? Why not?'

'Gunroom ain't broad enough.'

'Hhh-hhh-hhhn't-broad enough! Hhh-hhh-hhhf . . .' Tears of mirth wet Mr Loftus's cheeks.

'However, I will try the battle trumpet of the bull elk, if y'will permit me.'

He did so, and even Captain Rennie was obliged to smile, and chuckle, and nod.

Five bells of the afternoon watch. The gunroom dinner broke up, Lieutenant Tindall returned to the quarterdeck, and *Expedient* sailed on slowly north.

Lieutenant Hayter came on deck at four bells of the second

dog, in cockaded hat, undress coat, and his glass under his arm, to take the first – night – watch as officer of the deck, standing in place of the injured Lieutenant Trembath.

The wind had fallen to a gentle breeze, the moon had risen, and the sea lay crawling and silvery and calm, far into the distance.

*

At six bells of the morning watch Mr Leigh was on deck, and there was a slight haze over the sea. The wind had veered to the north-east, and was ruffling the waves, making an endless succession of rises and hollows and crested ridges, pewter grey, silver dark, glinting and sparkling in the early sun, slipping and folding and running as the haze slowly cleared. *Expedient* was close-hauled on the starboard tack, the pennant curling from her mainmast trucktop, her rigging a-hum. Norway lay days ahead, far to the north beyond the blurred separation of sea and sky at the horizon. No other ship was visible from *Expedient*'s quarterdeck, nor from her foremast, where James had posted two lookouts through the night, and another man at the main topsail yard.

'Three men in darkness, Hayter?' Lieutenant Leigh had asked, when James came on deck at the change of the watch to see the new men go aloft. 'What can three men see, that one could not?'

'I want to hear of anything ahead. A masthead light, stern lanterns, anything at all. And the further north we sail the earlier the sun, at this season. Men in the crosstrees may see a sail of ship in the first gleam of dawn.'

'Oh, very well. It ain't my business, I am merely officer of the watch.'

James had drawn Mr Leigh away toward the aft part of the quarterdeck, abaft the skylight, and:

'Look here, Leigh, I will never interfere with your duties as first, and as officer of the watch this morning, but I am charged

with my own particular duty, and I must carry it out as I see fit.
You see?'

'Oh, yes, I do see,'

James let out a breath, and made a further attempt:

'I know that this is all a damned awkward business for you,
and—'

'What? What is?'

'Having the erstwhile first lieutenant of the ship, her first
first, so to say, always in your sight about the deck, climbing
in the shrouds, and so forth, and in the gunroom.'

'I hope that I've never said anything untoward.' Lieutenant
Leigh, in usual the most amiable of men, felt his patience
sorely tested now. 'I hope that I am always gentlemanlike, and
officerlike.'

'Nay, nay, all I meant to say was – if there is any fault it is
entirely mine. I must ask your pardon for any slight y'may have
felt.'

'Slight? Good heaven, I am not some damned petulant girl.'
Petulantly.

James saw that he could only make things worse by continuing the conversation, and so broke it off, and went below.

As daylight broadened over the sea James again came on
deck and went aloft to the crosstrees of the foremast, today
dressed in his working rig, and his glass slung over his back in
its leather case. He nodded to his lookout, hooked an arm
through a stay, and focused his glass northward. The lookout:

'Only merchant ships sailing south, sir, that I have sighted
since dawn. Nothing at all before, no lights of any kind.'

'Very well. Are you ready for y'breakfast?'

'I am, sir. I mos' cert'ly am. But breakfast ain't piped yet.'

'Take this wedge of pie.' Pulling a piece of pie wrapped in
a kerchief from his jerkin, and handing it over.

'That is right kind of you, sir. I will, thankee.'

The lookout munched the pie, and nodded in appreciation.
James produced his flask, took a pull of raw spirit, coughed,
and handed the flask to his companion.

'I know it is cold work up here in heaven.'

'You are very good, sir.' Taking a pull himself, and handing the flask back.

'*Terces* has nearly gone in at Bergen by now, I'll wager – but just in case she has not, we must keep ourselves sharp. Y'hear?'

'Ay, sir. Sharp.'

'Very good. Let me hear you loud, the moment you sight anything ahead. I will like to hear you even if I am in the orlop.'

'Ay, sir.'

James stood a moment longer, shading his eyes in the morning light, and found his inner eye occupied by an immediate and vividly lifelike image of Catherine, her dark eyes turned on him, and in them a look of such intense, puzzled sadness that he felt his heart lurch in his breast.

'Oh!' An involuntary gasp.

'Sir?' The lookout turned his head.

'I – I thought I saw something there.' To cover his discomfiture he pointed ahead and raised his glass. 'Nay, it was nothing . . . just the flash of a bird's wing.' Lowering the glass. 'Sharp, now.' He nodded, stowed his glass in the case, grasped a stay and slid from the lookout's view.

The coast of Norway was sighted an hour before noon, three days after. The air was clear and bright, the wind brisk from the north-east, and the sea running a slight chop, but not rough, nor was there a heavy swell. However, *Expedient* was pitching in the headwind, a fault common to Perseverence class frigates because of a slight aberration in the design of the hull beneath the bow, abaft the cutwater. It had made one of the duty midshipmen, a boy called Glaister who was on his first cruise, puking ill, so that he was obliged to spend his watch doubled over the lee rail. The officer who had the deck, Mr Tindall, was for permitting the boy to go below, but Rennie – pacing his quarterdeck – refused to allow it.

'Work, Mr Tindall, that is the cure for seasickness. Work.'

'Very good, sir.' He touched his hat.

'Send the lad aloft. Give him something to do in the top. Oblige him to concentrate his attention.'

'I do not think he is capable of going aloft just at present, sir.' Indicating the small, hunched, heaving back at the rail.

'Well well, when he has given his breakfast to the fishes, then. When his stomach is empty.'

The hapless mid remained on duty, his face ghastly green, until at six bells:

'De-e-e-e-eck! La-a-a-a-nd ahead! Two points off the starboard bo-o-o-ow!'

Which bellowing announcement miraculously lifted the boy from helpless, hopeless misery into sudden elation. The very thought of dry land, solid and secure and welcoming, had cured him.

The stretch of coast ahead, as yet low on the line of the sea and sky, was the eminence at Farsund, wandering nor'-west toward Egersund and Naerbö, and a long series of islands, inlets and fjords. Rennie confirmed this on his chart, and by comparing the coastline with the topographical drawings issued with the chart by the Admiralty cartographer, which he had brought up to him at the binnacle by his steward. In the very far distance inland, no more than a faint smudge to the naked eye, snow-capped mountains. The sky near white at the horizon, deepening into sapphire blue on high. Rennie sniffed the wind, and thought he could detect the fragrance of pine forests. He breathed it in.

James had come on deck when he heard the lookout's hail, and was about to go aloft with his glass when Rennie:

'Do you know anything of Norway, Mr Hayter?'

'Dr Johnson said it had "noble wild prospects", sir. And I believe it is clean.'

'Clean? Ha-ha! Yes, yes, I like that very much. Norway is clean. Very good. Y'may go aloft and look at it, Mr Hayter, if y'please, and then tell me if your understanding has been confirmed.'

He did not comment on his Pursuit Officer's dress. The thought of clean snow and pine forests had lifted his heart, and James's piratical appearance, subjected to much satiric raillery in the past, was of no consequence today. When James descended and joined him on deck a few minutes later, Rennie said to him:

'Well – and is it?'

'Erm . . . is it what, sir? Oh, clean – I had clean forgot. I fear we are not yet close enough to be certain, but I will venture that it looks clean, ay.'

Rennie leaned closer to him. 'Have you been drinking, Mr Hayter?' A sniff.

'A drop of rum from my flask aloft, sir, to keep out the chill.'

'Ah. Hm. No sign of *Terces*?'

'Oh, no, sir. None at all.' Unslinging his glass.

'Well well, I cannot guess at such intelligence, you know. It is your duty to inform me in every particular.' A hint of acerbity.

'Oh. Well, I am very sorry I did not do so, sir.' Blithely. 'I had assumed, because I made no mention of her when I came down just now, that you had understood.'

'Understood?' Curtly, a frown.

'Well . . . yes, sir. In course the *Terces* ain't in sight. She is at Bergen, I expect, long since.'

'I will like an account of all your observations of today, if y'please, wrote out in full, when noon has been declared.' All lightness gone from his tone. 'Y'will attend me in the great cabin, properly dressed.' And he went forrard to divisions.

James duly brought his written report to Rennie in the great cabin, after the declaration, and waited, his hat under his arm, his undress coat fresh brushed, while the captain made a show of reading the report through. There was very little in the document, since there had been very little to see the past twenty-four hours. Presently Rennie sniffed, and:

'Very good.' He put the report aside, and looked aft through

the stern-gallery window. 'I think in future, Mr Hayter –
James – it will be more conducive to quarterdeck manners and
discipline if you was to wear correct uniform. In truth I
thought you had resolved to do so, and then today you was
again dressed – unsuitable.'

'D'y'mean . . . always dress in a blue coat, sir? Even when I
go aloft?'

'Y'may leave your coat at the binnacle when you go aloft.'

'Very good, sir.'

Turning in his chair to look across the table, Rennie: 'It ain't
that I am condemning your . . . your other clothes out of hand,
exact. It is merely the question of what will look officerlike on
deck. We must consider your standing in the ship, you know,
that cannot be ignored.'

'My standing, sir?'

'Yes, yes – your rank and duties and so forth.'

'Ah, well, yes . . . I had meant to say something about that
very thing, sir, before this. We had not quite established it.'

'In course we had established it, before we came to the
Nore.'

'Well, yes . . . but I have never had sight of my warrant of
commission, sir, and my duties have never been wrote out.'

'Why should they be wrote out, when I have given them to
you very succinct. How can there be any doubt as to your
duties? Are you in doubt?'

'Well, sir, I am not altogether certain as to—'

'You are Pursuit Officer, with the rank of lieutenant.' Over
him. 'I do not think it could be made plainer than that. There
is another matter I wished to address.'

'Sir?'

'Taking a flask aloft and drinking there, and handing the
flask to your lookouts.'

'It is often cold aloft and I—'

'An officer being passing civil to the people, in a merely
informal way, is not a thing I will ever condemn. However, I
will not like any of my officers to undermine discipline. This

is very painful to me, Mr Hayter – James – but I have begun to notice that y'are drinking more than is good for you.'

'Drinking more than is good for me . . . ?' Astonished.

'Ay. Ay. It is a fault that may develop at sea, if an officer ain't careful. I have seen it in ships' surgeons, and sometimes in pursers too. Even in post captains. You recall Captain Paxton, at the Nore?'

'Of the *Obelisk* seventy-four? The guard-ship?'

'Yes, he came to dinner. And returned to his ship so drunk he nearly stepped into the sea instead of into his boat. No doubt you recall it.'

'I remember Captain Paxton, sir.'

'He is a drunkard, I regret to say. He has lain too long at the Nore in his ship, with nothing to occupy him but inconsequential routine. He thinks himself passed over, and it has embittered him. I hope you will never emulate him, James. That would be a circumstance of great regret to me.'

James said nothing, not trusting himself to speak without anger. That Rennie should say these things to him was – he thought – damned near unforgivable. Rennie, who had often been in his cups in James's presence, who had never stinted himself in his intake of wine, nor spirits neither. Who knew all the particulars of James's career – that he had had his own command, and then had faltered – and yet had not had the decency to keep his views to himself: 'He thinks himself passed over . . . I hope you will never emulate him, James.' Christ in tears!

'We will sail parallel to the coast. Not off and on, like to a blockade ship, but keeping well offshore. We will wait . . .' Rennie paused and looked across the table. 'Are you listening, James?'

'Eh? Oh – yes. Yes, I am listening.'

'You will keep your lookouts aloft day and night. Their observations, and yours, must now be acute.'

'I hope that they have been acute since we weighed at the Nore, sir.'

'Yes, well, hm. I – I trust that you will take what I have said today to heart, James. You apprehend?'

'I think I understand you, sir.'

'Good. Very good. Then we will not linger over discommoding things, that are painful to us both. We will put them behind us.'

'I wish to be entirely certain . . . you forbid me wine at meals, sir?'

'Good God, when a man is eating his dinner it is the most natural thing, the most desirable thing, to drink a glass or two of wine. We all do it, in the ship. Forbid it? In course not, in course not.'

'Thank you, sir. Then . . . it is only the flask you will not permit?'

'Now then, James, I never said you could not carry your flask, like any other officer. I merely said . . . well well, you know what I said. Be careful aloft.'

'Aloft. Thank you, sir.' A polite bow, very correct.

When James had gone Rennie sat quiet in his chair a few moments, then he rapped the table hard and got up on his legs with a great sigh.

'He has made me the villain. He has cast me as the puritan, and contrived to make me sanctimonious. When all I wished to do was help him, God damn and blast the fellow!'

Then he was ashamed of himself, and looked for his cat to comfort him. Presently his steward Colley Cutton brought in the first course of his dinner, which today he would eat alone.

'What is it?' Looking at the covered tureen.

'As you see, sir . . .' He lifted the cover in a cloud of steam. '. . . hit is broff.'

'Yes yes, broth. What kind of broth, man?'

'I – I b'lieve Mr Swallow has called it "Surprise Broff", sir.'

'In little, ye don't know.'

'May I suggest that you tas'e it, sir, and then you will—'

'Be surprised?' Taking up his spoon.

*

As *Expedient* sailed northward along the Norwegian coast she began to encounter numerous other ships, and fishing craft, and Rennie ordered that they should stand well off from the shore, so as to see as few vessels as possible before *Expedient* came to Bergen. The wind now grew stronger from the north, and Rennie and Mr Loftus between them reduced sail to a single headsail and reefed topsails. Even though it was spring the wind produced a chilling effect in these northern latitudes which obliged men on deck to cover themselves in protective clothing. Those men going aloft to reef and furl found their hands and feet numbed as if they were in the depths of an English winter. The wind cut through any and all cloths and oilskins to make keeping the tops a misery, and duty midshipmen, going below from the quarterdeck at the changes of the watch, were rimed with salt from head to foot in the sweeping spray that flung back from the bow as the ship pitched into the wind close-hauled.

The ship herself began to suffer, and Rennie knew that if the pursuit continued in these conditions for many weeks together the strains placed upon her by the pounding of the sea, the constant spray, the fierce winds, would make the rigging, the caulking of the seams, and every part of the hull susceptible to further injury, adding to the damage already sustained at the hands of *Terces*. Every rope, every cable, halyard, stay, line and fall, down to the finest seizing of twine, would be weakened by the combined effects of pitching and rolling, of spray and salt, of sun and rain alike, until everything exposed to the weather started fraying and rotting. The ship's seams would begin to open and let the sea in, and the pumps would have to be manned watch on watch, exhausting the people.

Rennie recalled an earlier commission, when *Expedient* had sailed south into the Atlantic, and called at Tenerife in the

Canary Isles after a mere fortnight at sea. He had been obliged then to carry out quite extensive repair, even when his ship had been subjected to no more than the usual wear and tear of the sea. What would be her fate if she were to face storms in the North Atlantic? Could they reasonably expect to repair again at sea, in such conditions? Might not the ship, having already sustained severe shot damage, be vulnerable in the extreme?

'I cannot allow these things to deter me.' Rennie, as he paced his quarterdeck, his hat jammed down thwartwise on his head. He shook his head, sniffed, and wiped at his salt-crusted face with his kerchief. 'I must hold up my head without complaint, and continue.' Ducking his head as he turned forrard and was met by drenching spray. Thud, and the ship shivered under his legs as she met a heavy sea. Thud, as the bow dipped again, and another scattering storm of spray swept aft. Coming abreast of the wheel he saw one of the duty mids, and summoned him:

'Mr Glaister!'

'Sir?' Attending. He touched his hat, but did not attempt to remove it in the wind.

'Find Mr Hayter, and ask him with my compliments to come to me in the great cabin in half a glass.'

'Ay-ay, sir.' Turning to leave.

'Mr Glaister, are you feeling quite well today?'

'I am much better, thank you, sir.' His face chalky pale.

'Take a pull, Mr Glaister.' Handing the boy his flask. 'One swallow only, you mind me.'

'Thank you, sir.' The boy took the flask, lifted it to his mouth, steadying himself with his other hand on a backstay, and sucked down raw rum. He coughed, his face grew red, and his eyes watered. He gave the flask back to his commanding officer, coughed again, and got his breath.

'Warm, ain't it?'

'Very warm, sir.' Coughing.

'That is unwatered rum, Mr Glaister, to be took sparingly.

Nothing like it, though, when a man needs lifting up at sea. Very well, go and find Mr Hayter. Jump now.'

Ten minutes after, when James came to the great cabin, Rennie was waiting for him. Today James was correctly dressed, his hat under his arm.

'I have decided on a change of plan.' Rennie motioned him to a chair.

'Sir?' He sat down.

'We cannot simply wait outside Bergen for *Terces* to show herself. We do not know absolutely for certain she is there. We must discover it, yea or nay, but we cannot risk sailing *Expedient* in. I will like you as Pursuit Officer to take a boat into Bergen, and look for her.'

'Alone, sir?'

'Good God, no, it is too great a task for one man. You will take the pinnace with a small crew, step and bend, and sail in. I will give you six men, and my coxswain. Ample numbers to handle the pinnace, and adequate numbers to row you away, should the wind die. You will dress as fishermen, and in course fly no colours.'

'Very good, sir.'

'We will reach the latitude of Bergen a little before dawn tomorrow. I will like the boat lowered and got away by first light.' A nod, a breath, and: 'Will you drink a glass of wine, James?'

'I think I will like to keep a clear head in light of the task you have assigned to me, thank you, sir.'

'Come, one glass cannot injure you. – Cutton! Where are you!'

'Thank you again, sir. By your leave, I shall abstain.' Politely.

'Oh?' Raising his eyebrows. 'Well well, just as you say, it may be wiser in you to remain sharp. You will not object, I hope, if I drink a glass myself?'

'I do not think I could, sir.'

'Eh?'

'Object.'

'Ah. No. Why should you, indeed? – Cutton, damn you!'

His steward appeared, holding the captain's cat out in front of him. The creature looked discomforted and miserable. It squirmed and gave a mournful yowl. Rennie at once grew concerned.

'What has happened? What have you done to her?' Glaring at his steward, then transferring his attention to the hapless animal. 'My poor Dulcie . . .'

Cutton put the cat down on the deck, where it crouched staring straight ahead, then convulsed in a series of erupting heaves, and deposited a whole rat's body in a glistening, frothy slime on the canvas squares.

'Good God . . .' Rennie, in astonishment that so modest and small a beast could contain so large a rodent. 'How can she have ingested it?'

'Hit is a mystery, sir . . . ain't it, though?' Shaking his head in admiration.

'Has she done this before, good heaven? She is in usual such a clean, delicate— Do not smile imbecilic like that, damn you! Clean up this filthy mess, and take my cat forrard to the fo'c'sle until she is quite well.'

'Which shall I do first, sir?'

'Both, both! Jump now! – Christ's blood, what a damned repugnant thing.'

'Shall I bring your wine, sir?'

'I have not ordered wine. I am going on deck. I shall return in one glass, and by God the great cabin had better smell sweet, and all sign of repellent upset be gone entire, or I will know the reason why.' Getting up on his legs. 'Mr Hayter, are you still here? Should not you instruct the boatswain about the pinnace, and choose your crew? There is much to be done before the morrow, you know.' Taking up his hat.

'Very good, sir.' James, following Rennie from the cabin, and putting on his own hat.

'Ho, Dulcie . . .' Cutton retreated, returned with a pail of water and a cloth, picked up the cat and put her gently to one side, and began to clear up the mess. 'Ho, Dulcie . . . you has disgraced yourself, ain't you, my dear?'

The cat fell to washing herself, entirely unconcerned.

*

James lay in his hanging cot in his cabin, waiting for first light and reading by the glow of a small lantern. He had left instruction that he was to be called by one of the duty mids of the morning watch, at two bells – five o'clock. The decks would be washing in the grey breaking of day, holystones scuffing in a rhythm the length of the ship. He had ordered the pinnace hoisted out and towed overnight, so that it could be hauled alongside and he and his small crew could cast off and make sail easily and quickly when the moment came. He had slept poorly, his mind full of doubt and contradiction. He thought of Catherine. He thought of the increasing horrors in France, and his narrow escape less than a year since. He thought of why he was here in *Expedient*, now. In the name of God, what was his true purpose in the world? His mind began to blur and his head to spin. He shook his head and took a deep, steadying breath. He turned a page of his book, a notebook of his own rather than a published volume, bound in calfskin, one of half a dozen he had preserved from his first year at Cambridge, when he had had literary pretensions, and wrote copiously in his rooms late at night. A fragment of poetry stared up at him, long forgotten:

> Dancing through the lazy trees
> Insects on the drifting air;
> In the distance, bright beyond
> Lies the summer morning
> High and clear
> Above the green fold hill

The spilling land
Makes birds of men
That walk along the chalky height
And sweep their eyes ten mile afar
In glorious earthbound flight

A flickering
A lofting swift,
And on the softing wind
The creature's song
Hangs intimate
Above the quiet fields

'It is clumsy.' To himself, scarcely above a whisper. 'Why "glorious", good heaven?' He took up a pencil, and made a note in the margin. He lay back in the cot, letting the book fall in his lap, stared up at the deckhead and through it to that faraway world of youth, of nineteen years old and a yearning heart, of late nights and too much wine, of fiery thoughts and passionate debate, of headache and laziness in the morning, and a hundred resolutions to be chaste, and sober, and industrious – of poetry, and the river, and endless languorous days.

'Where is that boy, now . . .?' A sigh. 'I do not know him, any more.' He closed his eyes, and tried to imagine himself in a punt on the river on a summer's afternoon, the sun dazzling through the trees overhead . . . and was roused by urgent rapping on the slatted door of his cabin.

'Lieutenant Hayter, sir? It is five o'clock.'

And in confirmation twin strikes on the bell on the fore-castle, echoing dully through the ship. The muffled sound of holystones. A call from the chains as the lead was swung. Coughing from the hammock numbers forrard in the lower deck. James lifted himself, swung his feet to the deck, and:

'Very well, thankee, Mr Madeley.'

He found his flask and lifted it to his mouth, then did not

drink. He thrust the flask away in his jerkin. Five minutes after
he was in the waist, dressed in his usual working rig, but today
without the kerchief tied on his head. His crew was assembled.
Clinton Huff, the captain's coxswain, and six strong men.
Would they pass as fishermen?

'Huff, there.'

'Sir?' Touching his forehead.

'Pass round these hats.' He gave the coxswain seven round,
soft hats run up for him by the sailmaker out of old cloth, and
retained one for himself. 'You must all hide your pigtails under
these. We must look like fishermen, not seamen jacks.'

'Ay, sir. And I have got that netting, look.' And he dragged
across the planking a quantity of fishnet found in the cable tier,
and smelling distinctly of that part of the ship.

'Pooff . . . it stinks, don't it?' James turned his face away,
and then nodded. 'But it will answer. Keep it stowed under the
thwarts until we see other boats, and then we will deploy it as
if we were casting for fish ourselves.'

'Are we to go all the way into Bergen, sir?'

'Ay, we are. We must find *Terces*.'

'Yes, sir. Only she . . .' Hesitating.

'Yes, Huff?'

'Well, sir, happen she will fire on us . . . if we was rec'nised
as *Expedient*s. Ain't that likely, sir?'

'We shall not be recognised. Follow me, and don't talk
womanish.' He strode to the ladder, and ran purposefully up
to the starboard gangway. 'Mr Tangible! Haul the pinnace
alongside!'

'It is done, sir.' Roman Tangible, coming up the side ladder
from the tethered boat. 'Fore and main masts stepped. And I
has placed a pair of half-pound swivels in the stern sheets,
should other boats prove over-inquiring of your purpose, sir.'

'Swivels? Christ's blood, are they mounted in full view?'

'No, sir, no, they are hid under canvas. But they are there –
merely to warn other boats off, like – should they be required.'

'Oh. Very good.' Peering down at the boat, and then –

shading his eyes – eastward toward the brilliant beginning disc of the sun as it peered over the dark line of the coast.

James was on the point of sending young Madeley below to the great cabin to inform the captain of their imminent departure, when Rennie came on deck.

'The moment you have departed, Mr Hayter, the ship will stand away to the west. We will then keep station for four-and-twenty hours, and await your return.'

'Very good, sir. And if we were delayed beyond one day . . .?'

'Delayed?'

'Well, sir, bad weather may close in, and make it impossible for us to return to the ship. Should we then remain at Bergen, and go ashore?'

'Remain there? Good God, no. I am quite confident the weather will favour us. The question of going ashore therefore need not trouble you. You will go quietly into the anchorage at Bergen, find out if *Terces* is there, as I have requested, and return at once. You have your charts?'

'I have them, thank you, sir.' James showed him the charts rolled in protective canvas.

'Your Hadley's?' The old naval term for the quadrant, equally applied to the sextant, which replaced it.

'Charts, sextant, glass, and provisions, sir.' Confidently. 'All stowed aboard.'

'Rations for each man for . . . how many days?' Cocking his head.

'I thought it prudent to provision us for three days, sir.'

'Well well, I do not quite understand why. However, you are in command of the pinnace, Mr Hayter.' A glance at the rising sun. 'Time for you to be away.'

'Yes, sir.' Moving to the gangway stanchions at the top of the side ladder. Rennie stepped there with him, and thrust out his hand. James gripped it.

'Godspeed, James.' A brief smile, and a nod. James ran down the steps to the waiting boat, and Rennie went aft, and stood

watching from the starboard rail as the pinnace was shoved off
by a seaman standing in the bow with a boat-hook. Clinton
Huff gripped the tiller in the stern sheets, and James beside
him raised his voice in the timeless instruction:

'Make sail!'

The lateen yards raised and braced round, the sails trimmed,
and the thirty-two-foot pinnace, with her complement of eight
souls, found the wind and began to tack away toward the coast,
and was soon a small black silhouette against the glittering sea.

*

Mid-morning and the coast of Norway – the islands lying
outside the port of Bergen – now clearly in view from the
pinnace. Rocky shorelines, spruce and pine, and green slopes.
Beyond, inland on higher ground, the still unmelted snow.
The clear light of dawn had given way to a low, overcast sky,
with patches of mist on the hills. The air was chill over the
sullen sea.

They had encountered numbers of fishing vessels as they
neared the coast. James had ordered the pinnace's fishing net
deployed over the starboard gunnel. They had acknowledged
the shouts and waves from these fishing boats merely by
waving in distant salute, nothing more, and had kept to their
course. And now:

'Sail of ship to the south, sir, approaching.' Clinton Huff,
pointing.

James turned and peered, and raised his glass. He saw at
once that it was a brig, and that she carried Danish naval
colours, red with a narrow white cross. Since Norway was
subservient to Denmark, these were Danish waters. The brig
was making directly for the boat. A puff of smoke in her bow,
and then – alarmingly close – a fountain of spray as the
roundshot struck the sea. The thud of the gun.

'Christ Jesu.' James lowered his glass. 'We cannot outrun
the Danish navy, I fear. We must do as they wish directly, or

be smashed into splinters.' He gave the order to shorten sail, and the pinnace lost way. The cries of seabirds overhead. The faint whispering of the wind over the cold water.

'Ain't Denmark a friendly nation, sir?' Clinton Huff. 'Ain't Norway?'

'They have seen *Expedient* standing off, I am in no doubt, and guessed that we have come from her, and wish to know why.'

'What shall we tell them, sir?'

All eyes in the boat were on James.

'We shall say that we are fishing, to provision our ship.' With a confidence he did not feel. 'In the bow, there. Look to your net, now.'

Half a glass, and the brig now very near. A break in the cloud, and shafts of sun made dazzling pools on the dull metal of the sea, into which the brig sailed. James stood up on the stern sheet bench of the pinnace, and waved. No answering sign from the brig, and presently she sailed within speaking distance, out of the brilliance, came off the wind and lost way. Her gunports open, and her four-pounders run out. An officer at her rail, and the brief glint of his speaking trumpet as her boat was hoisted out.

'Boat ahoy! Are you coming from the English frigate?'

James cupped his hands to his mouth. 'Boat's crew from HMS *Expedient*! We are fishing!'

'We are going to board you, and take you in tow.'

'We have no need of towing, thank you. We must return to our ship.'

'You do not have a choice. Heave to, now. Do not resist.'

The brig's boat was now lowered into the water, and filled with a crew, who shoved off and began at once to row toward the pinnace.

'What shall we do, sir?' Clinton Huff, hardly above a whisper.

'Nothing.' Quietly.

'Are we to be took pris'ners, sir? On the open sea?'

'This ain't the open sea, though. It is Norway's waters, and
the Danes command them.' And he gave the orders for the
pinnace to heave to.

The boat came alongside, and two members of its crew,
each armed with a brace of pistols, stepped aboard the pinnace
with a towing cable, and secured it in the bow. The boat
returned to the brig, leaving the two men in the pinnace, and
after a brief delay the towing cable grew taut, lifting out of the
water in a curtain of droplets, and the pinnace fell in line astern
of the brig, bobbing and dipping in the wake as the brig got
under way.

'They will take us into Bergen,' murmured James to the
coxswain. 'Which was always our design.'

'But we is pris'ners, sir.'

'We ain't at war with Norway, nor with Denmark, neither.
We will see if *Terces* is moored in the harbour, and then these
fellows will be obliged to let us go, and we shall return to
Expedient.'

'Can we be 'tirely certain of that, sir?'

'They have no grounds on which to detain us.' Again with
a confidence he did not feel. 'I shall speak to the brig's captain,
one sea officer to another.'

'Ay-ay, sir.' Glumly the coxswain settled on his little stool,
and said no further word.

In the early afternoon the brig sailed in toward Bergen – the
sheltered harbour, the buildings and steeples of the prosperous
town, with steep green hills behind, and a scattering of snow
along the ridges – and made her signals.

When the pinnace had not returned to *Expedient* on the
following day, Captain Rennie overruled himself and decided
to hold station a further twenty-four hours. He summoned his
sailing master.

'We will go about, Mr Loftus, and continue to tack north
and south off the coast, and then anchor overnight. The
pinnace will return by noon tomorrow, I am in no doubt.'

'Very good, sir.'

The day passed, and the night, and when late in the morning of the day following there was no sign of the pinnace Rennie grew seriously anxious and dismayed. He was careful not to show it, however, but paced his quarterdeck steadily, as if he were entirely unconcerned. Mr Leigh had the deck, and when at last Rennie paused to make conversation, the first lieutenant made clear his own anxiety:

'Should we send in the launch, sir, d'y'think?'

'Eh? The launch? Good heaven, no.' A dismissive shake of the head.

'Sir, that Danish brig we sighted brief, the day before yesterday . . .'

'Well?' Glancing eastward toward the mist-shrouded coast. 'Was she the cause?'

'Cause of what?'

'Well, sir, the disappearance of the pinnace.'

'The pinnace has not disappeared, Mr Leigh. It has not vanished. It is delayed.'

'Yes, sir. But perhaps the brig has caused that delay. Don't you think so?'

'That is nonsense, Mr Leigh, you know. The pinnace wore no colours and was disguised as a fishing vessel, with nets and so forth, and all the crew in soft hats. Why should a foreign brig interfere with such a boat? Hey?'

'Well, sir, the brig ain't foreign, exact, in these waters. These are her waters.'

'Well well . . . well well.' Irritably. 'There could be no plausible reason for them to suffer interception in the boat, Mr Leigh. They are fishermen, going about their business. Fishing.'

'Yes, sir. Only they have been fishing a very long time, have they not?'

Rennie did not reply, but glared at his lieutenant, and then strode away aft to the tafferel, where he stood with his hands clasped behind his back. Presently:

'Mr Leigh.'

'Sir?' Attending him.

'I will inspect by divisions.'

'Very good, sir.' His hat off and on, and he went forrard to the breast-rail and gave the necessary instruction to the boatswain's mate, who raised his call and sent the high-pitched summons echoing along the deck.

When Captain Rennie had inspected his people, and his ship, and dealt with the small handful of defaulters, he waited on deck for noon to be declared, then went below to write up his journal. He was busying himself with the daily routines and tasks of command, but he was fully aware that to continue with these dutiful trivialities would not answer indefinitely. If the pinnace did not return very soon, he must act. He took up his quill and opened his journal, then:

'Cutton, there! Colley Cutton!'

'Sir?' Coming into the day cabin.

'Tea.'

'Not wine, sir? Before your dinner?'

'Are y'deaf, or just a damned fool? Tea, I said.'

'As you wish, sir. Only I has not prepared none. I must boil my spirit kettle in the quarter gallery, wiv your 'dulgence, sir.'

'Yes yes, get on, man. Cannot you see I am at work?'

'Very sorry, sir. I shall hendeavour to be silent as a mouse.'

'Do so.' Then, by an association of thought: 'What has become of my cat, by the by?'

'I b'lieve she has felt herself unwanted, sir, since the hepisode of the rat.'

'Unwanted? What nonsense is this? How are you able to ascertain whether or no a mere beast has such dainty understanding?'

'By her dee-meanour, sir.'

'Her what?'

'She shrinks away, and resides in dark corners, and don't like to converse wiv me.'

'Converse?'

'She don't miaow in greetin' no more, nor bump 'gainst my leg for her supper.'

Now from without:

'De-e-e-e-e-ck! Sail of ship to the east! It is *Terces*!'

'Christ's blood!' Rennie leapt up on his legs, upsetting his inkwell, snatched up his hat and glass, and ran to the companionway ladder.

'She will not like to be called "a mere beast", neither.' Colley Cutton, under his breath.

*

The small black-painted ship had already emerged from behind the long narrow island of Sotra – which sheltered Bergen harbour from the worst of the North Sea storms – and was running north, weathering the line of islands beginning with Askoy, Toftoy and Holsnøy. In the distance to the north lay Seloy and Fedje, and a host of small, rocky outcrops. Rennie peered at the pursuit through his glass.

'Shall we beat to quarters, sir?' Mr Leigh, shrugging into his undress coat as he joined the captain.

'Nay.' Rennie lowered his glass. 'Much as I wish to serve out that blackguard Broadman for what he has done to us, my orders are to pursue him, not to engage him in a sea action. Should he turn and beat toward us, and be so impudent as to attack again, time enough then to clear the decks, Mr Leigh. He will discover that I am no water plant, content to be chewed upon a second time. For the present we will simply . . . Good God, the pinnace! I had forgot the pinnace!'

He paced the quarterdeck a moment, then bellowed aloft to the lookout in the main crosstrees:

'Where does she head now, lookout?'

'North, sir! And cracking on!'

Rennie sniffed in a great breath, turned aft a moment, then:

'I do not like to abandon the boat's crew, in all conscience.

However, I cannot discover what has become of the pinnace, at Bergen, and at the same moment resume the pursuit.'

'De-e-e-ck!' The lookout, cupping a hand to his mouth as he bent down from his precarious position, hooking his other arm through a stay. '*Terces* appears to be towing a large boat, sir! Overly large for a small ship!'

The lookout resumed his observation of the *Terces*, raising his glass.

Rennie raised his own glass, could not see the towed boat, and turned to his first lieutenant. 'Go aloft, if y'please, Mr Leigh, and tell me at once what you see.'

'Very good, sir.'

Merriman Leigh shrugged off the coat he had just donned, removed his hat, slung his glass in its strapped case over his shoulder and ran forrard to the main shrouds. He jumped into the shrouds and ran nimbly up the ratlines, hung a moment in the futtock shrouds of the top, climbed easily over and up, and was soon in the crosstrees with the lookout.

'Would that I could do it so readily.' Rennie, murmuring to himself as he watched. 'Alas, I cannot.'

Presently Lieutenant Leigh called down: 'The towed boat has the look of a pinnace, sir!' He gripped a backstay and slid to the deck.

'A pinnace, Mr Leigh? Are y'sure?' Rennie, as the lieutenant joined him.

'I could not absolutely swear to it, at this distance, but I am nearly certain it is our pinnace, sir.'

'Yes yes, I understand you. But how in God's name . . . ?' He frowned, stared eastward toward the other ship, then Mr Leigh:

'When we sighted that Danish brig close inshore a few days since, sir, our pinnace had only just gone from view.'

'Go on.'

'I think now that it's entirely possible the brig came between us and the pinnace and hid it from view.'

'I suppose that is possible . . .' Then, thinking aloud: 'And the brig closed the pinnace and towed it into Bergen, or escorted it in, under the threat of her guns . . .'

'Yes, sir, exact.'

'Ay.' Nodding. 'Ay. Which would explain why the pinnace did not return – because it was held at Bergen, and the crew took prisoner. Took prisoner, and then brought from the brig into *Terces*, in the harbour, so that she might slip quietly away into the open sea, taking our boat's crew and their intelligence with them, in the hope that the escape would go unobserved. Mr Loftus!' Turning.

'I am here, sir.' Bernard Loftus was standing by the wheel, where Rennie joined him.

'D'y'know this coastline, Mr Loftus?'

'I have had some experience of it, years ago.'

'Hazardous waters, would y'say, standing in? Difficult to navigate?'

'The islands and the coast itself abound with rocks. I would not wish to attempt a passage along the coast in darkness. But in daylight . . . long experience of these shores by naval and merchant ships has given us intimate knowledge of the coast, and the Admiralty charts are more than adequate.'

'We are going to need all of that knowledge. If, as I expect her to, *Terces* shadows the coast northward until she is able to break clear and head west into the North Atlantic, we cannot afford to lose sight of her again. As it is, we have found her by pure good fortune. Had we been tacking on the southerly leg, standing off, it is probable we should never have seen her at all. Lay me in just close enough to weather those islands safe, Mr Loftus, so that we may track that villain near. The time for standing off and following at a distance is past. I am going to dog him.'

'Ay-ay, sir.' A hand to his hat. 'Mr Tangible! Stand by to tack ship!'

'When shall we make the attempt to free the prisoners, sir?' Mr Leigh.

Rennie did not know the answer. He had not wished to

confront that conundrum quite so soon. In reply he sniffed, nodded sagely, and:

'In due course, Mr Leigh. For the present our task – keep *Terces* in plain view ahead. You there, Mr Madeley. Go below to my day cabin and bring me the large chart laid out on the table. Jump now.'

Expedient swung over on the larboard tack, and began to sail east-by-nor'-east in toward the line of rocky islands, the sea like beaten pewter under a low grey sky.

As *Expedient* passed beyond the channel between Sotra and Askoy and swung north, mist swirled down from the hills and eddied over the shoreline, and another vessel emerged from that channel and began at a discreet distance to shadow the frigate. The Danish brig.

*

Rennie stood by the starboard knight's-head in the bow, his glass focused ahead on the pursuit. He was indifferent to the spray that flew up and round him and had already soaked his coat and hat, except when it interfered with the lens of his glass. Mr Leigh had joined him. Presently, without turning round, Rennie:

'Well, Mr Leigh? You have a question?'

'I wonder why *Terces* has took our boat's crew prisoner, sir, that is all.'

'To prevent them from returning to us with their intelligence, in course.'

'Well, yes . . . except that they could have been prevented from doing it by the brig, don't you think so, sir? Why did not the brig detain them at Bergen? Further, why does *Terces* tow the pinnace? Why tow a large boat that can only inhibit the speed of their little ship?'

'Well well . . . we shall discover that, Mr Leigh, when we rescue the boat's crew, and our Pursuit Officer.'

'You do not think – that they will be tortured . . .'

'Tortured!' Lowering his glass. 'Good God, don't talk so extravagant, Mr Leigh. They are held only as an expedient measure, I am in no doubt, and will be cast adrift in the pinnace when that purpose has been served.'

'Did you say "expedient", sir?'

'What? Oh.' Ruffled. 'Well well, it was neither an apt nor opportune description, Mr Leigh. Captain Broadman has done it for his own ends. Will that answer?'

'I beg your pardon, sir, I had only meant it as a joke.'

'This ain't the time for jokes.' Curtly, raising his glass again.

Islands and rocky outcrops ahead in profusion. Mist along the low hills, clinging to the tops of the trees, and swirling down along the indented, wandering shoreline. And always the pursuit – superbly handled, heeling a little as she harnessed the wind, her sails trimmed to an exactitude – found her way surely through the passage, and *Expedient* struggled to keep up. Mr Loftus referred constantly to the large Admiralty chart, and the seaman in the forechains with the lead was kept constantly at his work. Rennie had ordered that crews of waisters were to stand by at the chain pumps, in case of sudden emergency. He had kept to his decision not to clear the decks for action, but the gunner Mr Storey had loaded extra cartridge in the filling room of the forrard magazine, just in case.

The day lengthened, and grew old, and twilight descended over the coast and the sea. The mist lifted, and far inland snow turned red on the peaks as the dying sun was reflected there. A league ahead the pursuit lost way on the darkening water, and hove to.

'Thank God. They must anchor overnight, and so must we.' Rennie, as four bells of the second dog watch sounded on the fo'c'sle, and the ship prepared for hammocks down. He gave the order to heave to and anchor, and at last he came aft, stiff with salt and stiff in every limb from his long vigil, to the easeful respite of the great cabin, and a lifting glass of wine.

At a greater distance behind than that between *Expedient* and *Terces*, the Danish brig slipped unseen between two islands, and hove to as night fell.

Rennie consulted with his first lieutenant and his sailing master, in the great cabin.

'We know that *Terces* carries two stern lanterns and a masthead light, and that they have been lighted, because we can see them quite plain. This is a boon to us, because it means she cannot slip away at night without being seen to do so.'

'Clearly her master wished us to see him at night,' said Bernard Loftus.

'He has certainly made no effort to outrun us, nor hide from us, all the day.' Captain Rennie, nodding.

'Likely he believes that we will not attack him when our own people are held aboard his ship, sir.' Lieutenant Leigh.

'I am not hard at work to discover his motive, so long as we keep *Terces* in plain view, watch by watch.' Rennie laid out a second chart over the large one he had brought below, and examined it with his magnifying glass. '*Terces* lies . . . here.' Pointing to the place on the chart. 'And we are here.' Pointing again. 'Say to all the masthead men that I wish glass-by-glass reports of *Terces*' lights, through the hours of darkness. Any change, any movement, anything at all, is to be conveyed to me at once.'

'Very good, sir.'

'Very good, sir.'

'If I am asleep I am to be woke. Y'apprehend me?'

Rennie insisted on being given the names of the masthead lookouts as they would be on duty, watch by watch. In addition, he wished a man posted in the bow at all times, and anchor watches to be maintained in addition to the regular watches. When everything had been arranged to his satisfaction, he invited the two officers to join him for supper.

In the brief interlude between this invitation and the meal – when Mr Leigh and Mr Loftus had returned to their cabins to wash their faces and shift into clean shirts – Rennie allowed himself to reflect on the plight of the men held in *Terces*: his coxswain Clinton Huff, the six men of the boat's crew, and his Pursuit Officer Lieutenant Hayter. As he rinsed his face and neck in the basin of hot water Colley Cutton had brought to him in his quarter gallery:

'I hope to God they are not ill-treated.' Pausing to glance through the quarterlight.

'I do not fink she b'lieves that, sir.' Cutton, politely.

'Eh?' Turning distractedly to look at his steward, who waited in the narrow doorway with a towel.

'Dulcie, sir. I fink she may well have forgave you, now, for your treatment of her.'

'Dulcie? I was not talking of Dulcie, y'fool. Give me that.' And he took the towel and mopped his face.

'Beg pardon, sir. I fought you—'

'The cat has nothing to do with it.'

'No, sir?'

'No.' Mopping his neck, then: 'What the devil d'y'mean, forgive?'

'Well, sir – you shunned her, like, because of that rat.'

'Shunned my own cat? What nonsense is this?' Thrusting the towel at his steward and emerging from the quarter gallery to shift into his coat.

'I beg your pardon, sir. But cats is very sens'tive creatures, which takes 'ffence very common when they b'lieve theirselves wronged. She was sent to the fo'c'sle in disgrace. I carried her there myself.'

Rennie glared at his steward. 'Then it is you she blames for carrying her there, Colley Cutton, I am in no doubt. Bring me another glass of wine.'

'As you wish, sir.'

'And don't say "as you wish". This ain't a coffee house, nor a pleasure garden, neither. We are at sea in a ship of war. When I give you an order y'will respond: "Ay-ay, sir." And y'will jump, by God.'

'Fank you, sir.' Inclining his head with a show of humility. Rennie let it go.

*

The blindfold was removed by someone from behind, and James heard a door close. He blinked in the subdued light from a deckhead lantern, and saw beyond him on the canvas-covered decking a table, chairs, candles, and beyond that again a curved stern-gallery window. He was in the great cabin of the ship. A figure sat alone at one corner of the table, a sturdy black-haired man in shirt, breeches and sea boots, one of which was visible jutting at an angle by the table leg. James felt a waft of cool air on his face, and saw that one of the stern-gallery window panels had been lifted open and secured to the deckhead. From without came the creaking and dripping of an anchor cable as the ship eased a little on the tide. She was moored fore and aft, then.

'You do not object to the night air, I hope?' The tone neutral, but the voice firm and clear. The figure turned in the chair, and a pair of blue eyes regarded James with not quite stony detachment.

'Not at all.' James cleared his throat. 'After the stench of the orlop, I welcome it. I assume it was the orlop, where I was held?'

'It was.'

James glanced round the cabin, and took in other detail: a rack of swords, rolled charts, bookshelves, a stove, a small desk. It was very like the great cabin of a sloop of war of the Royal Navy, with perhaps a hint more of comfort.

'You are Captain Broadman, sir?'

'I am.'

'Will you release me from these bindings?' His hands were tied tight behind his back, and his arms were growing numb.

'Certainly . . . if you will give me your word as an officer not to attempt escape?'

'You have it.'

'Mm-hm.' The briefest chuckle. 'I should have said the same, exact, was I in your position. But would I have meant it, Lieutenant Hayter, hey?'

'You know my name?'

'You know mine.'

'No doubt my name was told to you by one of the boat's crew.'

'Nay, it was not.' Captain Broadman rose from his chair, produced a knife, and came to where James stood. He cut the bindings from James's wrists, and tucked the knife away. James rubbed his wrists and worked his arms vigorously to shake the circulation back into them.

'Thank you, sir. Where are my boat's crew?'

Captain Broadman did not answer the question, but instead returned to the table and indicated the chair opposite his own. 'Sit down, Lieutenant Hayter.'

James went to the table and sat down, and opened his mouth to ask the question again, but Captain Broadman:

'Yes, I knew your name from the beginning, before your ship began the chase. Also those of your captain and first lieutenant – Rennie, and Leigh, I think?'

'You are well informed.'

'Yes, I am.'

'Why did you think to attack us?'

'Think it? My dear Lieutenant Hayter, I did more than that. I engaged you, and prevailed.'

'You took us by surprise.'

'Come now, a frigate of the Royal Navy? Ain't His Majesty's ships expected to be ready for action at any time?'

James drew a breath, but then made no answer.

'Hm-hm. Your silence is answer enough.'

'You have not told me where you are holding my boat's crew, sir.'

'They are safe in the lower deck.'

'May I see them?'

'You may not, just at present. I had you brought to me so that I might give you supper. That is – if you would care to join me?'

'Care to? Have I any choice?'

'Certainly. You may join me, or return to the orlop.'

'Then I will join you willing enough – if you will tell me why you have kidnapped us in your ship.'

'Kidnapped? Nay, that is a very singular description of what was done. I am no slaver, I assure you. You was took prisoner, Lieutenant, and you are held prisoner, now.'

'Which enemy's colours d'you wear, Captain Broadman? Hey? England is not at war, sir.'

'Not at war? You have been at war with France a twelvemonth and more, have not you? You and Captain Rennie?'

'What? That is madness.'

'Is it, though? Did not you in effect invade France and undertake warlike activity there? Did not you engage French ships in a fierce sea action, in French waters, a year since?'

James stared in astonishment at Captain Broadman. How had he come by this intelligence?

'Are you an agent of France?'

Captain Broadman parried the question by countering: 'Why does *Expedient* continue to pursue me? I could have destroyed you, and yet did not.'

'Yes, why did you not?' James, genuinely curious.

'I sought merely to prevent further pursuit. And yet you have persisted. You hound me in foreign waters. Why?'

James sat silent a moment, then: 'Those were our orders.'

'In course I know that!' Fiercely, and he struck the table. 'My question is: who gave you those orders, and why?'

'I am unable to answer.'

'Unable, or unwilling?' Captain Broadman regarded James with a long unfriendly stare. A reluctant sigh, and: 'Well, perhaps Mr Brough Mappin has not told you, after all, but has simply required you to obey him blindly. He has dogged me ashore, I may tell you. I have been put to great trouble by that damned fellow.'

'Mapple, did y'say? Don't know the name.'

Again Captain Broadman struck the table, banging it so hard with his fist that a glass at his elbow bounced and tipped over, and rolled with a hollow sound back and forth in a diminishing half-circle, scattering red droplets of wine. Captain Boardman, governing his voice:

'If we are to dine together, we must treat each other with a modicum of respect, don't you think so, Lieutenant?'

'Conduct ourselves civilised, d'y'mean?' James, with an ease he did not feel.

'Indeed. Behave each to the other as men of intelligence and good sense. Yes?'

'I am in accord with that, certainly.' Politely, with a nod.

'Then pray do not keep to the wretched foolish pretence that y'don't know Mr Mappin. You was his agent in France, sir, and Captain Rennie aided you, at Mappin's bidding. You conduct yourselves at his bidding now. Well?'

'I follow my orders, as a commissioned sea officer.'

'God damn your bloody impudence!'

Captain Boardman had jumped up on his legs, and put a hand to the hilt of his sword, and for a moment James feared for his life. But then Captain Boardman chuckled, sat down again and: 'Hm-hm, I expect I should say the same kind of thing, was I in your position, Mr Hayter.' He leaned back in his chair. 'And I find that I cannot blame you, after all. I expect you are hungry?'

'Well, yes . . . I am, in truth.'

'Very good. We shall eat our supper, and be convivial.' Turning toward the door: 'Wilson! Wilson, there! Supper!'

'May I ask you a question, sir?' James, as Captain Boardman turned once more to face him across the table.

'Yes, yes, in course y'may. We are dining companions.'

'Have you ever served in the Royal Navy?'

'Eh?' His eyes narrowing.

'As a sea officer?'

'Why do you ask me that?'

'Well, sir, it is simply that you remind me of many officers I have known. Men used to command, that live in a particular way at sea in His Majesty's service, and behave – well, as sea officers RN always do behave. Disciplined, efficient, well ordered. Just as you yourself seem to do, in this ship.' Glancing round the cabin.

'This ain't a naval ship.' Curtly.

'No, sir, it is not. But it could very well be a small post ship, under naval command. It is certainly handled and fought like one.'

'Do you seek to flatter me, Lieutenant Hayter?'

'Nay, I don't. Simply to speak plain, one sea officer to another.'

'I say again: this ain't a naval ship. And I am no naval officer, neither.' Turning his head: 'Wilson, there! Light along our supper!'

James allowed himself a brief smile. 'If only I had past Navy Lists to hand I could look you up, Captain Broadman.' Not aloud.

Their supper arrived, carried in by a short, stout, chinless steward with a long pigtail. As the man began to serve the first course, James held out a hand palm up in refusal.

'Nay, I find I cannot eat, after all.'

'Not eat?' Captain Broadman, in surprise. 'Are you took ill?'

'No no. It is just . . . I would not feel quite comfortable dining here in the great cabin unless I knew that my boat's crew had been properly fed.'

'They have been fed.' Captain Broadman.

'How?'

'Eh? How? They was given food, Lieutenant, and they ate it.'

'What food?'

'The same rations served in the messes in the lower deck.'

'And how are they treated? Where are they berthed? Are

they permitted to go on deck, into the fresh air? You see, Captain Broadman, as the officer commanding these men I think it my duty to discover their condition of life in the ship.'

'Condition of life! They are prisoners! As are you, Lieutenant.'

'Indeed, so I am. Will you permit me to see my men, under the supervision in course of one of your own officers?'

'I will not.' Angrily, throwing down the napkin he had just taken up.

'Then I will not dine.' And James pushed away the dish in front of him, and sat back in his chair with his arms folded.

'All right, Wilson.' Captain Broadman dismissed his steward with a jerk of his head. The steward departed, carrying his tray at his side and closing the door behind him. The captain regarded his guest with stony disfavour.

'Upon my word, you are ungrateful, sir.'

'I do not mean to be. I am famished, and wish with all my heart – all my stomach – to eat my fill. But surely you will understand me when I say that I must look to the welfare of my men as my first concern.'

'Listen now, you had better understand me. Your wish to have sight of your men is naught but subterfuge. It is a stratagem to allow you to effect your escape, and I know it.'

'Escape? How could I escape? By diving into the cold sea, and swimming? You must think me a very hardy fellow, sir.'

'Your boat is moored directly astern, and your ship is not more than a league to the south.'

'*Expedient*?' Glancing toward the stern-gallery window.

'Ay. She pursues me yet. Or rather, she did, until we both dropped anchor tonight. Now she merely waits.'

'But . . . if she is so near . . . why has she not attacked?' Half to himself.

'Very possibly to preserve your life. A broadside of guns might well kill you outright. Who can tell? Or perhaps Captain Rennie does mean to attack – with a cutting-out party, under cover of darkness.'

James could not prevent a brief flicker of hope in his eyes. Captain Broadman saw it, and:

'So, you see, Lieutenant, I cannot afford to allow you any advantage. I must keep you under close scrutiny at every moment, and cannot accede to your request to roam about the ship. Pray eat your supper.'

James felt that Captain Broadman's logic was absurd – how could a prisoner under close supervision be said to 'roam about the ship'? – but felt equally that to argue with him would be demeaning and absurd, and so determined to say nothing more, but to eat nothing either, and he sat stubborn a few moments longer.

Captain Broadman attacked his food with relish, cutting and prodding, lifting and chewing. James, watching him and smelling that food, felt a nearly irresistible urge to emulate him. Presently, as saliva flooded over his tongue, his resolve faded and weakened. He leaned forward and looked intently at his knife and fork. All of the questions that had whirled and jostled inside him since their capture and imprisonment aboard *Terces* – What was Broadman's purpose? Who or what did he carry, and where? Was it America? How long did he intend to hold his prisoners captive? Would he cast them adrift in mid-ocean? And if he did not, would Rennie and *Expedient* attempt a rescue? – sank beneath the tide of his appetite, and he was about to seize the knife and fork, when:

'Captain Broadman, I must speak with you.'

A thin, fair-haired man had come into the cabin. Dark clothes emphasised deep-set, wide-apart grey eyes in a bony face, eyes so staring pale they burned like lights.

'You cannot come in!' Captain Broadman, very agitated, was up on his legs. His napkin fell to the deck. 'Did not I tell you, you was not to show yourself!'

James had remained in his chair, but now he too stood, and went forward to the intruder.

'Lieutenant James Hayter, RN.' Holding out his hand.

'Ah, yes. I have heard of you.' Affably, taking James's hand.

'Do not reveal your own name!' Captain Broadman, fiercely to the newcomer.

The gaunt man ignored Broadman, and with a little bow: 'Olaf Christian den Norske, at your service.'

*

'He cannot mean to take in further cargo.' Rennie, to himself, as he watched *Terces* bear east toward the mouth of the fjord ahead. This was the second day they had sailed north along the Norwegian coast, following *Terces*, and Rennie had yet to resolve the question of what to do about Lieutenant Hayter and his boat's crew, held prisoner aboard her. That the pursuit was developing into a fretful game of hide-and-seek Rennie had to put to one side. In the brief time they had sailed north, Rennie had come to understand the coastline as a long, asymmetrical glory, an aesthetic fracturing of land and sea into myriad islands and fjords, with mountains marching far inland, and distant staring slopes of snow. It had struck him that no one fjord was uniform with another, that many were not single narrow fissures at all, but much greater bodies of water, with spreading arms and several entrances among the scattered islands.

The immediate and most important thing was to keep *Terces* in plain view, at a distance sufficient to protect *Expedient* from a second sudden attack, but never so great as to lose sight of her. But this new development, of going into a fjord, dismayed him. Should he pursue *Terces* deep into the fjord, risking the safety of his ship in such unfamiliar waters? His charts of the coast were adequate, but as to the fjords themselves – including this one, the Dangesfjord – they were far from comprehensive, and probably inaccurate. The mouth of the fjord was scattered across with islands and rocky outcrops, and navigation within would be uncertain at best. A wooded headland jutted into the sea on the southern side of the fjord entrance, and soon *Terces*, tacking east, would run behind it. Dangesfjord was long and winding, and possibly had arms not marked on Rennie's charts, and another entrance to the north, among the islands. It must be assumed Captain Broadman had a working knowledge of the fjord, which Rennie did not. If Rennie followed him in, would not Broadman endeavour to outfox him, leaving *Expedient* entirely alone?

'But if I do *not* pursue him inside, I may lose touch with him altogether. If I simply wait here at the mouth, like to a blockade ship, will not he simply sail above those islands, or between them, and escape into the open sea to the north? Again, if I *do* pursue him deep into the fjord, overnight, might not he elude me in a hidden arm or inlet, further in, and simply double back?'

He paced his quarterdeck, then paused again at the rail. A sigh.

'God's love, I am damned whichever course I follow.'

He noted, as *Terces* began to pass behind the headland into the mouth of the fjord, that she was still towing *Expedient*'s pinnace. He lowered the glass.

'Mr Leigh!' Calling forrard to the breast-rail, where his first lieutenant stood.

'Sir?' Lieutenant Leigh came aft to Rennie at the starboard-rail, abaft the skylight. Rennie wished to appear doubt-free, and decisive. A breath, and:

'I think Captain Broadman will likely attempt two things. Firstly he will set free Lieutenant Hayter and the boat's crew in the pinnace, just at dusk, leaving us to pick them up. He may then attempt to give us the slip, either by sailing further into the fjord, or by going about and heading among those damned islands to the north. His object will be to delay and confuse us as darkness falls.'

'Is that why he has held them prisoner until now, sir, d'y'think?'

'I do, Mr Leigh. Else he would long since have scuttled or abandoned the boat, that can only hinder him. We will tack east round the headland, if y'please, and keep *Terces* in clear sight.'

Six bells of the afternoon watch, and *Expedient* had rounded the headland and was now sailing east into the fjord. Captain Rennie, now at the bow, focused his glass on the ship ahead. *Terces* was above a league distant, on the starboard tack, heading toward the distant snow-covered mountains. The wind had died away, the water in the fjord was much calmer than the open sea, and now Rennie saw what Dr Johnson meant when he talked of the 'noble wild prospects' of Norway.

Terces lay small and insignificant on the flat surface of the water, caught between great cliffs and steeps of rock, and their darkling reflection. Wooded slopes ran right down and into the glassy fjord in the nearer distance, and farther in there were farm buildings, red and white dots clumped on narrow green meadows low above the water. Farther still were massive mountains, rearing and marching to the horizon and trailed across with long dark scars, as if a huge beast had raked the snowy slopes with its claws. The clarity of the air and the depth of view were astonishing.

The fjord wound away to the north behind a jutting wooded spit, and then east again beyond that, toward the distant heights. Rennie consulted his charts, and could discover no detailed depiction of the fjord above the simple outlines of its length and width. He summoned his sailing master.

'Mr Loftus, have you any direct knowledge of these waters, beyond that spit of land ahead?'

'I confess that I have not, sir.'

Rennie sent one of the mids to his day cabin to fetch a final chart, but when it came he could learn nothing further from it. Dangesfjord was certainly marked, but as he had suspected, observations beyond the first mile or two were few. Hydrographical details – depth of water, shoals, islands, vegetation – were not given at all.

'How far in does he venture?' Murmured.

He raised his glass, peered, and confirmed that the pinnace was still towed behind.

Rennie remained in the bow watching *Terces* for a further hour, until eight bells sounded and the hands were piped to their dinner. He rolled his charts, and went aft. The second lieutenant had the deck.

'Mr Tindall.'

'Sir?'

'I am going below a short while. I wish to be informed at once of any change to *Terces*' course, any alteration at all, you apprehend me?'

'Very good, sir.'

'Keep a close watch. Every man alert.'

'Ay-ay, sir.' Touching a hand to his hat.

'Very well.' A last look at *Terces* far ahead on the flat water, and he went below.

*

Lieutenant Hayter had again been summoned to Captain Broadman's great cabin. He was brought there by an armed escort, and the man waited at the door. Captain Broadman looked up from the detailed chart of a fjord, weighted at each corner with leads on the table.

'I had thought to let you go, Lieutenant, in this fjord – deep in this fjord, in your boat. That was until you made the acquaintance inadvertent of my passenger, which was a circumstance very regrettable . . . for you.'

'Why so?'

'Olaf Christian den Norske is a valuable fellow, and his presence in my ship is a secret that must be kept.'

'Ah.' James nodded, then: 'However, you forget that I do not know why he is valuable to you, since you would not allow me to converse with him above a minute or two, and I have never seen him since.'

'Valuable to me? He is valuable to people elsewhere, but not to me.'

'Does not he pay for his passage?'

'No.'

'He don't? Then why d'you carry him?'

'That is part of the secret, Mr Hayter.'

'Yes, I see. And you think that if you were to release me and my boat's crew, and we were to be rescued by Captain Rennie in *Expedient*—'

Over him: 'Suffice it to say that Captain Rennie is very tenacious. No doubt he is provisioned for a long pursuit.'

James said nothing for a moment, then: 'May I assume that *Expedient* follows *Terces* still?'

'She does.'

James glanced at the chart on the table. From where he stood he could not discern details, and now he asked:

'And . . . we are presently in that fjord?' Nodding at the chart.

'We are. It is the Dangesfjord, one of the longest and deepest of all the great fjords of Norway, and the inner stretches are very remote. I was minded to put you ashore in your pinnace, without masts, sails, or sweeps, in one of the remotest parts of the fjord, in the Sonnylsvatn, where there are only scattered, isolated farms, and the people speak nothing but the old tongue, and never venture beyond their immediate surrounds from one year to the next. That would place you in grave difficulty, but in least you would have the chance of life and eventual return to civilisation. However, even had I done this in darkness, and slipped away subsequent upon a northern arm of the fjord, Captain Rennie – who as I've allowed is a very tenacious fellow – would likely find his way out and resume his pursuit of me. I could not take that risk, I cannot, I may not.'

James nodded again, as if conceding his captor's point.

'Thank you for your honesty, Captain Broadman.'

Captain Broadman inclined his head. 'I thought it best to

make you aware of you position, Lieutenant, so that you would dwell no more on the possibility of escape. There is no escape from *Terces*.'

'And my boat's crew?'

'None of you will be set free. That is my final word on the matter. You will now return to the orlop, and I will continue upon my present heading, leading Captain Rennie as deep into Dangesfjord as I am able.'

'And then . . . ?

'Ah. Then. Then, Lieutenant, I intend to turn and attack, and destroy *Expedient* forthwith, as I should have destroyed her on the open sea.'

James stared at the captain, and saw that he meant what he said. So far as Captain Broadman was concerned, *Expedient* was already smashed and burned. A breath, and:

'I think perhaps you do my commanding officer an injustice, Captain Broadman. You should have estimated him higher, you know, than merely tenacious. He will never allow himself to be approached and attacked a second time. He will fight you and outgun you, and prevail.'

'You think so? Even when I have assistance?'

'Assistance?'

'Indeed. The brig that took you into Bergen, Lieutenant, is on hand even now, following the pursuer.'

James made a conscious effort not to reveal his extreme dismay at this news. Instead, calmly:

'Will you tell me, then . . . why you continue to hold us prisoner? Why you do not send us ashore in our boat, to take our chance?'

'Because you are an experienced sea officer, Mr Hayter. When I am going to fight an action I do not want men like you against me, even in an open boat.'

'But how could we harm you, good heaven? A few men in a pinnace, unarmed?'

Captain Broadman leaned across the table. 'I will not like to leave *anything* to chance.' A grim little smile. 'Sentry!'

*

Dusk, and the magnificence of the fjord beginning to fade and darken. Mr Leigh had joined the second lieutenant on the quarterdeck of *Expedient*, and was peering at the chase through his glass.

'Is he going about . . .?' Half to himself, but Lieutenant Tindall heard him, and raised his own glass. In the diminished light he could barely make out *Terces* against the dark rock faces ahead. Was she altering course? He was about to voice the question himself when Lieutenant Leigh:

'Can you tell what he is doing, Mr Tindall?'

'Nay, I cannot. I can scarcely see her at all any more. But we had better be ready for anything, I expect. Mr Madeley!' To one of the duty mids.

'Sir?' Attending.

'Go below to the great cabin and with my compliments inform the captain that *Terces* is now – that she may be altering course.'

'Which shall I say, sir?'

'Eh?' Irritably.

'That she is altering course, sir, or that she may be about to?'

'Just as I told you, you impertinent dolt. That she is altering course. Jump, jump.'

'Ay-ay, sir.'

When the boy had gone the second lieutenant turned to the first, and:

'Look here, Leigh, if *Terces* is altering course, very probably we should beat to quarters, don't you think so?'

'The deck is yours. I will not interfere. However . . .'

'Yes?'

'If I was you I should wait until the captain comes on deck before you clear for action, and seek his opinion.'

'Yes? Very good, thank you, Leigh. I shall wait.'

'We do not know for certain that she is altering course, after all.' Again peering through his glass. 'I wish to heaven I had a night glass, so that I could make her out better in these conditions.' A sharp intake of breath, and immediately: 'She is going about, by God! I can see the pinnace swinging round astern!'

Mr Tindall sucked in a lungful of air. 'Boatswain's mate! We will beat to quarters, and clear the decks for action!'

The piercing shriek of the call, the rattling roll of the Marine's drum, and the ship came to foot-thudding, cursing, mallet-clattering life.

And now a cry from the tops, an astonished cry:

'Sail of ship to the west! Rounding the point half a league directly astern!'

Rennie came on deck, jamming on his hat. 'What ship lies astern of us? Where is *Terces*? She cannot have got astern of us, good God.'

'No, sir. *Terces* lies directly ahead, and is going about.' Mr Leigh, now focusing his glass astern over the tafferel. A moment, then: 'Christ Jesu, it is that damned Danish brig!'

'What! The brig!' Rennie had come on deck in a great hurry, and had forgotten his Dollond. He snatched Mr Tindall's glass without ceremony, and peered aft. 'Where? Where is the – ah, I have her. You are right, Mr Leigh, it is a brig. But is she Danish? How can we be certain it is the same vessel?'

'She must have shadowed us all the way north along the coast, at a distance, sir.'

'Damnation to that, the bloody villain. Where is *Terces*?' Swivelling round and peering forrard through the raised glass. 'Why was not I told at once that she had altered course, Mr Tindall?'

'I sent Mr Madeley below as soon as she—'

'Yes yes, well well, no matter, I see her now.' Over his second lieutenant, who shut his mouth. 'There is very little wind, at all. And the brig has the gage, which no doubt her captain thinks is to his advantage.' Turning aft again and peering. 'He is about to discover otherwise.' A decisive sniff. 'Mr Leigh.'

'Sir?'

'We will attack the brig first. I will like to smash her comprehensive our first broadside, and leave her crippled.'

'You mean to fire on her immediate, sir, in Norwegian waters? When she has not fired on us first?'

'It is plain both ships intend to attack me, Mr Leigh. I will not like to lie idle while they attempt it, and be caught a second time. You there, boy!'

A ship's boy attended him, touching his forehead. 'Yes, sir?'

'Go below and find the gunner Mr Storey, and ask him to come to me at his earliest convenience. Belay that. I wish him to come immediate, say to him. Jump now.'

In very light airs *Expedient* came about and began to run west in the fjord, directly at the approaching Danish brig. On either side the slopes and cliffs were fading and merging in the gathering gloom. To the east *Terces* ran in pursuit, but she was yet too far away to open fire with any accuracy, and Rennie was confident he could deal first with the brig, then turn to meet *Terces* in plenty of time. But dusk was fast becoming night. Could he fight an action at night, in a damned confining fjord?

Mr Storey came on deck. 'You wished to see me, sir?'

'Ay, Mr Storey. Our first broadside we will fire roundshot, long guns and carronades both, to smash that damned brig into splinters. Then I want grape, for the fight with *Terces*. I will like to kill men on her upper deck, at long range, before she can have at me with her smashers. But I do not want to disable the ship. I want her to limp away wounded and sore, but not crippled. You have me?'

'Ay, sir. Roundshot our first fire, then grape for *Terces*.'

'Very good. And Mr Storey?'

'Sir?'

'Have you a supply of rockets?'

'Yes, sir. There is both red and blue rockets.'

'Nay, I want white star rockets, the biggest you can make. Four-pounders, long cylinder and stick, able to shoot to a great height, and flood the surrounding water with light.'

'Christ's love, that is a tremendous weight of rocket, sir.' Scratching his head.

'Can you do it?'

'Well, I will do my best, sir, but—'

'That is all I ask. Make me a good supply. Eight or ten.'

'So many as that? I will try, sir, but I must mix antimony and isinglass, and spirits of wine and vinegar, in addition to the mealed powder, and that will occupy—'

'Then there ain't a moment to lose, Mr Storey.' Over him. I am relying on you to illuminate the action.' And he strode away aft.

*

Aboard *Terces* James Hayter was confined on the forrard platform of the orlop, in a storeroom adjacent to the sailroom and the boatswain's store. He had been able to convince his armed escort to leave him unshackled, by pretending to an attack of nausea and stomach cramps. By loudly groaning, retching, and spitting into a pisspot, he had driven the young man in grimacing disgust from the door to stand by the ladder a little way aft.

Before he had been taken up to the great cabin to be informed by Captain Broadman of his indefinite imprisonment, James had found lying under a pile of oakum a discarded marlin spike. Now in the reeking darkness he located the iron spike where he had hidden it, and tucked it into his waist. His plan was to overpower the guard, knock him senseless and seize his musket and pistol. He would then – if he could – find and release his boat's crew. His chief aim was to get aboard the pinnace. He was nearly certain that the half-pounder swivels Roman Tangible had concealed under canvas aboard the boat had not been discovered by the crew of *Terces*. There was powder and shot for the swivels. If he could only get aboard and mount the swivels on the gunwale, he could fight his way clear of *Terces* and make for *Expedient*, which could not be far away.

James groaned horribly, and made a commotion in the narrow storeroom, banging and thudding as if in slumping collapse. As he had hoped, the guard came to the door.

'Are you all right, sir?'

James was silent.

'Are you all right, there?' Anxiously now.

James answered with another dreadful groan, fainter and more piteous than the earlier ones, and followed it with a gasping, choking cough. The guard unlocked and opened the door, peered in, then ventured inside.

James seized him from behind the door, one arm fiercely round his neck, the marlin spike at his throat, and grabbed the musket with his other hand.

'Be very quiet, now.' Low and menacing, in the guard's ear. 'Else I will cut your throat.' Pressing the iron spike harder against the man's skin. The guard struggled very briefly, then was compliant. James felt for and removed the pistol at the guard's waist. He relaxed his grip on the guard's neck, and as the man stumbled forward James struck him on the back of the skull with the pistol butt. The guard dropped to the decking and lay still. James left him there, stepped cautiously out of the storeroom, locked the door, and a moment after was at the ladder.

He came up into the lower deck, musket at the ready, aware that he had no idea where his boat's crew were being held. There was nobody he could see in the forward part of the lower deck. Hammocks had not been sent down, because the ship was ready for action. Every man was at quarters. There was not a single lantern burning, and the light was very dim. James peered aft, then forrard again, and thought he discerned movement in the darkness. He moved forward. In a carrying whisper:

'Clinton Huff, there. Can you hear me?'

A scuffling movement, and the clinking of shackles.

'We are here, sir.' A hoarse whisper in response. 'Confined in the sick quarters right forrard.'

James's head bumped against a hanging lantern, and he found and struck a light, and lit the lantern. Held it up, and went forrard. He found his boat's crew lying very cramped in a row together behind a canvas screen, their hands bound with twine, and their feet shackled to an improvised bilboes bar set into the timbers in the small space of the sick bay. The bar had a stout padlock at one end.

'Thank God you has found us, sir. Can you release us from these irons?'

'I must find the key to that damned lock.' Holding the screen aside.

'One of their officers has that, sir. You will never—'

'Then I must smash the lock with the butt of the musket.' Decisively, putting down the lantern on the decking, and lifting the musket.

The sound of footfalls on the ladder aft, and James seized up the lantern and blew it out. A voice:

'Who is that forrard, there? Is that you, Joseph?'

James was silent. A figure came through the gloom, carrying a small lantern. The figure lifted the light, approaching the canvas screen, and as he did James struck him full in the forehead with the butt of the musket, and felled him. James snatched the lantern from his grasp before it could clatter to the deck, stepped over the unconscious form, and again lifted the screen. He raised the musket by the barrel and with a single smashing blow of the butt he broke the padlock open, and released his boat's crew from their split shackles, swiftly, one by one. He found a knife in the belt of the unconscious man, and cut the bindings of twine from his men's wrists.

'We must get into the boat.'

'Our boat, sir?' Clinton Huff, rubbing his wrists to ease the pain of returning circulation.

'Ay, the pinnace. It is towing astern, and I believe the swivels have not been discovered.'

'How will we pass along the deck without drawing notice to ourself, sir?'

'*Terces* will soon go into action against *Expedient*, which ain't far behind. We will wait until she does, and the great guns are fired. In the commotion and din of batteries firing and reloading, we will dash along the deck with sand buckets, water buckets, whatever we may find. There will be the usual shouting and cursing of an action. We will add to it – "Make way, there! Water lighting along!" – and so forth. You have me?'

'Yes, sir.' Dubiously. 'May I say something, please, sir?'

'Well?' Glancing at Huff in the light of the small lantern.

'The armoury in this ship is upon this deck, sir, behind a bulkhead aft. Whilst we was laying here we could hear the armourer preparing the small arms with his mate. New flints for the pistols and the like. If we armed ourself, sir, before we went on deck, we could make a proper fight of it, and give ourself a better chance of getting into our boat.'

'Fight?' James, cocking his head on one side. 'Make a fight of it? Christ's blood, man, we should be cut down at once.' Shaking his head now. 'Nay, we must make our escape by pure bluff. Follow me, and all of you will survive.' Glancing at each man in turn. 'Well, are you with me?'

'Ay, sir.'

'Yes, sir.'

'We are ready, sir.'

A general murmur of agreement. Except for Clinton Huff, who was silent.

'Huff?'

'I . . . no disrespect to you, sir, but I should prefer a brace of sea pistols and a cutlass.'

'That will not answer. I do not doubt your courage, but we must save ourselves by a trick, this night.' A breath, then: 'As soon as we hear the order to open fire, we will move. Follow me, and stay close. As we go on deck seize buckets, rope, anything that lies to hand, and look dutiful and urgent.' Glancing at each man again. 'For the present we will conceal ourselves behind this screen – and wait.'

And he blew out the light

*

'I believe the Danish brig has just now gone about, sir, and may be fleeing to the west, toward the open sea.' Mr Loftus, in answer to Captain Rennie's exasperated question as to why *Expedient* was not apparently 'closing the enemy'.

'What!' Rennie brought up his night glass, and peered ahead. And saw the retreating stern lantern of the brig. 'Hell's fire, the bloody dog. The cowardly cur.' He brought down the glass, and sighed. 'Well well, we cannot pursue her in darkness in these waters, that would be folly, Mr Loftus. We must turn and fight *Terces*, instead.'

'Very good, sir. Mr Tangible! Stand by to go about!'

The calls, high and carrying.

Presently, amid the urgent activity of turning the ship round, the gunner Mr Storey came on deck with his mate, who was carrying a bundle of rockets, and another man behind carrying a second bundle. Rennie went forrard to the waist to look at the rockets.

'I have made up a round dozen of white star, sir.' Mr Storey, touching his hat with blackened fingers. 'Four-pounders, as you asked, in three-inch cylinders and long sticks. I thought to fire them from the tafferel, sir, with your permission, well clear of all sails.'

'Very well, Mr Storey, thankee. I should prefer to launch 'em from the bow, but nay, we cannot risk our headsails catching fire. Carry the rockets aft, by all means.'

He turned to stride aft, and saw bright flashes in a line to the east. A brief, suspended moment, then the air droned and whined horribly all round the ship, followed by:

THUD-BOOM   THUD-BOOM
THUD THUD THUD THUD

Fountains of spray to larboard and starboard, and astern. Water cascaded across the deck. Rennie ducked his head, overtaken a moment by the sudden attack.

'Larboard battery, stand by to fire!' Lieutenant Leigh, at his station.

Rennie now recalled his earlier instruction to Mr Storey, ran to the breast-rail, and bellowed: 'Hold your fire, there! I do not want roundshot fired at *Terces*!'

At the same moment he bawled this instruction, Mr Leigh: 'Larboard battery! Fire!'

BOOM   BOOM   BOOM-BOOM
BOOM   BOOM   BOOM

The deck timbers shuddered under Rennie's feet, and acrid fiery smoke gusted the length of the ship, scattering powder grit and fragments of wad.

The broadside fell wide of the target, the roundshot droning away and smashing harmlessly into a rock face far beyond *Terces*. The echo of the guns sounded in a series of shock waves thudding back from rocky darkness along the fjord:

BOOM-B-BOOM-B-BOOM

In the sulphur stink of burned powder Rennie sucked in a deep breath:

'Mr Leigh! We will reload with grape! Grape, d'y'hear me!'

'Ay-ay, sir!' Calling in acknowledgement.

'Mr Storey!'

'Sir?' At the tafferel.

'Loose off two of your rockets right quick! Give me height and light!'

The hiss of fuses, sparks, and sudden tongues of fire as the rockets blasted up from the tafferel, and soared into the night:

CRACK   CRACK

and bursting, brilliant stars lit the whole of the fjord from side to side, lit *Terces* beating diagonally toward *Expedient* on the starboard tack, lit every line and yard and sail of *Expedient*, and every man on her deck.

In the brilliance the flashes at *Terces'* gunports were less explosively bright than in darkness, but the rushing balloons of smoke were all too clear. The immediate drone of roundshot going wide, and the shattering concussion of a single shot that had found its mark forrard. The larboard cathead and knight's-heads, several timber heads, and the fife-rail were shot away. The fished bower anchor writhed up, splitting in pieces, and fell into the water in a froth of splashes. A mortally wounded fo'c'sleman shrieked in agony, the sound deadened by the simultaneous echoing

BOOM-BOOM   BOOM   BOOM-BOOM-BOOM
THUD-BOOM

of *Terces'* carronades.

'God damn the bloody villain! I will teach him his lesson, by Christ!' Rennie stood at the breast-rail, his night glass pointed like a weapon. 'Larboard battery! Why don't ye fire, Mr Leigh!'

THUD-BANG   THUD-BANG   BANG-BANG-BANG
BOOM

As the larboard broadside thundered in response, and *Expedient's* timbers buzzed in vibration right through to her keelson.

*

A hail of grapeshot swept across *Terces'* decks. James and his boat's crew, emerging into the waist, threw themselves flat under a maelstrom of debris as fittings, shrouds, lines and rails were split, torn, smashed into fragments.

'Now is our chance, lads.' James, lifting his head after a moment.

Screams and wails, and fierce curses. The cracking crash of a broken spar falling. And bellowed from aft:

'Starboard battery reload!'

'Come on, lads.' James, getting up on his legs. 'Snatch up anything you find, and run aft.' He ran up the ladder and on to the quarterdeck, and found a scene of bloody confusion. Tangles of rope and torn canvas, smashed rails, broken men.

'Damage party! Make way, there!' he bawled, looping a length of rope over his shoulder and grabbing a bucket from where it had fallen by the breast-rail. He glanced over his right shoulder and saw that Huff and the others were following close behind. He ran on, dodging round a slewed gun carriage and two fallen men.

'Make way, there!' he bawled again. In the scrambling, cursing, urgent milling of men reloading guns amid the confusion of wreckage and the wounded and dying, James and his crew passed aft toward the wheel and the tafferel without hindrance. As he ran and swerved James became aware that the whole of *Terces'* deck was illuminated by a stark white light. As soon as he had noticed it the light abruptly faded and was gone, and darkness lay over the injured ship.

As he came abeam of the binnacle, James felt a hand on his left arm, and turned, thinking it was Clinton Huff. In the binnacle glow he saw Captain Broadman's face.

'By God, it is you!'

And he tried to seize James by the throat. James wrenched free and struck the captain a swinging blow on the temple with the butt of his pistol. The captain dropped to the deck and sprawled there. James ran aft to the tafferel, and peered astern. And saw not one boat but three, towing in line. *Expedient*'s pinnace was the last, two chain distant, at least.

'Christ's blood, we cannot quickly haul in the weight of all three.' Muttered. He turned to Clinton Huff, who was now at his elbow. 'We must all get into that first boat, and cut the cable.'

'Ay, sir . . . but how?'

'We must jump, and swim.'

'I cannot swim, sir.'

'Nor me, neither.'

'Nay, I cannot.'

Several voices together, in negative accord.

'Very well, I will jump and swim to the first boat, and—'

'Nay, sir. Let us all clap on to the line and haul together, and bring the first boat under the counter, and then drop down into it.'

'Haul the weight of three towing boats?'

This huddled conversation had been noticed. There were two stern lanterns, one at each side of the tafferel, and in their glow the knot of men could be seen. The confusion on the quarterdeck, as on the decks further forrard, was becoming order, and a figure now strode aft out of the darkness.

'You there, aft! Lend a hand here, to send this damned wreckage over the side! Jump, damn you!'

'Wait . . . wait . . .' James, softly, as the figure approached.

'D'y'hear me, there!'

James now stepped out of the light toward the figure, as if to obey, and swung the pistol butt. It connected with a sharp little thud, there was a gasping grunt and James caught the collapsing figure in his arms. Blood dripped over his hand as he lowered the sagging weight to the deck. Three seamen, shouting, now began to run aft toward James, and as he straightened two further star rockets burst over the fjord in a dazzle of light. Instantly followed by a further broadside of grapeshot.

'Throw y'selves down!' James, to his own men, as he flung himself to the deck.

Iron grape twanged and smashed across the quarterdeck, ricocheted whining from hammock cranes and guns, shattered the spokes of the wheel, and killed the helmsman even as he ducked to escape the onslaught of metal. One of the seamen running aft dropped in his tracks as his skull exploded. Blood sprayed aft over the skylight. The driver sail was pocked through in three places, and the boom hit in a spray of splinters. Debris rattled and scattered across the decking. The sound of the guns came following like a series of blows:

BOOM-B-BOOM   BANG-BANG-BOOM
BANG   BANG   BANG

And now the echoes, racketing and thudding along the rock walls of the fjord, and booming back on the night air.

More screams and groans, and hoarse curses. A loosened block fell to the deck with a clatter, and a length of line snaked after it, and whipped over the larboard rail.

'Cheerly now, lads. Clap on to the line and—'

But the boat's crew were already heaving, urgently and energetically heaving, hand over hand. James joined them, clapped on to the hawser-laid rope, and pulled his weight.

The first boat came nearer, and nearer, and was soon nearly under the counter. James continually glanced over his shoulder, but the damage and injury forrard were now so great that their activity at the tafferel was passing unremarked. The stark brilliance of the star rockets died into blackness as abruptly as a lamp blown out. Only the glow of the stern lanterns showed James and his men their task. Water rinsed and rode away from the rudder, and swirled astern round the line of boats. The tethering rope ran through the starboard chase port in the tafferel and was secured to the boom iron above the main brace sheave, inboard of the hammock cranes on the starboard side, and James now tied off and secured the slack. The leading boat lay riding and wriggling right under the counter immediately abaft the rudder.

'Now, lads.' James, a last glance over his shoulder. 'Into the boat, as quick as you like.'

One by one they went over the tafferel and slid down the rope into the bow of the boat, and scrambled aft over the thwarts. James dropped down last, pulled the stolen knife from his waist, and cut the line. The three boats rocked away astern, drifting free.

*

A cloud of black smoke rose from *Expedient*'s waist, lit from within by roiling orange fire. Captain Rennie had ordered his ship to go about, then to drift as if helpless. The smoke came from a tub of burning oakum and Stockholm tar placed in the waist on Rennie's instruction by the gunner Mr Storey.

'I fear she is heading away east in the fjord, sir.' Bernard Loftus, peering at *Terces*' stern lights. 'Shall we fire our remaining rockets?'

'No thankee, Bernard. We may need 'em at a later time.' Rennie lowered his glass. 'Mr Leigh!'

'Sir?' At the waist ladder.

'Y'may stand the hands down.'

'Stand down. Very good, sir.' And he stepped down into the waist and gave the order.

'We are . . . we are letting *Terces* go, sir?' Bernard Loftus.

'We are.'

'I thought you had ordered the fire and smoke in an attempt to draw *Terces* closer, and then press home our attack.'

'Nay, nay. I wish him to retreat, thinking he has crippled me. He will then attempt to give me the slip in darkness, as he did at the Nore. Only this time I shall be ready for him. Even as he flies to the open sea I shall lie in wait, then pursue.'

'Should we attempt to find those boats we saw astern of her, adrift, in that last star burst?' The master turned his head away from the acrid smoke drifting aft, and coughed.

'Hm. I should like to recover our pinnace, but unless the boats are close to I do not see how we may do it.'

As he finished speaking there came out of the darkness a hailing cry:

'Ahoy, there, *Expedient*!'

'Good God . . . it cannot be.' Rennie, running to the rail.

The sound of oars, and the pinnace came gliding into the glow of *Expedient*'s stern light.

In the great cabin James gave Rennie – at his request – an account of his time in captivity, and then of the battle.

'I struck down two of their officers, including the captain, as we made good our escape, sir. That – in addition to your broadsides of grape – I think decided them on their retreat. Captain Broadman had meant to destroy *Expedient*, certainly, but after he fell and they were leaderless, his people lost heart, and tacked away.'

'Ha-ha, then I had no need to make all that stinking damned smoke. I had thought to give them an opportunity to escape, but they needed no such persuading after all, hey?'

'No, sir. However, I cannot tell what Captain Broadman's mood will be when he comes to consciousness and finds his people have broke off the engagement. Likely he will wish to return and bring the battle to a conclusion.'

'A conclusion in his favour? Well well, he will discover that I am not the timorous weakling he supposes, if he attempts it.' A breath, and a suck of wine, then: 'I do not think he will attempt it, James. His task is to convey something, or someone, to America, and he will therefore—'

'I have met the man, sir.' Over him.

'Eh?'

'Yes, sir. I had meant to include all details in my written account, but you wished me first to tell—'

'You have met what man?' Over James, a frown.

'Captain Broadman's passenger, sir. Olaf Christian den Norske.'

'You met him? You conversed with him?'

'Very brief.'

'Then you know why he is in the ship! Why he goes to America! Good heaven, James, why did not y'tell me this at once!'

'No, sir, I do not know.' Shaking his head, holding up a hand.

'What?'

'I spoke to him only half a minute. He came into the great cabin whilst I was there, and Captain Broadman was very angry with him for doing so. I could discover nothing beyond his name.'

'Nothing at all? Good God, James, what a wasted opportunity!' Rennie was now up on his legs, very agitated. 'Could not you have put in at least a question or two to the fellow?'

'No, sir, I could not.'

Rennie turned away in exasperation, then turned back to James and: 'Indeed, could not y'have contrived to bring him with you, when you escaped in the boat? Hey?'

That would have been quite impossible, sir. The—'

'Why impossible? Why? You escaped, after all, and all of your boat's crew! Why could not you have—'

'Sir, with respect.' James, very firmly, over him. 'We escaped with our lives, yes. But we did so by pure good fortune, above anything else. Pure good luck.'

'*Luck!* There is no such thing, good or bad! I ask you again, why did not—'

'Sir, I had no notion where in *Terces* Mr den Norske was quartered! Nor had I—'

'Pray do not shout at me, sir! When I ask a question of you, you will reply in a moderate tone, and dutiful too, by God!'

'I beg your pardon, sir.' Stiffly correct.

'Yes, well well.' A sniff. A brief grimace. 'It don't do for two sea officers to talk vexatious, when they have exacting duties to perform, and a long cruise ahead. I accept your apology. Cutton! – *Cutton!*

'I am here, sir.' Cutton attended, carrying in a tray.

'Well, is that the pie I requested?'

'I was unable to ob-tain no pie, but I has found cheese, sir, and biscuits.'

'No pie, you idle bugger?'

'Cheese will be very welcome, sir.' James, looking eagerly at the tray, which Cutton set down on the table.

'This is infamous.' Rennie, persisting. 'There is always cold pie in the ship, kept in the pantry.'

'Yes, well, the pantry is locked, sir.'

'Then unlock it, man. Christ's blood, are ye helpless?'

'Really, it is quite all right, sir. I will gladly eat the cheese.' James was famished.

'We will neither of us eat cheese, Mr Hayter, while ever there is cold pie available. I will like a wedge of pie, myself. I find that I am hungry. D'y'hear me, Cutton?' A glare.

'Yes, sir, as I ain't deaf. Howsomever, the pantry is locked, and the cook Mr Swallow has got the key, sir.'

'Then go to Mr Swallow.' With sighing patience. 'Go to him, ask him to give you the key, and then unlock the fucking pantry with it.'

'Mr Swallow . . . is incapac'tated.'

'What? He is what?'

'He is drunk, sir.'

'Christ in tears. Sentry!'

'Sir?' The Marine sentry, opening the door.

'Nay, nay – never mind.' Another sigh, waving the sentry away. To Cutton: 'Leave the bloody cheese then, damn you, and bring us another bottle of wine.'

'As you wish, sir.'

'For Christ's sake don't say "as you wish". And don't sidle away like a crab, man. "Ay-ay, sir", make your back straight, and behave seamanlike.'

Presently, when they had eaten their cheese and drunk their

wine, Rennie spread charts, weighted them with leads, and took up dividers. Tapping and pointing:

'My charts ain't detailed eastward beyond the mouth of the fjord, or rather the two mouths, since the entrance is divided by these islands. No matter. In order to return to the open sea, *Terces* must sail west again. We will lie in wait for her. I have ordered a darkened ship, and absolute silence on deck. No calls, no bells, no orders given aloud. All instruction to be passed by signal of hand along the deck.'

A breath, a nod, and he pointed the dividers at another place on the largest chart.

'We must not forget that Danish brig, in course. Her captain was unwilling to engage me and my eighteen-pounders, with his much smaller guns. That was wise in him, very wise, since I would certainly have smashed him to splinters. Yet I do not trust him, James. He may well lie hid somewhere among these islands, ready to make mischief.'

'Mischief, sir?' James, putting down his wineglass.

'You was aboard the brig, James. You met her captain. How did he present himself? Is he intelligent, would y'say? Wily?'

'He did not say more than a few words to me the whole time I was held in the brig. I know nothing of his character, beyond . . .'

'Yes?' Glancing at him.

'Well, it is only a guess, you know. My sense was, sir, that he did not like performing that particular duty, bringing prisoners from a boat into Bergen, and then handing them over. It vexed him.'

'He was angry with you for inconveniencing him, James?' Puzzled.

'No, sir. I repeat, he spoke no more than a few words of English to me. Yet I detected his displeasure in having to undertake the duty he had been given . . . because I think he had been kept in the dark as to its purpose.'

'Ha-ha, well well.' A jerk of the head. 'It would appear the

Danish navy ain't dissimilar to the British, in that regard. Hey?'

'Not dissimilar, sir.' A smile.

'Sea officers are often kept blindfolded by those ashore, as we know to our cost, and the Danish fellow – did you tell me his name?'

'Captain Arbus, sir.'

'Captain Arbus don't know what this affair is all about, because he has not been told. Yes, all he has been told is that he must assist Captain Broadman, an Englishman in an English ship, and must keep watch on me, another Englishman in another English ship. I wonder if his duties do include any kind of belligerent action against *Expedient*. Do they include opening fire on me, perhaps from a place of concealment, among these damned islands?' Tapping the chart again with the dividers, and frowning.

'Surely he would not risk that, sir, for the reasons you gave just a moment ago. He cannot harm us with his little guns, and would not dare to try, since we would certainly smash him with ours.'

'In a direct confrontation at sea, exactly so. However, if he fired from a place of concealment astern of me – a narrow inlet, as an instance – he could smash my rudder and inflict other vital damage with one accurate broadside, James. Any ship, however stout, is weakest through her stern. He could cripple me, in truth, and my pursuit of *Terces* would in effect be finished. By the time I had repaired, *Terces* would be gone into the open sea and lost to me. I lost her once, and found her again, but I cannot trust to such luck a second time.'

'Luck, sir?'

'Eh?' Looking up from the chart.

'I thought that you did not believe in luck, sir.' Feigning surprise.

'Good God, when have I ever said that? Anything may happen at sea, and every man of us must hope for good fortune above all things.'

'Very good, sir.'

'I cannot imagine what gave you such an idea. A sea officer
that don't believe in luck? I will not like to sail with him, by
God. I don't want him anywhere near to me, not afloat nor
ashore, neither.'

'Oh, I am in accord, sir.' A vigorous nod.

A sniff. 'Now then, James, I had meant to ask you, and then
was distracted by Captain Arbus and his brig. What is your
opinion of Captain Broadman? Describe him to me. Leave
nothing out, I want to understand him in every distinction,
and you are the only officer that has met him face to face, and
conversed with him.'

'I will do my be—'

'And then I will like to hear an accurate account of his ship.
Tell me everything. Is she weatherly, what are her strengths
and weaknesses, how does her crew perform? How well do
they fight their guns? And so forth, and so forth. Leave
nothing out, you apprehend me?'

'Yes, sir. I will do my best.' And James continued his
account, interrupted at frequent intervals by his captain's
probing questions.

Expedient had proceeded, according with Rennie's orders
to his sailing master and first lieutenant, to the narrowest
place in the fjord, and then concealed herself – with much
application of the sounding lead – as near behind a high rocky
spit as Mr Loftus deemed safe in confining, dangerous
darkness. There she lay in wait, with an anchor watch and
lookouts in addition to the usual sea watches, through the
night.

'We cannot fail to notice *Terces* as she slips by. The moment
she has done so, we will follow, very discreet and quiet.'
Rennie, in a hoarse whisper to James as they had ventured on
deck after their supper.

'You are quite certain, sir, that Captain Broadman will not
notice us?'

'We are concealed, James.' A confident nod. 'Look to the immediate east. What d'y'see?'

'Erm . . . nothing at all, sir.' Peering.

'Exact It is a black rock face, as black as a dungeon. Now south. Well?'

'Nothing to the south, neither . . . oh, wait, though. Yes, just a glimmer of reflected light across the surface of the fjord.'

'When he crosses that place, when he slips through that "glimmer", James, I shall have him.'

'Very good, sir.'

'You have your flask with you?'

'No, sir. I left it below in my cabin.'

'Ah, well well, a pity. The night air is chill.' Sniffing in that chill. 'No matter.'

The two sea officers waited on the fo'c'sle – never talking above a whisper, always standing very quiet, or sitting next a gun – until the dawn sent grey shadows stealing over the cold still water beyond.

There was no sign of *Terces*. She had not passed.

'He cannot have got past us, for the love of God.' Rennie, as he and Lieutenant Hayter sat down to breakfast in the great cabin. Behind them Colley Cutton raised the shutters from the stern-gallery windows and secured them to the deckhead. Morning light lay across the table, and gleamed on silver.

'I do not think so, sir, no.' James sucked down hot coffee.

'Then where is he, damn his blood?' Rennie drank tea, rinsing it through his teeth before swallowing.

'Sir, I think you said our charts of this particular fjord were not very accurate.'

'Just so, they ain't. They are approximate only, at the entrance, and to the east. But if Broadman wishes to reach the open sea direct, surely he must return through these narrows, past us.'

'We are quite certain of that, sir?' Putting down his cup.

'Speak plain.' A jerk of his head.

'Well, sir . . . given that our charts show nothing but an

approximate outline of the fjord to the east, it may be that there is another arm of the fjord, that leads out to the north.'

Rennie got up on his legs and moved to the charts at the other end of the table. James pushed back his chair and followed, and pointed.

'All these islands lying to the north. Isn't it possible that among them lie other mouths, other entrances to this same fjord, which may have other arms or spurs, shown as separate and distinct fjords, here, and here – but all in fact part of the same one? Leading to other avenues of escape?' Tapping the chart with his fingertip.

Rennie glanced at him, ran a hand through his sparse hair, and rubbed the side of his neck. A sniffing breath, and:

'Yes, I must confess that did cross my mind, earlier, but then I dismissed it as far-fetched and improbable. There would be an indication, on at least one of these charts, of such connection between bodies of water. They may be incomplete, but I cannot believe such a glaring error could occur. I am certain *Terces* is still here, hiding in this fjord to the east. If she will not come out, we must go and find her, James.'

'Will not that defeat our intention of following her discreetly into the open sea?'

'I don't think Their Lordships will like me to lie idle. If I cannot follow *Terces* discreet, then I must follow her close. One way or t'other, she must be pursued.'

'Yes, sir.' Without enthusiasm.

'You don't like it, hey?' Lifting his head and looking at James.

An urgent knocking at the door. Rennie turned.

'Yes?'

Colley Cutton hurried to open the door, but before he reached it the door was thrust open and Lieutenant Leigh appeared, the Marine sentry at his shoulder.

'Sir, there is a Danish frigate in the fjord, heading east toward our position!'

'Surely you mean a brig, Mr Leigh?'

'No, sir, no! It is a frigate of thirty-two guns! Twelve-pounders, I believe!'

Rennie snatched up his hat, coat and long glass, and went on deck. James followed.

The frigate, wearing Danish colours, was plainly in view to the west, about half a league distant.

'Mr Leigh.' Rennie lowered his glass. 'We will weigh and make sail, and tack west into the fjord. The moment we are under way, we will then beat to quarters. I am going to meet this fellow head to head, with my guns run out, so there can be no mistaking my intent.'

Orders bawled, the calls sounding, and rushing activity through the ship. The anchor raised, the foresail unfurled and sheeted home, yards braced. Further orders as the ship began to move, and the rattle of the Marine's drum. The decks cleared, and great guns run out. Rennie stood at the breast-rail, his glass again raised, and watched the frigate approaching. Presently, to James at his side:

'Foreign waters or no, I am damned if I will be rushed at from all sides like a stag at bay. Any fellow that rushes at me will feel my horns at his throat, by Christ.'

James thought but did not say that he had never yet seen a stag at bay on water, nor indeed a stag at sea at all.

'Starboard battery ready, sir!' Mr Leigh, presently.

'Very good. Wait for my signal. I shall take off my hat and raise it over my head.'

A period of quiet as the two ships approached each other across the breeze-freshened, sun-glittering water. *Expedient* sailed into the centre of the fjord on the starboard tack, and James was newly aware of the magnificence of the spectacle, the snowy grandeur of the mountains away to the east, the steep shadows of the rock faces, the vivid green of the slopes and forests, all heightened and sharpened by the clarity of the air across great distance.

A puff of smoke at the Danish frigate's bow, and a column of spray ahead of *Expedient*. At the same moment the sound of the gun, and a series of reverberations.

James saw Rennie's hand go to his hat, and in alarm:

'Sir, I believe that was merely a signal.'

'It was a gun.' Rennie, curtly.

'Yes, to bring home his point, I expect, sir.'

'What point? That he wishes to engage?'

'That he wishes us to heave to and speak.'

'I cannot agree with you, Mr Hayter. I will not be rushed at and bested a second time.' And again his hand went to his hat.

'Sir, if you please, I will go in the pinnace and discover what her captain wants of us.'

'Go in the pinnace? When we have been fired upon? Have you gone mad, Mr Hayter?' Lowering his hand as he turned in exasperation to James.

'No, sir, indeed I have not.'

A second puff of smoke from the Danish ship's bow, and a second column of spray, this time immediately off *Expedient*'s starboard bow. The report, and its thudding echoes.

'God damn the impertinent wretch. I will not be fired upon without cause.' But Rennie's hand did not go again to his hat. Instead he lifted his glass, and peered.

'I think that had his intentions been other than peaceable, sir, he would already have given us a broadside with his larboard battery . . . don't you think so?'

Rennie made no reply, and continued to focus his glass on the approaching frigate.

'Could we not fire one gun in reply, sir?'

Rennie was silent a moment, then he lowered his glass, leaned over the breast rail, and:

'Mr Leigh! Aim ahead of the frigate, and fire number one starboard gun.'

'Ay-ay, sir!' The orders given, and

BANG

Flaming smoke from the gunport, boiling out over the water,

and a smash of spray so close to the Danish frigate's bow that for a moment her bowsprit was obscured.

'Christ Jesu, he will think that was a deliberately aimed shot.' James, half to himself.

The Danish frigate abruptly changed course, going over from the starboard to the larboard tack. A series of red-orange flashes along her larboard port strake, and twelve-pound roundshot sang and droned in menacing concert past *Expedient*'s stern, and made erupting fountains of her wake. Concussive echoes of the reports all round the fjord.

Rennie at once snatched off his hat and held it high, and at the same moment bellowed:

'Starboard battery, *fire!*'

'God's love, what have we done?' James, under his breath, as

BANG   BANG   BANG   THUD-BANG
THUD-BANG   BOOM-BANG

The deck timbers jarring and vibrating, fiery clouds rushing out from the ports. The sulphur stink of burned powder.

And miraculously – as James saw it – no shot went home. Spray shot up astern of the thirty-two, and a rock face beyond her was twice struck in a distant scattering of fragments, but nothing else.

'Re-e-e-lo-o-o-oad!' Echoing along the deck.

Rennie braced his knee against the breast-rail, his glass raised.

'Only let him think what he is doing.' James, again under his breath. 'What they are both doing. Let them desist, before it is too late.' Confidently, aloud:

'Well, sir, that will teach the fellow. Thank God neither of us has injured t'other.'

Now, from the mainmast crosstrees, a lookout's shout:

'De-e-e-e-ck! Sail of ship to the e-e-e-e-ast!'

Rennie immediately swung his glass eastward, and saw the

ship emerging from behind a jutting rocky spit, her masts and sails first, then her bowsprit and hull.

'It is *Terces*!'

Again Rennie swung his glass toward the frigate, and:

'Yes, yes, I see what they are about, by God. The frigate will engage me, while *Terces* slips away west to the open sea.'

Another shout from the lookout aloft:

'Sail of ship to the we-e-e-e-st!'

It was the Danish brig returning, her colours clear against the background of rock and steep slopes. Rennie focused there a moment, then lowered his glass and with a triumphant glare at James:

'There, d'y'see! I am rushed at from all sides, Mr Hayter!'

From the waist now:

'Starboard battery ready!'

Rennie again held his hat high. 'Fire as they bear!'

James gave an inward sigh, and in his head: 'Madness . . . bloody madness.'

The brig, as if by a prearranged design, tacked south-east in the fjord, using the thirty-two as a shield, toward the approaching *Terces*.

'How in God's name could they have arranged such a plan between them?' muttered James. 'How – when they could not have signalled to *Terces* in this remote place?'

'Why don't our guns fire!' Rennie demanded, leaning over the breast-rail. Before he had finished speaking:

BANG-BANG-BANG   BANG-BANG-BOOM-BANG

Through the boiling smoke, further flashes from the opposing frigate, and this time her twelve-pound roundshot did not all fall wide. Four of her shot struck *Expedient*, but even as they did eight of *Expedient*'s heavier shot struck the Danish vessel. This onslaught of iron, flying at 1,000 feet per second, did terrible damage to the smaller, lighter ship. Her foremast, hit low above the deck, sagged in the shrouds. The forestay drooped, carrying down with it the preventer, and tearing the crowsfeet out of the tilting top. The mast, broken through, fell away and crashed over the starboard side, crushing hammock cranes in a tumbling confusion of rigging, yards and canvas. The ship lost way. A moment of shocked silence, then the racketing, buffeting sound of the guns reverberated along the fjord, followed by screams.

Screams which James now perceived were close by, in *Expedient*. He had fallen to the deck without recalling how that had happened. Had he been knocked down? Blood dripped into his left eye, obscuring his vision. He wiped it away, clapped on to the still intact breast-rail and hauled himself up on his legs.

Rennie had not moved from his position, and looked exactly as he had a moment before, except that his hat had gone from his head. He was peering intently through his glass at the frigate, and seemed oblivious of the damage to his own ship. James looked down into the waist, and forrard along the starboard side, and saw injured men, smashed timbers, a gun carriage tipped on its side. To Rennie:

'With your permission I shall make an inspection of damage, sir.'

'That damned Dane is damaged, that is what counts.' Rennie, lowering his glass at last. 'He is crippled, in truth, and so cannot distract me from my pursuit of—'

'De-e-e-e-ck!' From aloft. 'The brig and *Terces* approach us together from the east!'

James now looked to the east through the clearing smoke, and saw the Danish brig and *Terces* heading straight for *Expedient*.

'Sir, I think that *Terces* has no intention to slip away. She means to attack us, with the brig in support.'

Rennie stared east and did not reply, and then:

'Sir . . . sir, if you please?' Mr Glaister, one of the midshipmen, had appeared at the waist ladder. Rennie heard his voice and distractedly looked down at him.

'Yes?'

'Mr Leigh is injured, sir.'

Rennie looked east again, and: 'Is he badly hurt?'

'He is lying in the upper deck by the capstan, sir.'

'Yes yes, what are his injuries?' Rennie, lifting his glass to peer at the advancing ships.

'I . . . I do not know, sir. He is in a dead faint on the deck.'

'Mr Hayter.'

'Sir?'

'Go to Mr Leigh, and discover his condition. If he is gravely injured, I will like you to take his place as first, immediate.'

'Very good, sir.'

'Report back to me, right quick. We must fight our way out of this damned fjord.'

'Ay-ay, sir.'

James jumped down the ladder behind the midshipman. The after part of the upper deck was a scene of confusion. Hanging smoke, sprawled men, great damage. One of the starboard guns had been destroyed, smashed off its carriage and the muzzle cracked wide by a direct hit. Lieutenant Leigh lay abaft the capstan, on his back. His left leg was caught up under his right, and he appeared lifeless.

'Leigh! Leigh! Can you hear me!' James, on his knees beside him.

There was no response. James now saw blood seeping dark through the shoulder of the lieutenant's coat. He lifted the standing collar, and saw the shirt beneath was a mass of glistening blood. He put two fingers to the pallid neck, and detected a pulse.

'He is alive. – You there! And you! Carry the first lieutenant below to the surgeon in the cockpit!' And as the two seamen approached through the hanging smoke: 'Take care, he is wounded severe. Cheerly now, lads. – Mr Glaister.' Getting up on his legs, and turning.

'Sir?'

'Reload, Mr Glaister. Jump now.'

'Ay-ay, sir.'

As James jumped up the waist ladder he became aware that the ship was tacking to larboard. Calls, shouts of command, yards bracing, and the ship swinging round. His head came level with the quarterdeck. An explosion of splinters and a shock of blasted air greeted him, and he ducked his head just in time to preserve it.

CRACK   CRACK   CRACK   CRACK-CRACK

The Danish brig's four-pounder great guns. James ran aft.

A further shock wave and eruption of splinters, and long lethal fractured staves, as *Terces* loosed a broadside of carronades. The deck trembling under James's feet. The air full of whirling, slashing fragments.

BOOM BOOM BOOM   THUD-BOOM
THUD-BOOM B-BOOM

The sound of that broadside, instantly after.

'Why don't our goddamned bloody guns *fire*, in the name of Christ!' Captain Rennie was now at the starboard rail of his quarterdeck. Catching sight of James as he came aft: 'Mr Hayter, y'will order the—'

His words drowned by *Expedient*'s reply, which had been made in spite of the confusion and disarray James had witnessed on the upper deck. Shattering din, the air choking dense with gritty, sulphurous smoke, and the deck jarring under their feet. The added numbing din of the quarterdeck carronades.

The Danish brig, veering away on the larboard tack, was caught amidships by thirty-two-pound roundshot from *Expedient*'s carronades, and eighteen-pound shot from her long guns. Caught and smashed with terrible force. She lost way at once, the water all about her rippling with the shocks running through her hull.

Expedient continuing to swing wide on the larboard tack. The creaking and groaning of timbers, stays, braced yards. A voice bellowing:

'Re-e-e-lo-o-o-ad!'

James's own voice.

He turned, and stared in wonder as a ragged window opened in the drifting smoke. A sudden entrancing view of the fjord far to the east. Dark cliffs, green wooded steeps, and the snow-streaked grandeur of the mountains beyond, all reflected with extraordinary clarity in the glassy water. Wind crawled across the water, dissolving the reflection, smoke whirled and obscured the view as the ship swung, and the moment of magical beauty was lost.

'Where are my junior lieutenants!' Rennie, bellowing through the last of the smoke, which wafted away as *Expedient* steadied on the new tack.

James found his voice. 'MrTrembath is forrard, sir. I have not seen Mr Tindall.'

'Haven't *seen* him? Why ain't he at his station!'

'Likely he has fallen, sir.'

Rennie brought up his glass to look at *Terces*, which now had altered course to close again with *Expedient*. Rennie beckoned to James, who joined him at the rail.

'We must allow *Terces* to escape, thinking she has destroyed us at last. Our ruse of thick smoke clearly did not hoodwink Captain Broadman, last night. Accordingly, we must devise a more effective method of deceit.'

'Sir, should not we take thought of the consequence of this. Aside from the—.'

'The consequence?' Over him. 'The consequence is that Captain Broadman will believe us, on this occasion. He will think we cannot pursue him, any more.'

'No, sir, I meant – the consequence of this action entire. We have fired upon two Danish ships of war, in their own waters, and severely damaged them both.'

'Good God, James.' Severely. 'They have damaged us. I did

not wish to fight them. They wished to fight me. Well well, be it on their own heads, then, the *consequence*. No sea officer of the Royal Navy may allow his ship to be attacked with impunity. It is his plain duty to defend his ship, and his people, and his king.'

'Very good, sir.' Politely correct. Aware of the absurdity of such an exchange in the middle of a fierce sea action.

'We will run.'

'Eh?'

'Are ye deaf with the guns, Mr Hayter? We will *run away!*'

'Are not we to fire at *Terces* again?'

'We will loose off a few guns, ragged and ill-aimed, and go about – looking very clumsy and unseamanlike, then make a dash for the open sea.'

'The frigate is coming about!' One of the lookouts still aloft. 'She is preparing to fire!'

'What! God damn the fellow! Ain't he took enough of a pounding?'

The answer came in gun flashes along the port strakes of the battered Danish thirty-two as she came beam-on to *Expedient* at a distance of a third of a mile.

The drone of roundshot, and the sound of the guns across the water. Explosions of spray. Buffeting echoes. And *Expedient* was not hit.

But the Danish brig, which Rennie had ceased to consider, was now astern of *Expedient*, drifting and apparently helpless – except that she had one long brass chaser, her most accurate gun. This gun she now fired. The nine-pound roundshot struck *Expedient*'s rudder, and smashed it off its pintles.

Rennie was distracted by the frigate, and at first did not notice what had happened, until *Expedient* began to drift. A gust of wind caught her stern, and she veered toward the northern shore of the fjord, and a steep rocky eminence.

Captain Broadman in *Terces* now saw his chance, even as Rennie was not yet wholly aware of *Expedient*'s helplessness, and that his plan of deception had become harsh fact.

'She don't respond to the wheel!' The helmsman, in terrible consternation, as if talking of a living creature. 'The tiller rope has broke, or a tackle sheave!'

'Nay, it is the rudder!' One of the carronade crewmen had hung far out over the tafferel to look. 'The rudder itself is smashed!'

BOOM   BOOM-BOOM   BOOM BOOM BOOM

Terces' carronades.

Rennie saw *Expedient*'s tafferel disappear in a spasm of disintegrating timber. The man who had been leaning there became a fleshy doll flung up in a violent tumbling arc, arms and legs flailing limp, and away to larboard out of sight. The punching crash of fragmented glass. Shocks and shudders through the body of the ship.

James, momentarily thrown off balance by the shock wave of a carronade ball flying within eighteen inches of his head, stumbled and fell, was deaf and half-blind, and found himself on his knees, his hands thrown forward on the sand-strewn deck.

The gusting wind now on her larboard quarter, *Expedient* veered drifting beyond the rocky eminence, and came in toward a low, rocky beach. A grinding crunch as her keel slid along a submerged arm of rock, then she floated clear, bottomed again briefly, drifted further in, then went aground with a series of shuddering jolts. Stays, shrouds and braces slackened and tautened and stretched gnarling as the ship finally came to rest, miraculously not listing, her starboard beam exposed to the fjord.

Standing at the starboard rail, his face streaked black with burned powder, his coat torn by splinters, Captain Rennie stared out at *Terces*, and:

'Well now, Captain Broadman, y'have a choice, sir. Close with me, and destroy me, or make good your escape.' As if mildly reflecting on what could be done in his garden today, weather permitting. 'I must tell you, however, that if y'do venture close, I shall be obliged – contrary to your expectation – to destroy you, you damned pox-addled wretch.' A little emphatic jerk of his head, and a breath. 'Mr Hayter!' Raising his voice.

'Sir?' James, his hearing returned, heaved himself up on his legs.

'Starboard battery reload, and triple-shot your guns.'

'We have lost near half our starboard guns, sir. With resp—'

'Kindly do as you are *told*, sir. Reload!'

'Ay-ay, sir.' And he ran down into the waist.

Minutes passed, and *Terces* tacked closer, then a little closer still.

James, on the damaged upper deck, called hoarsely to the crews at the remaining guns: 'Ready, now, lads . . .'

On deck Rennie lifted his glass, and saw a figure on *Terces'* quarterdeck raise a hand. A moment. Another moment. And *Terces* went suddenly and rapidly about, yards bracing, and heeled away close-hauled toward the west.

Rennie, softly to himself: 'He thinks me done, the villain. He will discover different, by God. He will discover different, another day.' A nod, a sniff, and presently he lifted his glass again, and saw that both the heavily damaged frigate and the brig had sent out boats ahead, and were being towed away. Murmuring as he lowered the glass: 'And that is wise in them, too, by Christ.' Turning. 'Mr Hayter!'

James appeared at the ladder. 'Sir?'

'We will stand down, and find out the damage to the ship – and the people.'

*

The rock face behind the narrow stony beach rose, pitted and rough, and scattered across with sparse green vegetation, to a sharp black peak several hundred feet above. *Expedient* lay stuck fast below, a pistol-shot from the shore. A narrow gorge ran between this peak and the next, and through the gorge roared and tumbled white water, which fanned out a little further east across the pebbly shore in a rapidly flowing stream. Rennie could see other white waterfalls half a league east, on the dark far side of the fjord. The high snows were gradually melting in the temperate spring air.

The nearest settlement of houses and barns was perhaps another half-league beyond the waterfalls. To the naked eye they were a few red and white blobs ranged across the sloping ground. In Rennie's glass they were clearly defined as well-kept little farms, perhaps eight or ten of them, and there was a small dark elaborately carved wooden church, with steep gables and spire.

'They cannot have failed to see and hear the action we was engaged in.' Rennie lowered the glass. 'Almost certainly they will be hostile to us, should they decide to venture closer in boats.'

'Yes, sir, you think so?' James felt able, now that Rennie had spoken to him, to go aft to where the captain stood near the smashed, gaping hole that had been the tafferel.

'Alert Lieutenant Harcher, so that he and his Marines are always aware of the danger posed to us from natives ashore.'

'Natives, sir?'

'These fjord-dwellers are primitives, James, I am in no doubt, scarcely more civilised than the cattle they tend.'

'You did not see their church, sir?'

'Yes yes, I saw it.'

James made no further comment, but instead simply made a neutral movement of his head, not quite shaking it.

'Ye don't agree they are savages, hey?'

'I hope they are not, sir, for all our sakes.'

'Well well, I shall not fire on them, if they do not give me cause.' A sniff. 'Ye'd better tell me what Adgett says, now.'

'Well, sir, we have suffered no great damage to the hull timbers, so far as Mr Adgett can judge, since there is no serious leak. It is probable we may have lost part of the false keel when we scraped over the rocks, and our copper may very likely have been damaged also. I should like to send a man diving down to look, with your permission.'

'Have not ye made up a working party already, Mr Hayter, and chose a man to go diving down? I am surprised that was not your first activity of assessment.'

'We have a great deal of repair to carry out on the upperworks, sir.' Nodding at the smashed tafferel. 'We are short-handed. A further difficulty is that the fjord water is damned cold. Cold enough to make a man insensible if he remains immersed beyond a minute or two. I felt it was my duty to ask your permission first, before risking a man's life.'

'Yes yes, very well, you have it, Mr Hayter. Let us find out what damage has been done to the bottom planks of the ship. Our guns will have to be hoisted out of her, I am nearly certain, and most of our stores too. But we must learn before we attempt to float her off whether or no such an action may cause water to flood into the ship, deep under the ballast, through timbers weakened by our going aground.'

'Then we may well have to get the ballast out of her, don't you think so, sir?'

'Eh? Good God, are y'certain? All the shingles, and the pigs as well?' Thoroughly dismayed.

'No, sir, I am not certain. I merely suggest it as a possibility. I will discover the facts directly, sir.'

Rennie looked at him sharply. 'Y'don't propose to make the dive yourself, I hope?'

'No, sir, I do not.'

'I cannot allow my officers to take undue risk. Where is the master? He should assist you in this.'

'Mr Loftus is in the hold, sir, with Mr Adgett.'

'Ah. Ah. Very good. Yes, Doctor?' Seeing the surgeon Elias Empson by the binnacle, his shirtsleeves very bloody. Dr Empson came aft.

'We have lost two more men, sir, I fear, and there is half a dozen others very gravely hurt.'

'I will go below myself in a moment or two, Doctor, and see the injured men, and attempt to cheer them.'

'Thank you, sir.'

'Aloft, there!' Rennie peered up at the lookout in the maintop. 'Keep a sharp eye on those dwellings to the east! Look for boats!'

James assembled a small party of three men to conduct the dive, as repairs were begun the length and breadth of the ship in a clatter of mallets and adzes. When they had fully understood why they had been brought from their other duties, all three men displayed reluctance, and assured James that:

'I cannot swim, sir.'

'Nor me, sir.'

'I should drown at once, sir.'

'But good heaven it ain't a matter of swimming at all. One of you would be lowered on a rope, d'y'see? You need only hold in your breath a short time, and look about you under the water, and—'

'I has never learned to hold my breaf, sir.'

'Nor me.'

'Nay, nor me, neither.'

'Then who is the best swimmer in the lower deck?'

'That would be Jess Skilton, sir, rated able. Only . . .'

'Yes?'

'Only his leg is broke, sir, and he is kept below under the surgeon.'

'Christ Jesu.' Quietly, then a resolute breath and: 'Very well, I will make the dive myself. You will assist me.'

James did not inform the captain of his decision. He felt that Rennie had more than a sufficiency of trouble to contend with at present, and would not welcome more from his disobedient acting first lieutenant. James was dressed in his working rig as he approached the task, and now shrugged off his jerkin, took off his shoes, and tied a length of hawser-laid rope securely round his waist. He climbed down the larboard side ladder, and waved to the three men above to lower him into the water. They were to allow him no more than two minutes. If he had not by then reappeared, they were to haul him up right quick.

The dark surface of the water, reflecting the ship's side, rose to meet him, and he felt its intense cold rising round his body. He sucked in a sharp, deep breath before the water closed over his head. Fully immersed he found the cold almost unbearable, and although he endeavoured to keep his eyes open at first he found it impossible. Blindly he pointed himself downward as the men above paid out more rope, and he kicked forcefully to drive himself to the bottom. His outstretched hands came in contact with a rocky shelf, and now he did open his eyes. The water was surprisingly clear, and he found he could make out the bottom planking of the ship without difficulty.

Several sheets of copper had been loosened by the heavy contact of the ship with the rocky bottom, but so far as he could see the planking beneath the copper was sound. He examined the ship's curved bottom a little way forrard, then kicked round and headed aft. There were no large splinters or loose strips of timber. He thought of swimming all the way aft to look at the rudder, but the cold was now so absolute that he felt his hands and feet going numb, and his face ached painfully. He kicked down against rock, and rose to the surface. He gasped for air, felt the rope slip up under his armpits and tauten as the men above hoisted him, and a moment after he was back in the ship. Rennie was standing directly alongside the diving crew on the gangway, his expression very fierce.

'What in the name of Christ was you thinking, Mr Hayter!'

James was shivering so violently that he was unable to form words. His numbed hands were useless, and one of the men had to untie the rope for him.

'Y'will answer my question, sir!'

James sucked in a shuddering breath.

'She is sound, thank God.'

And he fell in a swoon on the gangway. He would have

tumbled into the waist had not the man who had untied the rope caught him under the arms. Rennie's anger vanished, and became concern.

'Carry him into the waist. Handsomely, there, handsomely. – You there, boy! Fetch the doctor on deck! Jump now!'

And presently, under Dr Empson's attentive supervision – Rennie anxiously at his shoulder – James was carried below.

*

Two of *Expedient*'s four boats had been smashed in the first encounter with *Terces* in the North Sea, and the remaining two – the pinnace and the cutter – struggled to cope with all of the stores being hoisted out of the ship and taken ashore.

Dr Empson had insisted, in his quiet, bespectacled way, that Lieutenant Hayter should rest for the remaining hours of daylight, and so James took no part in the work of unloading and repair, but lay below in his hanging cot, fitfully dozing.

When the great bulk of the ship's stores at last lay on the stony shore – long rows of casks and a great quantity of other items under protecting canvas – all guarded by two Marines, *Expedient* was still firmly aground. Captain Rennie now had to decide how *Expedient*'s guns were to be got out of her, so that she was lightened enough to swim off the shelf. Mr Storey and Mr Adgett together made the suggestion that the guns should be floated ashore on a raft made from empty casks and planking. Rennie heard them out, but felt that such a raft would not be stable enough to carry the weight of even one of the eighteen-pounders, and rejected the notion.

'We must achieve it either by taking the guns ashore one by one in the pinnace, or by rigging a system of tackles between the ship and the rock face, and hoisting them ashore, again one at a time. Either method will be very consuming of time, but we must refloat the ship, one way or t'other.'

This to his sea officers and standing officers in the great cabin at nightfall. Mr Leigh was absent, still lying senseless below under the surgeon's care, but James – now wholly restored and hale – had joined them, and it was he who asked:

'Are we to resume our pursuit, sir, when we have refloated the ship, and carried out her repair?'

'We are, Mr Hayter. Just as soon as she swims.'

'Then would not it save us a great deal of valuable time – if we threw the guns overboard?'

'Lose all of our great guns?' Rennie, with a frowning stare.

'Well, not all of them, sir, no. Just so many as it takes to swim her off.'

'When we have only today suffered severe damage at Captain Broadman's hands? How in God's name d'y'propose we should defend ourselves against *Terces* on the open sea, should we need to?'

'It is my view, sir – with respect – that relieving the ship of the weight of perhaps half a dozen or eight of our guns would achieve our purpose. We would retain our smashers, and about half of our eighteens, as adequate armament. We could then stand a little way offshore, clear of the rocks, and safely take in our stores again.'

'Hm. Hm.' A sniff, a frown. 'Mr Loftus?'

'Sir?' Bernard Loftus looked attentively at Rennie, having exchanged a quick glance with James.

'What say you?'

'Well, sir . . . I think what Lieutenant Hayter suggests has very considerable merit. Relieved of, say, twelve or fourteen tons, the ship will very likely float, sir.'

'Mr Storey?'

'I will never like to lose great guns, sir. Howsomever, I do not think we has a choice, as we find ourself circumstanced.'

'Hm. Hm. Well well, so be it, then. We are all agreed.'

'In course, sir, there is still the question of repair.' James leaned forward over the table. 'We must undertake the—'

'We will repair at sea.' Rennie, over him.

*

Rennie did not waste time waiting until morning. As soon as consensus had been reached in the great cabin, he ordered that the work of jettisoning guns should begin, in lantern light. When six of the great guns had been hoisted out and dropped into the sea, the ship groaned, creaked, squirmed a little, and swam free. A hoarse, heartfelt cheer echoed through the ship.

Rennie ordered the boats to tow her clear of the underwater rock shelf, and then he anchored, the boats were tethered close, and the ship was quiet. All work ceased for the night. However, the Marine guard was doubled ashore to watch over the stores, and extra lookouts posted in case of a hostile approach from the water. Nothing untoward was observed, and at first light work was resumed. The day was misty and grey.

At six bells of the morning watch one of the lookouts sighted movement ashore, and presently a herd of animals came along a stony path out of the gorge, driven by a figure in heavy dark clothing. The animals proved to be sturdy, buff-coloured horses with stiff standing manes. Their keeper was an angular middle-aged man with a thatch of grey hair and a beard. He carried a tall staff, and spoke to the horses in a gentle, penetrating baritone that carried out over the water to the ship. When he saw *Expedient* the man stopped in utter astonishment, his blue-eyed stare taking in the ship herself, and the bustling activity on the shore and in the boats, as her stores were got back into her. The horses stood still, snorting and tossing their heads in the cool morning air. Presently their keeper turned the horses, waving his stick and issuing a series of gentle basso commands, and both animals and man retreated into the gorge, and disappeared.

Rennie followed their retreat in his glass. 'He will speak of this to his tribe, and more of them will come. We must prepare ourselves.'

'He looked peaceable enough, did not he, sir?' James, at his side.

Rennie lowered his glass. 'Never forget that Vikings came

to England from his region exact, and laid waste to much of the north country. They are a warrior people – savage, primitive, and fiercely predatory. We will mount swivels on the rail, loaded with canister. Say so to Mr Storey.'

'Very good, sir.' Thinking but not saying that the gentle fellow they had just observed was as like to a Viking as was a Dorset cowherd.

By five bells of the forenoon watch, all the stores had been brought back and hoisted into the ship, and the boats tethered, and work had begun on the replacement rudder, which Mr Adgett and his crew fashioned and fitted together and then lowered into the pinnace to be taken round the stern.

'Just as soon as the rudder is hung and we can steer, we will weigh and proceed, Mr Hayter.' Rennie turned from the shattered tafferel, which had been temporarily replaced by a canvas screen. He peered along the fjord a moment. A sniff. 'I shall not be sad to depart this place.' A slight, involuntary shiver. 'It may be handsome enough, but it is also chilling oppressive in scale, do not you find?'

'I think it is one of the most sublimely beautiful places I have ever seen.' James, quietly.

'Ah. Yes?' A brief quizzical look, another sniff.

At six bells, as the work on the new rudder continued from the tethered pinnace, men taking it in turn to go roped into the cold water to help hang it and secure the replacement spectacle plate and pintles in the gudgeons – a slow, laborious process, fraught with difficulty – Rennie had grown impatient, and was pacing his quarterdeck, sighing and muttering, his hands clasped behind his back. As he returned yet again to peer down over the counter, a scattering of fragments pocked and rippled the water all round the ship, and rattled on the deck. Rennie frowned, and turned to look toward the shore. A brief moment as the water settled and was still, then a further shower of fragments fell, and there was a deep rumbling sound, as if the air itself had trembled.

'What in the name of God . . .'

Rennie looked up at the rock face and the misty peak above, and at the same moment a tremendous rattling hail of stones, flints and other fragments descended on the deck, and turned the water frothing white all round the ship.

A further deep grumbling shock, and the air shook. Shouts of alarm.

'Mr Tangible!'

'Sir?' Roman Tangible appeared, his face pallid with fright.

'We must pay out the cables, and tow the ship well clear of the shore! Hands to the boats, double-banked oars!'

'Ay-ay, sir.' His call to his mouth, summoning men to action. The call echoed by the boatswain's mate forrard. Bawled commands. Activity in the cutter, and in the pinnace, as work on the rudder was abandoned. Splashing at the bow as hawsers were run out.

Another deep, ominous rumble, and a further cracking, rattling shower of fragments, bouncing on the deck and clinking and pinging on guns and hammock cranes.

'Give way together! Cheerly, now!'

The boats pulled out into the glassy fjord, oars dipping and lifting, the slack of the towing ropes was taken up dripping, and *Expedient* began to move, slowly swinging stern-on to the boats as she cleared, her loosened cables running from the bow.

When the boats and ship were two cables off, a tremendous concussion boomed and reverberated like a broadside of guns. A whole section of the dark rock face abruptly dropped, and collapsed in a tumbling sliding rush into the water. A huge wave bellied out from the shore, and *Expedient* and her boats were lifted up as it rolled under them. The hawsers held, the anchors digging into the rocky bottom, but one of the towing ropes aft of the ship stretched and parted in a twang of uncoiling strands, and the cutter was turned beam-on by the surging wave. The crew of oarsmen spilled into the swirling water. Three drowned at once, some of the others clung for their lives to the hull of the upturned boat, and two more were swept far out into the fjord still gripping their oar. The oar was caught in a powerful eddy of the surge and flung up tall and twirling, and the bobbing heads of the two men disappeared.

Expedient righted herself, as did the pinnace trailing aft of her. The echo of the crash sounded far along the fjord as the wave beat against the rocks on the far side. A flight of birds fled across the water, loud in retreating alarm. A last sprinkling shower of debris close inshore. Then the placid roar of the waterfall in the gorge reasserted itself on the late morning air.

Rennie rose on his legs from where he had fallen by the larboard rail, and found his voice. Shakily:

'Likely the thudding of our guns yesterday loosened the rocks high above us.'

James saw that he was clapped on to a backstay with both white-knuckled hands, and let go. And let out a long-held breath.

The cries of the men clinging to the upturned cutter sent both officers to the tafferel. Within moments the pinnace was pulling to their position, the rescue was effected, the bodies of the drowned men recovered, and the capsized, wallowing cutter taken carefully in tow.

The burial service was conducted for the drowned men, and for the men killed in the action of the day before, then Captain Rennie addressed his assembled officers and people:

'We have suffered much, and lost shipmates, but we here are alive, and the ship swims. We have a duty to perform. We must pursue the *Terces*, as soon as we are able. We must pursue her until we discover her port of destination, as we have been ordered to do, in the king's name. All our efforts must be directed to that end. We are all *Expedient*s, every man of us standing here. At sea, in peril, and storm, and action, we may rely only upon each other. I rely upon you . . .' Pointing at the upturned faces in the waist. '. . . and you, and you, and you.' Meeting each man's eye as his pointing finger moved.

He paused, leaning on the breast-rail, and lifted his gaze aloft, then aft, and then again looked at his assembled people. 'And we all of us rely upon our ship. We are all one together in her. She is our life, and our world.' A brief dramatic pause, and:

'Tell me now, what are we called?'

'*Expedient*s . . .' A ragged response.

'God's love, that damned great crash has deafened me, I think. Tell me again! What are we called?'

'*Expedient*s!'

'Mr Loftus!'

'Sir?'

'A double ration of grog for every man!'

Rennie and James ate a late supper together in the great cabin, which bore signs of the recent action. Several of the stern-gallery windows had been smashed, and were now shuttered. The work of repair continued on deck in the glow of lanterns, and the sounds of adzes and mallets filtered down to the two men. James was still in his working rig, having come direct from his duties on deck, and Rennie was in an old frockcoat. His cat Dulcie lay on the bench under the window, curled up asleep. Rennie and James had discussed the progress of repair, and James was preparing to return to the deck, but Rennie wished to talk a moment or two longer, motioned him to stay, and when James had resumed his seat:

'Yes, I had thought Broadman only came into this cursed fjord to give me the slip, to bamboozle me and tangle me up. But nay, the fellow all along meant to lead me into a trap, and then see me disabled or destroyed by his Danish friends.'

'He very nearly succeeded, did not he, sir?' James cut himself some more cheese.

'Eh?' A glare.

'Well, are we not fortunate indeed to've survived his—'

'*Fortunate?*' Over him. 'We fought the Danes to a standstill, good God! We smashed the buggers!'

'Yes, in course I did not mean—'

'And then we stood promptly away from the shore and prevented great damage to the ship by that damned rock fall. We have behaved seamanlike and courageous in all distinctions. Fortunate don't come into it.'

'No, sir.'

'As soon as we have repaired sufficient, we will weigh and make sail, head for the open sea and continue the pursuit, as I told the people.'

'Yes, sir. It will be as well to leave these waters before the Danish navy returns.'

'They will be licking their wounds yet awhile, before they will like to challenge us again, never fear.' A nod, a sniff, and a suck of wine.

'Yes, sir. So it is due west for us, between the Orkneys and the Shetlands?'

'West? Certainly not.'

'Not west . . . Lowering a piece of cheese to his plate.

'Nay, nay, James. South. We will sail south, into the English Channel, and thus save time.'

'He did not say anything of this to you, Bernard?'

'Nothing.'

Lieutenant Hayter and the sailing master Bernard Loftus were on the fo'c'sle, where the latter was getting some fresh air in his lungs after long hours supervising the retrimmimg of the ship in the hold. Around them the work of repair continued by lantern light, and they spoke in low tones.

'Well, that is his intention,' James continued. 'I thought perhaps he may have said something to you, and—'

'I cannot understand it.' Bernard Loftus, over him. 'He means to go south, to save time, when certainly *Terces* has headed west? Why not pursue her direct?'

'Ay, and that ain't the whole of it. He means to weigh and proceed *tonight*.'

'What?'

'Yes, tonight. He would say nothing further to me about our course, and then—'

'Why hasn't he spoke to me about these things? Good heaven, James, don't he trust me in anything? If we are to make sail in darkness, surely he—'

'Very likely he will send for you, directly, Bernard.' James, a hand on the master's shoulder.

'But, but . . . sail at night, in these narrow waters, that we do not know well even by day? When we have scarce repaired sufficient to withstand a damned little squall? What if a storm should blow in across the open sea, just as we cleared the fjord mouth? And I have not completed the trimming. Don't he comprehend that with all that weight of guns gone, I must—'

'I am sorry to have alarmed you so, Bernard. Only I thought I had better prepare you. He will send for you in a moment or two, I am in no doubt.'

'Ay, no doubt.' An agitated sigh. He turned to look aft in the lantern glow, then: 'South, hey? I wonder . . .'

'Eh?'

'Perhaps he intends . . . yes, now, that must be his intention, in course.' With relief. 'Certainly he wishes to save time. He wishes to go south to repair at Portsmouth, without further delay, because he has understood at last.'

'At Portsmouth? But that would mean . . .'

'Ay, it would mean this damned pursuit must go by the board, James. And good riddance. This commission carried a curse with it from the moment we weighed at Spithead, and in our present condition, with all of our losses and damage, it cannot be sustained. Thank God the captain has now understood it, and come to his senses.'

'Nay, I cannot agree with you, I fear. He has already declared he will continue the pursuit. If he meant to change his mind and make for Portsmouth, the pursuit abandoned – he would wait until daylight.'

*

The narrowest part of the Strait of Dover, between the South
Foreland of Kent and the French coast, the white cliffs visible
to the west, and the hazy lower bumps of France to the east,
and a brisk sou'westerly wind blowing. *Expedient* close-hauled,
pitching in the chop, and spray flying and sluicing along her
deck.

Lieutenant Hayter standing his watch, and Captain Rennie
on the quarterdeck. He joined his lieutenant at the binnacle,
his glass clamped under his arm and his thwartwise hat firmly
crammed down on his head.

'We make good progress in the conditions, Mr Hayter.'
Over the combined sounds of the wind and the sea. He ducked
his head as spray fanned up over the fo'c'sle and waist, flew
through the shrouds and stays, and smashed into drenching
fragments across the quarterdeck.

'Yes, sir.' A moment, then: 'Sir, may I suggest again that we
put our wounded ashore?'

'No, y'may not.' Curtly.

'Sir, with respect—'

'Kindly attend to your duties, Mr Hayter.' Over him, and
moving abruptly aft toward the repaired tafferel.

For a moment James stood irresolute, frowning at the
binnacle, then he turned and went aft to where Rennie stood
at the weather-rail, one hand on a hammock crane to brace
himself.

'Sir, I must speak to you.' James, immediately behind
Rennie, raising his voice over the wind and spray.

'What!' Rennie turned angrily, his private domain invaded.
'Mr Hayter, you forget yourself!'

'No, sir, no. I do not. If those wounded men – including
Lieutenant Leigh, I remind you – are not put ashore they will
certainly die. It will take only an hour or two to land them at
Dover, and—'

'No! I have said no!'

'Sir, in the confined sickbay below, with little clean air, and
the constant restless movement of the ship, they can have no

hope of recovery. If we continue this pursuit into the Atlantic, as I think you mean to do, they are doomed.' He had nearly said 'futile pursuit', and Rennie responded as if he had:

'Enough! Enough! Y'will go below, sir, and send Mr Tindall to me. I am appointing him acting first, and you will confine yourself to your cabin.'

'I will go, but I will speak my mind first. Dr Empson knows very well that he cannot keep those men alive in the—'

'You dare to defy me!' Furiously.

'God's love, cannot you see that all I wish to do is—'

'Mr Glaister!'

'Sir?' One of the duty mids, attending.

'Find Mr Harcher, and ask him to come to me with his sergeant of Marines and two men, at once! And then find Mr Tindall.'

'Ay-ay, sir.' A hand to his hat, and he ran forrard, kept his balance on the sloping deck, and disappeared down the ladder.

'You would place me under arrest, sir?' James, in astonishment.

'Be quiet, sir! Consider y'self under arrest already!'

'When all I have wished to do is save the lives of brave men . . . ?'

'God damn your mutinous insolence! Be silent, sir!' Clutching at the hammock crane as the ship lurched. Sea water swirled up over the lee hances, and fanned across the deck. James took a deep breath, and:

'Sir, I must speak, no matter the consequence. *Terces* has escaped us, and it will be impossible to find her again, even if she came south through the Channel to reach the Atlantic, as I think you suppose. Therefore what you attempt now is folly.'

'Be *quiet*!' Pale with rage, gripping the hammock crane.

'Nay, I will not, until I have spoke the truth to you. You risk our ship, in a very parlous condition of repair, and you risk the lives of all our people, not just those of the wounded men, for a damned shadowy scheme of Mappin's, that he never explained. We are plunging blind into danger and darkness, on one man's whim. It is folly.'

The ship crashed through another steep trough, shuddered and lifted herself, yawing, creaking and groaning, and water spilling from her scuppers. James raised his voice over the rushing of the sea, holding Rennie's eye with his own.

'I do not care what happens to me. My life don't matter, now. But for the love of God do not condemn two hundred souls, and our faithful ship, for *nothing at all.*'

Lieutenant Harcher now appeared, holding his hat in the wind, his sergeant and two Marines behind, and James allowed himself, with a last long look at Captain Rennie, to be taken below.

Presently Lieutenant Tindall came on deck, and when Rennie turned from the rail, saw him and nodded, the young man went aft.

'You wished to see me, sir?' A hand to his hat, partly to make his obedience, and partly to keep the hat from flying away.

'I do, Mr Tindall. Mr Hayter is – indisposed. He will no longer stand his watches, and Mr Leigh cannot. I am appointing you acting first, and Mr Trembath will be second. At eight bells you will come to me in the great cabin, and we will together arrange the new relief among the gunroom officers. Y'will find Mr Hayter's notations at the binnacle. Your course is west-sou'-west, and a point west. The deck is yours. Y'may carry on.'

'Ay-ay, sir. Thank you, sir.' His hand briefly again to his hat.

'Do not thank me, Mr Tindall.' Turning to go below. 'You are about to face the most arduous and testing duty of your life. As are we all.'

As if in confirmation a swirling gust of wind sucked Mr Tindall's hat clean off his head, and sent it spinning and tumbling far out over the tafferel and the line of the wake.

*

During the afternoon watch of the following day, when *Expedient* lay at 50 degrees and 9 minutes north, and 3 degrees and 9 minutes west, well south of Start Point, the westerly wind became a storm. At first Captain Rennie beat into it tack on tack, but made little headway, and in the end – when *Expedient* lay south-east of the Eddystone Rocks – he felt himself obliged to save his battered and limping ship from the certainty of foundering, and run north into Cawsand Bay to ride out the weather. Cawsand Bay was by no means the most comforting of anchorages in fierce conditions, but Rennie was now too far west to have gone into Torbay, and Cawsand was not at least to some degree protective against a westerly storm, if not an easterly, when it became a death trap for ships.

When James, confined in his cabin below, learned of their temporary place of refuge, he contrived through an inter- mediary in the person of the surgeon Dr Empson again to tackle the captain on the matter of the comfort and safety of the wounded men. Rennie was inclined to be angry, but the surgeon humbly and earnestly persisted, and the captain relented. When the conditions permitted, the day after, the wounded men – including Lieutenant Leigh – were taken ashore in the pinnace to the naval hospital at Stonehouse, on the narrow peninsula to the east of the imposing hump of Mount Wise.

The storm had not quite blown itself out, and Rennie found himself reluctant to venture beyond the bay into the open sea until it had. The enforced delay made him fret. He trod the heaving deck, and made himself busy in inspection of repair, which in turn made the repair crews nervous, and the boatswain and carpenter anxious, and the people in large – gloomy. Every man aboard her thought, and felt, and knew that *Expedient* was in no fair condition to go into the Atlantic, except apparently the captain himself. Every man thought, and felt, and knew that *Expedient* should put into the Hamoaze and there petition the dockyard master attendant for urgent repair. Captain Rennie refused even to entertain the notion. Then

James came to the door of the great cabin, on the morning of the third day. The Marine sentry knocked, and Colley Cutton opened the door. He was holding the captain's cat Dulcie close to him, and when the animal saw the faces outside she struggled in the steward's grasp, squirmed her way free and leapt down to the deck. Colley Cutton turned to try to recapture her . . .

'Dulcie . . . Dulcie, I am only going to feed you, you daft critcher!'

. . . and James slipped into the cabin behind him.

Rennie was seated at his desk, writing a dispatch. Half-turning his head, but not looking up:

'Do not harass the poor beast, you wretch. Treat her gentle, as befits her sex and nature. Blast.' Scratching at a word, and altering it. 'D'y'hear me?'

'As you wish, sir.'

'Do not say "as you wish", for the hundredth time. Who knocked at my door?'

'I did, sir.' James, advancing into the cabin.

'Eh?' Turning, then: 'Christ's blood, it is you.'

'May I speak to you?'

'Did not I confine you to your cabin? Do not answer. We both know that I did. Well?'

'You do wish me to speak, sir?'

'Are ye being insolent deliberate?'

James said nothing, and waited, his back straight. He had washed and shaved, and was neatly and correctly dressed, his hat under his arm. He was determined not to provoke, nor to be provoked.

'Well?' Rennie, again.

'With your permission, sir, I should like to offer my services.'

'Offer?'

'May I speak . . .?'

'Well well – go on.' A brusque nod.

'Thank you, sir. If we are to proceed into the Atlantic—'

'*If* ?! Over him. '*If* ?'

'When we proceed, sir, in pursuit of *Terces* – will not you need a Pursuit Officer?'

'Eh? Eh?' A jerk of the head. 'I had thought you was not in favour of such a pursuit, Mr Hayter. I had took it that you wished *Expedient* to be excluded from such duty, on grounds of incapacity.'

The ship rode a swell and swung a little on her mooring cables. Wind gusted and whistled round the quarter galleries.

'D'y'no longer hold that opinion, Mr Hayter?'

'If we . . . erm, when we continue the pursuit, sir, I think that I should not, as a commissioned sea officer, be idle below in my cabin. We are short-handed, the first lieutenant is gravely wounded and has gone out of the ship, and—'

A further knock at the door, and it was opened from without to admit Mr Madeley, one of the duty mids.

'With your permission, sir?'

'What is it, Mr Madeley?' Rennie.

'Sir, a squadron of ships approaches from the east into the bay, and has signalled us.' Reading from his notebook: '"Captain . . . Captain to repair aboard the flag."'

'What flag? What is the ship?'

'I do not know, sir. She is a seventy-four, and there are seven ships in all.'

'Did you acknowledge their signal?'

'Yes, sir.'

'Very well, Mr Madeley, thank you. I will go on deck.' Rising and taking up his hat. 'Mr Hayter.'

'Sir?'

'You will accompany me.'

'Ay-ay, sir.'

And James put on his own hat and followed Rennie up the ladder.

On his quarterdeck Captain Rennie looked at the approaching squadron through his glass, read the exchange of signals, and presently:

'Mr Tangible!'

The boatswain attended him, and touched his forehead. 'Sir?'

'We will hoist out the pinnace, if y'please.'

Half a glass later Captain Rennie, with Lieutenant Hayter beside him in the stern sheets, was rowed pitching and tossing and wet with spray across to the just anchored seventy-four. As she swung on her cables they saw her gold-painted name on the transom:

MALACHITE

The traditional question as the pinnace approached:

'What ship are you!'

And the traditional reply:

'*Expedient*!'

Indicating that the captain was in the visiting boat, and wished to be admitted.

'Come aboard!'

Captain Rennie waited until the lifting sea put his pinnace right up by the lowest step of the side ladder, then nimbly stepped from the boat and ran up the ladder, followed by Lieutenant Hayter. They were piped aboard, and taken aft by the *Malachite*'s first lieutenant.

'Who is in command?' Rennie asked him.

'Captain Davidson commands *Malachite*, sir, but Admiral Sir Jendex Lyle commands the squadron, and this is his flagship.'

'Lyle?' Rennie broke his stride. 'The same Admiral Lyle that had the *Argus* seventy-four, years since?'

'I believe *Argus* was the admiral's flag at one time, sir, years ago. I fear she was lost with all hands last year, in a storm at the Turks and Caicos Isles, under Captain Naismith.'

'Ah, was she? I did not know that.'

They came to the admiral's quarters, and were admitted by a steward. Compared to *Expedient*'s great cabin the admiral's quarters in *Malachite* were very splendid. There were silk hangings, pictures, books, fine furniture, a long, gleaming table and a wine cooler beneath it at the far end. Beyond, in the admiral's sleeping cabin, rich colours gave the impression of singular luxury.

The admiral laid aside his quill pen, rose from his desk, and greeted his visitors. He was a man above medium height, and spare – as spare in his figure as Rennie. There was no other similarity of appearance. A mane of pure white hair was swept back from his forehead. His face was very florid, and his eyes pale blue, and slightly bloodshot. His expression was polite, but with a hint of the autocratic. His undress coat was of very fine cloth and cut, and the buttons appeared to be gold rather than gilt brass. Rennie guessed that he was about sixty years of age.

When the formalities had been dispensed with, the admiral offered his visitors refreshment – Madeira. His offer was politely accepted, and the wine came.

The wind without was now markedly less gusting and fierce than it had been earlier in the watch, Rennie noted, and would soon moderate enough to enable him to weigh and make sail. This realisation made him anxious and distracted. He wished to send his dispatch – an explication to Their Lordships of *Expedient*'s brief delay at Plymouth – ashore in a boat, and be gone into the Atlantic immediately upon the boat's return. But he had not yet finished writing the dispatch, and—

'And now we come to our business, Captain Rennie.' The admiral was addressing him.

'Oh. Ah. Business, sir?'

'Indeed. I will like you to join my squadron, since you are at your leisure here, awaiting orders.'

'Awaiting . . .? Nay, sir, you are mistook. We are here simply to ride out the storm. Was here. We are already—'

'Mistook?' The admiral's demeanour had changed. It was a slight and subtle change – a tightening of the lines about the mouth – but Rennie saw it, and his heart sank. 'I am mistook?'

'Forgive me, sir, I meant no disrespect. I am commissioned – *Expedient* is commissioned – on a particular venture by Their Lordships, as an independent ship, and I had sought temporary respite at Cawsand Bay to wait out a fierce storm of wind, put my wounded men ashore, and attempt to complete repairing the damage to the upperworks. Therefore, I—'

'Damage?' Over him. 'Wounded men? Repair? What nonsense is this, pray? How can y'have been in such a sea action as to've caused these things, without we was at war? We are not at war, sir, unless I am *mistook.*'

'No, sir. With your permission, I shall endeavour to—'

'I will like to see your written instructions, Captain Rennie. Show them to me.'

'Show them to you . . . ?'

'Ay, sir. Let me see what has been wrote out by Their Lordships, exact.'

'I . . . I regret that I am unable to comply with your request, sir.'

'No, in course, you have not got the papers on your person.' A nod. 'We shall send for them. Your lieutenant will go, hey?' Glancing at James.

'No, sir. I fear the admiral does not quite apprehend me. I cannot – I may not show you the papers.' Why in God's name had not Mappin, or Lord Hood, written him an official letter of release for just such a moment as this, giving away nothing, but absolving him from all or any interference?

'Cannot? May not? Or *will not?*' Raised eyebrows, then a frown, and slight, vexed tilting of the head to one side. Rennie felt a twinge in his water. A breath, and:

'Well, sir, well well . . . it is simply beyond my authority. Further, my ship is—'

'You refuse outright, sir?' Over him. 'You absolutely refuse to show me your written orders?'

'Because I am forbidden to do so, sir, by direct indication of Their Lordships, and I beg that you will not insist. Further, my ship is in an indifferent condition of repair.'

The admiral shifted in his chair, and thrust away his glass on the table. A brief little grimace of a smile. 'Captain Rennie, I am being very patient with you, since you are my guest, and good manners must obtain at sea just as they do ashore. My squadron is engaged upon a mission of singular importance to Their Lordships. We have put into this bay because one of my ships – *Excelsior*, thirty-two, Captain Bagnold – has begun to leak so severe that she must at once go into the dockyard at the Hamoaze, or sink under Captain Bagnold's legs. Since *Expedient* is sufficiently seaworthy to undertake independent duties, she is seaworthy enough to join me, sir. *Excelsior* must be replaced. *Expedient* is conveniently here, and *Expedient* will accordingly replace her.'

Rennie was filled with such a potent mixture of emotions that he felt he must vent them, or explode.

'Sir, I am very sorry to speak so blunt – but what you propose is impossible. Quite impossible.'

The lines about the admiral's mouth became deep furrows. His florid colour deepened. But he did not shout, or rail. His voice was scarcely above a whisper:

'You dare to defy me, Captain Rennie?'

'I have no wish to defy the admiral. I merely state the facts of the case.'

'*Facts!* The sole fact y'have need of at present, sir, is your duty to obey me.' His voice now rising above a whisper into sharp, carrying authority. 'This interview is at an end.' Rising. 'You will return to your ship, gentlemen, and prepare to weigh. *Malachite* will lead. You will follow, taking your place in line astern of *Hermione*, thirty-eight, that follows me. Good afternoon.'

Rennie and James rose in unison, bowed, and departed the admiral's quarters. The lieutenant was waiting to conduct them out of the ship in the proper manner, but Captain Davidson was nowhere to be seen. As they came to the top of the side ladder, Rennie:

'Is the captain on deck?'

'No, sir. Captain Davidson is ill.'

'I am sorry to hear it. Will you give him my compliments, and say that I wish him a speedy recovery?'

'Certainly, sir.'

The two officers were duly piped out of the ship, descended the ladder into their boat, and were rowed away to *Expedient*. As they went they discussed their dilemma.

'I expect we must do as the fellow asks.' Rennie, ducking his head in the stern sheets, his face very grim. 'God damn and blast him.'

'Yes, sir. Erm . . . do we know, in truth, what we are asked to do?'

'Eh? We are asked join his bloody squadron, in course. You heard the fellow.' Glaring at the line of anchored ships. He noted the frigate limping into Plymouth away to their north. 'That must be *Excelsior*, I expect. Don't appear to excel, nor stand tall, hey?' Sarcastically.

'No, sir. Erm . . . perhaps there is a solution to this, after all.' James, *sotto voce*, glancing at Rennie.

'What? Speak up, James. Can't hear you.'

James bent closer to Rennie, keeping his voice low, so that neither the coxswain Clinton Huff, nor any of the seamen at the oars, could overhear.

'If I may suggest, sir . . . why do not we fall in line astern, as ordered, then simply lose way and lose the squadron – by design, but apparently by accident – in darkness, tonight?'

Rennie made no reply. He frowned, and looked north again at the retreating *Excelsior*. After a moment, James ventured to continue:

'I have every confidence that having lost way and fallen behind, in darkness, we would not be missed until first light. By then, well . . . we should be heading into the Atlantic and resuming our legitimate duty of pursuit. There would be nothing Sir Jendex could do to us, or about us, since we should be far away, out of sight. Vanished. Gone.'

Now Rennie looked at James, and at first his expression was dark and severe.

'What you propose is – it is mutiny.'

'Oh, no, sir. Nothing of the kind.'

'It is, though, by God.'

'Nay, it ain't, sir.' Confidently. 'It is tactics. We have a clear duty of pursuit we could not reveal to the admiral. We do not know his own duty, since he would not deign to tell us. Therefore, our sealed instructions must be our first and only concern, don't you think so? I am quite certain that is what Their Lordships would advise. Clearly, under the circumstances, we are obliged to employ tactics to achieve our design. We have no choice.'

'That is the most slippery, specious line of reasoning I have ever heard, Mr Hayter.'

James said nothing, and waited. Rennie glanced once more at *Malachite* and the squadron, then:

'Slippery, wretched, and underhand. Had y'not been instructed as an Anglican clergyman, I should have said your train of thought was Jesuitical.' A moment. 'But it is just what we require, by Christ! A splendid devious scheme! Well done, James!' And he gripped James's arm and nodded vigorously, his face alight.

'Thank you, sir.'

A moment more and Rennie's expression again became sober and stern. He released James's arm.

'We will conduct ourselves as if we was conforming in every particular to our new orders. No person in the ship, except ourselves, must have any inkling of what we are really about until the moment comes.'

'Very good, sir.'

Presently the pinnace came round under *Expedient*'s wooden wall, and the seaman in the bow hooked the boat in to the side.

Rennie did not send his dispatch ashore in a boat, but instead made a long entry in his journal, and put the dispatch aside among his papers for later reference. Then as the afternoon watch advanced, *Expedient* replied to a signal from *Malachite*, weighed and tacked into line astern of the frigate *Hermione*, thirty-eight. The squadron headed out of the bay and beat away west close-hauled into the moderating wind.

James Hayter, now restored to the position of Pursuit Officer – and acting first lieutenant – stood on the quarter-deck with Captain Rennie through the piping of the hands to their supper, and the first dog watch. Presently Rennie strode aft to the tafferel and motioned his lieutenant to join him there. The ship astern of *Expedient* was following close, yards braced, her sails taut on bowlines, and made bright by the westering sun.

Rennie sucked in a breath. 'I don't like it, James. Lyle is headed directly into the Atlantic. In the name of Christ how are we to evade him if he follows the course we wish to take ourselves?'

James made no reply.

The squadron beat west another glass, then at the first bell of the second dog watch there came the boom of a gun, and *Malachite* signalled the squadron to bear south-west by south. *Expedient* came over on the new tack.

Thank God.' Rennie took off his hat, wiped sweat from his forehead, and from the inner band of the hat. He replaced it thwartwise, then sniffed and peered aloft, hands behind his back. 'Our scheme will answer.'

'Yes, sir.'

'Tell it to me again, will you?'

'Very good, sir. In the dead of night, at four bells of the middle watch – as we agreed – the masthead light and the stern lantern are to be doused. With no shouts of command, only by quiet word passed along, we will shorten sail, come off the wind and fall out of the line. We will then wear, and beat nor'west, crowding on sail as soon as we are well clear. The whole to be accomplished within half a glass, so that the squadron has no time to notice our sudden absence.'

'Very good. Excellent. – We are favoured from on high, I think.'

'Favoured, sir?'

'Indeed. There will be no moon tonight, praise be.'

But as afternoon became evening James grew deeply perturbed, and felt that *Expedient* would not survive the voyage across the Atlantic in pursuit of *Terces*. *Expedient* was in no sounder a condition than she had been when she lay at anchor in Cawsand Bay. She was no less short-handed. Nor was the possibility of actually finding *Terces* and resuming the duty of pursuit any more likely than it had been when the admiral's squadron arrived, and subsumed *Expedient*.

Night came on and deepened. Captain Rennie continued to keep the deck, nervously pacing back and forth, and James kept it with him, his heart heavy. The plan they intended to execute had been revealed to a small number of the people only, and to the other officers. The first watch proceeded without incident, and *Expedient* kept station behind *Hermione*, observing the regulation distance of a quarter of a mile, *Hermione*'s stern and masthead lights riding clear in the darkness. In turn, *Expedient*'s lights were kept in plain view by the ship a quarter of a mile behind. The ship behind was the six-pounder frigate *Avril*, twenty-eight, and the other four ships were two sloops of twenty-two guns, and two brigantines.

'I have no knowledge of the admiral's duties or intentions,' Rennie had said earlier to James, as the sun sank red in the west, 'but I believe now that he may be going to Gibraltar, and the Mediterranean.'

'Very likely, sir.'

The first watch passed, and Rennie had sustenance brought to him and his lieutenant on deck by Colley Cutton, in the form of wedges of pie and flasks.

As James ate his pie, and sucked down raw spirit, his mood lifted.

'Why should I be obliged to fret and trouble my soul over

our plight?' To himself. 'Why should I doubt *Expedient*, as fine and stout a sea boat as was ever built at Chatham? Why, good heaven, to doubt her is to doubt her captain, and have not we always come through even the most hazardous peril and calamity together, strong and hearty? Hey? Well, we have – no doubt about it.'

It did not occur to him until much later – when his head began to ache and his tongue was dry and thick in his mouth – that the reason for the diminution of his doubts, and parallel elation, had been purely and simply the contents of his flask: several generous ounces of purser's rum.

But by then *Expedient*'s purpose had been accomplished, and the ship was alone on the sea, heeling tall into the Atlantic swell as the sun sent its first glorious gleamings over the horizon in the east, far astern.

*

Six bells of the morning watch, and the two officers still on deck. The deck newly washed, and hammocks up piped. Lieutenant Hayter, with the assistance of a duty mid, took the ship's bearings, 49 degrees and 33 minutes north, and 11 degrees and 45 minutes west, and reported them. Rennie nodded, and:

'I believe Captain Broadman is making either for New York, or Boston, James. We have headed nor'west sufficient long wholly to escape Admiral Lyle's squadron, and will therefore now come about on our new heading. Set me a course west-sou'west and a point west, if y'please.'

'Ay-ay, sir.'

The orders were given to the duty quartermaster, and James returned to Rennie at the after part of the weather-rail, where he stood at the newly packed hammock netting. As the ship came round on her new heading, petty officers bawling, yards bracing, the afterguard hanging their weight on the falls, Rennie:

'Breakfast, James? Or are ye dead tired? I will understand if
you wish to fall into your hanging cot.'

'Nay, I am wholly awake and alert, sir.' In spite of his thick
head.

'Then let us eat breakfast together in the great cabin, by all
means.'

They went below. As they came to the door of the great
cabin:

'Cutton! Colley Cutton! We are two starving men! Light
along our breakfast, cheerly now!'

Presently, when they had settled themselves at the table,
hats and coats off, and stocks loosened, Rennie called to his
steward:

'Where is my cat? Where is Dulcie?'

Colley Cutton appeared, holding a pan. 'I do not know, sir.
She is disturbed in 'erself, in my 'pinion.'

'Eh? Disturbed? Do not talk in riddles, y'fool. I asked you
where the animal was.'

'And I said, I do not ezackly know, sir.'

'Well well, find her and bring her to me, right quick.'

'As you wish, sir. In course, I cannot cook your breakfast at
the same moment as I am seeking Dulcie, sir. As you will
'preciate.'

'Do not be insolent.'

'I hope I will not never be insolent.' Then, muttering: 'Not
aloud this commission, anyways.'

'What? What did y'say?' Sharply.

'I said, I bow to your wishes, sir.'

'Bring us our breakfast, then. Find the cat afterward.'

'I bow to your wishes, sir.' Retreating with the pan.

'By God, I shall put the impertinent wretch ashore in
America, and sign a new man into my service. I swear I will.'
Rennie, glaring at the door.

James kept his face straight, and spread his napkin with great
care on his lap.

Their breakfast did not come, and after ten minutes Rennie

rose on his legs in a rage, and was about to bellow his steward's name when Cutton appeared, his eyes shining and his face cracked open in a gap-toothed smile.

'I knew she was out of sorts, and so she was!'

'What? What?' Rennie stared at him.

'She is a muvver, Gawd bless 'er!'

'Have you gone raving mad, man?'

'Ho, no, sir! No, indeed! She has become one, four times over!'

'What is the man talking about?' Rennie asked James.

'I think he means that your cat has had kittens, sir.' Calmly, then turning and raising his eyebrows: 'Yes, Colley?'

'Yes, sir, yes. And four de-lightful little critchers they is. De-lightful.'

'D'y'mean to tell me . . . that Dulcie has given birth, good God?'

'It would appear so, sir.' James, with a smile.

'Well, I'm damned. Ha-ha. My own cat.'

'Yes, sir.'

'D'y'know, I had not the smallest notion of anything of the kind. Well well. Well well. It is a miracle.'

'Perhaps not quite that.' James, with another smile.

'Eh?'

'More a simple, natural event, would not you say, sir?'

'Nay, nay, in course it is a miracle.' A confirming nod. 'Well well, where is she, Colley Cutton? Show me the mother and her babes.'

'Yes, sir.' Leading the way. 'They is residing in your sleeping cabin. In your . . . in your hat.'

'My *hat*?'

Rennie followed his steward into the sleeping cabin, and found Dulcie and four blind, mewling kittens nestled in his upturned foul-weather hat, beneath his hanging cot.

'When I seen she had made her nest in the hat, I did not like to disturb 'er, sir.'

'Nay, we must not. Dulcie, Dulcie my dear . . .' Cooing fondly, bending down.

James followed them in, looked and saw, and politely:

'Do you intend to keep them all, sir?'

'Hm . . . ?' Peering down still.

'The kittens.'

'What?' Turning.

'Often at home we used to drown unwanted—'

'Drown! Unwanted!' Fiercely.

'Not in every case.' James, hastily. 'Only if—'

'That will do, Mr Hayter.' Over him. 'I will not like to hear any more of your unpleasant musings on the question. There is no question. Dulcie and her infants shall have the best of care. You will make that your first consideration, Colley Cutton, above all else, these next days.'

'Even above my care of yourself, sir?'

'My care ain't important at all. You are to see to their comfort in every particular, d'y'hear me? – We must find them a proper bed. I will say so to Mr Adgett, who will make me a cot for them. Yes yes, no trouble must be spared.'

'As you wish, sir. Shall I move 'em now, then?' Cutton prepared to bend down.

'Move them! They must not be disturbed at all, good heaven! Did not y'pay attention to anything I have just said?'

'I fought you said you wisht Mr Adgett to make them their own bed . . . ?'

'Yes yes, so I did, but I don't want her upset, not now. – We must think of what to give her to eat. Delectable things, to please her. I will speak to Swallow. – Dulcie, dear little Dulcie . . .' Rennie again bent over her.

James and the steward exchanged a glance behind his back, and Colley Cutton gave a bemused, silent shrug. James jerked his head and the two men discreetly retired, leaving Rennie alone.

Two days passed, and Rennie was watching over his cat and

her kittens where they lay in a corner of the day cabin in their new cot. The cot had been made and delivered yesterday, according to Rennie's explicit instruction, and was lined with number six canvas, a quantity of oakum, and two of Rennie's older shirts.

A slow almost imperceptible swell was running, and the wind had dropped to a strange, wafting restlessness over the quiet sea. Mr Loftus came down from the quarterdeck, knocked, and ventured into the cabin when his knock was answered by the tiptoeing Colley Cutton. He waited politely, his hat under his arm, then when Rennie made no acknowledgement of his presence, he cleared his throat, and:

'Erm, may I speak to you, sir?'

Rennie now glanced at him, and raised a finger to his lips. Very quietly: 'Yes, Bernard?'

'A change in the weather is imminent, sir.' Lowering his own voice.

'Yes yes, I saw the glass. You have the matter in hand? Good, good.' Returning his attention to the cot.

'I should like your opinion of my intentions, sir. The first lieutenant and I have—'

'Pray keep your voice very low, if y'please.' In a whisper, his hand raised. 'The weather don't greatly concern me at present. I place myself in your capable hands, entire.'

'Will not you come on deck, sir?'

'On deck? Why? The weather is about to change, as it contrives to do at sea very frequent. You are my sailing master, Bernard, and a man of great and wide experience, as is Mr Hayter. I trust you both to press on, west sou'west.' A dismissive nod.

'You . . . you are quite certain that you will not come on deck?'

'Nay nay, I have said there is no need. West-sou'west, Mr Loftus, whatever the weather, hey?' Peering down and losing all interest in his sailing master.

'Very good, sir. Thank you.' He retreated to the door,

paused and was about to say something more, but was discouraged by Rennie's excluding demeanour, and made his exit.

On deck the sailing master said to the first lieutenant: 'It did no good at all. He would not listen to me. He made it plain I was not welcome in his quarters.'

James took his arm and drew him away from the wheel and the binnacle.

'He would not come on deck?'

'Nay, he waved me away. "West-sou'west, Mr Loftus, west-sou'west."'

'But this is damned foolishness, Bernard!' Vehemently, but with his voice instinctively lowered. 'I asked you to go below to him because he respects you in all matters of ship-handling – and this is his response? He has lost sight of the whole commission, and sails blithely into an Atlantic storm without the smallest sense of why he does it.'

'To find the *Terces*, I expect.'

'Find the bloody *Terces*? Hah. He does not give a fig for *Terces*, now.'

'But this mood of his cannot all be about his cat, though, surely, that he watches over by the hour?'

'In course it ain't. His cat is a convenient distraction.' A breath. 'He knows full well that this is a failed cruise, Bernard. That we accomplish nothing by westing like this, into the immensity of the sea, into God knows what calamities of wind and tumult. *Terces* is lost to us, as she was lost to us before we came south from Norway. Captain Broadman and his passenger Olaf Christian den Norske will never be troubled by *Expedient* again, and we will never discover their purpose.'

'Then in God's name . . . why do we continue?'

'It is Captain Rennie's pride. His sheer stubborn damned pride. He will not be told, and he will not allow himself to be bested, not by man, nor ship, nor stormy sea, neither. He would rather die.'

'Perhaps he would, but what about us? If he dies, so do we
– all of us.'

'Ay, Bernard, so we would. Unless he can be persuaded to
change his mind – believing that the notion to do so was his
alone.'

'Well, I am not the one to try.' A sigh. 'I dare not get
athwart his hawse.'

A sudden flattening fan of wind rushed across the slow swell
toward *Expedient*, and swept over the ship like a shiver.

The storm broke at seven bells of the afternoon watch, after an
uneasy period of gradually increasing wind and swell from the
west, the lifting waves streaming spray in long smoky drifts.
As the storm blasted in over her the ship rode down into the
troughs and lifted herself on the heaving shoulders of the
waves as hands shortened sail to foretopmast staysail, driver,
and reefed topsails. At first she made at least some headway,
tack on tack close-hauled, but soon her progress ceased and
she was driven back, making only leeway in the furious
onslaught of wind and sea. It became impossible to tack
through the wind at all.

Captain Rennie did nothing, and remained below in his
cabin. The conning of the ship was left to Bernard Loftus,
James Hayter, the duty quartermaster, and the four seamen
manning the wheel, fighting to keep her head up.

'We must wear!' James bellowed into the sailing master's ear.

'Shall I inform the captain?' Cupping a hand to his mouth
in reply.

'I will send one of the duty mids. Mr Glaister!'

'Sir?' The boy was pale and frightened in his foul-weather
cloak.

'Go below to the great cabin, and ask the captain with my
compliments—'

A tremendous sea smashed over the bow and flung deluging
folds across the decks. James ducked his head, clinging to a
stay, then:

'Say that we will like to wear ship, and run before! Jump, lad!'

The boy departed.

Another huge sea flooded up and over the bow, and slewed aft over the sloping deck. The wind whipped, whistled and howled in the rigging. Ahead the view was a wilderness of grey-green moving dunes, laced with runnels of spray, and spray whipped into smoking drifts from the quivering crests. *Expedient* ran shuddering down into another trough.

'We must rig lifelines, Mr Loftus!'

'Ay, we must. Mr Tangible!'

The boatswain did not appear.

'Mr *Tangible!*'

'Ay, sir?' He came lurching aft.

'Lifelines, Mr Tangible, fore and aft!'

'Lifelines . . . ay-ay, sir . . .' And he stumbled away forrard.

The sailing master stared at him, and turned to James, cupping his hand. 'I believe the boatswain is drunk!'

'I think y'are right, Mr Loftus!' James nodded, his face streaming. 'He reckons he is going to die!'

'But, God damn him, that is no excuse! We cannot allow a senior warrant officer to stumble about on deck in drink!'

'If I am not mistook, he is merely one of many.' James, shaking his head.

'But how has this happened!' In genuine dismay. 'I have the only key to the spirit room!'

'The only official key. Or perhaps they have broke the lock. I cannot say I blame them.'

'What? You do not mean that you approve of it!' Shocked.

'Ain't a question what we approve of, you and I. Any man has a right to dazing comfort if he believes death sits upon his shoulder.' The ship began to sag off, yawing and groaning. 'Bring her up, there! Keep your luff!'

'D'y'mean – we should all be drunk on deck?' Bernard Loftus, in further dismay.

'Nay, not quite! Else we could not fight to save the ship! –

We cannot wait for the captain's approval! We must wear, or be damned to hell!'

'I agree!' A brief nod, and: '*Stand by to wear ship!*'

But when a few moments after the ship began to come round by the stern, Captain Rennie appeared on the quarter-deck, and came aft:

'Why are we going about, Mr Hayter? Why do not we proceed west-sou'west?'

'The storm is too much for her, sir!' Over the wind. 'I sent one of the mids below with a message! We must wear and run before, and save ourselves!'

'We shall do no such thing, thankee! Our course is west-sou'west! – You there, quartermaster!'

And Captain Rennie began bellowing instructions to reverse the manoeuvre.

Even as he did so a tremendous sea smashed over the larboard side of the ship, swinging as she was beam-on, and this inundation was so severe that for a long, horrible moment it seemed the ship would founder. The whole of the forecastle and waist were under water, and the great weight of that water drove the ship lower and lower. By pure luck the force of the wave not only drove the ship sideways, but swung her round to head east, in the direction of the wave itself. She wallowed under many tons of sea water, then with a creaking, groaning, protesting shudder found her feet, and lifted herself. The great weight of water poured and tumbled from her decks, gushed from her scuppers, streamed from every part of her, and she lived, riding up out of the following trough.

Rennie and James had been thrown off their feet by the force of the wave, and had survived by clinging to the rail as the sucking rush of the sea swept them horizontal, like clinging seaweed on tidal rocks. Bernard Loftus managed to stay on his legs, clinging for his life to a backstay. His hat was gone from his head, and his coat torn at the sleeve. He had swallowed sea water, and was struggling to breathe. The quartermaster was gone from his place by the wheel.

The four seamen steering had survived by clinging to the spokes.

Captain Rennie was coughing violently, and choking, and could not speak. James found his voice, and roared:

'Mr Tangible! Hands to reduce sail! We will haul up the driver in the brails, and hand the maintopsail! We will scud on the foretopsail alone!'

He turned his attention to the men at the wheel. 'Your course is east-nor'east! Hold her steady, and let the wind do what it will! Handsomely now, lads!'

James fought his way aft in the fury of the wind, clinging on to falls and the rail, and made a search for the quartermaster, thinking he lay perhaps under the flag lockers, or tangled up behind one of the guns. The man was not there. James turned to face forrard, and dashed stinging spray from his eyes. To himself:

'The poor wretch is lost.'

He was not lost, however, and soon came stumbling up the ladder from the waist, where he had gone in an attempt to find the boatswain just before the freak wave struck. He resumed his place at the wheel. The after-guard clapped on to falls, and hauled up the driver in the brails, staggering on the wind-lashed deck as they worked.

Expedient, still streaming excess water, and sluggish in answering the helm, had survived.

But her captain was not content. In spite of the ferocity of the storm, he was determined to resume his original course. He attempted to give the orders, but because of a coughing fit was unable to do so for half a glass, and he clung to the binnacle, scarcely able to get his breath. Thus Lieutenant Hayter was able to prevail in the matter of the ship's direction. Only when Rennie had recovered his voice, if not his composure, was he able to attempt to countermand his lieutenant.

'Mr Hayter . . . hhh . . . Mr Hayter! We will—'

A hand at his elbow, tugging there, and Rennie turned in

astonishment to find his steward Colley Cutton, his body hunched against the storm.

'Oh, sir, if you please! The cot has tipped over, sir, and they has all gone!'

'What? What did y'say?' Cupping a hand to his ear. 'Speak up, man!'

'Dulcie and the kittens has vanished, sir!'

'What!' And Rennie at once dashed below, in fear and consternation.

When he burst into the great cabin it was just as his steward had said. The cat and her kittens were nowhere to be seen, and their new cot lay upturned on the canvas squares of the decking, in a scattering of oakum. Water had dripped through from the skylight into the cabin, the decking was wet, and the darkness of the storm had made the space gloomy.

'We must search for her, d'y'hear me, Cutton!'

'I has already done so, sir. She is gone.'

'She cannot have gone far, in a ship at sea. The cot tipping over has startled her, and she has found another place to hide and protect her infants. We will search for her, and find her. Jump, man, jump.'

'As you wish, sir.' Obediently turning about the cabin, bending and peering and bracing himself against lockers and racks as the ship rolled and lifted and spray battered the stern-gallery windows.

Rennie himself began a search of his sleeping cabin, and the coach, and found nothing.

'Dulcie . . . Dulcie . . .' he called. The shrieking wind mocked him, as if it heard his anxious calls from outside, and wished to make him despondent. He braced himself against a timber standard, and sniffed in a lifting breath. 'Dulcie . . .'

A faint sound, under the roaring and shrieking of the storm.

'Dulcie . . .' Returning to his sleeping cabin.

Again the faint sound, this time a little more distinct. The mewling of kittens.

'Dulcie, my dear, where are you . . . ?'

He knelt, bent very low and found them, the cat and her brood, huddled in, forrard of the quoin, under the carriage of the starboard gun. Safe.

'Thank God.' A heartfelt sigh – and then he felt himself a fool. In God's name what was he about, crawling on his knees below, when he should be in his place on the quarterdeck? What business had he, with his ship in danger, to be fretting over a cat, that could perfectly well take care of herself, good heaven?

'Up on your legs, William Rennie. Up, by God, and on deck.' His steward heard him, and thinking himself summoned, came into the sleeping cabin. The ship rolled heavily as Rennie got to his feet, and he staggered.

'Are you quite well, sir?' Colley Cutton, extending a supportive hand. Rennie thrust it aside.

'In course I am well.' Brusquely. 'The cat is there, under the gun. What a very great deal of fuss and commotion over nothing, Colley Cutton. I am going on deck. You will bring me a flask directly, d'y'hear. Three water grog.'

When the flask was brought to him on deck a few minutes after, Rennie found that it contained not grog but unwatered spirit. He was about to admonish his hunched, head-ducking steward, but thought better of it and dismissed him, and Cutton fled below.

Rennie turned his head out of the blasting wind and sucked down a mouthful of raw rum. He felt the benefit at once – a deep, grateful warmth that lifted him to his purpose, which he now saw clearly. To Lieutenant Hayter, at the binnacle:

'We will run before until this storm of wind blows itself out – a few glasses. "Small showers are long, but sudden storms are short." Hey, Mr Hayter? *Terces* is also running before, astern of us, I am in no doubt. We will thus lose nothing in the pursuit.'

'Ay-ay, sir.' James touched a hand to his hat, which was wedged firmly on his head. Happily he had been vindicated in his opinion that Rennie would wish to run before and save the ship, so long as he believed it was his notion to do it.

Expedient ran before the wind four-and-twenty hours. The wind and the waves began to diminish and decrease late in the afternoon of that following day, and Captain Rennie paced his quarterdeck in eager anticipation of being able to go about very soon, and run west-sou'west once more. A shout from the maintop lookout:

'De-e-e-e-ck! Sail of ship to the east! Three points off the starboard bow!'

Captain Rennie brought up his glass, and focused. The ship lay perhaps two leagues ahead. Three-masted, square-rigged.

'Can you see her colours, there!' Lieutenant Hayter, calling aloft. A brief delay, then:

'No colours flying . . . she has the look of a frigate, sir!'

'A frigate?' Rennie peered again. The lookout was right. She was a frigate. The sinking of *Expedient* into a trough cut off his view, then as the sea lifted he saw the frigate again. She appeared to be drifting.

'She is in trouble.'

'With your permission, sir, I will go aloft and see for myself.'

'By all means.'

James Hayter ran forrard to the main shrouds, his cased glass slung over his back, jumped up the ratlines and was in the maintop in half a minute. He unslung his glass, slipped it from the case and focused it. A moment after, he pushed the glass back in its case, clapped on to a backstay and slid to the deck. He came aft, steadying himself as the ship rose steeply on the shoulder of a wave.

'Well, Mr Hayter?'

'I believe she is the *Hermione*, thirty-eight, from the admiral's squadron. She looks to be severely damaged, sir, lying low in the water, and drifting.'

'Very good, thank you. Mr Tangible!'

The boatswain came aft, looking haggard. 'Sir?' A waft of stinking breath.

'Hands to make sail, Mr Tangible. Courses and t'gallants, in addition to our topsails. We must crack on. The frigate ahead of us two leagues is in danger of sinking.'

'Ay-ay, sir.'

The calls, echoing along the deck. Topmen aloft, furled canvas loosed from the gaskets on the yards and sheeted home filling, and soon *Expedient* began to pick up speed across the hills and vales of the rolling sea, where before she had been merely scudding.

When *Expedient* reached *Hermione* and hove to, a glass after, Rennie and James saw that her maintopmast was gone, her rudder broken, and she was obviously leaking badly, so low and sluggish did she lie. The cable of what presumably had been a sea anchor lay limp and useless, trailing over the stern.

'I will send a boat at once,' Rennie decided. 'The sea is heavy, still, but we must take the risk.'

'With your permission I will go in the boat myself, sir.'

'Very well, thankee, James. I will send Mr Adgett and a repair crew with you, to do what they are able in the immediate. Take my coxswain Clinton Huff, and one of the duty mids – Mr Madeley. Give her captain my compliments, and say to him that I am at his disposal, and will do my utmost to aid him in any way I can. – Mr Tangible! We will hoist out the pinnace, if y'please! – I will like a comprehensive report on her condition of repair, the number of men injured and so forth, by the change of the watch, James.'

'Ay-ay, sir.'

When James came alongside the wounded frigate he saw that she was even more heavily damaged than he had thought. He could hear the clanking of pumps, and water was sluicing from her scuppers, but the pumps were losing the battle. Her rudder had been torn completely away. There were very few men on deck, and her fore yards were not braced. Square sails not in the brails hung down torn and flapping, falls trailing.

Her mainmast was little more than a stump. *Hermione* was in a very bedraggled condition.

Clinton Huff had some difficulty in bringing the pinnace into the side of the frigate in the heaving sea. They had not been hailed from the deck, and went aboard uninvited, jumping up the side ladder as the pinnace nudged and scraped against the wooden wall of the ship.

James found and reported to the officer of the deck, Lieutenant Grantham, who was severely hampered by a broken leg, to which a crude splint had been bound. He was obviously in great pain, and yet contrived to hobble about the deck with the aid of a crutch, and even up and down ladders. He took James below to the great cabin, where to his surprise James found *Hermione*'s captain writing up his journal, a square, solid figure in his chair. He turned, revealing a dour face, devoid of any hint of relief or pleasure in being rescued.

Lieutenant Grantham began to introduce the visitor, but was curtly interrupted:

'Captain Hallam Woodall, RN, His Majesty's frigate *Hermione*, thirty-eight. And you are, Lieutenant . . . ?'

James made his back straight, his hat under his arm. 'Lieutenant James Hayter, sir, His Majesty's frigate *Expedient*.'

Captain Woodall threw down his quill. 'We was sent to find you, Mr Hayter, when *Expedient* disappeared so mysterious from the squadron line. When the storm struck we suffered great damage, lost our rudder, and a sea anchor. Many of my people suffered bones broke, and my surgeon himself lies injured.'

'Captain Rennie has sent me to say – with his compliments, sir – that we will—'

'Be quiet, sir. You will kindly take me to *Expedient* in your boat, and we will then take *Hermione* in tow, and return to the squadron without the loss of a moment.'

'Very good, sir. Captain Rennie has asked me – required me – to make a report as to *Hermione*'s state of repair. With your permission, I—'

'I will make the report myself, Mr Hayter.' Over him, and getting up on his legs.

As he conveyed Captain Woodall to *Expedient* in the pinnace across the short, pitching interval of sea between the two ships, James thought but did not say that there was as much likelihood of Captain Rennie obeying an instruction to tow Hermione back to the squadron as there was of the great god Poseidon appearing at supper to pour their wine and offer his blessings.

The meeting of the two commanders did not go well.

Rennie attempted to be amiable, and solicitous, and sympathetic to his fellow captain in his plight. And was cut off.

'Don't want to hear your blandishments nor your excuses, sir. You are, both directly and indirectly, the cause of my present predicament. Do me the kindness simply to listen, and then to comply with my instructions.' Flinging his hat down on Rennie's table.

'Instructions, Captain Woodall?' Frowning, beginning to be irked.

'Ay, instructions, sir. I am senior to you by ten years on the list. You will send me some of your people to aid with the pumps, and take me in tow. We will then proceed east-sou'east, forthwith, and rejoin the squadron.'

'Take you in tow? Well well, I do not think I am able to do that, you know, even granted your seniority on the list. We have—'

'Evidently you do not apprehend me, Captain Rennie.' Again over him. 'This ain't a question of *choice*, sir. It is a direct order from Admiral Sir Jendex Lyle himself.'

'Ah. Well well, I fear that both you and the admiral will be disappointed.' A brisk nod, and a sniffing breath. 'I cannot do as you ask.'

'What! What did y'say, sir!'

'Are ye deaf, Captain Woodall? I will aid you in repair to the best of my capacity – replacing your rudder and so forth – and then I will make sail to the west.'

'You will defy me and the admiral both?' Outraged and astonished.

'I may not defy Their Lordships – that I think you will concede take precedence.'

'I concede nothing of the kind, sir. You are under the direct command of the admiral, since we departed Cawsand Bay. And by God you had better obey him, and explain to him why ye've absented yourself, or know the consequence!'

'Captain Woodall.' Very firmly. 'I am endeavouring to be gentlemanlike, but you try my patience, sir. If you will give me a list of your injured people and what they need, a list of urgent repairs, and the number of hands you require – temporary – to aid you with these, and with your pumps, I will endeavour to assist you, one sea officer aiding another. Beyond that, I cannot and will not go.'

'By God, sir! By God, I have never heard—'

'Let us get to work, if y'please.' Over him. 'I cannot lie here indefinite, rolling my masts out on the swell.'

*

On the day following, *Expedient* had resumed her original course into the Atlantic and her pursuit of the *Terces*. At noon she lay at 43 degrees and 21 minutes north, and eighteen degrees and 55 minutes west, the wind moderate from the south-west, the sky clear, and the glass steady at fair. *Hermione* was now far astern, left to manage her own business.

Captain Woodall had been outspoken in his disapproval of Rennie's intentions, and Rennie in turn had grown vexed and at last wholly impatient, and had sent his visitor back to his own ship. With him went *Expedient*'s surgeon, and further hands to aid *Hermione*'s people at the pumps, even as Mr Adgett and his crew stopped the worst of the leaks below, rigged and hung a new rudder, and patched up two of her yards and the spanker boom.

These *Expedient*s remained in Hermione overnight, working

by lantern light, and returned to their ship in the morning watch. *Hermione* now lay higher in the water, and her pumps were holding. Dr Empson had treated the injured men, and revived *Hermione*'s ailing surgeon sufficient to get him back on his legs. Rennie had judged *Hermione* to be self-sustaining, and able to proceed. He saluted her with a gun, made sail, and swung away west.

Rennie took divisions, inspected his ship, and made some comments to his first lieutenant when the declaration had been made and the hands piped to their dinner.

'I will like you to resume the roster of your own lookouts at the mastheads, as Pursuit Officer. I think you should consult daily with Mr Loftus, also, in all distinctions of the conning of the ship. Charts, tides, wind, headway, leeway. We must crowd on as much canvas as the masts and yards will safely bear. We must know to a certainty that we are gaining.'

'Is that possible, sir?' Raising an eyebrow.

'Eh? In course it is possible. You and Mr Loftus between you will calculate the speed *Terces* makes each day, and the exact distance she covers. We achieve no less in our own ship. Why cannot we apply the same calculations to *Terces*? It is simple mathematics, simple trigonometry.'

'I have never found trigonometry simple, sir, I confess.' James, with a smile. 'And so far as *Terces* is concerned, surely we can only make a rough estimate of her progress?'

'I do not regard this pursuit – any part of this pursuit – as a matter for levity.'

'No, sir, I did not mean—'

'I know what y'meant, thank you. We will crack on, and gain, and you will calculate that gain, glass by glass, watch by watch, and day by day.'

'Very good, sir.'

'There is another motive for it.' A glance at James.

'Another . . . ?'

'Ay. Admiral Sir Jendex Lyle sent his principal frigate in

pursuit of us. When that frigate returns alone to the squadron, I think the admiral will decide that he cannot and will not be thwarted. I think he will send other ships to pursue us, and I wish to be far away, out of his reach.'

'With respect, sir, d'you really think he will be so vindictive? We were never part of his original squadron. We were merely a convenient replacement when one of his ships was obliged to drop out at Plymouth. When *Hermione* returns—'

'When *Hermione* returns without us,' over him, 'the admiral, I repeat, will see it as direct defiance of his authority. That is his nature.'

'May I venture an opinion, sir?' Politely.

'Well?'

'I think that it is in Captain Woodall's nature not to admit defeat, neither. Therefore I think he will say that he never saw *Expedient* at all. That he was caught in the storm, suffered great damage, and was obliged to desist or founder. The admiral will then take thought of his own design, his own commission – to go to the Mediterranean – and he will forget all about us.'

'You think that?' In frowning doubt.

'I am certain of it.'

'Hm. Well.' A sniff. 'But that don't alter our need to crack on. Let us do so, if y'please, without the loss of a moment.'

'Ay-ay, sir.' As he put on his hat and left the captain's cabin, James thought but did not say that in all probability *Hermione* would not make contact with the admiral and the squadron until she reached Gibraltar, since the squadron would not have lain at anchor on the open sea, awaiting *Hermione*'s return, but would have pressed on south. Nor did he say what he most wished to, that to proceed with the pursuit of *Terces* deep into the Atlantic was pointless, hopeless folly.

Rennie sat down to write up his journal, then sighed and thrust the quill irritably aside. Muttering:

'He don't believe in this pursuit. Nay, he don't. He will seek to undermine me in this, and yet I cannot afford to remove him again. We are far too short-handed, and I need him. Christ in tears, what a cruise . . .'

Another sigh, and he rose and paced the canvas squares, glanced out of the stern-gallery window, then went into his sleeping cabin. The cat's cot had been placed by the gun carriage, and she lay there quiet, her kittens close against her, all asleep. A momentary fear that they were overly still and quiet gripped Rennie by the throat, and he crouched low. One of the kittens stirred blindly, and was licked and soothed by its mother. Rennie's fear passed.

'Safe.' Rising. 'You are quite safe, my dears.'

He stood watching a moment longer, then returned to the day cabin. Again he paused to look out of the long window. Quietly:

'Is any of us safe, in the vastness of the sea?'

He thought of Sylvia, at home in Norfolk, of his peaceful garden, and the view across the shallow rise to the copse beyond, under the wide bird-soaring sky. He thought of these things and was both reassured – and saddened.

'Why downcast, William Rennie?' Whispered.

The long run of the wake astern, through the angled window, the creaking and easing of timbers, and the ceaseless gliding wash of the sea.

'Look to your duty, man. Find a way to prevail.'

And he lifted his head, and made his back straight.

*

Expedient had developed a slight list to larboard, a difficulty of trim, and the sailing master and the first lieutenant went below into the hold with a crew to shift and secure casks in the tiers. During this work, which occupied nearly the whole of one watch, James Hayter motioned Bernard Loftus to follow him up the ladder into the forrard part of the orlop, where they could not be overheard.

'I am speaking first to you, Bernard, rather than to Mr

Tindall or Mr Trembath, because they are younger, less mature men, and we two have served together many years and understand each other.' All spoken in a quiet tone. He paused to look about, making sure they were entirely alone in the gloom, then continued:

'Will you give me your candid opinion of our condition?'

'D'y'mean . . . as to the trimming of the ship?' Keeping his own voice low.

'Nay, not that. Nor the state of repair in general. I meant, your view of what we attempt.'

'The continued pursuit of *Terces*? I had hoped you would not ask me that.'

'But I do ask it, Bernard.' Earnestly.

'Well . . . the Atlantic is a very broad ocean, and the ship ain't in an ideal state of repair, but we have survived worse.'

'And . . . ?'

'Well . . . if you wish me to be candid, I think what we attempt . . . ain't perhaps altogether wise.' Reluctantly.

'And . . . ?'

'And if you press me further, I think it unlikely that we will find *Terces* again. Nor do we know to a certainty where she is headed. The captain thinks the United States, but he has admitted that is merely a guess. We do not know.' A shrug.

'And since we have lost all contact with *Terces* upon the sea, we do not in effect "pursue" her at all.'

The sailing master was silent, and James continued:

'In truth, all of the captain's talk of calculating *Terces*' speed, of gaining upon her, and so forth, is flat nonsense, since she is altogether lost to us.'

'I believe she is – yes.' A troubled sigh.

'Good, very good. Then we are of the same mind.'

'D'y'mean that we are of the same opinion – or something more?' Looking at him in the dim light, and growing more uncomfortable.

'Something more, I hope.'

'Then you must hope in vain, James.'

'Eh? Surely we have both thought the same thing, since the storm?'

'I will never be party to mutiny.' Shaking his head.

'And I have not used that word. Would never use it.'

'But that is what you meant, though, ain't it?' Bluntly.

'Mutiny is an ugly business, wild, anarchic and foolish. I would never countenance it, no more than would you. But we cannot simply continue in this way, watch by watch, indefinite. Do not you agree?'

'"Cannot continue in this way." Which way? D'y'mean on this course, west-sou'west?'

'You know very well what I mean, I think. Not just our present course, but the pursuit entire. That is nothing but a futile, stupid, dangerous pretence.'

'Dangerous?'

'Certainly. Each further mile we sail puts all of our lives more deeply in peril. As you admit, the ship is in a poor condition of repair. We are desperate short-handed. *Terces* lies we do not know where, far beyond our reach. What in the name of God is our purpose! Hey?'

'And this is not mutiny?' A vehement whisper.

'In course it ain't. It is plain common sense, as you know very well.'

'I do not like this conversation, James. It troubles me sorely, and I will like to forget we ever had it.'

'More pretence, Bernard? Hey? The next storm we encounter – and there will be such a storm, by God – may well sink us. Our one chance of survival, as I see it, is to go about now, before it is too late, and steer a course for home.'

'He will never agree to it.' Flatly.

'Not if it came from one man, nor even from two. But if all officers, commissioned and warranted, went to him in the great cabin, and earnestly enjoined him—'

'He would call it mutiny.' Over him, and holding up a hand. 'I want no part of it.'

'That is your final word?'

'It is.'

James looked at him, looked away a moment, then:

'May I hold you to your wish?'

'My wish?'

'To forget that this conversation ever took place?'

'I certainly wish it had not.'

'Then you will say nothing?'

'I am sorry you think it necessary to ask.'

'I did not mean to impugn your honour, Bernard. But I must be entirely certain. If you are not with us – you will say nothing?'

'Us? You have already spoke to others of this?'

'Nay, not yet. But I am going to, very soon.'

'I wish you would not. I ask that you will not. It is *mutiny*.'

'We must agree to differ, as to that. Will you take my hand, Bernard?' Holding out his hand. 'And give me your solemn oath that y'will not interfere?'

Bernard Loftus shook his head, and kept his hand by his side. 'If I did that, it would be just the same as agreeing to your scheme. I want *no part of it*.' And he stepped away to the ladder.

Captain Rennie pre-empted his first lieutenant. He himself summoned all of his commissioned and warranted officers to the great cabin, a most unusual occurrence. When they were assembled, Rennie surveyed them a long moment, until the silence was nearly oppressive, then:

'I am going to address the people directly, as to our purpose. Many of them, and perhaps some of you, have begun to wonder what we are about, alone in the immensity of the sea, and the ship we pursue far out of sight. I intend to lift the people up, and urge them to their task. I intend to call upon their courage, and fortitude, and strength. I intend to make their hearts swell with pride, and manly emotion, and the determination never to be defeated by a cowardly dog that fired upon us unprovoked, killed and maimed their shipmates, and has schemed and behaved in every way underhand, piratical, and villainous. When I am done, no task will seem too arduous, no duty too irksome, nor wearying, nor harsh, if only it will bring us in sight of our prey! They will feel to a man that they cannot wait to catch him, the damned pox-raddled wretch, and make him rue the day his mother gave him life!'

He paused, looked at all of them searchingly, then:

'And I will then call on you, Mr Loftus.' Looking at him.

'Yes, sir?'

'I will ask you, in my behalf, to give all hands a double ration of grog, to gladden them and stiffen them to their duty.'

'Very good, sir.'

'That is the moment you, Mr Tangible,' looking at the boatswain now, 'will raise a cheer. "Three cheers for the captain! Huzzay! Huzzay! Huzzay!" You apprehend me?'

'Ay-ay, sir. Three cheers, after the double ration is pronounced.'

'Exact.' A nod. 'Very good, thankee, gentlemen. Will ye join me in a glass of wine before we go on deck? – Cutton!'

Everything went just as Rennie had said it would, and later, as he took his watch, Lieutenant Hayter was obliged to admit to himself that he had been comprehensively outwitted and outgunned, and that his scheme of obliging Rennie to turn back was now quite smashed to pieces.

*

A week passed. A week of variable winds, occasional calm and modest headway, while essential repair continued. On the first day *Expedient* sailed 119 miles, on the second day 112 miles, on the third 123, on the fourth 81 miles and on the fifth a mere 38 miles, in very light airs. The fifth day the ship was becalmed, and on the sixth she made 77 miles. A total for the week of 550 miles.

When Lieutenant Hayter and Mr Loftus brought their detailed log of the ship's progress to Rennie, as requested, the captain discovered that no accurate calculation of the *Terces'* progress had been included, only an estimate, and he demanded to know the reason why. James Hayter responded:

'It is 550 miles, sir, as you see.' Nodding at the pages.

'But that is our own travelled distance.'

'Yes, sir.'

'Is it also an exact figure for *Terces*?'

'No, sir, it cannot in course be an wholly precise figure, since we can only know the approximate total of miles *Terces* has travelled, based upon our own—'

'In short, you have guessed at this.' Over him.

'Well, sir, with respect, I do not see—'

'What say you, Mr Loftus?' Turning his eye on the sailing master.

'I would submit, sir, it is more than a mere guess. Assuming that *Terces* matches us in speed, given the prevailing weather was very similar for both ships, we did not see how we could arrive at a more accurate total of distance travelled through the sea, unless we—'

'I repeat, ye have made not an accurate record, but a damned paltry guess. Hey?'

'Sir, with respect—' began James, and was cut off.

'Did I not require you to *calculate*, sir?' Glaring at him.

'And we have done so!' James, raising his voice, then: 'I beg your pardon, sir, I did not mean to shout. We based our calculations upon the fact that *Terces* has nearly the same sailing capacities as ourselves, and therefore—'

Over him: 'She is smaller, leaner and lighter, and therefore is likely faster across the open sea. What you are saying is that we have not gained a single mile. I required *Expedient* to gain, even as we continued our repair, and you have failed in this specific duty. *Terces* is likely moving further and further ahead upon the sea, so far ahead that we are in danger of losing her altogether. And you do not mind about that, neither of you, hey? Because you do not believe in this pursuit. Well well, that will not answer, by God!'

Both James and Mr Loftus were silent. James thought but did not say that by any sane reckoning or estimation *Terces* had been lost to them the moment she escaped at Norway. He did not say it, but Rennie read something in his eye, and:

'You have an opinion y'wish to express, Mr Hayter?' With menacing calm.

'No, sir.'

'Come, now. Your mouth twitched a little as I spoke just now, and your eye gleamed. I am not so unobservant that I cannot see when one of my officers harbours doubt and dissent. Well well, let us hear it.'

'I – I had rather say nothing, sir.'

'Your request is denied, sir. Y'will not say nothing, you will express your doubts to me, right quick.'

'I have no wish to be impertinent, nor ungentlemanlike – sir.'

'You suggest that *I* am impertinent, sir? That *I* am ungentlemanlike!'

'Sir, if you please—' began Mr Loftus.

'Be quiet, sir!' Angrily. 'I asked Mr Hayter a question, and by God I will have a reply. – Well?' Glaring at James.

'I do not know how I may reply to the captain, without causing him offence.' James, staring straight ahead, his back straight.

'D'y'not? D'y'not? Without offence?'

'I heard your voice, sir, and I come at once.' Colley Cutton, bustling in with a tray.

'Go away, damn you.' Rennie, a brief ferocious glance at his steward.

'As you wish, sir.' Bowing his head. 'Only I fought I heard you summ'n me, very clear.'

'I did not. Go away.'

He waited until the steward had made his exit and shut the door carefully behind him, then:

'Well?' To James.

'Sir?' Staring straight ahead.

'I trusted you, Mr Hayter, you and Mr Loftus both, as my most able and experienced officers. I trusted you to aid me in this endeavour, and left you to carry out your duties over an entire week without interference because I had no wish to hound, nor hector, nor overbear. I was mistook in this leniency. You have failed me. I should have been more exacting and severe, and I have paid the price. The ship and the commission have paid it, and now in consequence we are—'

'D-e-e-e-e-e-ck! Sail of ship a point off the starboard b-o-o-o-o-w!'

Rennie broke off in mid-sentence, snatched up his hat and glass and ran out of the door, and jumped up the ladder. The others followed him on deck.

Without waiting to gain Rennie's permission, nor ask it of the officer of the watch, James jumped into the main shrouds, ran up into the top, and thence to the crosstrees, where he joined his lookout. The lookout pointed, and handed him his glass. James took the glass, hooked an arm through a stay to steady himself, and focused on the sail ahead.

The ship was a long way ahead, six leagues or more, but he could see that she was a three-masted square-rigger, under a full set of canvas. He could not make out her colours, nor the paintwork. Could she be the *Terces*? He lowered the glass and rested his eye a moment, then again lifted and focused. Nay, it was impossible to tell. He returned the glass to the lookout, clapped on to a backstay and slid to the deck.

'Well?' Rennie, eagerly and anxiously. 'Is it *Terces*?'

'She is a three-masted ship, but I cannot say more than that with certainty, sir. She is far ahead – twenty mile, I reckon.'

'Then we must catch her, by God. – Mr Trembath.'

'Sir?' The officer of the deck, attending him.

'Hands to make sail, Mr Trembath. I will like reefs shook out, and stunsails low and aloft, if y'please. We must crack on.'

'Ay-ay, sir. Low and aloft. – Mr Tangible! Hands to make sail!'

Soon the ship bristled with activity. Topmen swarmed in

the shrouds, and moved out along the footropes of the yards. Canvas dropped, bellied and filled, on yards and booms. *Expedient* picked up speed, heeling under a great spread of sail.

By eight bells of the afternoon watch *Expedient* had gained a little on the far ahead sail, but in Rennie's view not enough.

'We must overhaul that ship and discover whether or no she is *Terces*, Mr Hayter.' Lowering his glass.

'We cannot safely bend any further canvas, sir, when—'

'Good God, the ship has undergone very extensive repair. Adgett and Tangible between them have made good nearly all damage to rigging, yards and upper works, and you and Mr Loftus have retrimmed her. The ship is sound, and now we *must crack on*!' Turning in agitation, and pointing aloft. 'Look ye there, as an example. Why ain't there a stunsail on the weather fore t'gansail yard?'

'I had noticed that myself, sir. It is yet repairing, as I understand it.'

'Well well, but that is damned bad seamanship. It should have been replaced long since, as a matter of urgency. Look to it right quick, Mr Hayter. *We must crack on!*'

'Ay-ay, sir.' A hand to his hat.

As the sun sank gleaming low over the sea and night approached, gradually diminishing the stretching immensity to a few acres of glimpsing, darkling water around *Expedient*, and then merely to the restless sound of that water as the ship washed through it, Rennie grew ever more anxious and impatient. A brief relieving trip below to his quarter gallery, and he returned.

'Have we gained?' To the officer of the watch Mr Tindall, on the quarterdeck. 'Can we see her light?'

'I think we may have gained a little, sir, before hammocks down.'

'Yes? You think so? What was our speed, at the last glass?'

Mr Tindall checked his notation. 'Seven knots, sir.'

'Too slow, Mr Tindall. Too damned slow.'

'Mr Loftus has been very attentive, sir, as have I, to the trimming of the sails. I believe we have got every last half a knot out of her, sir, these many glasses.'

'Yes yes, well well, it ain't enough. And what of the chase's light, I asked you. Can we see her light?'

'I – I do not think so, sir.'

'Do not *think?* I require the officer of the deck to *know*, Mr Tindall, one way or t'other.'

'Yes, sir. I will just—'

'Very well, thankee, Mr Tindall.' James, appearing in his working rig. 'I am going aloft myself, and I will discover the light, if it is there.' Slinging his cased glass on his back. To Rennie, politely: 'With your permission, sir?'

'No need to request my permission t'do y'duty as Pursuit Officer, Mr Hayter.' A nod, a sniff. 'I will like to hear at once when y'see the light.'

'Very good, sir.' And he went forrard and jumped into the mainmast shrouds.

'Your tea, sir.' Colley Cutton's voice.

'Oh, Cutton, yes.' Grasping the handle of the hot can, and sucking down a draught. 'Thankee.' Another sucking draught, and he coughed. 'Very welcome.'

James presently returned to the deck, as usual sliding down a backstay, and made his report. 'The ship's light is visible, sir, far ahead. She will not escape us tonight.'

'Very well, thankee, Mr Hayter.' A moment, then turning to Lieutenant Tindall: 'Y'may stand down both batteries, Mr Tindall.'

The orders given, and to their great relief the tired gun-crews were permitted at last to go below.

Rennie then required rather than invited Lieutenant Hayter to attend him at supper in the great cabin, and when James duly appeared, his face washed, his undress coat newly brushed and donned, it was clear to him that the captain had something of importance in his mind. His overly solicitous demeanour made James alert, and wary.

'A glass of Madeira, my dear James? Or will you like claret, in preference?'

'Claret, if you please, sir.'

'He took the filled glass. Thank you, sir.'

'It is a very fair wine, that, I think. I laid in six cases at Portsmouth, when we was obliged to store at a moment's notice, and the wine merchant – not my usual fellow at Norwich, in course – chose admirable well when I told him what I wanted, at a very reasonable rate, too. Taste the wine, and see if ye don't agree . . .'

James dutifully sipped, and did not like what he tasted.

'Nay, dear fellow, take a good deep draught, else you will never taste anything of the grape.'

James drank off half the glass, and suppressed a desire to gasp and cough. The wine was harsh in his throat, and left an acid taste on his tongue.

'Very fair, would not you admit?'

'Hm . . . very . . . very distinctive, sir.'

'Ay, that is the word – distinctive. I am glad you think so.' He poured a glass for himself, and sucked most of it down in one gulp. 'Ahhh . . . nothing like good wine at the end of a long day, hey?' He refilled his glass, and pushed the bottle.

James, feeling himself duty bound to respond to Rennie's hospitality, refilled his own glass, but left it standing on the table. Rennie took a deep breath, studied his glass a moment, pursing his lips, then:

'I have changed my mind about catching *Terces*.'

'Yes, sir?'

'Ay. I knew she was *Terces* from the moment we sighted her, in course. I haven't changed my mind about that. But I no longer wish to overhaul her.'

'No, sir?'

'No, I don't. With any luck she has not seen us. We are far behind – twenty mile and hull down from her deck, just as she is hull down from ours. So long as we keep her in sight, I will like to hold station at this distance, and simply follow her.'

'Yes, sir. And . . . if she ain't *Terces*?'

'You doubt it? You doubt my opinion?'

'I have no wish to doubt you, sir, in course not. However . . .'

'Well? However?' Frowning.

'The Atlantic is a very broad ocean, sir. Many ships cross it to America. Unless we can establish beyond doubt that the ship we presently pursue is *Terces* – well, we may chase her all the way to Boston, or New York, and find she is the *Primrose*, 400 tons, with a cargo of passengers for the New World.'

'*Primrose*? You know of a ship of that name?'

'No, sir, I merely wished—'

'Then why use it?' Over him. 'Never mind, do not answer.' An irritable sigh, and he rose and paced, then again sat down. James waited, his glass untouched. Presently Rennie sniffed in a breath, and:

'We both know you have had grave doubts about this pursuit into the Atlantic, there is no point denying it. I have never entertained such doubts myself, and now that we have *Terces* in sight you must cast yours aside. That is why I asked you to attend me at supper tonight.' A quick glance at James, who said nothing.

'I have decided upon something else, in addition,' Rennie continued. 'I believe we must do more than simply discover where *Terces* is headed. I think we must make every effort to learn why her passenger goes to America. In little, when *Terces* makes landfall, and her passenger goes ashore, so must we.'

'Will not we greatly exceed our orders in doing that, sir?'

'Nay, I do not think so. Our written orders are exact, certainly. We are required to follow and learn *Terces*' destination – and yet within that instruction there is surely another meaning, another implication. We are sea officers. We know very well that we must always use our best endeavours under any and all circumstances. Well well, I think the circumstances have changed, and accordingly it is our duty to discover as much as we are able about the *Terces*, her master, and her passenger – given what they have cost us in blood spilled and lives lost.'

'With respect, sir, ain't that reading things into our orders . . . that in truth cannot possibly be seen there, under any circumstances?'

'You disappoint me, James. I had thought you was a man of deeper perception. In course, I will never doubt your courage. But I had thought you was a man who could see things for what they are.'

'See things for what they are, sir . . . ?'

'Indeed. This is all to do with the French.'

'The *French*?'

'Certainly. Anything that Mappin touches has to do with France, and what has happened in France since the year '89. Captain Broadman and his passenger in *Terces* have connections with France – deep, intimate, dangerous connections, I am in no doubt, else Mappin would never have sent us on this little cruise. Would never have offered me that spurious bribe of 2,000 of money, to quicken my interest.'

'If I may be candid, sir, it puzzled me that he would offer such a bribe to a serving sea officer. Surely he must have known you would refuse it outright.'

'The world Mappin inhabits, my dear James, ain't made up of honourable men. So accustomed is he to chicanery, cunning, bribery, and general viciousness of character among his professional acquaintance, that he will always assume the worst of a man rather than the best.'

'I have no particular reason to love him myself, sir, as you know.'

'In course, in course, just so. But that don't mean he is not honourable in his own devious way, in the nation's interest. He sees a war approaching, and so do I, and so do all perceiving and sensible men. That war will be fought with France, and any and all allies she may draw in. It will be a fight to the death, this time.'

'But what has Norway to do with France, nor Denmark for

that matter? Olaf Christian den Norske – in the little time I saw him – seemed to me a pleasant, open-faced, honest sort of fellow, not given to—'

'Pleasant? Open-faced?' Over him. 'I am in no doubt the world is filled with pleasant-featured fellows that would cut my throat for a shilling, the moment I turned my back, good God. If he is linked with the French, and I have every reason to suspect it, then he is our enemy, just as certainly as Captain Bloody Broadman.'

'If what you say is true, sir – then you must also believe that America will side with France, since that is evidently where *Terces* is going.'

'Not all in America, not every man and woman. Nay, by no means. But there is sufficient numbers in America that hate us with a passion, and wish us ill, to be a great trouble to us, and they will side with France, and her allies. Denmark, I believe, will be her ally. It is the Danes who control Norway, and her shipping routes. Broadman and his passenger are a vital part of it all. And that is why we must remain a shadow behind the *Terces*, never showing ourselves, and why we must discover what they are about when they arrive in America, and whom they meet.'

'I have no stomach for being a spy again, sir, after what happened to us in France the last commission.'

'This can scarce be called *spying*, good God.' Irritably.

'What else, then?'

'It is part of our duty of pursuit, as I've said very plain.'

'I will not like to argue with you, sir.' A little shrug.

'Eh?' A querulous look.

'Instead, if you will permit me . . . I will make a suggestion.' Leaning forward.

'Well?' A sniff, leaning back.

'*Firethorn.*'

'Fire what?'

'I suggest we disguise ourselves as the *Firethorn*, sir. Or any name we choose. A large merchantman, bound for the United

States of America. That we overhaul the ship ahead of us, discover whether or no she is *Terces*, and then sail—'

'It is fanciful.' Dismissively, sitting forward again. 'What you suggest would involve an absurd and elaborate masquerade, a great deal of painting, and rearrangement of the upperworks . . . good heaven, I cannot and will not even begin to entertain it.'

A breath, and a polite grimace. 'Very good, sir.'

'Beside, it simply ain't necessary.' Impatiently. 'The ship *is* Terces, I am entirely certain – as I said to you.'

'Very good, sir.'

'We will follow her, then follow Broadman and his passenger ashore.'

'Very good, sir.'

'*Firethorn*? Disguise?' Again looking at James with a frown. 'You have drank too much of my wine, James. Excellent though it is, it must be took in moderation.' Retrieving the bottle.

'Perhaps you are right, sir.' James, pushing away his full glass with a show of reluctance.

He made no further suggestions, and ate his supper largely in silence, responding to Rennie's attempts at congeniality with brief, polite, but unconversable replies.

Presently, when Rennie had drunk a glass of Madeira and eaten his cheese, and James had politely refused both, Rennie gave up, and James went away to his cabin.

*

On the next day an ordinary seaman, Nately Thoms, fell ill of fever on the lower deck, and was confined by Dr Empson in the sick berth forrard. Within twenty-four hours four other hands had fallen ill. The mood of the lower deck, already fractious because the ship was so short-handed, grew fearful and dark. On watch the hands were surly and reluctant, and at divisions refused to meet the gaze of their officers.

Rennie ordered the ship to be washed and smoked between, and sent for the surgeon.

'Doctor, I will ask you quite blunt. Are you able to prevent further cases?'

'I fear that may be . . . difficult.'

'In little, ye cannot.' A grim nod. 'How many cases, now?'

'Two more, this morning. Seven in all. But I fear there may be more, perhaps many more. It is ship fever, very hard to eradicate once it has took hold in the confined space of—'

Over him: 'When y'say "ship fever", Doctor, d'y'mean – typhus?'

'It is a form of typhus, yes.'

'Christ's blood.' Quietly.

'I will do my best, sir, to quarantine those infected forrard in the sick berth, but with other men among the hammock numbers nearly certain to fall ill, the—'

Again over him: 'We must wash and smoke daily. All hammocks to be scrubbed in chamber-lye and triced up to air in the girt-lines, not left damp in the netting.'

'Scrubbed – daily?'

'Nay, not the hammocks every day, that ain't practive. But they must be scrubbed today, certainly. I will say so to Mr Tangible.'

'Very good, thank you, sir. Erm . . . any change in diet?'

'Diet? Nay, I don't think so.' Looking at the surgeon. 'The men must keep up their strength.'

'I meant – in the matter of drink, sir, not food.'

'I do not apprehend you, Doctor.'

'Should not the men forgo their grog, sir, until the fever has burned out in the ship?'

'Forgo their grog, Doctor? To what purpose?' Shaking his head.

'To aid in their resistance, sir. Grog can only inflame and weaken them, surely?'

'Nonsense, Doctor, stark nonsense. Grog strengthens seamen, not merely in their physical beings, but in their souls.

We are far at sea, upon a hazardous venture, and the people need lifting up. Without their grog they would grow listless and despondent.'

The doctor took a deep breath, and: 'Sir, Captain Rennie – I think with respect that your own view is nonsense. Fever is a disease that inimically heats the blood, and can only be made worse by the—'

'*What didy'say?*' Glaring at the surgeon.

'Because *grog* heats the blood, sir. Cannot you see that? It can only make the fever infinitely worse!'

'Do not raise your voice to me, sir.'

'I – I beg your pardon, sir.' The doctor checked himself, and looked away.

'Your duty is one of healing, Doctor, not of discipline nor command.'

'Yes, sir. Very good.' Not meeting the captain's gaze.

'Kindly have the good manners to look at me when I address you, sir.'

'Yes, sir.' The surgeon turned his head and looked the captain in the eye.

Rennie in turn looked at him a long moment, then: 'We must trust each other, you know, within these narrow wooden walls. I trust you to do your best for those that are ill. And you must trust me to know what is best for those that are hale. Thankee, Doctor. Report to me again at the change of the watch.' And in dismissal he turned away to the stern-gallery window, his hands behind his back.

'Very good, sir.'

When Dr Empson had left the cabin Rennie's resolute, upright demeanour deserted him, and his shoulders sagged. He sat down frowning at his desk, and took up his quill to make lists. One of those lists was of the numbers of men left available to him to sail the ship and if need be to fight the guns. The list was far short of the ideal, so far short in fact that Rennie felt fear in his guts, flexing its needle claws.

He laid aside his quill with a sniff, and murmured:

'If this fever takes hold severe, and takes its toll, *Expedient* could become a sort of ghost ship – a three-masted wraith upon the wide, uncaring sea, slowly sailing toward oblivion . . .'

A sigh, and he stared unseeing at the sword rack. A movement at his calf. He looked down, and saw his cat Dulcie. For the first time since she had littered she had come to him now and rewarded him with her familiar affectionate bumping.

'Dulcie, my dear.'

Answered with a miaow, and an upward look.

'Where's your brood, then, my dear? Sleeping, hey? Are you hungry?'

Another miaow, and he rose from his chair and busied himself with finding titbits for his cat, and a saucer of milk, and was relieved for a few moments of all the hard, vexing, worrying exigency of command, and became simply a domestic being, seeing to the needs of his closest companion.

In the second hour of the afternoon watch, Nately Thoms died. By eight bells, two further men had died, and a third was near the end, sweating and retching in his hammock, his skin speckled with the telltale rash.

Dr Empson came aft to the great cabin, and duly reported this news.

Rennie stood silently listening and staring out of the stern-gallery window, his back to the surgeon. When the surgeon had finished, Rennie at last turned round.

'Very good, thankee, Doctor. Return to your duty, if y'please. I must find a way to lift the people.' A nod of dismissal, and the surgeon bowed and withdrew.

But Captain Rennie could not think of a way to lift his people. Although *Expedient* was still in pursuit of the far ahead ship, the importance of the pursuit was beginning to recede in his mind, to be replaced by something like dread. In God's name . . . what was he to do?

*

"'. . . for the resurrection of the body – when the Sea shall give up her dead – and the life of the world to come, through our Lord Jesus Christ; who at his coming shall change our vile body, that it may be like his glorious body, according to the mighty working, whereby he is able to subdue all things to himself.'"

A nod. The rattling drone of the drum. The tipping of the boards, and the canvas-shrouded corpses plummeted into the sea. Subdued splashes in the gently rolling swell, the ship hove to out of respect for the dead, her pennant running long from the mainmast trucktop on the rippling wind.

Captain Rennie closed the book, put on his hat, thwartwise upon his head, and:

'Mr Hayter.'

'Sir?'

'We will get under way, if you please.'

'Ay-ay, sir.' His own hat on. 'Mr Tangible! Hands to make sail!'

And now something happened – did not happen – that at first shocked Rennie, then made him angry, then dismayed. The hands assembled in the waist did not disperse. Mr Tangible's piping call, repeated by his mate's call forrard, went ignored, the high, piercing sounds echoing over the deck as unremarked as the calls of a passing seabird.

A long moment, as Rennie at the breast-rail of the quarterdeck stared at his motionless, surly crew. And then, one by one, slowly and reluctantly, the men began to move. Rennie quietly let out a long-held-in breath, and turned aft to the companionway ladder. A seaman of the afterguard moved to the weather-rail by the hammock cranes, and stood there. He had clapped on to a sheet, but was not pulling his weight, the hawser-laid rope hanging loose in his hands. He met Rennie's gaze and returned it unblinking, neither defiant nor deferential. For several seconds Rennie was utterly non-plussed. Was the man being insolent? Or was he asking a silent question: what is to become of us? Rennie came to himself with a sharp sniffing intake of breath, and pointed at the seaman, who immediately turned his back and began hauling on the rope.

'That man!'

The seaman took no notice, and continued hauling down on the sheet with both hands, his back turned.

'That man, there!' Rennie's voice now raised to a full, carrying, quarterdeck bellow.

And again the man ignored him, busy with the rope.

It had become a contest of wills on the open deck, a contest Rennie knew he could not afford to lose.

'Master-at-arms!'

The man was seized, taken below, and put into the bilboes.

Captain Rennie paced aft to the wheel, and to the officer of the watch, loudly:

'Mr Tindall!'

'Sir?' Attending, his hat off and on.

Again loudly, for the benefit of all within earshot, Rennie gave his instruction:

'Mr Tindall, I will like you to impress on every man of the watch that I will not tolerate insolence, idleness, nor disobedience on deck. Nay, nor anywhere in the ship. Any man that shows reluctant, nor slow, nor slovenly, neglectful and vicious, will be clapped in irons directly, d'y'hear me, now?'

'Ay-ay, sir.'

'We are short-handed, and engaged upon a long and vital pursuit in the service of the king. No man that is defiant of good order and discipline will escape harsh punishment! He will be tied upon a grating and flogged, and his grog stopped indefinite! You apprehend me, Mr Tindall?'

'Yes, sir. Very good, sir.'

'Very well. Your deck.'

And the captain strode aft and stood at the tafferel, hands clasped behind his back, every inch of him the stern disciplinarian, upright, determined and strong. Within he was quaking and nauseous, twinges of fear in his guts and in his water. He had not lifted his people at the burial service, as he had meant to. Somehow the right words – heartening, gathering, encouraging – would not come to him as they had always come in the past, when he had wished to unite the ship in a common purpose. And within moments of this failure he had been obliged to chastise and confine a man who was very likely as fearful as himself – with every good reason.

'Men are dying.' In his head. 'Men are sickening and dying. And even when I told James I was certain of *Terces* ahead – in truth I was not, and am not yet.'

Captain Rennie stood watching the wake – outwardly resolute, inwardly quaking – for several glasses together, and then he went below.

During the night the pursuit disappeared. One moment the distant light was there, visible from the mainmast crosstrees, and a moment after it had vanished. The lookout informed the deck, and presently Lieutenant Hayter went aloft to see for himself – that there was nothing to be seen.

Lieutenant Hayter remained in the crosstrees a further glass, hoping against hope that the light would reappear. It did not. He debated descending to the deck, going below to the great cabin to wake the captain and inform him, and decided to wait until first light. Perhaps the lantern had simply gone out on the mast of the distant ship, and not been relit.

At first light, the pale gleaming of the sky reflected in the bleak wilderness of the rolling sea, there was no sign of a sail.

James slid to the deck by a backstay, and went below.

'She must have cracked on, sir, when the—'

'God damn your reckless neglect, Mr Hayter!' Rennie flung himself out of his hanging cot, stubbed his toe against a timber standard, and stumbled against the gun. In a fury:

'You was obliged to tell me *at once* of any development, any change, and you did not! You skulked there aloft, fearful and irresolute, like some fucking little mid in his first year at sea!'

'Sir, I do not think that is quite fair, when I—'

'Be quiet, sir! Christ knows how far ahead *Terces* has gone by now! Christ knows if we will ever find her again! Why was not I informed *immediate*!'

'I was not certain, sir. I could not be certain, when the ship was so far ahead, and perhaps the masthead light had simply—'

'Silence! Y'will be silent, sir! I will not hear these damned piddling middy's excuses on your lips! They sicken me! Sicken and disgust me! Cutton! – *Cutton!*'

'I has just boiled my spirit kettle, sir, and shall bring your tea directly.' Cutton, pushing his head round the door of the sleeping cabin. Rennie thrust him aside, and strode into the day cabin, pulling on his breeches. The ship lurched a little, and Rennie steadied himself against his table, and again turned on his lieutenant:

'What o'clock did she disappear, hey? Can you remember even that little fact, I wonder? Or has it escaped you, as *Terces* has escaped us? Hey!'

'The masthead light of the pursuit vanished at three minutes past six bells of the middle watch, sir.' Checking a note with studied care, then looking up directly into Rennie's eye.

'What o'clock is it now?'

James fumbled for his pocket watch, and at the same moment the ship's bell sounded on the forecastle. Three bells. Half past five.

'So we have lost two hours and a half!' Rennie, in something like triumph.

James made no reply.

'Well!'

'Well – what, sir?'

'You acknowledge that we have lost all that time? Two hours and a half?'

A light knocking now, at the door of the cabin. Rennie ignored it, and it was repeated – tap-tap-tap.

'Cutton!'

His steward did not appear, and in a fury of irritation Rennie strode to the door and flung it wide.

'Well!'

It was the surgeon's mate, a thin, apologetic man with the face of an aged boy.

'I humbly beg your pardon, sir, for disturbing you so early, but the surgeon—'

'Yes yes, well well, Dr Empson has sent you to say there is more fever cases? Yes?' Interrupting him.

'No, sir, he has not sent me. I came of my own accord, sir. The surgeon himself has been took ill.'

'The surgeon? Is it the fever?'

'I – I wish it were not.'

'Damnation.' Softly, turning away to the window. Presently he faced the cabin again, his face sombre, and: 'Very well, thankee . . . what is your name?'

'Dart, sir. Eloquence Dart.'

'Elo— Hm. Thankee, then. Are there any further cases of fever this day?' Anxiously.

'Only the surgeon himself, sir – so far.'

'Ay, so far.' A brief grimace – his attempt at a smile. 'Will you do your best for him, Mr Dart, and say to him that I wish him a speedy recovery? Please to carry on with the surgeon's duties in aiding the other sick men, and report to me again at noon today, will you?' A nod of dismissal.

When the surgeon's mate had gone, Rennie thought a moment, a finger to his lips, then strode to the door, and:

'Sentry!'

'Sir?' The Marine in his red coat.

'Send word for the sailing master Mr Loftus to attend me in the great cabin at his earliest convenience.'

'Ay-ay, sir.'

James waited, and when after a minute or more Rennie had said nothing further to him, he asked:

'Do you wish me to remain, sir?'

Rennie looked at his lieutenant, frowned, and curtly:

'I do.'

'I am expected on deck, sir, as officer of the watch, at eight bells.'

'Y'will remain here until I dismiss you, Mr Hayter.'

'Very good, sir.'

When Bernard Loftus came to the great cabin a few minutes after, fully dressed but his eyes still muzzed with sleep, Rennie greeted him with another of his brief grimaces.

'Mr Loftus, good morning to you.'

'Good morning, sir.'

'I am making you Pursuit Officer, Mr Loftus, effective immediate. Mr Hayter will take his instruction in all matters pertaining to the pursuit from you. Your first task is to find her.'

'D'y'mean – find *Terces*, sir? Ain't she there . . . ?' A glance at James.

James opened his mouth to speak, but Rennie, over him:

'Mr Hayter has contrived to lose her in the night.'

'At any rate, she has disappeared.' James, glancing away toward the window.

'A fact he did not report to me until a few minutes since. We have lost not only *Terces*, therefore, but a very great deal of time, whilst he deliberated, and procrastinated, and neglected his duty to inform me at once. Your task, Mr Loftus, is to make up that time and find me *Terces*, right quick. You have me?'

'If indeed the ship that vanished was *Terces*.' James, as if to himself.

'Do you apprehend me, Mr Loftus?' Rennie, ignoring James.

'Yes, sir. Erm . . . are my duties as sailing master to be—'

'Y'duties as sailing master will not be in any way interrupted. Your duties as Pursuit Officer will be consonant with them, entire. Thank you, Mr Loftus. Good morning.'

'Very good, sir.' His hat on, and he departed. As he did so

eight bells was struck on deck. When the door had closed, Rennie:

'Are not you expected on deck, Mr Hayter? Ain't it your watch, sir?'

'Yes, sir, it is. But I—'

'Then why d'y'linger below deck, sir?'

'I wished merely to ascertain my standing in the ship, sir.' Not quite defiantly.

'Your "standing", sir, did y'say? You are a commissioned sea officer, with the rank of lieutenant, and your obligation is to perform your duties accordingly. "Standing" don't come into it.'

'Thank you, sir. You said I was to take instruction from Mr Loftus. Did you mean that I was to confer with Mr Loftus about his new duties, or that he was to confer with me?' An inquiring smile so icily polite it was nearly an outright rebuke, and at last Rennie reacted.

'Take your watch, sir!'

'Very good, sir. But may I—'

'Not another word! Not one! Go on deck!'

When James had gone Rennie sat down at his desk, and found that he was trembling with anger. His hands shook, his heart was thudding in his breast. Muttering furiously:

'God damn and blast the bloody fellow! Cannot he see the gravity of our position? Cannot he grasp the extremity of the hazard we face, with fever raging in the lower deck, the pursuit lost, the people increasing fearful and reluctant, and *Expedient* far from any safe haven? Why must he take the adversarial role in any and every damned discussion, good God! Why does he look on me as his enemy, when I have strained every sinew to aid and assist him in his career! What has provoked this wretched, lunatic disloyalty! I do not deserve this treatment! Nay, I do not, I do not!'

He was so angry that tears started in his eyes, and he banged the desk with his fist.

Three days passed, during which the ship was increasing

slow, in lighter and lighter airs. More men fell ill, including men clapped in irons for open disobedience on deck. The pursuit was not sighted again, and the mood of the people grew ominously sullen. Then in the early morning of the fourth day the wind gave way to a breathless stillness, and *Expedient* lay altogether becalmed on the pale vastness of the sea. The surgeon's mate came to Rennie's cabin, his lined boy's face ashen.

'Dr Empson has died, sir.'

*

The sound woke James as he lay in his hanging cot, the book he had been reading open on his breast where it had fallen. He raised himself on an elbow, and the book fell to the deck. His lantern had gone out.

The sound came again. A deep, dark rumbling, as if a great gun were being hauled along the deck on its trucks.

And now it came to James. Roundshot were being rolled.

'It is mutiny . . .' Whispered.

Very quietly and carefully he swung his legs out of his cot, and stood on the deck timbers. Movement overhead, furtive, hurried scuffling. James froze, then reached for his clothes in the darkness, and slipped them on, but remained barefoot. He reached for his sword, and his pistol case. A few moments, and he was about to venture out of his cabin when the door was opened and the captain's face appeared, lit by the subdued glow of a small dark-lantern.

'James?' Whispering.

'I am here, sir.' Also whispering.

'Thank God they have not took us all.' Coming in.

'It is mutiny certain, then?'

'Ay.' A nod, a brief sigh.

'Which other officers have been took, sir?'

'I cannot be certain, but I think they have took Mr Trembath, who had the deck, and Mr Tindall, who was relieving him. You heard the roundshot rolling? That was the signal.'

'How many are the mutineers? Who leads them?'

'I do not know, James. I do not know. But as soon as I heard the rolling shot I knew what was afoot, and straightway crept from my sleeping cabin down the ladder, and hid behind the gunroom bulkhead. I heard them go to my cabin to look for me, and no doubt take me, but I was too damned canny for them, by God.'

'Are you armed, sir?'

'Nay, I am in my nightshirt, as you see. All I have is my dark-light.'

James gave him a spare pair of breeches, a shirt, one of his pair of pistols and his spare blade, a plain hanger. Rennie shifted quickly into the clothes, tucked the pistol into his waist, and jerked his head.

'We will go on deck, James, and find out how things lie.'

He shut the lantern, and James followed him out of the cabin, reflecting that the one good thing about this new emergency was that all bitter difference between them could now be put aside. Both barefoot as they were, neither made any sound on the deck timbers. They opened and went through the gunroom door to the ladder, and crept up.

When they reached the upper deck, Rennie halted and held out a warning hand to halt James behind him. For a few seconds they listened. Silence, except for the eternal sounds of a ship at sea – creaking timbers, the slap of water, the easeful stretching of shrouds and stays as the ship moved almost imperceptibly on the slow swell. Tonight, no wind. No wind at all.

'Should we go forrard into the waist?' James, whispering.

'Nay, I want to see my quarterdeck, and who is there.' Rennie, crouched behind the lower capstan. He tapped James on the arm, and they crept forward past the capstan to the companionway ladder, and cautiously on up.

Rennie lifted his head above the level of the deck, just high enough to look aft through the stanchions and past the capstan toward the wheel. There was a figure manning the wheel, and other figures abaft the mizzenmast, but he could not make out who they were in the dim light. He swivelled his head, and nearly cried out in shock when he saw a figure immediately above him, just forrard of the ladder, leaning on a stanchion. He ducked down below the level of the deck, and whispered in James's ear.

'Christ's blood, there is a man just above, right by the ladder. If we are to go on deck, we must take him and silence him.'

'Which way does he face, sir?'

'Forrard, I think. Ay, it must be forrard, else he would have seen me.'

'A blow to the skull from behind, then, and he must be caught as he falls.' James, decisively. 'I will do it, sir. I am taller.' He thought but did not say – 'and more powerful built'. Rennie made way for him on the ladder, without demur.

In his head: 'Thank God we can put aside all difference, and work as one again.'

James silently rose to his full height on the top step of the ladder, immediately behind the man who stood with his back to it. Lifted his pistol and brought the butt down with a sharp snap of his wrist. A subdued crack, and the man slumped. James caught him, and lowered him to the deck. But the sound and the movement had been noticed, and three figures now appeared from aft, and began running forrard. James just had time to see they were armed with muskets, before

crack

Rennie fired his pistol, and the leading figure reeled and fell with a moan.

James now lifted his own pistol, and fired at the second figure

crack

careless now of concealment. Battle had been joined. The second man fell, shot through the head, and slumped away against the larboard rail.

Shouts and flurries of movement, both fore and aft. The third man in the party that had run forward from the wheel discharged his musket. A flash and the report, and the ball sang away harmlessly. The man dropped his musket and attempted to draw a pistol from his waist, but James stamped two paces straight at him and ran him through. The man went down with a gasp, and James's blade sucked clear with a subdued ring. Blood dripped on the deck timbers.

Musket shots from the fo'c'sle, now, flashes in the darkness and

crack   crack-crack

James ducked as a ball fizzed past his head and struck the capstan in a shock of splinters. Lifted his head again, and at first could not see Rennie. Then he heard him.

'You damned mutinous wretch!'

And saw him in mortal combat on the gangway with a tall seaman wielding a cutlass. Rennie's short hanger clashed with the heavier blade, and it was clear to James at once that the captain would be bested if he did not make more of his swordsmanship, instead of merely swinging and bellowing in a red mist of rage.

It was as if Rennie had heard the admonition, silent though it was. He parried a scything sweep of the seaman's cutlass, thrusting it wide with a sawing clash of steel on steel, and slid his shorter blade clear with a sudden extra jerk, leaving the seaman slightly but fatally unbalanced. Rennie stepped back neatly and slightly to one side on the gangway, and as the heavier built seaman lunged again Rennie brought up his blade straight, caught him full in the sternum, thrust deep and severed his aorta. The man coughed, gasped and clutched his chest as Rennie pulled his blade clear. The dying man dropped his cutlass, staggered against a hammock crane, and pitched overboard. Half a moment, then a heavy splash.

Rennie beckoned from the gangway. 'We will go forrard, James!' And he began to advance toward the fo'c'sle. A flashing, cracking fusillade of musket and pistol shot. The air sang with lethal metal, and Rennie felt balls rip through cloth at his waist and thigh, and a ball whirred past his ear – but he was unharmed. He ducked, fell back, and joined James crouching behind the capstan.

'They have took the fo'c'sle, sir.' Keeping his voice low.

'How many are they?' His own voice low.

'At least a dozen, by the muzzle flashes. Perhaps twenty.'

'Only twenty? Then where is the rest of the people, good God? Why have they not resisted, and fought back?'

'I expect they are held below, sir, under guard. And I think we must assume the mutineers have got hold of both arms chests from below, and carried them forrard with them.'

'Ay, very like.' Soberly, a nod. 'Which makes it very probable they have also took the forrard magazine, and hold the gunner Mr Storey.'

'Almost certainly.'

'God damn the bloody villains. We must make a plan, James.'

'Even if we are alone against them, sir, just the two of us?'

'I wonder if they have took the after magazine, James . . .? If they have not, by God, we may have a chance . . .'

'Chance, sir?'

'Ay. It is a very great risk, but I believe we must take it. One of us must go below, and discover yea or nay whether the aft magazine is took.'

'What can we do, even if it is not? The great guns are of no use to us.'

'I am not thinking of the great guns, James . . .'

'Not thinking . . . ahh, I see. Swivels.'

'Ay.'

'I will go.' James, decisively. 'If the magazine is held, so be it. If not, I will find and bring swivel cartridge and canister, and our scheme may just have the ghost of a chance.'

'Very good. I will remain here, and observe the fo'c'sle, and wait for your return. Try to be quick, will ye?' He touched James's arm briefly, nodded, and James rose stealthily and was gone.

James descended the ladders with infinite care, his bare feet soundless on the treads, his sword held ready to thrust. He had no light. The dark-lantern had been lost somewhere on deck in the first flurry of fighting. He was virtually blind, but he knew every inch of *Expedient*, from her truck tops to her pigs and shingle, and every moment of his descent he knew exactly where he was. He was now on the after platform, facing the stern, and the doorway of the aft magazine lightroom was immediately ahead. Through that doorway was the second door, into the magazine itself, and the cartridge racks. He listened, holding in his breath. Surely if there was a guard, James would hear his breathing, or some little shuffle of movement? There was nothing.

'It is not took, then.' In his head.

Just to be certain he waited a further whole minute, then ventured to the small doorway, and found that it was locked.

'Christ's blood . . .' Whispered.

Should he attempt to shoulder it down? But that would not answer. These doors, and all bulkheads and timbers down here, were as solid and strong as any in the ship – on purpose. The magazine of a ship of war must be secure at all times. The lock would not burst, even were he to crash his full weight against it repeatedly for the whole of a glass. He did not have a whole glass, nor even half of one. He must find the key, right quick, or desist.

Not quite two minutes later, James joined Rennie again at the capstan.

'You have got cartridge?' Excitedly.

'Nay, I have not. The magazine was unguarded, but the lightroom door was locked.'

'Locked! Why did not ye kick it down, for Christ's sake!'

Footfalls now on the gangways, larboard and starboard. The fo'c'sle party were venturing aft. Oaths and threatening talk as they advanced, as if to lift themselves. The rattling of small arms, and cutlasses.

'A magazine door cannot be broke down, sir, as I think you know. We must go aft, now, and find the swivels where they are stored under the flag lockers.' James, urgently whispering, and glancing forrard.

'Ay, the swivels are stored there. Storey has put them there himself. But can they possibly be *loaded*, James? Without cartridge and canister we are lost.'

James fled aft, doubled up, running on the larboard side of the quarterdeck, and Rennie followed him. There were two men at the wheel. James dealt with one, and Rennie with the other.

They reached the flag lockers together, and dragged one of the one-pound swivel guns from the storage place beneath, just as the fo'c'sle party began to advance aft on the quarter-deck. The gun was over three and a half feet long with the tiller attached to the pommelion, and was very heavy. The forked yoke had been removed, but the small flintlock mechanism was attached, under a lead shroud. Rennie tore off the shroud.

'We will heave the gun upon your shoulder, James. You will stand steady, and I will aim and fire. We will both pray to God that the damned thing is loaded.'

'And that there is just enough powder in the pan . . .' James, muttering.

The mutineers were now advancing in force on either side of the mizzenmast. Rennie helped James heave the gun up on his right shoulder as he stood facing diagonally across the quarterdeck from the larboard corner of the tafferel. James

heard Rennie cock the mechanism with a sharp double click.
  'A ragged row of flashes across the deck, and:

crack   crack   crack   crack-crack

Musket and pistol shot whirred and sang and ricocheted.
James felt a sharp tug as Rennie pulled the lanyard.

BOOM

  The deafening concussion of the charge, and the gun
jumped on his shoulder. He was nearly blinded by the flash,
and the whole of his right cheek was scorched. He could hear
nothing, and for a moment could see nothing.
  Then it became clear that seven, eight, ten men lay scattered
across the deck timbers in a bloody sprawl. The numbness in
his head resolved itself into a black singing hush, then into the
hideous groans and shrieks of mortally injured men. Everything stank of burned powder. The weight of the gun tumbled
from his shoulder, and he heard it thud to the deck. He turned,
and saw that Rennie had fallen. He knelt at Rennie's side, and
heard him grunt with pain as he tried to lift himself. James
took his arm.
  'Sir? Where are you wounded?'
  'My shoulder. Leave me . . . and go forrard.'
  'I cannot leave you lying wounded, sir. I will get you below.'
  Rennie shook away James's hand, and with an effort again
attempted to rise. He was unable to do so, and fell back.
  'Sir, let me help—'
  'Nay, leave me! We cannot go below until the deck has been
secured!'
  The groans and cries of the wounded now filled James's
ears, and he was forced to look at them more closely. In all
there were a dozen men lying on the quarterdeck in the area
of the skylight. Three panes of the skylight had been shattered,
and there was blood splashed across the glass. Six of the men

were clearly dead, sprawled motionless. Of the other six only two were not horribly injured, and both of them had been caught in the legs and were now unable to stand. The four others were all covered in blood from multiple canister shot strikes. One of them, who laying gasping and jerking, had had the left side of his head shot away. James stood tall to peer forrard and could see no other men on deck. This was the core of the mutiny, bloodily cut to pieces with a pound of canister. He knelt again beside Rennie.

'There will be no more fighting on deck this night, sir. I will go below and fetch the surgeon's mate.'

'Don't – hhh – don't be a damned fool!' Rennie, pushing himself up into a sitting position, and clutching at his right shoulder, where his shirt was now soaked with blood. 'There is more of them holding the bulk of the hands below, under arms. You cannot tackle them single-handed.'

'I do not intend to, sir. I will tell them the facts, and they will surrender.'

'They – hhh – they will not! They will cut you down!'

'Sir, there are men here that need medical aid, including yourself. I must go below and find the surgeon's mate.' And he left Rennie, and went to the ladder.

As he descended, unarmed now and his shirt stained with Rennie's blood, he became aware that he was trembling in every part of him. His foot slipped on a tread, and he realised that both his feet were slimed with blood from the deck. His cheek was fiercely painful from the powder burn of the swivel gun. He came to a swaying halt on the ladder, and nearly fell.

'I am going to faint . . .'

The dark-lantern – which he had discovered lying on deck and had relighted – began to slip from his hand. The need to save the light brought a strong effort of will, he sucked in a deep breath, clung to the ladder and consciousness, and the moment of dizziness passed. The trembling had also diminished, and he was again able to descend. As he did so it struck him as very odd that the men who were holding the other hands below had not reacted to the fighting on deck – the pounding feet, shouts, gunfire, and screams of pain. Why had they not come on deck to aid their fellow mutineers?

'Because there is too few of them, and they are deathly afraid.' Whispering to himself.

A moment after he was obliged to bring that notion to the test. From halfway down the ladder to the lower deck:

'You there, below! This is the first lieutenant! Your mutiny has failed, and all your friends lie dead and wounded upon the deck! Lay down your arms and come up into the waist right quick, or know the consequence!'

Silence.

'D'y'hear, there! Send up the surgeon's mate, to treat your own wounded! Then come up the ladder into the waist one by one, unarmed, and surrender! Cheerly, now!'

Silence.

To himself, James: 'I'm damned if I will go down among them and allow them to kill me. I will go on deck, and wait for them to see reason.'

He retreated up the ladder and went on deck, and looked for the captain. To his surprise Rennie had managed to get to his feet, and was at the flag lockers, attempting to pull clear from the storage space beneath another of the one-pound swivel guns. Blood from his shoulder dripped on the planking.

James, going to him: 'Sir, you must not tax yourself. You are wounded severe, and bleeding.'

'Help me with – hhh – this swivel, James. We – hhh – must be prepared for a further assault from below.'

James took the swivel from him, and heaved it on his shoulder. It was so heavy he staggered, nearly fell, clapped on to a stay to steady himself, and then went purposefully forrard. Rennie followed him toward the breast-rail, stepping round the dead and wounded. As they passed the unmanned wheel, Rennie:

'Christ in tears, who is conning the ship? We are drifting.'

'I will return and take the wheel myself, when we have dealt with the remainder of the mutineers, sir.' James, effortfully, over his shoulder. 'I ordered them to come up into the waist, and surrender.'

They waited, James with the swivel still on his shoulder, Rennie panting and clutching at his wound. Nothing happened. Silence except for the groans and whimpers of the wounded aft.

'God damn the bloody wretches – hhh – I will make them respond . . .' Rennie, advancing to the starboard side of the breast-rail. James at last thought to relieve himself of the burden of the swivel, and lowered it with a thud to the breast-rail. Rennie, startled by the sudden noise, turned to look, and at that moment a man appeared at the lower deck ladder, under the shadows of the boats, raised and aimed his musket and was about to fire, when James:

'Look out, sir! Throw yourself down!'

Rennie instinctively ducked his head, just as there came the flash of the musket.

crack

The ball thwacked into the breast-rail.

Another man appeared in the shadows beneath the boat skids, and James heaved the swivel round by the tiller, aimed it into the waist, cocked the flintlock, and grasped the lanyard.

'Lay down your arms! If you do not, I will blow your guts all over the deck!'

crack

The ball struck the breast-rail, and slurred into James's left arm. He gasped, and pulled the lanyard. A blinding flash.

BOOM

The unsecured gun leapt from the rail and tumbled heavily into the waist.

Smoke hid James's line of sight a moment. Pain seared his left arm, and his knees began to buckle. He clung to the breast-rail with his right hand, and held himself upright. As the smoke cleared he saw that the two men at the ladder had been flung across the forrard hatch grating, their upper bodies smashed to pulp.

Soon after, a white shirt tied to a handspike was lifted up the ladder, and four men came into view in the waist, and carefully laid down their muskets and a brace of pistols each, and stood quietly waiting.

James turned.

'It is over, sir, thank God. The ship is ours.'

*

The aftermath. The dead were buried, and Rennie took stock. Of the twenty-two original mutineers – whose wildly optimistic aim had been to take the ship to South America and there begin a new life – fourteen had been killed outright in the battle on deck, four more had been critically wounded, and four had surrendered. With the surgeon dead and many fever cases in the lower deck, Rennie was faced with a dilemma. He was now so desperately short-handed that he could not afford to confine these four remaining mutineers. Should another storm occur, or any of the myriad emergencies common to a long cruise, the safety of the ship must be his paramount concern. He convened a captain's court in the great cabin, and the four men were brought before it under Marine escort.

Rennie presided, his arm in a sling, his dress coat draped at his shoulders.

'Do you wish to remain in irons below, until we reach a place where a court martial may be convened, according to the Articles of War . . . or will you be tried before this court, here and now, today, and accept the findings and rulings of this court, and any punishment decided upon as a result?'

'Captain's court, sir.'

'Ay, now.'

'Ay, this court, sir.'

'Today, sir.'

All four men.

'Very well. Mr Hayter, you will read the charges, if you please.'

'Very good, sir.'

Under number XIX of the Articles of War 1749, the four men were charged with making a mutinous assembly, and by reason of their open admission, duly and immediately found guilty.

Rennie addressed the convicted men:

'Now, then. I cannot hang you, since this ain't a court martial. I am in no doubt that you would be hanged, all of you, was you to have been brought before such a court. Nor can I punish you beyond two dozen lashes, according to the book, since any greater chastisement also requires the sanction of a court martial. However ... I am going to take it upon myself, in the interests of discipline at sea, to sentence you today to four dozen lashes each, punishment to be carried out immediate. You will then resume your duties in the ship, and consider yourselves very fortunate indeed.' A pause, and he looked hard at each man in turn, then: 'Mr Hayter.'

'Sir?'

'All hands to witness punishment.'

'Ay-ay, sir.'

Later, when the punishment had been completed, and each man – his back flayed bloodily to the bone – had been carried below, Rennie summoned Lieutenant Hayter to the great cabin. As James came in, removing his hat, Rennie:

'I expect you think I was lenient?'

'Forty-eight lashes?'

'I could have ordered a hundred each, and been more than justified, by God. But I did not, because I need those men. I need every able-bodied man I can muster, and was therefore obliged to be lenient.'

'Those men cannot now be called able-bodied, sir, surely. Each one cut down in a dead faint?"

'You do not mean I hope that I was too harsh with them?' Staring at him. 'Damned mutinous wretches that fired on us, and wounded us both?' Nodding at James's bandaged arm.

'The men punished never fired a shot, sir. They surrendered.'

'By God, you *do* think I was too harsh!'

'Nay, nay – I don't.' Shaking his head.

'Then what *do* you mean, hey?' Angrily, then wincing at the pain in his shoulder.

'I certainly did not mean to make little of our wounds, sir. We are both of us fortunate to be alive and on our legs.'

'Just so. Well, what else? Speak plain.'

'Well, sir – when a man is flogged severe he can be of little use on watch, laying aloft, nor anywhere on deck, neither. He is crippled.'

'Crippled? What nonsense is this? In a short time his back heals, and he resumes his duty.'

'Yes, well, I . . . I expect you are right, sir.' Politely.

'Damnation to that! I asked you to speak plain! For Christ's sake say what y'mean!'

'Very well, sir.' A breath. 'Our surgeon is dead. The surgeon's mate is hard pressed in the lower deck. He is a good fellow, well-meaning and diligent, but he lacks proper help in the sick berth. He has many fever cases, and now those wounded mutineers, leave alone our own wounds, that must be dressed if they are not to fester. To tax him with four further cases is . . .'

'Is what?'

'Would not it have been more prudent to punish those men when we had reached a place of safety? Now they cannot be of any use on watch, when we are desperate short-handed as it is.'

'Good God, it is only a flogging. They are young and strong, and they will heal.'

'One of them has not come to himself. He still lies unconscious. Dart thinks he may die.'

'Dart?'

'The surgeon's mate, sir. Eloquence Dart.'

'Ah, yes, I had forgot that curious name . . . Well well, never mind. He is talking nonsense, whatever he is called. As are you, James. Womanish nonsense. Those men will heal, and they will resume their duty – or by God they will be flogged again. D'y'hear me?'

'Very good, sir.'

'Cutton! – *Cutton*, damn you!' Wincing again.

'Yes, sir?' Cutton, coming into the cabin.

'Bring me a pint of three water, right quick.'

'As you wish, sir. Shall I bring Dulcie and the kittens to you, or simply Dulcie herself, sir?'

Rennie glared at him a moment, then, softer:

'I had not thought once of my poor cat in four-and-twenty hours. She was horribly alarmed by the fighting, I am in no doubt, and has hid herself away. Has she?'

'She is in the coach, sir, as you will remember. Placed there at your pacific requess, her and the kittens and the cot.'

'She was not frightened?'

'I could not say, sir. As you know, I was took by the mut'neers when I went to the fo'c'sle to smoke, sir, and was held susbequent under their muskets in the lower deck, and I was in a state of very great fright myse—'

'Yes yes, well well.' Over him. 'Bring me my grog. Jump now.'

When the steward had gone, James cleared his throat, and:

'May I return to my own duties, sir?'

'What?' Turning from the window. He had wished to consult with his lieutenant about new watch bills, and many other things consistent with the management of the ship, given their greatly reduced circumstances, and to share with him his feelings of profound sadness and disquiet about the mutiny and all of the foolish men killed, but he was now out of temper, too tired and and in too much pain. 'Oh – yes. Yes, by all means, James. Return to your duties, if y'please.'

'I am your first lieutenant, am I not, sir?'

'Yes *yes*, in course you are.' Looking at him.

'Not – not Pursuit Officer, again?'

'That post is – I am setting it aside. There will be no Pursuit Officer in *Expedient*, in the immediate. I will say so to Mr Loftus. Hm. Hm. Your course is west-sou'west, by a point west.'

'West-sou'west, and a point west, ay-ay, sir.' His hat on.

'Bring me to Boston, without further mishap, and let us hope we may find *Terces* there, and thus be able to report her destination, as ordered.' And when James had left him, he added under his breath: 'Pray God, without further mishap.'

James for his own part was so numbed and bemused by the events of the past few days – in truth by all the events of this most taxing commission: the bitter actions; the long chase; fever; the loss of the pursuit; the mutiny – that he felt able to keep the deck, and his journal, keep up his lists and inspections, and take his meals in the gunroom, only by remaining in a kind of purposeful daze. Rennie had ordered him to bring the ship to Boston, and he would do his best, he would do his duty, and simply leave it at that.

As to the people themselves – those who had survived the fever and the mutiny – they too were numbed and dazed by events, but seamen are stoical beings by nature and calling. What could have been the source of conflict and division among them – the slow return to duty of wounded, flogged and disgraced mutineers – was simply accepted as a necessity in the survival of a short-handed, damaged ship, and the harsh fact of the mutiny receded into near insignificance as the long voyage continued.

*

Three days, and three nights, in returning light wind. On the third night, in the quiet of the middle watch, James paced the deck, deep in his thoughts. He paused and glanced aloft into the moon-bright, moon-shadowed canvas towers. So sharply were the sails and rigging defined, white and black, that he felt for a moment as if he were in a vivid dream, a living magic-lantern show, in which absurd creatures might appear, their painted faces jerking and whirling above him in grotesque pantomime.

He reached out a hand to a stay, and put his other hand to his head. His hat fell to the deck with a muffled sound that was like an ominous thud in his ear. His forehead was filmed with sweat.

'Oh, Christ . . . am I fevered?'

But his brow was not hot, nor even warm. It was cold and clammy. He shivered, and bent down to pick up his hat. Straightened, and drew a deep breath. A slight dizziness, and his head cleared. The moonlight was no longer a threatening brilliance, stark and striped, but merely the soft radiance of a warm night at sea. Another breath, and he felt the sweat drying on his brow. He put on his hat, and again he began to pace. Passed the wheel, and glanced into the binnacle. To the helmsman:

'Steady.'

'Ay, sir. Steady it is.' Half a spoke, and back.

The sighing of the wind. The sucking, slipping wash of the sea. The easeful creaking of timbers, and hawser-laid rope. The smell of tar.

James paced to the tafferel, and looked at the line of the wake. Under his breath, in order that the duty mid half-asleep nearby, or the other members of the watch, should not hear him and think him beginning mad:

> ' "All nature is but art, unknown to thee;
> All chance, direction which thou canst not see;
> All discord, harmony not understood;
> All partial evil, universal good;
> And, spite of pride, in erring reason's spite,
> One truth is clear, whatever is, is right." '

The glistening, washing, eternal sea, broad under the moon.

A figure approached, hesitant on the quiet deck. James peered and saw that it was the surgeon's mate, Eloquence Dart.

He beckoned to him, and:

'Yes, Mr Dart?' Adding the courtesy, since Dart was now acting surgeon.

'I – I had thought to wake the captain, and say something, but then I reflected that he – he may not be in the most welcoming mood, was he to be woke sudden in the middle of the night.'

'What is it?'

'It is a thing of some significance, I believe. Two of the men I had made certain would die tonight have recovered their senses entire. And their fever has broke.'

'Well, they are lucky, that is all.' A shrug.

'Nay, that ain't the whole of it, sir.' A sharp intake of breath, shaking his head.

Four bells, the sound echoing clearly along the deck from the belfry.

'Go on.' James, looking closely at Dart. Was the fellow drunk?

'There have been no further cases these past four-and-twenty hours. Nay . . . eight-and-forty, near enough. Two whole days, and now two men that was near dead are awake, and speaking. I believe . . .' His breath catching in his throat.

'Yes, Mr Dart?' Was he laughing, the fellow? Nay, good heaven – he was in tears.

'I believe – oh, thank God – I believe we shall soon be free of fever in the ship.'

'My dear fellow, you are done up.' Kindly, taking his arm. 'Here, sit down on the flag locker.'

'I'm sorry . . .' Snuffling.

'There is nothing to be sorry for, Mr Dart. You have worked nobly, to the point of exhaustion and beyond, in saving men's lives. Here, now, take a pull.' Producing his flask.

The acting surgeon took the flask gratefully, and sucked down raw spirit. A cough, and he wiped his mouth.

'Thank you, Lieutenant. You are very kind.'

'Take another pull. It will lift you.'

'I am all right, now.' Handing back the flask. 'I have had very little sleep, but I am hale enough.'

'Let me say again, in gratitude, that I know the very taxing work you have undertook, unaided since the surgeon died, binding up the wounded, and caring for all of the fever cases. You have bound up my own wound, after all, and the captain's, and I know he is very grateful also. We are all in your debt, Mr Dart.'

'You are kind.' He tried to say more in response, but again his breath caught in his throat, and he turned his head away and was silent, his narrow shoulders trembling with emotion and exhaustion.

James looked at him, and was aware that he had always found something odd about Eloquence Dart. He had the voice and manners of an educated man, and was clearly intelligent, and yet here he was in the position of surgeon's mate, scarcely above loblolly boy in the naval hierarchy. How had he come to this?

'Is this your first ship, Mr Dart?'

'First ship? No no, it is not, Lieutenant. This is my – my third ship.' A tired frown, then a confirming nod. 'Ay, my third.'

'Could not you have qualified for a full surgeon's warrant by now? You are not without the skills, certainly.'

'Nay, I have not sought advancement.' Shaking his head.

'But good heaven, why not?' And when the acting surgeon made no reply: 'How came you into the navy?' James took a swallow of rum himself, and again held out the flask, but his companion shook his head.

'I – I was a clerk. And I – lost my situation.'

A sudden instinct, and: 'Not by any chance . . . a clerk in holy orders?'

His companion stiffened, shot him a glance, and was prepared to be defensive. Then, relaxing a little:

'You have guessed correctly, Lieutenant.'

'Yes, do not think me prying, you know. I asked because I was nearly a cleric myself, long ago, and know something of the life.'

'You, Lieutenant?' Astonished.

'Ay.' A smile. 'It was a calling I had already decided to abandon by the time I went down from Cambridge. I should have made a terrible curate, and a worse vicar.'

'Perhaps . . . And yet in a way a sea officer's duties are not altogether unlike those of a clergyman, now that I think on it. You must tend to the needs of your flock, Lieutenant, as must he.'

'Nay, I do not think there is any similarity at all, you know. A clergyman attempts to lessen and eradicate the sins of his flock, in the name of God. That is holy orders. My duty is to *give* orders, in the name of the king. A clergyman may fail. A sea officer may not.'

'I failed.' Quietly.

'Oh, I beg your pardon.' James, discomfited. 'I did not mean that as direct criticism of you, Mr Dart. It was a passing observation, that is all, and a damned clumsy one.'

'None the less . . . I did fail.' A sigh.

'What happened ashore long since ain't my business, nor the navy's neither.' Regretting now his searching questions, and adopting a deliberately light, dismissive tone in an effort to deflect the acting surgeon from unburdening himself. 'What is past is past, and best forgot.'

'I am – I am not as other men.'

'Eh?'

'If there is anything I have learned from life it is this: we cannot change what we are, and it is folly to assume the contrary.'

'Nay, you are quite right. A short, uncommon stout man cannot become a tall, uncommon thin one. However, what of it? We make the best of ourselves, and you have clearly done so, Mr Dart. Hey? You have found a new calling at sea.'

'Perhaps I have.'

'There can be no doubt of it.'

'In least I cannot come to further personal disgrace.' A breath, held in, then: 'That was the cause of my dismissal from the parish, you see. Personal disgrace.' He shook his head, and clearly wished to continue with his revelations, but James:

'Well, I must find out the speed of the ship, I fear, and how she lies, and make my notations.' With an exhalation of breath, as if reluctant to break up the conversation. 'Duty calls. I will convey your very welcome intelligence about the fever to the captain, at the change of the watch, Mr Dart. Thank you again, and goodnight to you.' And he went forrard to the binnacle, feeling relief, and calling for the duty mids to attend him.

The acting surgeon, left on his own at the flag lockers, sat quietly for a time and then went below to care for his patients.

At the change of the watch James went below to the great cabin, and found the captain already awake, drinking tea in his nightshirt. He conveyed the acting surgeon's opinion that the outbreak of fever was now on the wane.

'He is certain?'

'I would not say certain entire, but the signs are greatly encouraging.'

'Hm.' A swallow of tea.

'You do not find them encouraging, sir . . . ?'

'What? No.' Distractedly, then: 'Well well, it's simply that I find it very difficult to allow myself to believe that anything at all will go right with this commission. And Dart ain't a surgeon. He is a surgeon's mate, or as we used to call them when I was a mid: "the butcher's apprentice".'

'Your wound is healing, ain't it, sir?'

'What?' Touching his bandage. 'Well well, it ain't stinking of gangrene, in least.'

'He has had an education, you know.'

'Dart? What – brief, sing-song tutoring at some damned dame school, in infancy? That ain't an education.'

'You have not conversed with him, while he dressed your wound?'

'Nay, I have not. What could we discuss, good God?'

'For what it is worth, in my estimation he could pass for surgeon tomorrow, and serve in any ship with distinction. He is very far from the ignorant man you suppose him to be.'

'Well well, if you say—'

'And I for one believe him about the fever.' James, running on. 'My wound heals, as does yours, sir. That is all the proof I need that he knows what he's about. I trust him just as I trusted Thomas Wing. By result.'

'Now then, look here, I never said the fellow was a fool. He – he has done tolerable well since Empson died, but I cannot be guided by his opinion alone. He is only *acting* surgeon.'

'Then will you go into the lower deck yourself, sir?'

'I am not a qualified medical man, neither. I can be of no use to sick men.'

'It would cheer all of the sick-berth men to see their captain, sir. And you could see for yourself the recovering fever cases.'

'What you mean is that I have neglected my duty, hey?'

'Nay, I meant nothing of the kind.'

'I have kept away from the sick berth quite deliberate,

because I did not wish to catch a fever myself. I am the captain of this ship. I must remain hale, and in full possession of my strength and my faculties, if ever we are to reach safety.'

'Yes, sir, and that was sound sense – so long as the fever raged. But now that it is fading and receding, do not you think—'

'No, I do not.' Over him, forcefully. 'We have only the unsupported opinion of the acting surgeon that the danger is past.'

'Yes, sir. No doubt you are right to be cautious. The men must be wholly returned to health before they may be returned to duty. I do see that.'

Rennie drank off his tea, and went into his quarter gallery. Presently he emerged, drying his face with a clean towel.

'Yes, well well, I have considered what you said just now, James.' A sniff, and he dried his neck and ears.

'Yes, sir?'

'Yes, I have. I will make an inspection of the sick berth before breakfast today. I wish to discover if there is men recovered sufficient to be added to the watch bills. In usual I should wait until divisions, but in a matter so important as this I cannot afford to wait even a minute longer than I can help. If what Dart says is true, there may be men ready to resume their duties almost at once.'

'Very good, sir.'

'And then I will like you to eat breakfast here with me.' He threw the towel over the back of a chair, and with renewed energy in his step returned to his sleeping cabin to dress. From the doorway:

'Cutton! More tea! Cheerly, now!'

*

Expedient had altered course and had been sailing due west several days, and now lay at 42 degrees and 17 minutes north, and 55 degrees and 29 minutes west. She was still more than

900 miles east of Boston, and well south of St John's. The nearest point of land by calculation was Sable Island.

Fever had diminished in the ship to the degree that no man had died of it recently, and there had been no further cases at all. And all those that had succumbed but had not died were now recovering well, and some had even returned to duty.

Rennie summoned James again to the great cabin, to dinner.

'We never did have that gunroom dinner, did we, James?' As they sat down.

'Gunroom dinner . . . ? Oh, yes, I recall. No, sir, we did not. Events intervened. In course we should arrange it as soon as you like, and—'

'No no, I was not chiding you. I should have proper dinners here in the great cabin. Officers, middies, a full table, now that there is some semblance of normal life returned to the ship.'

'Yes, thank God, we are nearly free of the fever.'

'Ay, by the time we reach Boston we will be free of it, entirely free, and therefore able to land without quarantine.'

'Yes, sir. I – I have been pondering our arrival.'

'Have ye?' Pouring wine. 'Well?'

'Well, sir – surely we cannot just sail into Boston Harbour and blithely drop anchor? What is our purpose? We have no official business there.'

'No, no official business.' Nodding, pushing the bottle toward James across the table. 'But as we are an independent ship of the Royal Navy, unattached to any fleet, why cannot we pay a friendly visit to a leading American port, and take in provisions, finish all of our repairs, and so forth? After all, England ain't at war with America, and Boston of all American cities is the least likely to resent our arrival.'

'Was not Boston the place where the revolution began?'

'To be strictly accurate it was Lexington, I believe, although I grant you, the notorious "tea party" took place at Boston, ay. But good heaven, all that is far behind us, now. Bostonians like and admire England, now.'

'Sir, if your earlier surmises were correct, as you expressed them to me, and Captain Broadman and his passenger have connections with revolutionary France, then there must probably be powerful elements in Boston society ready to help them in that cause, else why have they come? Did not you say there were people in Boston who hated England with a passion? Surely that cannot be the same as liking and admiring, can it? The two things ain't reconcilable.'

'Fill your glass, James.' Mildly.

'Oh . . . yes. Thank you, sir.' James dutifully filled his glass, but did not immediately drink.

'Yes, you have merely posed the same question I wish to know the answer to myself. You recall, I said we should go ashore and seek out that answer?'

'Yes, sir, I do recall that. And I said – if you recall, sir – that I did not much like the notion of again being a spy ashore in a foreign country. But leaving that aside a moment . . . what if *Terces* ain't there, after all?'

'Well well, let us deal with one question at a time, hey? Until we reach Boston we will assume that *Terces is* there. And if she is, then we will have met our obligation to Mr Mappin, and Their Lordships, by discovering her final destination. We may either send a dispatch by a merchant ship, or return to England ourselves with the intelligence. I favour the former, since as you know I believe our obligation don't end there. We owe it to ourselves to discover more, given the very heavy price we have paid in this commission. That ain't spying, not at all. It is merely searching out the truth.'

'Owe it to ourselves?'

'In course it ain't only ourselves, James. It will be in the nation's interest, in addition, if we can discover more.'

James nodded, drew breath, then said nothing.

'Drink your wine.' Rennie drank from his own glass, with evident pleasure.

James took up his glass and drank it off, in order to dispense with the harsh acid taste all at once, rather than in a series of polite sips. He set the glass down with a hearty thud, and just managed not to wince.

'Ahh . . .' In feigned appreciation.

'Excellent, ain't it?' Rennie refilled his own glass, and again pushed the bottle.

To please him – because he had difficult things to say to the captain, that must be delicately put – James poured a little more of the wine into his glass, and pushed the bottle back. A moment, then:

'Sir, may I speak frankly?'

'By all means.' The bottle. 'I hope that y'will always be candid with me, James, when we talk together like this.'

'Thank you, sir.' Another pause, and:

'We do not know anybody at Boston, we shall be strangers there. If we proceed beyond our orders, if we exceed them as you suggest, sir, do not we run the very great risk of undermining the whole purpose of our commission? Of endangering our ship, and ourselves?'

'Every day at sea in a ship of war is a risk, James, every watch, every glass. We are sea officers, obliged to take such risk and face such dangers as we may find by our warrants of commission.'

Aware that he was being deflected, and warned, James cleared his throat, and nodded. And persisted.

'Yes, in the ordinary run of things at sea, in course that is true, sir. What troubles me is how we may justify taking very great additional risk – ashore.'

Rennie opened his mouth to speak, but James continued before he could.

'Sir, hear me out, I beg you. We have sustained very considerable damage to the ship, as you have acknowledged, leave alone injury and death among the people, fever and mutiny, and near despair. I ask you, in all candour, in view of all these things – have not we done our duty, and suffered enough? Will not Their Lordships look askance at us, weakened as we are, if we seek to interfere in this matter, ashore in a foreign land, where we have no authority to act, and nothing beyond conjecture to act upon?'

'You persist in talking of America as if it was remotest Araby, or Africa. A foreign land?' Raising his eyebrows. 'Our former colonies, with whom we maintain friendly relations in all distinctions – trade, commerce, and so forth?'

'Sir, forgive me, but I must now be very direct.'

Rennie put his head on one side – an ominous quirk of attentiveness James recognised and understood. He persisted.

'In little, I think we should return to England as soon as we are able, whether or no we find *Terces* at Boston.'

'And so we shall. We shall return.' A sniff, and he straightened his head, sat back in his chair and regarded James a long moment. 'When we have found out the truth.'

'I see.' Quietly. 'And if *Terces* is not there, at Boston . . . ?'

'In the unlikely event she ain't – then we will continue to search for her elsewhere, until she is found.' A menacing little grimace of a smile, then: 'Cutton! Bring our first remove, as quick as you like!' And Captain Rennie drank off his wine.

*

Terces was not at Boston.

Expedient arrived on a sunny morning, in light airs, the sea glittering under a high blue sky as the ship passed between Deer Island on the north and Long Island on the south. *Expedient* observed full maritime protocol, followed all the formalities, was visited by the port authorities – including the quarantine officer – in their boat, and cleared, and given permission to enter the inner harbour and drop anchor at a designated mooring number. The port agent, to whom they at once applied, was able to provide Captain Rennie and his officers with the names of appropriate victualling agents, and a shipyard that could supply such *matériel* as they might need, and artificers, should they be required.

While these things were being arranged, and he busied

himself ashore in the port, a message came to Captain Rennie
from a Mr Leyton Hendry. Would he and his officers care to
come to Mr Hendry's house on Oak Street, at Beacon Hill,
for dinner? The message was delivered to Captain Rennie by
a black servant in livery.

'Mr Hendry's carriage will attend you here at the dock, suh,
at five o'clock this evening, if you is willing . . . ?'

'Willing? Yes – yes, indeed. We are most willing, say to him,
with my compliments and thanks.'

Rennie returned to *Expedient* in his launch. Another boat
had been sent from *Expedient* to traverse the harbour, and
venture into the Charles River. There was no sign of *Terces*.
The port agent had known nothing of her, nor had any of the
other men ashore with whom Rennie had dealt during the
course of the day.

'*Terces?* Don't know of any such ship, lately.' Heads shaken.
'She ain't been here to Boston, Cap'n Rennie.'

'There is no trace of her anywhere, sir,' Lieutenant Hayter
greeted Rennie as the captain came up the side ladder into the
ship. 'We have searched very thorough. We even ventured to
speak to the officers of a small armed brig on the Charleston
side. They knew noth—'

'A naval brig, d'y'mean?' Over him.

'No, sir. I was informed by the officers that there is no
American navy now, it was stood down following on the war,
and the ships sold out of the service. What remains is simply
former officers manning armed vessels for merchant protection and the like.'

'Ah. Hm. And they had had no sight of our pursuit?'

'None, sir.'

'Ay, well well, it would appear that either she has not come
here, or . . .'

'Or?'

'Perhaps she may have come under another name, and has
already gone away.'

'You think that likely, sir?'

'I think it is certainly possible, even probable.'

'Well, I expect anything is possible.' His tone neutral.

Rennie looked disapprovingly at James's working rig, made a face, and: 'You must shift out of that abominable piratical disguise and into your dress coat, James, if y'please.' And he told his lieutenant about the invitation to dine at Beacon Hill.

'Is this gentleman known to you, sir? Mr Hendry?'

'Nay, he ain't. But when I have heard "Beacon Hill", which I am told is the finest district of Boston, I knew we could expect a splendid dinner, and I did not hesitate.' Looking at his pocket watch: 'Come, James, y'must shake a leg. We are to be at the dock at five o'clock, in five-and-twenty minutes. Mr Hendry is sending his carriage.'

'Is he, by God?' An appreciative little jerk of the head. 'Very good, sir. I shall make haste, by all means.' Unwinding the blue kerchief from his head, and going aft to the companion.

Ten minutes later both officers were in the boat, in their dress coats and cockaded hats, and wearing their tasselled swords. As they took their seats in the stern sheets and the duty mid called 'Give way together,' James thought but did not say that there must certainly be people in the port who would not look kindly on the blue dress coats, with proud white facings and gilt buttons, of the Royal Navy. Just to the north of the harbour, after all, lay Charlestown, burned to the ground in the late bitter war by British forces, and yet rebuilding.

As they were rowed in toward the wharf, Rennie was silent, apparently lost in his own thoughts, and so James remained silent. Having searched the harbour and found nothing, and and having got only blank looks when *Terces* was mentioned, and negative replies to questions, he was nearly certain – unlike Rennie – that she had never been at Boston. He did not believe she could have come there 'under another name'. Nay, she had never arrived. Unless . . . the idea came to him like a pebble thrown in a pond, sending out wide ripples . . . unless she had indeed come and gone, and the whole port of Boston, collectively, was concealing the fact.

'Ay, perhaps *that* is possible . . .'

'Perhaps what is possible, James?' Rennie, adjusting his scabbard.

'Oh, nothing, sir. I was thinking aloud.'

'About what?'

A scattering of spray from the blade of an oar. James ducked his head.

'About what?' Rennie, persisting.

'I – I was thinking that it's very possible we shall remember this evening a long time. How welcome it will be to eat good food at a steady table, on which the wine don't tilt in the glasses, a table at which – very likely, sir – we shall be seated beside pretty women.'

'Eh?'

'Come now, sir, surely you will not tell me the thought of feminine company had not crossed your mind?'

'Hm-hm, well well.' A smile, a nod. 'I will not deny it, James. I do not forget my dear wife in saying so, you mind me? But to be in the company of the opposite sex again, after long days at sea, lifts any man's spirits, hey?'

'It certainly lifts my spirits, sir.'

'And somefing else, besides.' Murmured forrard, and a suppressed guffaw. Another scattering of spray as oars dipped and lifted.

'Silence, there!' The middy. 'Row dry!'

James kept his face straight, and dismissed all speculative notions about *Terces* for the moment. Tonight he would only endeavour – to enjoy himself.

*

Following on the American Revolution, and the subsequent War of Independence, the merchants and bankers of Boston decided upon a policy of wholesale renewal. Charleston to the north was already being rebuilt, and Mr Harrison Gray Otis's Mount Vernon Company undertook the task of relandscaping and developing the hills of Boston itself, and vast quantities of earth were removed, carted, and used elsewhere along the riverbank. Beacon Hill became the epicentre of refurbishment. Great new houses were designed and built, and plans were laid for a new and imposing State House. The leading young architect among the several that tendered for the work was Mr Charles Bulfinch, whose practice quickly became the most favoured in the city. He secured the contract for the State House, proposing a magnificent golden dome, and designed many of the larger private houses. His chief rival was another coming man, Mr Napier Templeton. Mr Leyton Hendry had engaged Templeton to design and build his new house on Oak Street, with a view over the river. The house was newly completed, and Mr Hendry was eager to establish it as a place of social significance.

Oak House was built in the high Georgian manner, of brick, with a steep mansard roof, tall windows, tall chimneys, and a grand stone architrave above the columns of the entrance. To the rear was a spreading walled garden, with newlaid lawns, dozens of newly planted trees and one enormous old oak tree that had survived the relandscaping and given the house its name.

Mr Hendry had made his fortune in shipping. He was thus of a mind – when he learned of *Expedient*'s arrival – to honour the sea officers of a nation with whom he now had no quarrel, a nation with whose merchants he conducted the greater part of his very profitable business. He had enquired among his official acquaintance in the port, learned the names of those officers, and sent his invitation. He was a tall man, grey-haired, with the strong features and black brows that in another man might have been forbidding. His clothes were beautifully cut. He had assembled a large party to honour *Expedient*, and greeted Rennie with affable formality, and:

'But my dear Captain Rennie, sir, are there but two of you? I meant that all of your officers should come to my house.'

'That is kind in you, Mr Hendry, most generous kind, but

a ship must be governed, you know, even when she lies in harbour, and some of my officers have that duty tonight.'

'Are you hurt, Captain Rennie?' Mr Hendry, anxiously, noting Rennie's slight wince as they shook hands, and a stiffness in his shoulders, the result of his wound during the mutiny, now bandaged under his coat.

'It is nothing, nothing – a slight mishap at sea.' Rennie made himself smile, and: 'May I introduce Lieutenant James Hayter, RN, my first officer?'

'Lieutenant.' An exchange of bows, and Mr Hendry noticed the scar on James's cheek, but said nothing. 'Welcome to Oak House, sir. Please think of it as your home while you are here, both of you.' Including Rennie.

'You are very kind, sir.'

'All of your officers, in fact. Oak House is open house to HMS *Expedient*.'

A great many introductions, and quantities of Sillery and Madeira. The party was largely made up of other merchants and their wives, but when Rennie enquired after Mr Hendry's wife he learned that his host was a widower.

James had already noticed an exceptionally pretty, dark-haired young woman in a very becoming blue dress among the throng, who did not appear to be attached to any of the younger men present. He contrived to find himself in conversation with her, and having not caught her name during the general introductions discovered that she was their host's niece, Miss Constance Amelia Dunne, of Lexington.

'And which do you prefer, Miss Dunne?'

'Prefer, Lieutenant?'

'Of your two Christian names – Constance, or Amelia?'

'Oh. The first.' A glance, then averting her gaze. A slight flushing of her cheeks as she felt his eyes on her.

'I agree. Constance is by far the prettier name.'

'What is your own Christian name?' She caught sight of the scar on his face as he turned his head in the candlelight, and: 'Ohh, you have been hurt!'

'What? Oh, no, that is – it is a little scorch.' Touching his face. 'I was clumsy with a lantern, in heavy weather.'

'I hope it is not painful?'

'Not at all, I had forgot all about it. And to answer your question, I have two names – James Rondo. Like you I prefer the first.'

'James.' She turned to him, and once again averted her gaze, since James's own eyes were still very directly upon her.

James contrived to take her into dinner, and was gratified to see that she had been seated on his right at table. Miss Dunne by contrast was clearly disconcerted.

'Oh, but I had made sure that I was to be seated between Mr Ingleby and Mr Prior. I made my uncle promise.' Frowning, looking up and down the table.

'They are particular friends?'

'Oh, I have known them both a very long time. I wished particularly to ask Mr Ingleby's advice on a matter, and to gain Mr Prior's support.'

'Perhaps I can help.' Gallantly.

'Oh, no. You could not.'

'Ah.' James felt himself unaccountably disappointed and discommoded by this blunt response. As they sat down the soft candleglow, and the sparkle of silver and crystal along the table in that glow, were suddenly less welcoming. He tried again.

'Will it wait until after dinner?'

'Wait?' Miss Dunne turned her face toward James as a liveried servant poured wine.

'The matter on which you seek advice?'

'Oh, yes. I wish to buy a riding pony, that is all.' Lightly. 'Yes, it will wait.'

'I am glad.' He smiled at her, and she returned the smile, then her smile faltered and again she averted her gaze. Quietly, under the bursts of conversation beginning along the table:

'Please, Lieutenant. You stare at me so. I wish you would not.'

'Was I staring? I am very sorry.' Making no effort to desist.

And when she glanced quickly at him again he continued to regard her unabashed. He saw her blush, and at last he looked away and took up his glass. Then: 'I cannot help it.' Quietly.

'Well, you must not, all the same.'

'You are the loveliest girl I have ever seen in America.'

'But you have only just arrived!' Blushing deeper. 'How can you be so discriminating when you have never met any other American girls?'

'None of them could compare to you, Miss Dunne.'

'Lieutenant, you are very disgraceful. And now I command you to be quiet, so that I may be comfortable.'

'Then I will be quiet – for the moment.'

Presently Miss Dunne was engaged in conversation by her other neighbour, and James by his, and the flirtation was thus postponed – but not forgotten.

Captain Rennie was seated at the high end of the table near his host, and was engaged in lively conversation there, drinking deep, and all the cares of the commission falling from his shoulders. The lady on his right in her low-cut gown was very handsome. Her name was Mrs Quincy Burrell, and she had put him at his ease at once, smiling and drawing him out. He allowed himself to be drawn out – to a point. Beyond that point he became inventive.

'And this is your first visit to Boston, Captain Rennie?'

'Indeed it is, madam. And I am duly impressed. A very fine city.'

'What has brought you to us, Captain Rennie? Are you here on official business?'

'Nay, Mrs Burrell. We are here by a happy accident, merely calling in, you know, to pay our respects, among other things.'

'Surely you cannot have come all the way from England by accident?' Another smile.

'Well well, you are quite right. The truth is very mundane, I fear. It is charts.'

'Charts?'

'We are an island race, and we depend on the sea for our living. From time to time it pleases Their Lordships – out of necessity – to send single ships on long cruises such as ours, to make and provide accurate charts for our fleets.'

'Surely there are accurate charts of Boston, are not there?'

'Certainly, madam, but we had weathered a fierce storm at sea, and was in need of repair, and since Boston was the nearest port convenient to our duty, we came here. We also required victuals, water, wood, and the like. And – happily – it has led to this very splendid occasion.'

Mrs Burrell looked approvingly round the table, as if she herself had arranged the dinner, then:

'I hear you wish to find a ship named *Terces*, Captain Rennie.'

Rennie glanced at her sharply, then as sharply recovered his composure.

'I have enquired about *Terces* in the port, ay.' A nod. 'We spoke in the Atlantic, you know, and she was headed to Boston. When we came in I thought to find her here.'

'My husband has never heard of the *Terces*, among the many ships that come and go. He is a merchant in the town,' she added.

'Well well, I know *Terces* very little myself – except for that chance encounter at sea. I made some few enquiries in the port, and then had forgotten all about her until this moment, madam.'

A servant came discreetly into the room, looked for Captain Rennie and saw him. After a moment he came round the head of the table behind Mr Hendry's chair, moved to Rennie's place, and bent to his ear:

'A gen'man outside has axed me to give you this message, suh.' He handed Rennie a folded note, and slipped away before Rennie could ask him who the gentleman was.

Rennie unfolded the note, and read:

*Using all discretion, meet me in the garden
at the rear of the house, by the great oak, in
five minutes.*
                 A friend

'A friend?' Only half under his breath, bemused.

'Not bad news from your ship, I hope?' Mrs Burrell.

'Eh? Oh – no no.' Tucking the note away in his coat. Mrs Burrell was being overly inquisitive. He must be on his guard, now. He must discover what was afoot. 'How am I to slip away discreet, that is the question.' Not aloud. He waited four minutes, politely conversing with Mrs Burrell, but scarcely noticing what she said, then drank off his glass, shifted a little in his seat, sniffed in a breath and:

'You must excuse me, madam. Wine lifts the heart, but it has another effect.'

This naval directness had the desired consequence of disconcerting Mrs Burrell, and deflecting her curiosity. Rennie rose from his place, tried to catch Lieutenant Hayter's eye further down the table and failed, caught the eye of the servant waiting quietly by the door, and left the dining room. The servant guided him to the rear of the house, and opened a door that gave on to the twilight of the garden. Rennie saw the great oak at once, and went quickly there by the stone path.

'Are you there . . . ?' Careful to keep his voice low.

Silence.

Rennie ventured closer, and stood right beside the thick, furrowed trunk, under the spreading branches. The smell of slightly moist earth.

'Is anybody there . . . ?' Again quietly.

Silence.

Rennie now went round behind the tree, peered in the fading light – and found nothing.

A tap on his shoulder, and he whirled, clutching in reflex for his sword – and remembered he had taken it off when he came into the house. There was nobody there, and now

Rennie saw that a low branch had brushed his shoulder, not a human hand. Thoroughly disconcerted now, and in rising anger, effortfully controlling his voice:

'Now then, if you are here, reveal y'self right quick! I am in no mood for hide-and-seek!'

Silence, except for a sudden flurry of wings as a small bird escaped in alarm above him, and flitted away across the garden. Rennie sniffed in a sharp impatient breath, turned back toward the house – and Brough Mappin was standing on the path.

'Captain Rennie.' His voice low but clear. 'Thank you for coming out to me.' As always his appearance was flawless, from his combed hair to his buckled shoes, but tonight he wore not his customary immaculate grey, but black.

'Good God. Good God.' Utterly astonished. 'How in the name of Christ have you appeared in Boston, Mr Mappin?' Allowing his voice to rise for the first time. 'And how did y'find me at this house? Hey?'

Mr Mappin raised a finger to his lips, glancing toward the house. 'Pray speak soft. I have bribed the servant to say nothing, but his loyalties do not lie with me. We must be quiet, and quick. I have much to tell you in a very short time, and then you must return to your dinner, else be missed.' Coming forward as he spoke, taking Rennie's arm with another glance toward the house, and guiding him deeper into the garden.

At table Lieutenant Hayter had resumed his flirtation with Miss Dunne, and was wholly absorbed in this delight when Captain Rennie returned. Again Rennie tried to catch James's eye, and again failed.

'We had almost given you up, Captain Rennie,' said Mrs Burrell.

'I must apologise, madam, and . . .' turning to his host '. . . to you, sir.' Briefly resuming his seat. 'But I fear that I must go away at once to the wharf, and return to my ship.'

'Return to your ship?' Mr Hendry, dismayed. 'But the night

is young. I had hoped you and the lieutenant would dance, later, and—'

'Dance?' Rennie, over him.

'Why, yes. I have engaged musicians, and—'

'You are very kind, sir, most generous kind, but a difficulty has arose that requires my immediate attention, and I want Lieutenant Hayter with me.' Glancing down the table toward James.

'The difficulty is with your ship?'

A little sigh, and again getting to his feet. 'It is a question of men riotous in drink, fighting and rebellious, that must be dealt with immediate. I cannot say anything more at present, forgive me. I should be very much obliged to you, Mr Hendry, if you will allow us your carriage to take us to the wharf.'

'Why, yes, certainly.' He called a servant, gave instructions, and presently Captain Rennie – and a very reluctant Lieutenant Hayter – departed Oak House, to the consternation of their host, and the general disappointment of his other guests, not least Miss Dunne.

In the carriage, as they proceeded in darkness down to the wharf, James:

'I rather think Mr Hendry had expected us to sleep at his house, sir.' Settling back into his seat with a sigh, and adjusting his scabbard. 'With respect, could not this drunken fighting – or whatever it was – could not it have been dealt with on the morr—'

'There has been no drunken fighting.' Over him. 'Mappin is here.'

'What!'

'Ay, Mappin.' And briefly he explained the circumstances of his meeting with Mr Mappin in the garden, then continued:

'He heard of the fierce action at the fjord in Norway, and thought *Expedient* was lost. He then took ship for Boston himself, thinking to discover *Terces* here, and her passenger.'

'Olaf Christian den Norske.' All irritation with his captain gone.

'Just so. And in course when he came to Boston *Terces* was not here – as we ourselves discovered. However, he made further enquiries, and learned that a ship similar to *Terces* in every particular – exactly similar – had briefly visited. People could not remember very much more about her, except that she dropped anchor in the harbour one day, and was gone two days after. This ship was called *Mermaid*. Her master – Captain White. She neither unloaded any cargo, nor took any in. She put a passenger ashore. Mappin is certain Captain White was Broadman, and his passenger den Norske.'

'What is Mappin's interest in Mr den Norske, sir? Did he describe it to you? Why have we been obliged to pursue this man clear across the Atlantic? How—'

Rennie held up a hand, and:

'I know you have a great many questions, James – as had I, indeed. Let me proceed, and all will become clear.'

'I beg your pardon, sir.'

But before Rennie could continue the carriage turned down into the area of the wharf, the wheels rattling over the cobblestones. The two sea officers descended, lifting their swords clear of the fold-down step.

'I will tell you all of the rest when we are in the boat, James. Then as soon as we are aboard ship we must make our plans.'

'Plans . . .?' As they crossed the wharf to the stone steps under the light of a single high lamp.

'Ay, Mappin wishes us . . . Good God, where is the boat?'

They stared down the steps. Lapping black water glistened uneasily in the near darkness. The iron mooring ring lay free of rope.

'Did you instruct Huff to wait, sir?'

'In course I did! You heard me do so, when we came ashore. Christ's blood, where is he, the villain!'

'Evidently the coxswain mistook your meaning, sir.'

They searched along the length of the wharf, but *Expedient*'s boat was not there. Several other boats lay tethered at the northern end.

'We will borrow a boat,' decided Rennie, descending the steps.

'Who is to row us, sir?'

'Good God, James, we are not merely sea officers, we are right seamen, ain't we, that have not forgot how to ship an oar?'

'In course you are right, sir. I will row, while you steer.'

'Damnation to that. We will both row.'

And they went down the steps together and into the smallest of the three boats tethered there. Presently they cast off, and began rowing out into the harbour.

'Handsomely, now . . . hhh . . . handsomely, James . . . hhh . . . let us row dry.'

'Ay-ay, sir.'

To conserve his breath and his energy Rennie did not speak again until they came to *Expedient* half a glass after, and James did not press him. They found the missing launch tethered to a stunsail boom, secured their borrowed boat, and came up the side ladder into the ship. James was all for admonishing the coxswain and boat's crew for disobeying orders and returning to the ship, but Rennie:

'Nay, that will keep until morning. I must tell you everything that Mappin has told to me, and then we can decide upon a stratagem.'

'Very good, sir.'

In the great cabin, over fresh-brewed tea, Rennie repeated everything Mr Mappin had revealed to him.

'According to his intelligence, Olaf Christian den Norske is a designer of guns. Perhaps the most gifted and far-seeing in a generation. Reputedly – nay, certainly – he has drawn up the plans for an entirely new kind of cannon, that can be used either in ships as a great gun, or ashore as a field weapon.'

'Ah . . . well.' James, a nod and a brief grimace.

'You know this?' A puzzled frown.

'No, sir, no. It's simply that we were obliged to take just

such a new gun into *Expedient* our first commission, sir – with calamitous consequence.'

'Yes, the Waterfield pattern, that proved a failure, and cost lives. I do not think this new gun can be compared to anything that has gone before, James. According to Mappin it will change the nature of warfare.'

'Ah.'

'You are sceptical, I see. I was myself, until Mappin revealed a detail or two.'

'If den Norske is indeed here, sir, then presumably he intends to interest the Americans in this gun?'

'One American. George Wynn Holbourne, a man who made his fortune trading with the French before and during the War of Independence. He owns a large merchant fleet, with which he imported great quantities of munitions and other *matériel* during the war, and men – mercenary soldiers. He resides on Chestnut Street, in the same district as Mr Hendry.'

'Is Mr Hendry associated with him?'

'Nay, Mappin thinks not. Hendry is quite genuine in his fondness for England. Holbourne's mother was French, and he has deep and lasting connections with France, above the purely commercial. He means, in little, to support her in the coming war. To this end he wishes to purchase den Norske's design, and manufacture the gun at his own foundry, here in the United States.'

'But surely, sir – surely if den Norske wished to aid the French with his design, he would already be in France, would not he?'

'Nay, James. According to Mappin, Mr den Norske believes that his gun should and will be used purely for American defence.'

'He has no wish to aid the French?'

'None. He could raise no interest in his design at home in Norway, nor Denmark. Then Holbourne offered him the opportunity to see his design realised here.'

'Where is the foundry? At Boston?'

'At Lexington.'

'Lexington? That is where—' He broke off.

'Eh?'

'No, nothing. I did not mean to interrupt.'

Rennie glanced at him, then continued: 'As you may imagine, I asked Mappin pretty forceful why we was told nothing of this before we weighed at the Nore, but was instructed merely to pursue, and make a report of where *Terces* went.'

'And . . .'

'He would only say that he was not then in possession of sufficient intelligence, that he had heard rumours, and had suspicion, but no more. The important thing now, he believes – and I agree with him, James – is that he should get hold of den Norske's design before Holbourne does.'

'Oh, but surely Holbourne has the design in his hands already, sir, if den Norske is here?'

'Mappin's information is to the contrary. Mr den Norske is in hiding, and has evidently made some very particular conditions that he expects Holbourne to meet, before he will relinquish the design.'

'D'y'mean – he has doubts about Holbourne's motives?'

'Ay, Mappin thinks that after the action at the fjord, and *Terces*' escape, den Norske became deeply distrustful of Captain Broadman's motives, and Holbourne's, and reluctant to proceed with the arrangement, and thus when *Terces* came to Boston he straightway fled ashore and hid, and Broadman departed in *Terces*, having fulfilled his part of the bargain to bring den Norske to America. Negotiations continue between den Norske and Holbourne, but den Norske is very far from satisfied. Mappin is having Holbourne's house watched.'

'How has Mappin come into possession of all this intelligence, when he has been here so short a time?'

'We may not think very high of Mappin, James, but this is his profession, and he is a very resourceful fellow.'

'By "resourceful" you mean money, sir, do y'not? Large sums of money?'

'I do. A great part of that money will be offered to den Norske, as soon as Mappin can discover where he is hid, and go to him.'

'What is our place in this, sir? What role are we expected to fill?'

'We are to transport Mr den Norske, and his design, to England, as soon as Mappin can arrange it. Mappin will come with us.'

'And . . . that is all? We are to lie idly here at our mooring until Mappin brings den Norske aboard?'

'Ay, James. That is Mappin's scheme.'

'I see. But you said that we must have a stratagem of our own, sir, did not you?'

'I did.' A grim half-smile, and a nod. James waited as Rennie refilled his cup, drank it off, set it down with a sniff, and:

'Now then. We—'

The muffled bumping of a boat against the side of the ship.

'What's this . . . ?' Rennie rose from his chair, and reached for his sword. 'Sentry!'

'Sir?' The startled sentry on duty at the great cabin door.

'Alert Mr Harcher! An attempt is being made to cut us out!'

Rennie and James jumped up on deck, swords drawn, and saw that Lieutenant Tindall, who had the deck, and the two duty mids – had noticed nothing.

'Mr Tindall!' Rennie, running aft to the tafferel. James ran there with him, and they both peered over the counter, and at once saw a small boat, occupied by two men, being rowed rapidly away into the glancing darkness of the harbour. Lieutenant Tindall joined Rennie and James at the rail, and peered in dismayed surprise at the retreating boat.

'Ahoy there, the boat!' bellowed James. 'Who are you!'

There was no response, and the boat was soon lost in the gloom. The clatter of feet and the rattle of weapons as Lieutenant Harcher, his sergeant and their Marines came running on deck, shrugging into their coats and carrying their muskets.

'A false alarm, Mr Harcher. Y'may stand down.' Rennie strode forrard from the tafferel. 'A boatman that had lost his way, nothing more.'

'Very good, sir.' Mr Harcher put his hand to his hat, found it was not there, and was briefly embarrassed.

'Mr Tindall!' Rennie, at the companionway ladder.

'Sir?' Lieutenant Tindall, again attending him.

'You will write a full account of what has occurred tonight, and bring it to me at the change of the watch.'

'Full account, sir . . . ?'

'An account, accurate in every distinction, as to why you, and by God the anchor watch entire, failed to notice the approaching boat.'

'I – I . . . very good, sir.' His hat off and on.

'Further, y'will be doubly vigilant hereafter. Do you apprehend me?'

'Yes, sir.' Clearing his throat.

'Are ye suffering from a cold, Mr Tindall?'

'No, sir.'

'Then kindly do not cough in my face when I am addressing you. Return to your duty.'

Rennie and James went below to the great cabin.

'What did they want, I wonder?' Rennie, laying aside his sword.

'You do not believe, then, that they had merely lost their way?' James.

'In their own harbour? Nay, I do not.' Firmly.

'Perhaps, instead, they came looking for the boat we borrowed, sir – don't you think so?'

'By God . . .' a chuckle '. . . can you be right, James? We took a boat, they thought we had stole it, and came to find it.' A pause, a sniff, then: 'But why did not they reply when we hailed them? Why did they flee into the darkness, if they had a perfectly legitimate reason to come to us? Nay, on second thought, those men did not come looking for a missing boat, James. They had another motive.'

'They could not have come to attack us, when they were only two.'

'I think Mr Holbourne has sent them, or associates of Holbourne.'

'But would Holbourne be interested in *Expedient*, sir? He could not link us to den Norske, when we have had no contact with him here.'

'Holbourne may have heard of our enquiries about the *Terces*. If he has even an inkling of a plot to deprive him of den Norske's design, it is very likely he has arranged to have us spied upon.' Before James could interrupt: 'Any British ship of war, coming out of the blue to Boston, will arouse Holbourne's suspicions, because of his hatred of England and his love of France.'

'D'y'think he has discovered that his own house is watched?'

'I am in no doubt Mappin has enjoined his men to go very careful, but nothing is certain in an affair of this kind.' A moment, a sniffing breath, and:

'By the by, James, who was that young woman you engaged in such close conversation at dinner?'

'Young woman?' Innocently. 'Oh – d'y'mean Miss Dunne? She is Mr Hendry's niece, sir. I thought it good manners to draw her out, you know, since her uncle had gone to such trouble to be kind to *Expedient*.'

'Hm. Hm. And is her home, by any chance, at Lexington?'

'Lexington . . . ?' A thoughtful frown. 'Yes . . . yes, I think she did say—'

Over him: 'Think? Come, James, you blurted out "Lexington!" when I mentioned that Mr Holbourne's foundry was located there.' Another sniff. 'Ye'd better have no further dealings with Miss Dunne.'

'No further . . . but good heaven, why not?'

'She may be a spy for Holbourne at Lexington, and elsewhere.'

'With respect, sir, I think that is just wholly absurd. You said yourself that Mr Hendry was a good friend to England. Why should not his niece fall under the same distinction, exact?'

'Well well, I noticed you was becoming infatuated with her, James. This ready inclination in you has led to very grave consequence in the past, therefore y'must be protected from yourself. I forbid you to see Miss Dunne again while we are engaged in this vital matter.'

'*Forbid* . . . ?'

'That is the word. It is my instruction to you, and my wish.'

'Sir, again with respect, I think you have clearly mistook a harmless conversation at dinner for something else entire, and that—'

'I have mistook nothing. Declare to me now that was you to go below to your cabin and there discover Miss Dunne naked in your hanging cot – you would turn her out of it, and out of the ship. Well? Would you?'

James had gone pale with anger.

'Sir, I really do not think I will countenance such an attack on my honour, nor upon the lady's, neither. What you have just said to me is a damned insult.'

'Be quiet, sir.' Curtly.

'Nay by God, I will not, unless you offer me an apology.'

'Apology! What fucking dishwater is this, when I am trying to save you from utter wretched foolishness, that could put us all in mortal danger!'

'You have accused Miss Dunne of being an harlot and a spy, merely because I behaved gentlemanlike to her. In other circumstances that would be tantamount to an outright challenge. I therefore demand—'

'James, James . . .' Rennie held up a hand '. . . before you overreach y'self, and say something y'will only regret, I have no wish to quarrel with you. We must stand together as *Expedient*s, and think of our duty. Our duty is to aid Mr Mappin in taking den Norske and his design out of Holbourne's reach, and away to England.

You agree?'

James was furiously silent.

'You agree?' Insistently, raising his eyebrows and looking at James very direct.

At last, James: 'I agree.' Averting his gaze as he said it.

'Very good.' A nod. 'Thankee, James.'

Rennie now noticed a sheet of paper lying on his desk, and took it up. Presently, half to himself: 'Ah. Yes. The doctor's amended list of men that are restored and fit for duty.' He put the list down, took up a quill and added something to the bottom, then: 'By the by, James . . .' Laying down the pen.

'Sir?'

'I had forgot it until now. Mappin brought some welcome incidental news from England. Thomas Wing has made a full recovery, and is presently assisting Dr Stroud at the Haslar.'

'That is excellent news indeed, sir.' Bending a little.

'Ay. Wing is better off where he is, I think.'

'You would not want him back?' Puzzled.

'I would not wish anybody with us this cursed commission that was not obliged to be.' Quietly. 'I fear the worst of it is ahead of us.'

'Do you wish me to remain, sir?'

'Eh?' A frown.

'You wished to discuss our own stratagem . . . ?'

'Oh, yes. Yes, I did, and we was interrupted. I will like something stronger than tea while we talk. Cutton! Colley Cutton!'

His steward did not respond, and Rennie found a bottle of Madeira and glasses in his pantry, and brought them to the table. James joined him there, and the two sea officers, restored for the moment to amity, fell to earnest conference over their wine.

*

'Mappin wishes us to remain aboard *Expedient*, ready to weigh and depart the moment he comes to us with den Norske. He wishes us to stay aloof from the town and its society. I do not think that will answer, James. We must play a more active part in this, and we can circumvent Mappin's instruction easily enough. Because of our continuing repair, one or both of us must go ashore frequent to see about timber, rope, nails, and the like – copper, even. And we need not remain always in the confines of the wharves. We can move about the town.'

'Yes, sir, during the hours of daylight. And we may very probably receive other invitations to dine, which we could not in all conscience ignore – could we?'

'Well well, possibly. I cannot imagine that Mr Hendry is overly pleased with me, when I have broke up his carefully arranged dinner. Perhaps he will convey his displeasure to others in Boston, that was thinking of playing host to us, and dissuade them.'

'That was not my impression of Boston society, sir.'

'Was it not? Was it not?' A nod, a little grimace. 'What was your impression?'

'Very welcoming, I should have said, sir. Eager to please, with open arms, and open hearts.'

'You are thinking of one young woman in particular, I am in no doubt, as illustration of your case?'

'It was my sense of the gathering as a whole, sir.' James, carefully neutral and polite.

'Was it? Very good.' A breath, a pull of wine, and: 'The reason we cannot simply stay aboard *Expedient* all the time and wait, James, is that I do not believe Mappin has told me the whole truth, even now.'

'D'y'mean – about den Norske, or Holbourne?'

'About the whole damned business, James. From the moment we began the pursuit of *Terces*, and Broadman first turned on us and fired without warning – I have been ill at ease.'

'Well, yes, indeed. A discreet pursuit became hot action, bloody action, we lost a great many of our people, and—'

'Nay, James, I have never shirked an action at sea, and nor have you. Great guns and blood are a sea officer's lot, and we have snuffed burning wad since we was mids with voices yet unbroke, and our dirks shining new. Nay, action don't make me ill at ease. It is what lies behind. Olaf Christian den Norske is here in Boston, ay. But is he here in truth to offer this new gun to America, and to negotiate favourable terms for its manufacture here? Or does he know very well that Holbourne – just so soon as he casts the first example of the gun – will offer it to France?'

'In effect then, den Norske is helping France? But he is a Norwegian. Why should he wish France to have his gun before Norway, or her masters in Denmark?'

'Don't forget that Norway spurned his design, as did Denmark. Perhaps he then offered it in Sweden, and was again turned away.'

'Yes, but why? If this gun is so wonderful, miraculous effective, why did they reject it?'

'You may have hit on the reason. Perhaps it is so radical in concept, defying all conventional notions of ordnance, that the qualities den Norske claims for it are – in the conventional wisdom – mere fantasy. I say perhaps.'

'Yes, but—'

'Pray let me finish, James. It is pure speculation, I grant you, but I believe agents of Holbourne – who has wide mercantile interests in Europe through his fleets – or agents of France, heard of this design for a new gun, and alerted den Norske to the possibility of its manufacture in America.'

'Ain't it likely, sir, if what you say is true, that the French would already have made an offer for this gun, if they believed in it?'

'No, no, no.' Rennie held up a hand, breathing through his nose, his eyes closed. 'Y'see, James, I do not think Mr Olaf Christian den Norske is altogether the mild, polite, diffident-seeming young fellow you described to me, after one brief meeting aboard *Terces*. I believe on the contrary that he is a most ruthless, determined and ambitious fellow, with two things in his head. He means to see his gun realized, and he means to make his fortune. In this he is neither Norwegian, nor Danish, nor French in his sympathies, nor American. He does not care a fig for any of them. His colours are those of one Olaf Christian den Norske. Another possibility occurs to me, James.' Holding up a finger. 'Supposing the ships that was apparently protecting *Terces* in the fjord had other notions. What if they was merely trying to prevent den Norske and his design from escaping Norwegian waters? What if he had, after all, engendered strong interest in his gun in Denmark – but had not received a handsome enough offer? Hm? What if he and Broadman, in the fleet-footed *Terces*, was obliged to outrun those ships when *Terces* had eluded us in the action? Hey?' Nodding, warming to his theme. 'And accordingly, what if he has shown a full and complete set of these plans to nobody as yet? Has merely *described* his idea? He will vouchsafe the full design for his gun only to whomsoever will give him what he wants, entire, in gold. And for the moment – with reservations – he believes Holbourne offers him his best opportunity. Ay, that is the most plausible explication.'

James had listened attentively, but now he could not conceal the depth of his doubts.

'Well, sir . . . I will not like to argue with you, but as you yourself have said . . . most of what you suggest is pure speculation.'

'That don't mean it ain't true, though.'

'No . . . perhaps it don't . . . but I do not see, neither, why Mappin has done most of the things he has done, in quite the *way* that he has, sir. It is—'

Over him: 'Good God, James, we may never know everything to an exactitude. That is always so with men like Mappin. And it is why, in this instance certainly, we cannot leave things to Mappin alone. His mind is a maze. It is a tangle of concealment, trumpery and dark make-believe, and will likely lead, therefore, to a confusion of action. I do not care for all this talk of "negotiation", and houses watched in the dark, and waiting, and so forth. Mr den Norske must be found and seized, and his plans seized. He must be brought to *Expedient* by force, and took to England a prisoner, right quick.'

'Take this man in a foreign city, and carry him bound and gagged into the ship? *Kidnap* him? When he ain't an enemy of England, nor of America neither?'

'Pish pish, James. In course he is an enemy, if he has designed a gun that could be turned on Englishmen in the coming war. Far better that we should make the gun ourselves, and turn it on the French, hey?'

'Well, yes, I expect so . . . but ain't that what Mr Mappin is trying to achieve, sir? By more circumspect means?'

'Damnation to circumspect. Has Mappin found den Norske? Nay, he has not. Has he got the design of the gun in his hand? Nay, he has not. Will Mr Holbourne have it in *his* hand, if we do not act? He will, by God.'

'Very good, sir. Erm . . . how do you propose to act?'

'We will create a diversion, James. A diversion on a grand scale.'

*

Rennie studied the list before him on the table, and ran the undipped quill of his new pen down the numbered items. Murmuring:

'Two dozen large rockets, red. Two dozen bombs. Six small fire-rafts. Six buckets of oakum and tar. One dozen smoke-balls. Red cartridge for two blank broadsides of guns. Hm. Hm.' Shaking his head. 'Two dozen smoke-balls.'

He dipped the quill in ink, altered that item, drew a line under the last, and initialled the list. A scattering of chalk powder from the pouncebox. A sniff, and he looked up at the waiting gunner, and handed him the list.

'Well well, Mr Storey, can you do it?'

Glancing at the list: 'Oh, I can do it, sir. Only it will take me all of four-and-twenty hours.'

'Very good. Then everything will be in readiness by tomorrow nightfall, without fail. Yes?'

'Is that an whole day and night, sir?' As he spoke eight bells sounded on the fo'c'sle. 'Midnight, sir. Asking your pardon, but that don't give me—'

'It gives you no time to lose, Mr Storey, just so.' Over him, and a quick little grimace and a nod.

The gunner saw that he was dismissed, suppressed a shrug, put the list away in his coat, and left the great cabin. Rennie stood up, paced to the stern-gallery window, paced back, and:

'Sentry!'

The Marine sentry on duty attended him. 'Sir?'

'Pass the word that I will like to see all officers here in my cabin, in . . .' His pocket watch. '. . . five minutes.'

'Five minutes from now, sir? Tonight?'

'With my compliments.'

'Ay-ay, sir.' Making his back straight, and departing.

'Cutton!'

No response.

'Colley Cutton, wake up, you idle wretch! I required you to remain on duty until I wanted you, tonight! Rouse y'self right quick, and attend me!'

His bleary steward, hair on end and shirt crumpled, emerged from the coach.

'I fell asleep, sir, askin' your pardon. I has been so attentive to Dulcie and her brood, sir, that I was—'

'Bottle of Madeira, and decant it.' Curtly. 'And bring glasses.'

'Now, sir?' Peering at him.

'Ay, *now*! Christ's blood, must I repeat every instruction I give in the ship?'

'As you wish.'

*

The stern lights of moored ships rode in reflection on the oily blackness of the harbour. Two brigs lay moored alongside the wharf immediately to the north, separated by a gap of perhaps half a cable from the wharf which *Expedient*'s boat now approached.

Lieutenant James Hayter, dressed in his working rig, ran lightly up the stone steps and looked along this wider, deserted wharf. They had come ashore at the northern end, out of the glow of the single lamp halfway down. A moment of lapping calm as he stood there. A waft of cool wind across the open water. He felt it on his face, and sniffed in a long breath. Glanced down the steps, saw that the boat's painter was being secured to the iron ring, and gave a low whistle. His party of men came up the steps, and followed James across the open space into the deep shadows by the wall of the dockside building.

Keeping his voice low, James: 'Huff . . . Thomas . . . Hill . . . Enderby . . . Cole . . . Lacey . . . ?'

Each man answered in turn.

'Remember, keep your pistols and knives concealed, lads. We are merely members of the gaping crowd that will come flocking here when the fun commences.'

'May we smoke, sir?' Clinton Huff, the coxswain.

'Nay, better not. We must keep ourselves wholly concealed until the moment comes. There may be a watchman about, and even a whiff of tobacco could give us away.'

'How long must we wait, sir?'

'Another glass. Here, pass this among you.' And he gave his flask to the coxswain.

'Thankee, sir.'

'One pull per man. And from this moment we will keep silent.'

'Ay-ay, sir.'

And the waiting began.

Almost exactly thirty minutes later a series of flashes lit the harbour to the east. Utter quiet, then the tremendous sounds of the explosions over the water.

THUD-THUD-THUD-B-BOOM

'Wait!' James, urgent and low, holding out a restraining hand as one of his men began to move out of the shadows. 'We must wait until a throng begins to assemble. We must not be associated in any way with what is happening on the water.'

Further great flickering flashes, lighting the harbour surface, the moored ships, and the wharves.

THUMP-THUD   THUD-THUD-BOOM

And now *Expedient*'s masts and rigging could be seen outlined against roiling fire, and the bulk of her hull was wreathed in dense smoke.

Soaring trails of sparks, and red brilliance broke across the sky, and fell in radiant balls of light.

CRACK   CRACK   CRACK

Fire now shivered and roared all round the ship, sending up clouds of spark-bright smoke, until the whole ship was enveloped in thick fiery fog, with only the tops of the masts clear above.

A crowd had now begun to gather, streaming down to the wharf from the town. James permitted his men, one at a time, to drift out of the shadows and join the townspeople. James retied the blue kerchief on his head, pushed a clay pipe into the corner of his mouth, and emerged from the shadows himself. He had dusted his face with charcoal before coming ashore, and was confident that he was unrecognisable as Lieutenant James Hayter, RN.

'How can we be certain that den Norske will come to that

particular wharf, sir?' James had asked Rennie when they first discussed the plan in detail.

'Because it is the wharf nearest to the ship. The other wharves are cluttered with casks and so forth, and there is not much room for a crowd to gather, anyway. He will come to our wharf, James, I am in no doubt.'

'But how can we be sure he will venture out at all? If he has remained hid so long, why would he break cover? To gape at a fire?'

'A great fire is entertainment, James. It provokes both horror and fascination in equal measure, and is thus irresistible. After close confinement will not den Norske welcome just such a public occasion, safe and unremarked in the press of people – part of life again? And when he sees it is the visiting English frigate that burns, will not he rejoice? "That difficulty has been removed, in least!" Hey?'

Now James casually joined his men. Gasps and cries from the crowd as another rocket soared on the night sky, and burst in dazzling red stars over the whole wide harbour. *Expedient*, apparently burning fierce, could plainly be seen a little to the east of the other ships. The rocket was followed by a series of orange flashes through the thick smoke, and:

BOOM BANG BANG B-BOOM BOOM THUD BOOM

The air itself seemed to shudder. More gasps. And a voice in the crowd:

'Them's her guns exploding! That means she is burning terrible bad!'

'An attempt must be made to save those poor sailors!' Another voice.

'You cannot get near to a ship afire. She may blow up any time now.'

'Ay, they must save themselves, poor devils, if they can.'

James smiled to himself, and began moving slowly through the press of people, looking for Olaf Christian den Norske.

There were groups of men from the taverns, some of them boisterous. There were families, including children, who had heard the explosions and come hurrying down to the harbour. Several hundred people had already crowded on to the wharf. James slowly shouldered his way from one end of the wharf to the other, but the man he sought was not there.

On the harbour two or three boats from other ships had bravely gone across to aid the burning frigate, but had been driven back by the intensity of the fire.

An immense eruption of flames and shivering sparks from the far side of *Expedient*.

'Those are Mr Storey's fire-rafts.' James, to himself.

He began to move back along the wharf toward the southern end, pretending to watch the conflagration, but in truth watching the crowd. He was near to the end of the wharf when he saw a hatless figure wrapped in a dark cloak, standing next to a family group, a solid, prosperous-looking man and his wife, and their two small children. It was as if the figure had attached himself to this group, like a bachelor uncle, but clearly the man and his wife were quite unaware of him as they pointed at the burning ship, and talked animatedly to their children. The figure beside them was equally fascinated by the spectacle, but was silent.

James jerked his head at the nearest of his men, and moved a little closer to the end of the wharf. The fire on the harbour flared up a moment in a quivering tower of flame and sparks. The figure turned nervously to look about him, James saw his face quite clear, and recognised – Olaf Christian den Norske.

James fell back from the press of people at the front of the wharf, and moved into the deep shadow of the building, where his crew presently joined him.

'Olaf Christian den Norske is the man standing with that family at the southern end.' James, pointing. 'On no account will any one of us approach him. We will wait until our burning ship has by design drifted away down the harbour, and the crowd has begun to disperse, and then we will follow him. His lodgings cannot be far – if he came on foot.'

An hour passed. The burning ship drifted away down the harbour to the south-east, the fire diminishing. At length the ship was lost from view in a great pall of smoke, and the crowd began to break up. Children, brought from their beds by indulgent parents, were carried – some asleep – away from the wharf. The men from the taverns were now subdued. Excitement and wonder and dread had been dissipated by the gradual diminution of the drama, and by the lateness of the hour, and soon the wharf was nearly deserted. Olaf Christian den Norske followed the family of four away from the wharf, separated from them and cut away up a narrow street with the spire of a church at the top. James and his crew discreetly followed. Their quarry turned left, continued past a second church, then turned right up another narrow street, and went in at the side of a double-fronted brick house halfway along. There was a single lamp at the far end of the street, but the rest of it was dark, and there were no lights in any of the windows.

'You all saw the house he entered?' James, whispering.

'Ay, sir.'

'Ay, we did.'

'Very well. We shall wait here at the corner five minutes, to allow him to be comfortable within, and then we will go in there and take him.'

They waited, and presently James gave the signal to move up the street. They went in single file, keeping to one side, careful to tread light on the cobbles. When they reached the house they saw there was a narrow space between it and the next house – and that there was an iron gate. The gate was locked.

'Christ Jesu . . .' James, under his breath.

'Should we break it open, sir?' Clinton Huff, whispering.

'Nay, the noise would wake the whole street.'

'Should we go in at the front, then, sir? Break down the door, like, and—'

'Nay, nay, that would be even worse. He must be took, but very quiet. We must be stealthy, d'y'hear me, now?' Glancing at each man.

'Ay, sir.'

'Ay, sir.'

'There will be an alley behind, I am nearly certain, where we will discover the rear entrance to the house.'

Leaving Cole and Thomas behind to watch the front of the house, they returned to the corner of the street, cut left, and found the alley. Dark and narrow, windowless brick walls, the smell of drains. James led the way, counting the number of properties, until they came to the right house. There was another gate. James seized the ring handle, twisted it, and found it was locked.

'God's love, what have we done to deserve this?'

'What shall we do, sir?' Clinton Huff.

'We must climb over the gate.' James seized the ring handle again, inadvertently twisted it the opposite way – and the gate swung open.

Hill was deployed as lookout in the alley, and a moment after James, Huff, Enderby and Lacey were at the narrow rear door of the house. James wished to have a party inside large enough to overpower their man quickly and easily, but not so large as to trip over themselves in the confines of the house.

The rear door proved to be locked, but a small window to one side was not. The four men squeezed through it, and found themselves in total darkness. The lingering smell of cloves told them they were in the kitchen.

'Should we risk a light, sir?' Clinton Huff, whispering.

'No!' James, also whispering. 'We will move deeper inside the house, and search it room by room.'

'Without no light, sir?'

'We are all used to moving about below deck at night, without lights. Keep close.'

An inner door led to a steep, narrow stair, lit by the faint glow of a lamp somewhere above.

James and his men crept up the stair, James in the lead. The top of the stair gave on to a short passage and a small entrance hallway, the front door beyond. James stepped cautiously into the passage, and stood still. He noted the central main staircase. Doors on the left and right gave on to the lower rooms of the house. A single lamp burned on the wall in the entrance, the flame turned very low. All was quiet.

Over his shoulder James whispered: 'We will search the lower rooms first. Should we disturb anyone, do not hesitate to subdue them at once. A hand over the mouth, and a sharp blow to the skull with your pistol butt.'

'Even if it's a woman, sir?' Huff, moving to his side.

'Certainly. A single scream could destroy our purpose.' With a ruthlessness that surprised him even as the words came out of his mouth.

'Ay-ay, sir.'

'And remember, we must not only take den Norske, but also find his strongbox.'

'What is in the box, sir?'

'Something of great value to England. And now we must keep silence.'

Moving quickly and quietly James led the way to the door on the left.

The downstairs rooms were all empty. There was no furniture, the floorboards were bare, the windows shuttered. In most of the rooms there was the sour odour of damp.

James led them back to the hallway, put a finger to his lips, and pointed up the central staircase, which rose between elegantly turned balusters. They went up in single file, stepping softly on the wide treads.

It took them a mere five minutes to discover that the upper rooms were also empty. When they had reassembled on the wide landing, James allowed Huff to light the small dark-lantern he had brought with him.

'Can we have come into the wrong damned house . . .?' James, half to himself.

'Where does that lead, sir?' Huff, whispering and pointing to a door on the left. 'We never seen it when we first come up.'

Through the door a long dark side passage led to the rear of the house. Their shadows strode enormous on the walls in the subdued glimmer of the lamp. At the far end was a very narrow, steep stairway leading up to an attic door, tight under the slope of the roof. Beneath the door, a sliver of light.

'So that is where he is hid, by God.' Whispered.

They stood staring up at the narrow door. James touched the coxswain on the shoulder.

'Huff, you come with me.' To Enderby and Lacey: 'You two remain here. Should we fail to come down with our prisoner two minutes after we break down that door, you will come up and assist us.'

'Two minutes – ay-ay, sir.' Enderby.

James led the way up the ladder, using the thin stair-rail like a mast shroud. Huff went up immediately behind, carrying the lantern. At the top James braced himself on the rail, raised his right foot, and kicked the door off its hinges.

Olaf Christian den Norske was seated on his narrow campaign bed in his shirtsleeves, studying documents by the light of a single candle. A canvas partition had been erected, separating his living area from the rest of the attic. The canvas billowed with the force of James's entry, and den Norske leapt to his feet with a cry, and grabbed for a pistol that lay on a stool by the bed.

'No! Do not!' James, presenting his own pistol at den Norske's head. Huff moved forward from behind James, snatched up den Norske's weapon, and tucked it into his waistband.

'Good God . . . you are Lieutenant Hayter.' Den Norske, staring at James.

'We met very brief aboard the *Terces*, Mr den Norske.'

'But . . . I saw your ship explode and burn. How have you escaped?'

'Our ship has not burned, you know.'

'Ahh . . .' Den Norske nodded, and gave a wry little smile. 'Pyrotechnics, yes, I see . . .'

'You must come with us, now.'

'Come with you? D'you mean to take me to England?'

'We do. And I hope that you will submit with good grace. I will not like to use physical force when it ain't necessary.'

'But you will use it – should I not submit, hm?'

'I will.'

A shrug. 'Then in course I will come with you. May I just shift into my coat?' Nodding to his coat lying draped over a chair at the end of the bed.

James nodded, and den Norske stepped to the chair, and reached for the coat.

Huff had moved back to the door to signal to the two seamen waiting below that all was well, and James was momentarily distracted by this. Den Norske turned from the chair with a pair of pocket pistols in his hands, and was at James's shoulder before he could react. The muzzle of one pistol was thrust into James's right ear, and the muzzle of the other pointed at Clinton Huff's broad back. As Huff turned

crack

he was shot dead. Blood sprayed across the wall and the canvas partition, and the body slumped. Powder smoke. The sound of blood leaking. Shouts from below.

'Now then, Lieutenant.' In James's other ear. 'You are going to assist me in leaving this house. Yes?'

'I – I will do as you say.'

'Then drop your pistol.'

James allowed the weapon to fall from his grasp. It clattered on the bare boards.

'Very good.'

More shouts from below. Rapid footfalls on the stair.

'Tell them to abandon their weapons, and go back downstairs, and wait. Tell them I will kill you if they do not obey at once.'

James opened his mouth, and called out the instructions. 'There is a pistol at my head!'

'Very good.' Den Norske. 'D'y'see that box under the bed there?'

James looked, and saw a small black strongbox nearly concealed by a folded blanket hanging low at the end of the bed.

'I see it.'

'Pick it up, and carry it in both hands before you. On no account drop it, or I will certainly shoot you. Do you have me?'

'I understand you.' James went to the bed, always aware of the pistol at his head, and he pulled the strongbox out from under the bed, and hefted it up in front of him.

'Ahead of me, move to the top of the stair, and go slowly and carefully down.'

James did as he was told. Behind him he heard the rustle of den Norske's coat being removed from the chair, and of papers being thrust away in a pocket. For an instant he thought of turning, flinging the heavy box at den Norske, and over-powering him. Den Norske seemed to read his thoughts.

'Go on down, if y'please, Lieutenant. Do not entertain foolish notions of counter-attack.'

James could see Enderby and Lacey waiting at the bottom of the stair. He began the descent, holding the box clear of his chest so that he could see his feet and keep his balance in the light coming from the attic. As he reached the bottom of the stair, James saw that Enderby, the younger and taller of the two seamen, was concealing something in his left hand, which hung down at his side. Was that a pistol butt? His sea pistol lay on the floor, with Lacey's pistol.

'Where is Clinton Huff, sir?' Enderby asked him.

From behind James, den Norske: 'He is killed. As will your lieutenant be killed, if you do not obey me in every particular.'

Enderby pretended to take the news very hard. His shoulders slumped, then he leaned suddenly forward, thrust James powerfully aside with his right hand, lifted the small pistol in his left, and fired it directly at den Norske:

crack

The ball struck him in the neck. He clutched at his neck, his eyes staring, the pistol in his other hand discharged harmlessly into the wall, scattering plaster dust, and den Norske fell, blood welling through his fingers. The pistol clattered away across the floor. Powder smoke. James, thrown off balance, instantly recovered. He threw the strongbox aside, and jumped to prevent den Norske from attempting escape. The wounded man was beyond escape. He gave a desperate groaning gasp, and lost consciousness. Blood leaked from his neck on the floor, pooling under his head.

James knelt, tore the kerchief from his head, balled it up and pressed it against the wound. The bunched cloth grew sodden with blood, and James saw that his effort to keep den Norske alive was pointless. He was already dead.

'Is he dead? Did I do right, sir?' Enderby, peering down, the smoking pistol still in his hand.

'Ay, ye did right.' James, with a sigh, and he got to his feet.

'I know we was supposed to take him alive, sir, but I couldn't see no other—'

'Ye did right.' James, over him, reassuringly. 'And now we must get out of this house at once, or be took. The sound of shots will have raised the alarm. We will go downstairs to the kitchen, slip out through the alley and away to the wharf.'

'Cole and Thomas is still at the front, sir.'

'We will call to them as we reach the corner of the street. Take up that strongbox, now, and run. I will follow you.'

Enderby took up the box, and he and Lacey ran down the passage toward the landing. James knelt again and felt inside the dead man's coat. Found the papers he was looking for, and thrust them away inside his jerkin. Rising, and looking down at the corpse:

'You have got me into a pretty fix. I will be blamed for your death. But I cannot mourn over you, that killed a good man this night.'

A last glance up the steep stair, then he turned and ran along the passage. Less than a minute later he joined Enderby, Lacey and Hill in the alley, and they proceeded cautiously to the corner of the street, and whistled to Thomas and Cole. Presently they were all assembled in the shadows. A dog barked nearby, but otherwise there was no indication of alarum. Keeping his voice low, James:

'We had better not return to the wharf as one party.' To Enderby: 'Give me the strongbox. I will carry it, and go on ahead alone.' Enderby handed him the box. 'You will follow singly, at intervals of two minutes, and we will all meet at the wharf in one glass. D'y'have me?'

'Ay, sir.'

'One glass, sir.'

'Ay.'

'Very good.' James glanced both ways along the street, then he stepped out, carrying the box under his arm, and hurried away in the direction of the harbour.

When he arrived at the wharf twenty minutes after, not a single person remained of the crowd that had earlier watched the floating conflagration. The harbour was again dark and peaceful, the only evidence of the fire a hint of sulphurous smoke on the air. Keeping to the shadows James made his way to the north end of the wharf, peered down the steps, and was confounded. The boat was gone. And where was Mappin?

Captain Rennie had earlier sent a message to the address Brough Mappin had given him, outlining his independent plan to take den Norske, seize the complete set of designs for his gun, and bring them to the ship. He had required Mappin – if he desired to return to England in *Expedient* – to take no notice of the fire in the harbour, but to come to the wharf at a particular time, wait there for James and his crew to return with den Norske, then embark in the boat with them.

'Could he have took the boat?' James, muttering. Then he shook his head. Nay, Mappin would never have proceeded alone.

James put down the box, and ran down the steps. Then had the boat drifted? There was only the lapping water, and the mooring ring flat on the stone. His forehead was damp with sweat, and a breath of wind was pleasantly cooling. Nothing else was pleasing or comforting. He ran back up the steps, and leaving the box ran down the length of the wharf. There were two other sets of steps, one halfway along, the other at the southern end. No boats were tethered at either.

'God damn the thieves and villains of this port! May they rot in hell!'

He returned to the northern end, retrieved the box, and retreated into the shadows to wait. As his anger faded he was obliged to admit that, even though it had been sent back next day, he and Rennie had taken a boat from this very wharf in order to return to *Expedient* the night of Mr Hendry's dinner. Was it fair, therefore, to blame whoever had taken *Expedient*'s boat tonight? Likely it would be returned in the morning – but too late. A sigh, and he crouched down to ease his tired limbs.

The others came one by one to the wharf, at intervals of a few minutes, crept into the shadows and gathered round James. When all were present:

'Well, lads – we must make a new plan. Our boat has been took.'

'Christ, and the coxswain dead . . .'

'What are we to do, sir?'

'Ay, tell us, sir.'

'Just as I said, lads.' With a confidence he most certainly did not feel. 'A new scheme. Since our own boat is stole, we will steal one in our turn.'

'Is there other boats moored here, sir?' Enderby, doubtfully.

'No, not at this wharf. We will go round to the next, and find a boat there.'

'Ain't that a loading wharf, sir? There will be watchmen there.'

'Ay, there will. But we are strong, and determined. Any unwise persons that attempt to thwart us will be dealt with very severe. We will prevail, and return to *Expedient*.' A deep breath, and he took up the box. 'Come on, then.'

*

Expedient at sea, at seven bells of the middle watch. Captain Rennie pacing his quarterdeck. Although no part of the ship had been burned, the acrid reek of extinguished fire lingered everywhere in her, and in the sails and rigging. In accordance with the scheme Rennie had agreed with Lieutenant Hayter, the ship was now well outside the harbour, clear of all boats and ships that might otherwise have attempted to come to her aid as the fire died down. And if any such vessels tried to find her after daybreak, *Expedient* would by then have stood off the coast, and made for sail for England, her boat having returned to her under cover of darkness.

But the boat had not returned, and Rennie was increasingly anxious. Everything hinged on its safe return, everything. Was Mappin even now waiting at the wharf, waiting in vain? Had James and his men fallen foul of the authorities in Boston? Had they been took, and the scheme wrecked?

'God knows . . .' Rennie, at the tafferel.

The boat, mast stepped and sails bent, came to *Expedient* at three bells of the morning watch in grey pre-dawn light. The wind had freshened, and James had made good time once clear of the inner harbour. *Expedient* was hove to on the slow-riding, ruffled swell, maintopsail aback. Rennie had grown anxious to the point of despair, and had been about to call for his boatswain to make sail when the lookout's call came.

'De-e-e-e-ck! Boat approaching from the nor'-we-e-e-e-st!'

Rennie hurried forrard to the gangway as the boat came off the wind and lost way, and came in alongside. Lieutenant Hayter stepped up the ladder, carrying something under his arm. His face under the smears of charcoal was pallid, and he looked exhausted. Rennie peered down into the boat as sails were lowered, looking for passengers.

'Have you brought them with you?' As James came up into the ship.

'If you mean Mr den Norske, sir – he is not with us.'

'And where is Mr Mappin?'

'He is not with us, neither. And we had to steal a boat. It is a long story, sir.'

'Then for Christ's sake make it a short one, and tell me.' Again peering down into the boat. 'You *stole* this boat? Where is my coxswain?'

'Clinton Huff was shot dead, sir.'

'Good God.'

'By Mr den Norske, who was himself then killed.'

'Christ Jesu – then the mission has failed.'

'No, sir, not entire.' He held out the strongbox. 'I believe what we sought is in this box.'

'You are certain? You have opened it?'

'Nay, I have not.'

'Bring it to the great cabin.' Turning on his heel, then checking himself, and turning awkwardly back to his lieutenant. 'That is, that is – if you please, Mr Hayter.'

In the great cabin James put the box on the table, and stood waiting for the captain to invite him to sit down and make his report, but Rennie was preoccupied and left his exhausted lieutenant standing. Rennie sent for the armourer, Ishmael Jupp, and marched impatiently round the table peering at the box from different angles. When the man came Rennie instructed him to break it open right quick. The lock proved difficult to break, and James – uninvited – at last slumped down in a chair at the end of the table. Rennie did not notice. To the armourer:

'Cannot you wedge that damned chisel *under* the lock, Jupp?'

'Yes, sir, I am attempting to do it, but the fu— I mean, the lock itself is peculiar stubborn, sir. It is all turned, like, with no hard edges.'

He adjusted the position of the chisel, lifted the mallet, and fell on the lock with a series of rapid ringing blows. James shut his eyes, and rubbed his forehead.

Five minutes of pounding, then a harsh metallic snap, a pinging clatter, and the lid of the box jumped up half an inch.

'Done, sir!' The armourer, standing back.

'Very good, thankee, Jupp. – Cutton!'

'Sir?' His steward, attending bleary-eyed.

'An extra ration of grog for the armourer. Say so to Mr Loftus.'

'Me, sir?'

'Yes yes, you. Jump now.' Waving them both away out of the cabin.

When they had gone Rennie noticed James slumped asleep in the chair. For a moment he was inclined to leave him be – it was clear the poor fellow was all in – and then he changed his mind. They must discover what was in the box, and then Rennie had a great many questions for his lieutenant. Sleep must wait.

'James! – *James!*' Rapping his knuckles on the table.

James roused himself, rubbed his face, apologised, and stood beside Rennie as the captain opened the box. What they saw astonished both men. Wedged in the box between blocks of wood was a coned black shot, the base ringed by an inch-wide strip of steam-turned timber, and tied to a green flannel cartridge by several tightly wound threads of twine. At the top of the metal cone was a neat hole of about an inch and half diameter, and several inches deep. Lying in the bottom of the box, under the wooden blocks, was a wood-and-metal plug painted black and red.

'What the devil is it, James? A mortar bomb?'

James, peering: 'Nay, I believe this may be the combined
cartridge and shot den Norske designed for his new field gun.
That plug may probably contain an explosive charge of some
sort.' Pointing. 'Don't you think so, sir?'

'But where is the design, James? Where are the draft plans
for this bloody gun?'

'I was near certain they were in the box.'

'They are not.' Curtly.

'Wait, though.' James had removed his jerkin and hung it
over the back of his chair when he sat down. He retrieved the
jerkin now, and thrust his hand into an interior pocket. 'Yes,
I have them still.' And he withdrew several sheets of paper
folded into a tight bundle. 'I took these letters from den
Norske's coat after he was shot, and had thought no more
about them until now.'

'Well?' Rennie.

James unfolded the sheets, and spread them out on the table.
The first two sheets were indeed letters. The others were a
series of beautifully executed drawings.

There were six drawings in all. In carriage plan, side
elevation, breech elevation, muzzle elevation, section, and
overall plan, they showed the full details of a brass six-foot field
gun, with a rifled barrel, four and five-eights inches diameter
at the muzzle, and an ingenious hinged breech. The carriage
was of an extraordinarily clever design, with a pivot enabling
the gun to be swung and locked at a dozen points through a
wide arc of fire, without compromising its stability. The
breech elevation included, at one side, details of the projectile.
The cone shell had an empty weight of seven pounds, and a
charged weight of fourteen, with a one-pound bursting plug
fitted into the top of the cone. Also included on this sheet were
brief notes about a new type of cartridge powder. These gave
no indication of its ingredients.

Both men studied the drawings, and at length James, half to
himself:

'I see that the cartridge and shot are meant to be inserted in the opening breech, rather than rammed in at the muzzle, but I do not see any provision for a flintlock . . .'

'Loaded at the breech, good heaven?' Rennie. 'Nay, it cannot answer, James.' Shaking his head, a grimace. 'The fellow was clearly a lunatic.'

'With respect, sir, I must disagree. The thing is entirely plausible, and quite wonderfully inventive.'

'Y'said y'self there was no flintlock, James. Such an oversight is typical of men such as den Norske. They are elaborate and ingenious in their glorious fantastications, and they forget the fundamentals.' Tapping a drawing dismissively.

'No, sir. I never said there was no flintlock, merely that he had not included it upon the drawing. Here is the vent.' Pointing. 'There must be a place for the lock above it . . . Ah! Here it is, on the side elevation! But . . . it ain't a flintlock, though. It is some other kind of lock. What is that word, sir, can you make it out?'

Rennie, peering: '"Fulminate", I think. So far as I am aware, that means to strike by lightning. As I told you, the fellow was stark mad.'

'Mad or no, these drawings deserve close examination by the Ordnance Board, sir. As does the shot itself.'

'Possibly. It will be for Their Lordships to decide. It ain't our business to deal with the intricate contrivances and doodlings of fellows like den Norske, thank God.'

'If you will permit me to express an opinion, sir, I believe the seizure of these drawings – after all our tribulation – has made the commission a great success.'

'Well well, you are entitled to your opinion, James. I must tell you it ain't an opinion I share. I think we have wasted our time, at terrible and unconscionable cost.' A sniffing breath, a glance at his lieutenant. 'You are tired, and I will not detain ye long. However, I must have your report, and answers to all of my questions, before you go to your rest. – Sentry!'

'Sir?' The duty Marine, attending.

'Pass the word for Mr Loftus, and Mr Tindall. I wish to see them both, at once. With my compliments, say to them.' To James: 'We must make sail, and set a course for England. Mr Mappin will have to make his own way, now, the fellow.'

And presently, as the captain and his lieutenant sat down to their business at the table in the great cabin, HM frigate *Expedient*, thirty-six, heeling a little as her sails filled, began her long journey homeward.

*

At six bells of the forenoon watch, *Expedient* heading east-nor'-east and a point east, in a steady topsail breeze. From aloft:

'De-e-e-e-ck! Sail of ship two leagues directly astern of us, in pursuit!'

Rennie came on deck, roused from a nap by his steward. His first Lieutenant followed soon after. It was a fast brig, rapidly overhauling them. Her colours could not clearly be seen.

Rennie peered at the brig through his long glass at the tafferel, then strode forrard.

'Mr Tindall!'

'Sir?' The officer of the deck, attending him.

'We will beat to quarters, and clear for action.'

The brig was very fast indeed, and by three bells of the afternoon watch she was little more than a mile astern. Her colours, rippling in the wind, had now been identified by Lieutenant Hayter, who descended to the deck from the mainmast crosstrees by a backstay.

'She wears the red, white and blue bars of an American merchantman, sir, and on closer examination I can say with confidence she ain't armed.'

'Not armed? Then why does she presume to dog us, a ship of war?'

A puff of smoke at the bow of the brig, at once carried away floating and dispersing on the wind.

BOOM

'Not armed, Mr Hayter?'

'I believe that was a signal gun, sir. Very likely they wish to speak.'

'What does her master want of me, God damn him? I am going away from America.'

'Since his brig cannot be a threat to us . . . should not we discover his purpose, sir?'

'Hm. Hm.' A sniff. 'Very well, very well. – Mr Tangible!'

And *Expedient* came off the wind and hove to, topsails aback.

The brig soon followed suit, a boat was lowered and rowed across. A solitary seabird circled curious overhead. As the boat drew close, James focused on the figure in the stern sheets.

'I see who it is, now, sir.'

'Eh? Who?'

'It is Mr Mappin.'

Brough Mappin had not been at his address in Boston when Rennie's message to him had been delivered there. He had been away at Lexington, and had returned in the morning. Thus he had seen and known nothing of the fire. As soon as he had read the message he dashed to the port and engaged the brig to pursue *Expedient*. All this he vouchsafed to Rennie the moment he came aboard and was taken to the great cabin. Then:

'I trust you have Mr den Norske safe in the ship?'

'Nay, Mr Mappin, I have not.'

Mr Mappin now grew very pale, and his mouth set in a thin line. All of his usual composure and self-possession were gone in that moment.

'Your damned impetuous decision to proceed independently in this venture has caused it to fail! Fail entire!'

'Olaf Christian den Norske is dead.' Rennie, quietly.

'*Dead!*'

'Ay. He shot one of my men, and was then instantly killed

himself. For a fellow whose life was so took up with guns, he had little understanding of the price to be paid for their intemperate use, I think.'

'Damnation to your feeble jokes, Captain Rennie! It is you that is intemperate, sir, and wretched irresponsible. You have cost—'

'Will you care to look over the plans?' Over him.

'What?'

'The draft plans for the gun. Mr Hayter in course secured them, and an example of the shot.'

'You have the full design . . .?' Staring at Rennie.

'Oh, yes. Yes, we have it.'

'Let me see it.'

'Yes, yes, I will like you to see everything, my dear Mappin – all in good time. But in the immediate I have some questions for you – as to why, and when, and how, concerning this "venture", as you call it – and I will like to hear your answers.'

'To hell with your questions! I demand that you show me the plans for the gun! I wish to see them *at once!*'

'Well well, you are a peremptory and insistent fellow, Mappin, but I think we will do better altogether if you understand me in this distinction: I am in command of this ship.'

'I demand—'

Rennie, over him, very firmly: 'And if you wish to return in her to England, you will not dare presume otherwise. Should you so presume, by God, I will put you in irons in the orlop, and ye'll spend the voyage in stinking darkness, with rats your only companions. Do you apprehend me, sir?'

'Do not cross me, Rennie – I warn you.'

Rennie smiled, shook his head, and: 'Sentry!'

'Sir?' At the door.

'Kindly ask Mr Harcher to come to the great cabin with his sergeant and a party of Marines. Ask them to wait outside.'

'Ay-ay, sir.' Retreating.

Mappin, deathly pale and furious: 'Have you the smallest understanding of what will happen to you if I—'

'*Be quiet, sir!*' A quarterdeck bellow.

Mr Mappin, in spite of himself, was shocked into silence.

'Now then, now that we understand each other, we may begin.' Rennie smiled at him, and indicated a chair: 'Pray sit down.'

A moment, then Mr Mappin did as he was told, and sat down. Presently the boat returned to the brig, the brig turned away toward Boston, and *Expedient* resumed her course – east-nor'-east and a point east – for home. And Mr Mappin began to answer the questions put to him.

In the hour and more that followed in the great cabin, over tea, Rennie learned that his instincts about Olaf Christian den Norske had been largely correct. The young man had invented a remarkable weapon of war – as yet untested, but with the potential to influence the outcome of entire battles – and had then attempted to attract bids for it. The governments of his region could not match his price. It was remarked of him that he was both charming, and arrogant – arrogant to the point of ruthlessness. He did not really care who purchased his design, so long as his genius was recognised, and his fortune assured.

The British government, through 'diplomatic channels', had made an approach – and had been summarily rebuffed. The matter was then dropped. However, it was clear to a small number of far-sighted men in England that the design for this gun must be obtained, by all or any means. Mr Mappin was given that task.

Rennie listened carefully to all of Mr Mappin's replies, but now he interrupted:

'Why did you offer *me* money, Mr Mappin? I am not a spy, nor am I seized by the desire to manufacture guns. I am a sea officer, serving the king.'

'My sincere apologies, Captain Rennie. It was a mistake. My mistake.' He drank tea, put down the cup, and: 'I had prevailed upon Their Lordships – Lord Hood – to allow me to offer you money, and he had agreed, because he had given you unqualified assurance that you would not be ordered into perilous waters so soon after your ordeal in France, and thus he felt in all conscience that you ought be compensated. However, he did not wish his name associated with the offer direct . . . and he quickly came to regret the notion. And so did I, indeed. I had no right to offer a serving sea officer what amounted to a squalid bribe, and therefore the offer was withdrawn, and formal instruction issued by Their Lordships, as Lord Hood would have preferred, I know, from the beginning.' He drank off the last of his tea, and gave a little sigh. 'I am in no doubt that I have made other errors in the course of this affair. Perhaps I have been overly . . . overly secretive in my dealings with you, Captain Rennie, and with others, in causing them to be overly secretive in turn. That is one of the perils of my calling, I fear.' A breath, a brief smile, and: 'I hope and trust that you will receive your proper reward in due course, when the Prime Minister, and Their Lordships, learn what you have achieved.'

'I do not care about rewards.' Stiffly.

'Come, Captain Rennie, do not naval men rejoice in prizes, in time of war?'

'That is entirely different. It is wholly unlike.'

'Ah. Then again – my apologies.' A little bow.

'In course, I should not object if my officers was favoured, and my people, that have suffered very grave this commission. As for myself . . .'

'Hm. Well, you are the best judge of that, sir. I cannot influence you, as to that.'

'Nay, ye cannot.'

Three weeks later, on a day of grey skies and rain showers, *Expedient* tacked safely under the Isle of Wight, headed north round the Foreland, and signalled her request for a mooring number as she arrived at Spithead. This was granted, and presently Mr Brough Mappin went ashore with the folded plans for the late Olaf Christian den Norske's gun, and the strongbox.

Captain Rennie waited for the boat to return, and then went ashore himself, carrying a full written account of the commission, and Mr Mappin's letter of unstinting praise and commendation. Lieutenant Hayter went with his captain in the boat. As they stepped ashore at the Hard, in a brief respite between showers, Rennie sniffed in a breath, and:

'That is England under our legs, James.'

'Ay.' James shook his hat free of droplets, and glanced about. A sudden dazzle of sunlight, and the carrying cries of gulls.

'Do you go to Dorset?'

'I – I don't know.' Shading his eyes, thinking of that last letter to Catherine.

'I should go to Dorset, if I was you, my dear friend.' His hand at James's elbow.

'You think so?' Looking at him.

'Without the loss of a moment. And I release you, accordingly.'

'You are very kind, sir.' A moment, a deep deciding breath, and he put on his hat. 'Then I will go.'

'I am glad. Good luck, and Godspeed.'

The two sea officers shook hands, and went their separate ways across the wide shallow incline.

HMS Expedient

Peter Smalley

1786: Captain William Rennie and Lieutenant James Hayter are on the beach and on half pay when they are given a prime commission: *HMS Expedient* is a 36 gun frigate which is to be sent to the South Seas on a scientific expedition.

But there is something odd and disturbing about the nature of their task. They sense that they are not being told the whole truth about the forthcoming expedition? Why is their voyage through the Atlantic dogged by sabotage and why are they followed by a mysterious man of war? And what are the secret orders which may only be opened once they round the Cape of Good Horn?

The answers lies on a beautiful uncharted island, in the remotest corner of the Pacific immensity, to which the storm-battered Expedient limps for desperately needed repairs. Soon the dangers of the voyage will pale in comparison with what the crew discover there, across the limpid waters of the lagoon.

'Smalley has written a real page-turner, engrossing and enthralling, stuffed with memorable characters. Highly recommended.' *Daily Express*

'Following in the wake of Hornblower and Patrick O Brian . . . there is enough to satisfy the most belligerent armchair warrior: cutlasses, cannibals, as well as a hunt for buried treasure. All this plus good taut writing gets Peter Smalley's series off to a flying start' *Sunday Telegraph*

arrow books

Port Royal

Peter Smalley

1788. An uneasy peace exists between Britain and pre-Revolutionary France. But French spies are already abroad in the British Colonies planning attacks that will take place when war is declared. One of the places most at risk is the island of Jamaica.

HMS Expedient is dispatched to Port Royal. There her crew finds a society founded on the unimaginable riches of slavery and the plantations; a society threatened by sexual intrigue, scandal and the ever-present threat of fever. But soon murder is added to the mix and it falls to Captain Rennie and Lieutenant Hayter to unravel a complex enemy plot taking place at the Governor's residence at Spanish Town; a plot that will end in a bloody and unexpected sea action.

'Salute a new master of the sea' *Daily Express*

arrow books

THE POWER OF READING

Visit the Random House website and get connected with information on all our books and authors

EXTRACTS from our recently published books and selected backlist titles

COMPETITIONS AND PRIZE DRAWS Win signed books, audiobooks and more

AUTHOR EVENTS Find out which of our authors are on tour and where you can meet them

LATEST NEWS on bestsellers, awards and new publications

MINISITES with exclusive special features dedicated to our authors and their titles

READING GROUPS Reading guides, special features and all the information you need for your reading group

LISTEN to extracts from the latest audiobook publications

WATCH video clips of interviews and readings with our authors

RANDOM HOUSE INFORMATION including advice for writers, job vacancies and all your general queries answered

Come home to Random House

www.rbooks.co.uk